LOVE ENTER

LOVE ENTER

Paul Kafka

HOUGHTON MIFFLIN COMPANY
Boston / New York 1993

Kaf
c1

For information about permission to reproduce
selections from this book, write to Permissions,
Houghton Mifflin Company, 215 Park Avenue South,
New York, New York 10003.

Library of Congress Cataloging-in-Publication Data
Kafka, Paul.
   Love enter / Paul Kafka.
      p.   cm.
   ISBN 0-395-60478-8
   1. Americans — France — Paris — Fiction.   I. Title.
PS3561.A362L68   1993   92-44194
813'.54—dc20   CIP

Printed in the United States of America

Book design by Robert Overholtzer

AGM 10 9 8 7 6 5 4 3 2 1

The author is grateful for permission to quote
from "I Walk the Line," by Johnny Cash, copyright
Johnny Cash, BMI, 1956.

5/93

With thanks
to B.W.,
to Julian Bach,
and again and again
to Janet Silver

BOU.DOC

Jennifer Sandler is the magician here tonight. Renee Gilbert plays the role of her beautiful, silent assistant. Soon a baby will spring from the trick box of Renee's belly. Sandler prepares for her performance to the accompaniment of the hidden infant's own heartbeats, which come thudding through the internal monitor with the steady rhythm of a galloping horse. The shining instruments are set out, the brilliant lights focused. At the last moment the internal monitor is removed, and in the thick new silence Renee is curtained off from her own abdomen by the blue drape, which the nurses hang from two IV stands so that it falls just above her navel.

What's going on? Renee's eyes immediately ask. She knows she's going to miss the good part. I want to tell her, but I'm new here and afraid to speak unless spoken to. With a crowd-pleasing sweep, Sandler draws the blue triangle of the scalpel forward. The attending physician, Gus Grant, is letting her lead. He follows her with the pad, catching the surge of blood. Sandler's fingers glide and turn, face his, bow, and glide again. Red seeps across until Grant catches it.

Renee's nose twitches. She's the only one in the room not wearing a mask. She wrinkles her nose again and I have a strong urge to reach over and adjust her epidural. I'm sure she's in pain.

"An itch?" the anesthetist asks.

She nods. The woman scratches Renee's nose.

*

Sandler uncovers the pink dome of the uterus, which pushes up against the eye-shaped window in the transversus abdominis. She nods to Grant, and he hands the bladder blade to the scrub tech while he and Sandler lean back and pull hard. I hold my breath, wear my poker face. The window in Renee's belly only yawns an inch wider, the uterus rising higher toward the white light. Renee's eyebrows form question marks.

"Almost there," I whisper, stepping forward. I can't help myself. I'm not doing a damn thing. It must be my job to talk to Renee. I try to ignore the silence that surrounds us.

"How you holding up?"

"I'm glad it's almost over," she tells me. She's been in the hospital since one this afternoon. She was only at twenty-nine weeks, so when she came in contracting, Grant checked for ruptured membranes and urinary infection, then hydrated her and put her on terbutaline to stop her or at least slow her down. He also gave her a shot of betamethasone to accelerate fetal lung maturity. At twenty-nine weeks, the air sacs of the lungs don't hold enough surface tension for the lobes to expand. Betamethasone stimulates the production of the surfactant. Renee's contractions didn't slow, so Grant put her on magnesium sulfate to supplement the terbutaline. Her membranes ruptured and then, at six o'clock, the baby scared the pants off everybody with persistent late decelerations. That's what finally reserved Renee this prime, dinner-hour table in OR.

"Have you picked names?" I whisper. We're the two youngest in the room, not counting whoever's inside.

"Jordan."

"How about a girl?"

"Jordan. Thought we had another week or two," she says, her mouth turning down in a mock pout. She thought she had another ten.

"I like Jordan."

"My father's name," she says. She speaks in the slow New Orleans style, as if the two of us are strolling beneath the live oaks of a peaceful avenue. She's a thin woman where she isn't pregnant. Her wrists are thin. She's the color the nurses here call cream.

I step back to look past the drapes. Sandler's hands turn, lean, glide. Her steel wand deepens the crescent in the uterus. Sandler and Grant work faster. Their hands pass, dip, pass. Sandler stops, nods. They lean forward until their masked noses almost touch. The silence is complete. One of Sandler's hands disappears, then the other.

The baby leaps, blue, green under the lights. Renee's eyes find it in midair. For an instant we all disappear. There's only Renee and her baby floating above her. Sandler suctions the baby's nose and mouth. Grant clamps and cuts the umbilical cord and passes the kid, who is a boy, to Chris Spellman, the neonatal attending. Spellman lays him firmly in the middle of the table. We go to work.

"Eight forty-one," the circulating nurse calls. I wipe glistening vernix off Jordan's belly and back. Spellman holds the oxygen catheter to his nose.

"One minute," the nurse calls out.

She's waiting for Apgar scores, which summarize a baby's condition. Spellman ignores her. We can see the baby's condition. He's pale and his chest sucks in with every breath. I put a mask on him and push air into him with the bag. He turns a shade or two darker, and Spellman's worrying shoulders drop an inch. The same nurse who called for scores comes over to bracelet the kid's ankle and ink his feet and finger, as if this were a normal delivery. Spellman frowns her right back across the room. He wants to get this boy dry and warm before we take care of the bookkeeping. The baby's crying now, but not well. Spellman holds him up for Renee. She looks. Her eyes carry him right through the air to her.

Now it's midnight, Bou. I'm on call. My hands walk up and down this keyboard like Jennifer Sandler's own. Green words dance across the screen, the way they have since I thought of you an hour ago. It's four years, four months since we said goodbye, or whatever we said. You're still the one I want to tell about my day. That makes this a love letter, doesn't it? I'm writing you a love letter.

I just can't get used to Labor and Delivery. For one thing, the colors up here are ridiculous. Hospitals are supposed to be white, but the narrow corridors of this wing are yellow, the floor is speckled black, white, and pink, and inside the miniature delivery rooms the walls are tiled to breast height, bright pink above. For another thing, I can't adjust to the rhythm of this place. Delivery's like a nursing home crossed with a fire station. For hours nothing happens, then all at once everything goes crazy. There are two separate and supposedly equal teaching hospitals under this roof, Tulane's and Louisiana State's. This morning there were five births in an hour, just on the Tulane side. But tonight after the C-section, there was absolute silence on both sides of the delivery hall.

Sandler sewed up Renee's uterus and tucked it back inside. Grant left for another delivery and the third-year resident, Tim Clinton, came in. He sewed up Renee's belly while Sandler chatted with her about Renee's five-year-old, Marcy. Turns out Marcy doesn't want a baby brother or sister to come live in her house and use her old crib. She asked this morning if the new baby couldn't live down the street at her friend Jamie's house.

Clinton's another one of my new bosses. He asked me who I was and if I knew anything about outboard motors. I told him no and that I was a fourth-year subintern who'd been in neonatal and was starting OB. *Good to have you aboard,* he said, and then told me all about his motor anyway. He's pretty sure he's got a sticking carburetor, and from the symptoms he described, I had to confirm that diagnosis. He imitated engine noises while stitching up Renee as delicately as if he were embroidering a pillowcase. Finally Renee's belly was crossed by a single stitched line. The circulating nurse and the scrub chanted inventory in a soothing nursery rhyme. They have to make sure no instruments are left inside the patients.

I told Renee goodbye, as if she were the guest of honor, and left her chatting with Sandler and the nurses. I watched a Monopoly game in the unit clerk's office until I got sleepy. The RNs, LPNs, aides, and scrub techs all hang out in Unit Clerk, which looks like a big kitchen, with two phones and a copy machine next to the sink and a school clock on the wall. Finally I wandered toward the residents' room to lie down, but instead found myself in Nurses' Conference in front of this computer. No one ever uses the machine, or this room. I pulled a sweater and a jacket off the monitor and flipped on the CPU. Up out of the hard drive flew the winged-staff-and-serpent caduceus, then a full-screen banner saying WELCOME TO MEDWARE, and finally a menu. I picked CHART, which gave me a divided screen, the bottom half filled with medical abbreviations and a list of lab result tables, the top half blank except for a pulsing cursor. I started writing to you. The words just poured out. I started describing the C-section. I knew you'd want to know everything. I had to type as fast as I could, just to keep up with your questions.

Kate, the head night nurse, came in fifteen minutes ago. She told me this IBM arrived with the Great Cash Transfusion of 1990, after the Joint Commission on Accreditation of Health Care Organizations nearly shut Charity down. The commission found a few minor problems with the hospital, such as poor blood banking, thirty beds together in undivided wards, no fire doors between corridors, and no significant records on the patients. I exaggerate, but Kate says this PC, the steel doors between wards, and the cloth partitions inside the giant rooms were supposed to drag Charity into the modern era.

To my eye, the results are only so-so. I'd say the hospital is now hovering in the late '50s, but then I'm in no position to criticize. Who knows where I am. All I can say with confidence is that I'm not in New Orleans, I'm not in October 1992, and I haven't even decided if I want to be. I should make use of this computer and these scattered hours of something like leisure, because I probably won't have this opportunity again until I retire. Over the next ten weeks I could update my records and try to figure out what's wrong with me. I think it's a memory problem. I've got to free up some working memory, or I'm always going to function in the fog that has surrounded me since last spring. My trouble is backlog. The records for one year in particular — a year you know everything and nothing about — are such a mess that my only chance of sorting through them is to toss everything out and start from scratch.

I'll go high-tech and put the whole year into this computer. Perhaps in that way I can create an order not my own. I'll work at night and during the day, whenever it's quiet. There's nothing I won't tell you, except how much I'm still thinking about you, which you know. I'll write about my New Orleans and especially about that Paris we knew, which stubbornly refuses to stay in the past.

I'll conjure you right up into the air, Bou, the way Sandler abracadabraed Jordan out of Renee's belly. Then, when you're floating in front of me, I won't reach out. I'll just look, while everything else disappears.

Water Castle Street

At eight o'clock in the morning, Rue du Faubourg St.-Denis was in full light. Men stood at the counter of Le Brady throwing back shots with their coffee. Outside his *poissonnerie,* an aproned man arranged blue shrimp, beheaded cod and pollack, speckled mullet, octopus *gros* et *petit,* and squid with startling, white-wall-tire eyes. Two turbaned teens came flying out of the Passage de l'Industrie behind rolling racks of cheap blazers. I stepped aside and found myself nose to nose with a dead pig, who hung from the pegs of what, elsewhere, could have been a coat rack. In the glass tanks below were flattened lengths of rib and half-gallon blocks of blue-mottled lard. I walked on, more awake than I wanted to be. Barrels of olives stood outside a store whose shelves were crowded with jars of *harissa maison,* couscous in cloth sacks, dates in cellophane. I reached Rue du Château-d'Eau. The light and the commotion faded all at once. In this shady, narrow street, like a cave down whose mossy walls water inaudibly trickled, was the studio where Madame Lafontaine taught ballet.

Where, I asked the receptionist, is the *men's* dressing room? She left her post and led me through the third floor of the silent building. She pointed to the room I'd already discovered, where a naked woman stood searching through her dance bag. I thanked her and made my way to the back corner. While I dressed, three other women arrived, and paid me no more mind than the first one had.

I crossed the hall and lay in the band of sunlight that fell through the open studio window. My head swam, my heart raced, and I felt like a whole day had passed since I'd woken up in the loft and climbed past Beck's cot. He'd been lying flat on his back, his erection stretching his red-and-white-striped boxers like a circus tent. Now I envied him his oblivion.

The dancers wandered in one by one, threw their bags under the piano, and stretched out across the room from me. They had their own private beach where they lay, pulling their legs overhead and talking only to one another. I did my lumbar stretches and tried to convince myself that I'd once been a dancer, if only an amateur. A plump woman came in and sat on the floor near me to adjust her pink slippers. I crawled over.

"Good day," she said, before I could. "You are here for the first time?"

Gratefully, I told her I'd heard about the class from a friend in Syracuse, in the United States. I was a modern dancer and had had only two years of ballet classes, after two years of modern ones. She looked concerned.

"You will find Madame Lafontaine impatient. Perhaps she will not let you remain. This is her superior course. She instructs the debutantes in the afternoon."

Debutantes, I understood, meant beginners, not society girls. With her round face and cushioned limbs, Paola didn't look like a ballerina. She spoke in formal constructions that sounded like Latin crossed with French. She told me she'd come all the way from Verona to study with Madame.

"Do not be fragile when Madame abuses you," she told me. Before I could worry what that meant, Madame herself rushed into the room. The performance photo of her in the foyer was dated 1954, which made her at least fifty, but she had a teenager's body. She stood at the piano, looking over her notes. She glanced down at me but didn't ask my name or offer a smile.

That was when I knew I was in trouble. Ever since I'd started ballet junior year, I'd been desperately behind. I was trying to learn in my early twenties what I should have figured out in my early teens. Madame Lafontaine, if that was her real name, seemed unlikely to have the sense of humor I required in all my ballet teachers. I was wondering how I could make a quick getaway when a short, barrel-chested woman appeared in the doorway and felt her way along the mirrored wall to the piano.

"*Commençons,*" Madame Lafontaine said. I jumped up and followed Paola to the barre. The short woman, Rose, sat and raised her large head as if sniffing the breeze. Madame whispered a single word to her. The blind woman began to play.

After class, half the fifty dancers stripped and lined up at the two showers. The other half threw on their clothes and hurried off. We were three men among the women. Two of us were showerers.

I leaned my weight on my left leg and suddenly it wasn't there. I sat on the bathroom floor, watching a white sheen dissipate from the faces above me. Paola's appeared among them. She lifted me to my feet with surprisingly powerful arms.

"Chocolate," she told me.

"Chocolate," I mumbled. The tile wall was cold on my back. I concentrated on that.

"Also two liters of mineral water. *Gazeuse.*"

Class had been a disaster. During the endless barre, my legs and back reached for positions they could not achieve. I accumulated small injuries. Madame Lafontaine ignored me so absolutely that by the adagio, I was no longer sure I existed.

"You are stabilized?" Paola asked.

I nodded.

"I must render myself to rehearsal," she said.

I noticed only then that in the midst of the naked throng, she was fully dressed. She placed my arm into the grasp of a tall blond man.

"Thierry," he said, and smiled.

"Dan," I answered.

Project Bohemia

"May I remind you, my dear Margot," Beck intoned, "that you are, technically, a senior?"

I'd just come back from my seventh ballet class. I counted each day's victory carefully. From this end, Beck's phone call sounded legitimate. It wasn't his mother or his brother. And it wasn't for the apartment owner, Claude Villeneuve, or Beck would already have slammed down the phone as he'd sworn he would until the day Claude bought us our toilet.

"No, I don't exactly have a job. More of a residency. Got it through an old Skull 'n' Bones buddy who's covert operations now. Of course you didn't know. It wouldn't be a secret society then, would it? Cover? For safety, I've got two. First is college punk hanging around Paris. Second is expatriate jazz phenomenon like Powell and Webster, only white and about thirty years late."

Beck's spirits were on the mend. The day before he'd landed a gig playing Caribbean music. His fellow trombonist, Julien, had given him a gram of Tunisian hash on credit. That had cheered him considerably.

"You still with that big girl?" he asked Margot.

I threw my tights in the sink, shot a stream of liquid detergent into them, picked up the wrench, and turned off the water.

"Boo," he was saying. "That's right."

In my mind I spelled your name Boo. I didn't learn about the Boutique until the next night. Beck remembered you perfectly well, but pretended he didn't.

"Not premed? Well, what *is* she planning to do?"

Whoever you were, you didn't conceive of your life as a medical mission. That made Beck nervous and I suppose it bothered me, too. At that point in our lives, we thought that everyone was, would be, or should have been a doctor. This was what our parents, who either were doctors or had married doctors, had taught us. At college, while we pretended to expand our horizons, we spent all our time with people who believed, as we did, that doctors led significant lives and everybody else was just fooling around.

"Tell me all about Boo, and I do mean all. This is business."

I shut off the water with the wrench, then went to the half-height fridge on which Beck was perched, lifted his legs, and pried open the door. That first two weeks we drank Belgian beers. The whole bottom shelf was covered with Gueuze, Stella, and Rodenbach, which we were too stupid to drink at room temperature.

"Only Wendy Isler. She called herself a performance artist, but really she was an actress who could just barely get along with other people."

He was speaking in a way I'd never heard before, but then I'd never heard him talking with an American woman. I knew only the Beck of the Centre Médical de Recherche et de Traitement Diététique de Forcilles, the hospital where I'd worked in his shadow all summer. At Forcilles, he'd been the friendly American, the Yale boy who had efficiently wowed everyone with his lab skills and his uncanny ability to guess medicine he hadn't studied yet.

"That's why I'm interested," he said. "Since personality is a construct, actors are all spies, and vice versa."

It had been nearly three months since Beck had accosted me at the bus stop outside Hôpital Forcilles. I'd flown in from Poughkeepsie the night before and was standing in the sun, jet-lagged, trying to figure out why my lab coat felt like a sweatshirt on backwards. Beck marched up and talked to me for five minutes in his frightening French before I could tell him I was an American and, furthermore, his roommate.

"I had my first inkling of the implications of this for the intelligence community two years ago. Wendy and I had been together for — well, two weeks. She'd always been a quiet one. Eyes wide, hands squeezing and releasing, occasionally a little squeak. Precisely. Silent-pleasure type. Then came one rehearsal for a new part, and suddenly she's a neighbors-be-damned type. You've got it. Fortissimo woofs and woompahs. Insistent, minimal shrieks, way up in the right hand. Very Meredith Monk."

There was nowhere to go in our one room, with the loft bed at one end and the long window at the other. I spread a sheet of *Le Monde* and sat on it, then held up another sheet and read the same sentence over and over. It concerned dockworkers.

"I do not have a confession compulsion. I've loved. I'm not ashamed."

He'd already been at the hospital a week when I arrived on June twenty-second. I never had a chance of catching up with him. By the end of the month he'd met the entire medical and nursing staff. I attached myself to his wide wake and soon understood why people like him were successful. No one could ignore Beck. Most people liked him.

"I'd always been Sloppy and Teaser. She was Creamcups. After that night, I was just Lover."

One afternoon the doctors fetched Beck along on rounds to the gastroenterology ward. I followed and studied him. He wasn't out of line, the way he is in real life. He charmed everyone from Docteur Falloux, chief of ward, to Madame Brull, most unapproachable of nurses. He was shameless about speaking awful French and greeted everyone by his or her first name. No one minded.

"Exactly. *Is that you, Lover? Come to me, Lover.*"

In the kitchen, I gave the blue tights a prod with a ladle. Our apartment belonged to the stepson of a doctor at Forcilles, who had agreed to let us live in the place for free while we renovated it. The floor had two years of dirt in it, and the south wall was streaked where I had naively rubbed a few lay-

ers of dust off it. The worst was the floor of the toiletless bathroom, which had acquired a form of mold that acted a lot like
brown shoe polish. The cleaning supplies I'd bought three
days before stared up at me from the corner.

"I will write this up for Langley. That's why I'm asking if
Boo is, well, *role-specific*?"

Soon the doctors called Beck upstairs whenever anything
was going on. In July he diagnosed a hydatid liver cyst that
the chief had thought was adenocarcinoma. Beck interviewed
the patient, a retired foreign legion officer who must have
picked up the Echinococcus in Algeria. Beck quietly suggested
that the boss take another look. From that day on, the doctors
treated Beck like a visiting specialist. They showed him interesting cases, then asked his advice. I'd find him up on the third
floor, diplomatically conferring with Docteur Falloux or Pu-
chault. He was efficient and polite. I was soon known simply
as Beck's friend, the other American.

"Only Peter Pan? Come on, Margot. I don't care if it is technically personal. This is a national security issue."

I stood at the open kitchen window and drank my icy
Gueuze. Swallows dropped from the sky, then boomeranged
up and away from the zinc roofs across Rue Roubo.

"Well, I think you have a discretion compulsion. Sticks and
stones."

He slid from the refrigerator to his piled clothes, among
which were all the colorful boxers his girlfriend, Val, had given
him. Beck's top three boxers, in my opinion, were the green
pair with the blue dolphins, the navy pair with the brown vio-
lins, and the yellow boxer boxers, with the angry red boxing
men on them.

"Valerie's fine. I'll tell her you said so when I write. Just a
hop, skip, and a jump from Wuyün. She was alternate, but it
turned out that the first-choice boy couldn't sustain life outside
Sterling Library. No, but we're seeing other people."

I rinsed my tights and hung them in front of our window.
They would dry overnight. One day during the next week, I'd

dance in a cloud of the green peppers, onions, and beef I fried that night.

"Val said I'd just have to put up with it. True, but at least they're Manchurian. I don't expect any awkward scenes in theater lobbies."

Beck was surrounded by his open suitcases, his cassette tapes in three dented biscuit tins, his tape deck, the French book I'd never seen open, his chem, bio, physics, and MCAT books, issues of his jazz magazine, *Coda,* a few French *Penthouse*s, and the latest *France Football.*

"Not tonight, then. No, you're right. I'd probably perform in an unforgivably male fashion. Hard to say in advance. Spray the furniture. Rub the walls with my molting head."

He could have talked forever, but Margot was trying to wrap things up.

"Yes, ma'am. Tomorrow. Wine."

He didn't mention me at all except to say that he'd bring his roommate. I was the other American again.

"*Bises, bébé,*" he told her, and hung up. He turned to me, still talking a blue streak. Wildest thing, he said. Letter this morning from Brook, trumpeter at Yale. Brook said Margot was in Paris, Margot the tenor and alto sax, gay premed he knew from chem and Jazz Ensemble. Brook sent her phone number. Turns out Margot was working in a brainwaves lab at Pasteur for the year. Dinner, he told me in his manic race, was tomorrow in the sixteenth, a classy neighborhood. We were bringing wine. He said nothing about you.

"Who's Boo?" I asked.

Beck lay back on his cot.

"Boo's tall," he said.

This was a remarkably concise answer, given his mood.

"Tall?"

"I met her at a party," Beck said.

I decided to try another tack.

"How can they afford that neighborhood?"

"Boo's loaded," Beck told me. "She's from Lincoln, Mass."

He rolled to the side and started a small avalanche of belongings.

"Golden ghetto," he said. "Also retirement community for British spies when they leave counterintelligence. The boys don't need new accents there. They can bring their polo ponies — with new faces, of course."

"You'd know all that because you're a spook."

Beck sighed. He dropped his head back over his doubled pillow until his bottom chin disappeared and his top chin pointed straight away from his body.

"You're beyond suspicion," he whispered. "I'll speak freely. I'm part of a mobile target force."

His voice had a metallic, Deep Throat quality.

"Project Bohemia. We're scattered through Europe. Pose as subway guitarists, action painters, café poets. Our goal," he rasped, "is a new cold war that will make détente look like rapprochement."

"I knew you were holding out on me."

Beck's sea-lion chest arched to the ceiling.

"If I disappear," he said, "call HQ. Ask for Kleenex Man. Tell him I've gone to the Spelling Bee. To find Treacle for the Porridge."

American women, I thought.

Boutique Mademoiselle

"Bless us," Beck called up the stairwell. "If it isn't the Sax Machine."

I followed him to the landing where you towered behind Margot. Beck picked Margot up and whirled her around, then set her down and kissed her with loud smacking noises, as if she were his six-year-old niece. I stood in front of you, Bou, and my soul ran at a fast clip up to my eyes and leapt in a shallow, long-jump arc across the air into your eyes and was gone. I felt my metatarsals bow up and open, my lungs widen. I longed to take your hands in mine, lace my fingers in yours, squat and rock on my heels with you. We'd begin, eye to eye, forehead to forehead, knees wobbling, to balance and whisper together. Instead I stood to one side. *Bou?* I asked. *A hat store,* you said. Really two, both called Boutique Mademoiselle. The main branch was under the table where your mother and her friends played bridge. They had all called you Bou.

That made no sense at all, but Margot was greeting me now, her hands under my elbows, her cheek against mine. A loose, lost-and-found arrow surged up and through me. I kissed Margot with closed eyes, and didn't need to see her because I already knew the high Eskimo curve of her cheeks cresting above me, the blue of her eyes, the trill of her tongue speaking, the spiral fall of her hair, the weight of her breasts not in my hands. I listened for my heart and found it plashing away inside her, and I realized I'd lost that, too. And so it was there on the landing during that first long moment that I learned I loved you and Margot, not indistinguishably but inseparably, and always.

Margot led us into the apartment, poured out mugs of wine, and sat me on a sofa with a rounded back at one end, which she told me was a chaise longue. The whole place was full of battered antiques with names. Under a tall candelabrum with forty-watt bulbs in orange hats stood an inlaid writing desk, its broken hood rolled two thirds of the way up. A scarred wooden table with legs like ironwood trunks grew across the alcove by the kitchen. In the living room grate was that fossil of a Pathé Marconi TV, a little Sputnik, complete with vacuum tubes and a bell fuselage. The apartment was surprising and intricate, and Beck jumped on the subject while I was still trying to decide what had just happened to me twice, or once.

"Most excellent crib," he told Margot in the kitchen. "One imagines a lock of chestnut hair tied with velvet ribbon in that defunct *écritoire,* and a dried rose petal between the pages of a musty Baudelaire in the study. Down the hall, beneath a tear-stained photograph of a young officer, a last letter from the front, cut by a single gold-rimmed bullet hole. Why else comes faint but unmistakable lamentation from high in the corners of this twilight salon, which heard such laughter, saw such love? Yes'm, truly a mysterious and alluring rental property. Ours is a little simpler. *N'est-ce pas,* Daniel?"

Beck pretended you didn't exist, as was his way when he wanted to get to know a woman more than he thought she might want to know him. The music of Thelonious Sphere Monk moaned from the tiny cassette player in the kitchen. Margot chopped and sautéed mushrooms. You told me about Yale and how of course you remembered Beck, he'd danced with you at a party once. You were concentrating in modern European history and theater, and I was concentrating on the symmetrical and economic grace with which you moved through the room. I stood and helped set the table, and you told me about your family while I looked at your cinnamon lashes and the strength of your forearms and hands, which held an invisible bridle together with forks and spoons. Your father was a financial counsel, which was actually a kind of lawyer, and your mother a preschool teacher and perpetual student of early childhood. My father was a doctor, I told you, and when you didn't ask what kind, I had that sinking feeling that always comes before I talk about Mom. I was about to go through with it when you said that you had two brothers, but that the middle one, Nathan, had drowned. We stopped setting and looked at each other.

"He was seventeen," you said. Mom was thirty-four, I told you. We didn't need to whisper because we weren't telling secrets, and both Beck and Thelonious were at full volume. But we leaned across the table and once more looked into each other's eyes, as if to glimpse those always present, always absent ones. In your tensed shoulders, Stonewall Jackson chin, smoky eyes, and cropped blond hair, I found him.

Beck went off to the toilet, and for the first time Margot tried to teach me how to fold napkins. I still work at it every once in a while. What amazes me is that in five years I've never repeated the same mistake. My napkins are like snowflakes. She was patient and thought I wasn't just watching her eyes and lips above the conical nests of linen she wove while her unpredictable, low-high voice spun instructions in the air like birdsong. She was busty and sturdy, and she looked up at an angle that included my middle but took in all of me, so that standing in front of her, I was entirely present.

Beck returned full of enthusiasm. Plumbing, he told me right past you, was an astonishing invention. We should look into it at once. We three sat down and ate the mushroom omelet and salad while Margot made a second omelet. We ate that, two yogurts, and all the bread while Margot got out a leftover chicken. We picked the chicken apart and finished the second and half of the third bottle of wine, along with a hunk of *reblochon* and a box of toasts. Margot nibbled the salad.

It happened that fast. We'd been at Rue Berlioz just over an hour. The pattern of feasting, and of who loved and nourished whom, was already firmly in place.

Two hours later I soaked myself and my tights in Berlioz's lion-footed, rowboat-size bathtub. When I was dry, I went to your bedroom and hung the tights over the glowing sconce, which clung like a phosphorescent barnacle to the wall. I set a towel on the cracked marble table to catch the drip, and lay my muscle shirt over the radiator. Margot's two saxes, one taller than the other, stood by the hall door like a big and little brother. Opposite them was the oak armoire with the handles like saucers. A row of books ran from its feet to a knitting basket in the corner. Threadbare velvet drapes were roped back to expose the middle halves of the balcony windows, which reflected the olive-and-royal-blue madras spread tucked under the wide futon. A worn, eyeless elephant lay in the deflated cleavage between the missing pillows.

I tiptoed down the hall. You and Margot spooned like a beautiful dwarf and a handsome noblewoman in the TV moonlight. You held one hand protectively under Margot's head, her dark hair falling across you. Beck, too, was asleep, leaning back against the chaise on the dried-out herringbone floor. His head was tilted past what looked comfortable, and his knees were Egyptian left. He wore a bleached Texaco attendant's shirt, which said *Jess* in once-red thread above the pocket.

I stood first watch.

Through the narrow window, the New Orleans dawn is orange and rose. I'm tapping away, alone and wide awake for once. Delivery has been quiet since an hour ago when Laskin, Boy, slid effortlessly through his mother's birth canal as if on a toboggan run. Not so last night at around ten when Joel Nash and I performed three deliveries, two hitchless, the last one outlet forceps, in a single athletic hour. When that third baby decided not to be born, we paged Jennifer Sandler, but she was busy in OR with the attending, Gus Grant. Joel and I were on our own.

Joel's my fellow fourth-year subintern, along with Steve Tsintolas. Joel would be a doctor by now if he weren't on a full ride with Uncle Sam. In his second year, Army shanghaied him to Saudi, where he did nothing, from what he says, except learn to make all kinds of macrobiotically acceptable foods. He's a nonlacto-ovovegetarian, and though born Baptist is a self-proclaimed Brahmin. He looks like a cross between Colonel Sanders and Yoko Ono. He has Yoko's features and her hair except blond, but he has the Colonel's smile and twinkly blue eyes.

Last night he briefly attempted a vacuum-assisted delivery. This is a procedure in which a device like a sterile plunger attached to a pump is planted on the baby's head. To put it crudely, one draws the unwilling infant onto the great, peopled stage of life with something resembling a Hoover Convertible. The problem is the suction doesn't always hold, and when it does, the baby isn't always pleased. Like last night. The baby's head was barely crowning with each contraction, then disappearing again, in a most provocative manner. Joel gingerly applied the rubber bell, but as soon as I turned on the pump, the kid's pulse dropped to seventy. We removed the cup and the baby's heart rate came right back up. Joel was slower to recover, having turned as pale as one of those slabs of tofu he eats with soy and chopped scallion.

Just then the dreaded Dr. Grant arrived from surgery, took one look at Joel, and sat him in the corner. I had the forceps in my hand, and I was too worried about what I was going to do with them to care about the boss. Joel always has time to worry about Grant because Joel's a white southerner and Grant's an African-American southerner. Grant turned his impatient eyes on us, his lips twisting with dissatisfaction before we could even tell him what had happened, and Joel quaked like a schoolboy. I didn't care. I'm a Yankee.

There were no more decelerations once we got the vacuum off, but there also wasn't much progress with the mother's pushes. We had an asynclitism, which is when the baby's head hits the floor of the birth canal at the wrong angle. I held the left forceps blade in my palm like a violin bow, then guided it into position with my right glove. That was only about as hard as reaching into the trunk of a car packed tight for a camping trip and finding a jar of peanut butter. Then I placed the spoon of the right blade in front of the baby's other ear. This was tougher, more like going back into the trunk in the dark and coming up with two slices of unsquashed bread. Luckily the mom, Judy, who was only twenty-four but was having her third, did all she could to help me. She said I was doing just fine. Once it was clear her baby wasn't in distress, she even asked Joel if he was feeling better. I thought that was a nice gesture.

Her introitus was distended like the mouth of a fish, not soft the way you'd expect. Between contractions the baby's head jammed up against her perineum so tight I could feel the ridge of the eyebrows. To my amazement, I closed the forceps. Grant checked their placement, then I started the gentlest traction Charity Hospital has ever witnessed. I wasn't moving that baby at all, just standing there sweating, all my chest muscles in a knot. The head started to move, slowly, and lined up all right. I knew where the baby was, even though I couldn't see it. I could sense it pivoting in there. Grant whispered that I should have done an episiotomy and that I'd better do one now. Kate held the forceps while I gave Judy a shot of lidocaine and then, under Grant's guidance, carefully made the cut.

I took the forceps again, but I still wanted to let the baby come out by itself. I bent my knees to get the gentlest angle of leverage, and tried not to let Grant see that I wasn't doing anything. I leaned over the invisible baby and prayed to it to hurry up. With the next contraction the head came all the way clear, facing down toward Judy's bottom. I thought I'd done it. Then Judy's perineum snapped shut around that baby's neck, as if there were a ghost between her legs trying to strangle it.

I froze. The baby wasn't breathing yet, was still on the umbilical cord, but for an endless second I forgot that. The next contraction didn't arrive. Grant opened the forceps and carefully removed them from the baby's head. Then he pried the handles out of my numb hands, while I tried with telepathy to help Judy figure out in what direction to make the baby go. Grant lifted Judy's feet out of the stirrups and guided her knees up and apart. The whole room closed in. Joel and Kate were telling Judy, *Push! Push!* I could hardly hear them. Judy, the baby, and I, we were all waiting to be born together, the baby from Judy, Judy from time, me from that silent place where I stood.

Another inch of the baby's neck appeared and my ears opened. Grant placed Judy's feet back in the stirrups. The left shoulder worked free. Kate and Grant came in closer and I made a basket of my hands and forearms. The baby's right shoulder popped clear, and with a squirt the whole creature followed. She lay in my hands and on my arms, her hair matted, her nose chafed and flat. I saw the red pucker of her pudendum and realized that I'd known all along that she was a girl, though there was no way I could have known.

Grant took her from me. Kate clamped and cut the umbilical cord. I stood still. Joel was back on his feet, and he and Grant worked on the baby. Kate cleaned up Judy and told me to sit down.

On his way out, Grant said I'd done fine. That was all. No wonder Joel's scared of him.

Below my window on Gravier, a crowd of doctors and nurses on the day shift slows as it reaches the hospital entrance. I study these people as if they are the natives of a country where I once lived, a distant place where I spent my nights asleep and my days with other people.

In half an hour I'll drive home and snooze if I can. Sometimes it takes a while to wind down. This afternoon when I wake, I'll stretch out and jog down Glencove and around Oakdale Park. If it were a Monday, Wednesday, or Friday, I'd have ballet class with the high school girls at Giacobbe Academy, but this afternoon it's running again or nothing.

I used to have a life. The problem is I built it with Dana. Now she's gone and I can't find much to do when I'm not here. Dana and I spent Monday through Wednesday nights at my house across the river, and Thursday through the weekend at her place on St. Charles Ave. Usually when we went out it was just the two of us. The rest of the time it was mostly people from Dana's class and me. Now the whole Saturday night crowd, except for Mike Lewitt and Eileen Chu, who are my year, is scattered in residencies all over the country. I don't see Mike and Eileen too often because they just got engaged and I just got disengaged, and it's a little awkward.

What scares me about working all the time is that I don't mind anymore. When I was a kid, Dad used to tell me war stories about his internship at Mount Sinai, how he worked every night and hardly ever slept. All through elementary school I had nightmares about having to go to school at night. In my dreams I was still in the lunchroom at midnight, waiting for recess. I was miserable, knowing how tired I was going to be the next day, wishing I was home with Mom.

Now my nightmare has come true. I live at work, emerging from the hospital only to feed and sleep, and not for very long even then. I used to pretend I was still a dancer. I used to keep up my French, renting movies and reading books so I could go back to France and work for a year someday. Now I don't do a thing except trudge back and forth to this hospital. What worries me is that every week it gets easier to be alone.

I started working with babies in the summer, when I did an elective in diagnostic ultrasound. I went from that to high-risk pediatrics. Now I'm in my OB subinternship. I've spent so much time with babies this fall that I'm thinking of just packing a suitcase and moving into that wretched call room on thirteen, with its peeling paint, its roaches, and its ceiling fan for air conditioning. Then at least I could stop pretending I have any other place to be.

Now the last of the seven-to-seven shift are hustling over from the parking lots on La Salle, mostly women nurses in white. Walking slowly along the same route are the earliest birds of the eight-to-fivers in civvies, a few in lab coats. I should envy all these people. They slept through the night in their very own beds in Metairie, Chalmette, the Ninth Ward. They didn't have to get up once. But you know, I don't envy them. All I can think about is how much they missed.

Behind Einstein

After she realized I was Jewish, our new concierge, Madame Lagache, took to me. But right from the start she didn't like Beck. I couldn't understand it. Almost everyone at Hôpital Forcilles had been wild about his clumsy, American-abroad ways. Only Madame Lagache resented his assaults on French syntax and found no charm in the rags he carefully threw on each day, his tattered smoking jacket, his gas station shirts and retirement pants. She didn't see him as a jazz personality with a new look. She thought he was immodest.

"*Monsieur,*" she called to me from her doorway that first week. "Will you and your friend be staying long?"

She was a small woman with round shoulders, a ruddy complexion, and hennaed brown hair worn in an abridged pageboy that just covered her large ears.

"Until we have finished the renovations."

Madame Lagache could have had us thrown out with a single phone call to the building plumber, whose *atelier* was directly across the street. The plumber would have strolled over, taken one look at the pipes, and told us the apartment was illegal until he installed the fixtures. That would have taken a few weeks if Claude Villeneuve agreed to pay, which he might not have. That was why I had to win our concierge over immediately.

"What is your occupation?" Madame Lagache asked.

We were students, I told her, and friends of the Villeneuve family. Claude hadn't returned my calls that week and I was doing nothing, but I said *les travaux* were under way. Madame Lagache squinted suspiciously at me with her steady left eye, while the right one bobbed exotropically.

"What is your field of study?" she asked in an icy tone. Perhaps I was squatting in the apartment with no purpose or permission. Perhaps Claude did not want me to stay, and so had engaged no plumber.

It was too late to turn back. Beck and I were students of medicine. I didn't mention our interests in the arts. I told her we'd just graduated from Yale University in the United States, which was half true, and that we were taking a year to learn French. Her door opened further and one of her arms snaked out and pulled me into her apartment. In her other hand was a book so old it looked like a sponge. She saw my glance and handed it to me. *Ars Moriendi, The Art of Nourishment,* first published in 1492. I looked up and saw that her tiny flat, as narrow as a section of the stacks at the top of Carnegie Library at Syracuse, was blanketed with books.

"*La médecine,*" she repeated. "Have you explored a cadaver, then?"

I translated the question as best I could. In France, at my age, I would have been well into medical training. Yes, I said, I had explored a cadaver, and wondered if this meant examined. I thought of the frog, the two rats, and the eel I'd brutally dismantled over the previous years. Madame Lagache set the porous book aside, grabbed my hands, and held them to her face.

"You have the fingers," she said, sniffing them, "of a form weaver." Her own fingers were cold and rough. My French wasn't nearly up to this kind of talk. It was more on the level of "How long have you been in Paris?" and "American food is less good than French food." I decided to let the remark about my fingers alone. Would she please, I hazarded, tell me about her books?

She grinned with such force that I snatched my hands away and bumped the back of my head on her door. She put on her reading glasses and started hauling volumes off the shelves with both hands. The first one she opened for me was Bourrit's account of the first ascent of Mont Blanc, by Paccard and the "cowardly peasant" Balmat, in 1786.

"Paccard returned blind and without the use of his fingers," Madame Lagache mentioned as she pressed the binding to my chest. "Neither Balmat nor Bourrit ever forgave him."

What did I like to read? she asked. I told her I enjoyed Ionesco and Camus, these being two writers from my French class whose names occurred to me. Madame Lagache asked why I didn't study *this world* and told me that she herself had stopped reading literature fifteen years before. Now she investigated healing, astrology, and history, which were all one subject. She knew the poems of her youth by heart and looked at them only when she wanted to *write* them.

I was sure I'd missed an important transition. Write what? Then she brought down a volume of Apollinaire in which someone had crossed out and revised a number of verses in a pointy, backward-leaning hand. She glanced over these, her lips moving, as if to reassure herself that the corrections were justified.

"Before writing," she assured me, "I consult the originator." She kept talking while I decided she meant original. What bothered me was the familiar way she kept calling out "Guillaume," as if Apollinaire himself were right there with us. The greater part of her collection, she told me, was in storage in the *cave*. This was only the material currently on display.

"You may borrow what you like." She used the familiar *tu*. I had become a borrower and a *tu* at the same moment. I bowed as far as space permitted.

"You are too kind," I murmured, still employing the *vous*. This was a little different from my relationship with my landlord at school, a gentleman by the name of Julius Beggs, on Allen Street, who read only *Soldier of Fortune*. When I once asked him to fix my front steps, which had crumbled into a pile of brick, he offered instead to fix my dumb college ass for me.

"Are you interested in the Greek medicine?" Madame Lagache now inquired. She handed me a long volume wrapped in blue paper. I undressed it and examined its illustrated pages. A color plate detailed the removal of a tooth in a Golden Age tableau, complete with a marble dental chair and a cloud-covered Parnassus. The Greeks employed a hot iron rod for a cautery. She lifted a dozen books from a cutting board, the topmost of which was the *Calendrier Solaire et Lunaire* of Bai Niam Li. Then she opened a drawer and pulled out a jar of rusty nails. She put up water as if for tea. She was entirely friendly now. Another woman had been staring accusingly out the window at Beck and me every time we entered or left the building.

We sat side by side at her small table. Lace doilies marked her end of it as the tea table. A fountain pen, a pile of books, a block of heavy paper, and a maneuverable lamp topped by a magnifying glass transformed my end into the desk. Under the lens was *Poésie, Musique et Graphologie* by Docteur Jean-Charles Gille-Maisani.

"What do you know," Madame Lagache asked with studied disinterest, "about the Masons?"

I cleared my throat. I said I believed the Masons were a fraternal order of craftsmen who had built the great cathedrals of Europe. Above her toothy smile, Madame Lagache's left eye fixed me. My schoolboy's knowledge amused her. It was as if I had said I believed the moon was made of Jarlsberg.

"The Masons are the Lost Tribe of Israel. They constructed a lunar capsule in Egypt three thousand years before Jesus of Nazareth."

I nodded as if I'd suspected as much. Germaine, as I called her after that day, pushed aside a half-dozen sheets of cryptic scribblings to reveal a shiny new paperback, *La Pierre et la Foi,* by Noah de Rocca. She turned the pages with callused fingers.

"You are a Jew," she announced. She used the archaic *hébreu* instead of *juif*. I hesitated, wondering just what a Jew was in Germaine's mind. Perhaps it was like a Mason, mysterious and powerful. If so, how would this affect my chances of keeping the apartment?

"*Oui.*"

Germaine pulled a second book from beneath her notes. It was called *Les Juifs et l'Empire.* On the cover was a drawing of a king with a large gold cross suspended from his neck. Beside him stood a white-bearded man bearing a staff and whispering in his ear. The kettle lid rattled. Germaine rose and dropped a few of the nails into a teapot, then added water.

I leafed through *The Jews and the Empire.* On one page I learned that Christopher Columbus came from Spanish Jews living in Genoa. On another page, a doctor of theology in Lucerne argued that Charlemagne had been disastrously counseled by Père Cordovero, an Umbrian Jew masquerading as a Benedictine friar.

We sipped what looked and tasted like dirt mixed with clam juice. Germaine explained to me that the Jews were not only the ancestral Masons but had reached other worlds at key moments throughout history. She said the contributions of Einstein could only have been the result of contact with a higher intelligence in the Triangulum galaxy. She hauled a book from the floor and hunted in it until she found his astrologic chart. Together we pored over the text, which explained that Einstein had been a mediocre student and then had inexplicably become the most brilliant physicist of the century. I hunted up and down the column for a synopsis of what Albert had done during the years between his pitiful showing in his first year of high school in Aarau and his acceptance of the Nobel prize in Stockholm. I also looked for some mention of the physics think tank in the Triangulum galaxy, where diverse life forms cooperated in the spirit of enlightened inquiry. From what Germaine said, the galactic nucleus, defined by its small disk of neutral gas and its three averagely bright suns, was an interstellar Los Alamos. There was nothing about Triangulum on our page. I concluded that Einstein's visiting professorship there was Germaine's own contribution to the history of ideas.

She lifted away the pages to where a strip of felt-backed fur marked her place. On the lefthand page was Rigaud's portrait of Louis XIV. The Sun King wore yellow knee garters and tomato-red high-heeled sandals. On the right was his birth constellation. Dozens of planets were diagrammed in their orbits on the morning of September 5, 1638, at 2:38. Germaine bent over the chart and explained the correspondences that had governed the life of *le Roi Soleil*. As far as I knew, Louis XIV was not a Jew. We had apparently left *les Hébreux* to go about their interplanetary affairs. Germaine spoke and pointed here and there in the packed pages, which linked the Franco-Dutch War, the Great Winter of 1709, and the deaths of the beloved Duchess Adelaide of Bourgogne and two of her three sons to sinister aspects in Louis' royal sky.

"Will you take over your father's practice?" she asked out of the blue. I blinked at her. I hadn't mentioned that my father was a doctor. How could she have known I was planning to be an ear, nose, and throat man? Now that I actually have to decide on a specialty, I don't know what to do. But back then, I just thought of Dad's demanding golf schedule and of the way he reads *American Journal of Otolaryngology* on the john Sunday evenings, and said to myself, *Why not ENT?*

But how had Germaine known? And why had she asked me about my father when we were in the end of the seventeenth century? I told Germaine my plans. Still she studied me intently, as if she hadn't understood my pronunciation of *oreille*. For the first time, I wondered if she knew more about my future than I did.

"You are Pisces?"

"Aquarius," I told her. She nodded as if that was what she'd meant by Pisces.

"You have the courage," she said, "to enter the other."

Other what? I wondered. But Germaine just left the word floating in the air.

"You possess a transparent soul."

I fingered Germaine's bookmark, which I fervently hoped was rabbit. I was remembering the feel of the tumors, hard as pebbles, beneath Madame Puget's skin when I'd washed her each morning in August at Hôpital Forcilles. During those weeks I'd worked in the terminal ward, I had felt that my soul was . . . transparent was as good a word as any. But I'd never thought of this as an advantage.

You cross thresholds of time, Germaine told me now. My *shadowlight* bore *energy seeds*. In particular, if I understood her, I would be good with ailments of the liver. That meant something to me. I was glad Germaine saw a gastroenterologist in me, even if she was officially only a janitor. I was just getting started studying for MCATs then.

Out in the hall, the elevator groaned and rattled to a halt. The grillwork doors squeaked open, footsteps approached, and a fist pounded Germaine's door. We sat in silence, then Germaine rose and ponderously walked two steps, as if passing down a long corridor.

"Bonjour, Chérie!"

A squash-shaped woman with a bronze helmet of hair peered into the room. She raised her eyebrows high when she saw me, then looked away. It was as if I were buck naked and lying in a feather bed, not sitting at Germaine's table in front of a teacup. Shouting, the woman informed us that her toilet was blocked through absolutely no fault of her own. She swore she had put neither grease nor *trop de papier* down it, and then asked whether *Chérie,* as she again called frowning Germaine, would please call the building plumber *at once.*

"I will see to it," Germaine answered. She closed the door so quickly the woman had to jump back. Germaine didn't call the plumber at once. Instead, after the elevator had risen, she placed her telephone in a drawer, which she then closed on the cord. Her fingers twitched murderously and her weak eye ping-ponged off the side of her head. She didn't stop frowning until she'd finished a second cup of tea.

"Your mother misses you," she told me. In French this came out *You are missing to your mother*.

"But my mother is —"

Germaine dismissed my mother's death with a wave of her hand.

"She will visit you. I have already contacted her."

I didn't ask what Germaine meant by *visit* or *contacted*. I was afraid to undermine the new bond between us. Now that the topic of plumbing had been so harshly reintroduced by the helmet head, I felt much less confident of Beck's and my tenure.

Later in the week, when I brought Germaine one of the delicate bouquets of violet skullcaps sold at the Faidherbe-Chaligny métro exit for twenty francs, she told me more. As soon as Mom's soul had been liberated from Saint Francis' Hospital, it had traveled to the sixth Cepheid-type star in the globular cluster Omega Centauri. From there, Germaine gradually led me to understand, Mom had followed my progress through life with earnest, but in no way anxious, interest.

None of this surprised me. I'd known it already, the night Dad picked me up from Onkel John and Tante Clara's in Schenectady. For two weeks I'd been staying in the attic room with Curt, going to school with him and Mina. Onkel John had given me two dollars allowance, even though all I did was make my bed and help clear the table. Dad didn't drive up to their house until almost ten o'clock at night. He helped me pack my duffle bag and held my hand all the way home in the car, driving with his left hand the way he always had when he wanted to play with Mom's hair. I didn't have to ask him where she was. I knew I wasn't going to see her anymore, but I also knew that I'd never be without her.

"Come again soon," Germaine told me that first day, when at last she ushered me into the hallway.

"With pleasure," I answered, and bowed for the second time in our brief acquaintance. Germaine was starved for good manners. Her lonely days of cleaning and guard duty were interrupted only by the offhand greetings of passing tenants.

"You are in love," she told me. "Walk cautiously in the streets."

I thanked her and told her I would. She summoned the elevator, which sobbed like a wounded beast as it wended its way down from the fourth floor.

"Above all," Germaine told me, "watch for buses."

Window Glass

"The cauliflower's fresh," Margot explained, "and not that cabbagy, so that's for the salad. The carrots are plenty stiff, but they're not sweet."

So those went into the curry pile along with the tomatoes, which looked fine from where I sat. I sat in the declined empire chair, looking into the balcony window. We listened to a World Saxophone Quartet tape that Margot adored and that I thought sounded like sax players making fun of folks who buy cassettes full of squealing nonsense.

I could never make Beck understand how I kept falling in love with both you and Margot during those weeks. It didn't need explaining, I thought. Every other day or so I sat by the window looking through the iron balustrade along the ancient wall of tan-and-amber fieldstone, over which grew the dark, cordate leaves of vineyard ivy. I talked with whichever of you was there about whichever of you wasn't. You were lovely separately and you fit together perfectly, not in spite of but because you were tall and Margot was short, you were moody and Margot wasn't, you were messy and Margot was a housekeeper, a scientist, and a jazz person all rolled into one.

"She's having a tough week," Margot said, chopping all the wrong vegetables.

"Her brother?"

Margot shrugged. Nathan had been dead for seven years.

"That's part of it. That's always there."

Her hair hung in black curlicues over the navy sweatshirt

she wore three days out of four. When she looked up from the cutting board she lifted her thick eyebrow — her monobrow, Beck called it — and her eyes drew mine.

"So what do you do?"

"I wait," she told me. "Bou talks eventually. When I can't stand it anymore, I rush her. Then we get into these terrific arguments about whether I want to discuss everything because I want to be a shrink, or whether she's like the rest of her family and never talks about anything difficult. What bothers her is that I came out to my parents and she hasn't and won't. She's competitive about everything."

I could never think of Margot as being the same age as the rest of us. She looked a whole epoch more mature, the way the senior girls at Arlington High did when I was in ninth grade. Margot made me wish I'd had an older sister back then, so that she could have had Margot for a friend. That way I could have fallen in love with her when I was fourteen and she was seventeen, and she could have pretended that it was just a game, while really she would have been mad for me, too. But I didn't have a sister, I didn't meet Margot until I'd finished college, and I was fifteen months older than she was.

"She's even competitive with you. You know she did ballet when she was little, before she started riding all the time. The other day she said she wished she hadn't quit so she could take class with you."

"That's not competitive."

"You don't know her," Margot said. "What she really means is that she wishes she could dance better than you."

All at once I saw you. You were three feet tall, hopping around a lawn in a pink tutu over white tights.

"Her riding teacher said she wouldn't improve if she kept missing saddle time. The ballet school said riding would deform her legs."

There you were again, an eight-year-old rider in a hard cap, boots, tiny jodhpurs, like a young Princess Anne. Everything Margot said, I saw instantly. I had Bou the ballerina, Bou the horsy girl. From what Margot had told me two days before, I especially knew Bou the shy Andover junior who didn't go on dates, smelled permanently of manure, and thought lesbians were transvestites who smoked cigarettes in holders and flattened their hair with brilliantine. Often that fall I felt like my own medium-landlady, Germaine. I was absorbing too much information from sources that were not apparent to me.

"Bou said she didn't care how her legs came out. When she was six, Mam took her down to New York to see this famous rider, Rodney Jenkins. He was an old friend of Mam's, and he took Bou up on his saddle and rode her around the edge of the jump course. That was it for ballet. Only now she's jealous of you."

From the moment I met Margot, I felt as if I'd been in Hebrew school with her every Saturday of my life. Yet I knew I'd never known anyone like her. She did what she wanted to do, she thought about things I'd never heard of, and still she listened to me attentively, which made me smarter than I was. She had quick hands for cooking and touching. She could walk up to wherever I stood and fit herself against me like a cat. She loved women and men.

"Is Beck still having wet dreams?" she asked. It was after six. The last of the previous night's wine tasted like pencil shavings. From the once regal chair by the window, I could look toward the courtyard and at the same time see Margot reflected in the glass. The window glass aged and mellowed what occurred inside that apartment, like instant barrel wood.

"Haven't heard any. He probably has them after I leave for ballet."

"Does he miss Val?"

"I suppose so. He talks about her body for hours."

We all gave away each other's secrets, but Beck was difficult to rat on. His confessions were so detailed and personal that there was almost nothing left to give away. He'd already informed you and Margot about his earwax problem, the way he bullied his mom, what occurred or didn't occur each day in his bowels, the tantrums he threw when his dad beat him at tennis, his feverish need to make money, his obsession about women whose breasts were widely separated, and his guilt over Ralph Powers, the boy in his fourth-grade class whose lost eye he felt responsible for, though it had never been conclusively established that it had been Beck's jump from the sled that had sent Ralph into a fire hydrant. The only topic about which Beck was stubbornly mute was his brother, Brian. Still, I did my best.

"He's secretly glad she's in Manchuria," I said. "Dreaming her has got to be easier than dealing with her."

Margot laughed like a silly little girl with a chest cold.

"Valerie," she said, "is truly a pain. Talk about arrogant."

She took the challah out of the oven and set it on the table. In the window, the bread was golden. After a moment the air smelled like summer. I curled deeper into the faded needlework roses.

It had been only two weeks and a day since Beck and I had come to Rue Berlioz. That night I'd watched over the three of you, then gone and fallen onto the striped bedspread. I'd woken in the morning with the bald, eyeless elephant, Phunt, tucked under my chin like a violin. I was sleeping between love and love, you and Margot warming me with your bottoms, your backs curled away from me like a pair of wings. I nuzzled your hair and Margot's hair, and before either of you had woken I decided I would stay encamped in that nest forever. I loved the perpetually mild season, and the potential for flight.

"I really only know Valerie from self-defense," Margot told me. "She was just there the first week."

"They threw her out?"

"She wouldn't shut up. She had the goalie from the soccer team with her. They did Moe and Curly routines with all the little whoops and chuckles when we were learning eye jabs. The instructor asked Val if she thought she could control herself. She said no and left, taking her partner with her. I think she has an attention problem."

Valerie did sound like the ideal mate for Beck. It was natural, too, that even at the beginning of October, Margot believed that Val's inappropriate behavior indicated an attention disorder. This was right in the beginning of Margot's attention fixation, when she was just starting to see everything in terms of her lab job. She hadn't yet gotten around to dividing up all learning activities into global or selective attention categories. It would be over a month before she put those colored cards on everything to increase her French vocabulary, and two months before Beck would stay up all night writing dirty limericks on the cards and switching them around. I can't look at a thick-slice toaster without seeing bright green paper and thinking SALT SHAKER (*SALIÈRE,* f.) and *There once was a boy whore from Ipswich,* et cetera, in that order.

"Are they going to get hitched?" Margot asked.

"Who knows. Beck talks."

Margot thought Val was the only woman on earth who could tolerate prolonged exposure to Beck, and vice versa. She told Beck and he agreed. Beck and Val were both overachievers intent on being totally independent together. He was the musical premed meteor, she the soccer and Chinese studies star. Each was attractive in an overinflated way, to judge from the picture of Val on the wall by Beck's cot.

"I'll bet she already has a pair of Chinese boys doing her bidding," Margot said. "She's been there two months. If she wanted Beck, she'd be here."

"She was supposed to come to France with him," I said, pleased that Margot didn't know. "He was going to put off med school and follow her wherever she wanted to live next year. She changed her mind when she got the Fulbright."

People on their way home from work filed down Berlioz. None of them was you or Beck.

"No Westerner has ever been to her town for more than a night. She couldn't pass it up."

"They'll have a lot of use for English, then," Margot said.

She put down her knife and disappeared into the kitchen.

Then she came out along the wall, spun on her right foot, and dropped back into her chair with her arms full of green peppers and an eggplant. Margot's figure — her wide hips and low butt, together with her breasts, which filled her sweatshirt a few inches closer than I ever expected to her suddenly narrow waist — gave her the overbuilt, road-hugging grace of an early '70s Corvette. Especially the '72 Stingray coupe.

"He runs downstairs for the mail every day," I contentedly ratted. "He sends Val long letters on Mondays and Saturdays. They're so thick he has to tape them closed. Every once in a while he gets a postcard from her with big writing."

"The nerve."

"He wants a Paris woman to make him forget. Or at least help him wait."

I abused Beck as well as I could. It was my way of forgiving him for the casual put-downs he threw my way whenever the four of us were together. I knew he was just being entertaining, but his jibes still hurt. I was forever playing Zeppo to his Groucho. I took my straight man's revenge.

"He can't find the girl," I said. "His charms don't translate. Here he's just a fat guy with a red face and a terrible accent."

"What's he usually?"

"Suave and accomplished."

"Oh, come on," Margot said.

She knew I was right. In English, Beck was physically acceptable and intellectually intriguing. Women found in him a sort of egotistical Yogi Bear, with brains and a trust fund. But in French his lunkish form overshadowed his wit. The foreign women he'd met during the summer were not impressed. He'd first tried his moves on two Austrian substitute nurses, Hilde and Berthe, who were perhaps the only two members of the Hôpital Forcilles staff not to be bowled over by him. Beck invited them on a day excursion to Versailles, with me along to make it look like he wasn't trying to seduce both, or rather either, of them. The next Sunday he took all three of us to lunch on Rue de Paradis, and then to the Musée du Cristal to look at the Baccarat perfume bottles that were Berthe's obsession.

It turned out that Berthe was engaged and not kidding about it, and that Hilde was frightened of being touched below the waist. This didn't definitively bother Beck until he found out that she was also frightened of touching anyone else below the waist.

"He claims he was busy at Yale."

"Beauty and the Beast appeal," Margot said.

"He told me Val had to fight for him."

"It's true," Margot said. "I don't understand it, but he was in demand."

Not so in Paris. For a month I'd watched him try to pick up women in bars, on the métro, at the bank where he could flash his dollars. Even there he had no luck. A few days after we moved to the city, he met a Dutch philology student at the library at Beaubourg. Meanwhile he was dropping in on an Argentine waitress who worked at the *tabac* on Rue Paul Bert. Neither responded, and in desperation Beck went after an actual native at the BNP in Reuilly while drawing on his bottomless credit cards. I watched him sidle up to the prospect, who looked like a slightly elongated Demi Moore, and speak a few words of his patois to her. She told him quite loudly she was not free Friday night. He didn't understand and went after her again. She broke down and said, in unaccented English, that she would never be free, not on a Friday, not on any day of the week. Beck went home and wrote a long letter to Val.

"You don't think he's attractive?" I asked, thrilled.

"He's not my type."

I didn't know how to interpret this.

"Have you ever, you know —"

"Screwed guys? Sure. In high school I was with the jazz band director. He was married."

I was immediately granted a picture of a dark, popular, sixteen-year-old Margot in faded cords and untucked flannel shirts. She spent all her time with the boys in the jazz band and with the band director. She had breasts, and she was brilliant at trigonometry. Margot hadn't told me any of this, but it all turned out to be accurate. My Germaine Lagachian powers were not limited to your past alone.

"He said he loved me. He wanted to get a divorce."

She crushed garlic.

"You were sixteen."

She stepped to the kitchen.

"We would have been cool for a few years, until I graduated."

I saw the young Margot at once, pretty and efficient, making decisions that most grown people can't handle. In the afternoon she did math, had sex, played sax. She always played sax.

"Where would I be now? In Newton, married to a high school band teacher, that's where. I loved Wayne, but I wasn't a pinhead. Besides, Dad wanted Yale for me."

Margot and I were from the same background, both middle-class Jewish onlys with a hard-wired success wish. My dad had made it out of Opa and Oma's teetering little house in downtown Poughkeepsie to a golfer's split-level in Brentwood. Hers had made it all the way from Jersey City to a dental practice in Massachusetts, with a two-car garage and a boat in the driveway. Margot had told me her dad was so proud of her he could hardly bear to let her explain what she'd accomplished last. He was always too busy trying to repeat the success story to Margot's mom. That was true even on Thanksgiving of her first year at Yale, when Margot was telling him, while she helped cook, that she'd figured out she liked sleeping with women. Bobby was about to say to Miriam, *That's our girl.* Instead he turned to Margot, offered her a spoonful of cranberry sauce, and said, *I don't think there's any reason to worry, honey. This is very common at your age.*

I'd never sprung any comparable revelations on Dad and my almost stepmom, Brenda. I did startle them when I started taking modern dance five days a week freshman year. I made the switch after I realized that if I trained as hard as I could and didn't injure my knees or shins again, I might be the seventh fastest sprinter on the JV squad. Over the phone, Brenda said she loved dance. Dad was silent, but I could hear him wondering if his great nightmare, the Gay Son, was about to be visited upon him.

But my point was that Margot and I were from the same caste, whereas you and Beck, well, you know who you are. Beck says your father's people arrived in New England on a wooden boat, swapped beads for Beacon Hill real estate, and settled down to wait for you. Meanwhile your mother's folks went on up to New Hampshire, cleared the land, and named it Logs.

"Did you date guys at Yale?"

"I went out with my physics section leader," Margot said. She braised eggplant.

"What's this with you and teachers?"

"That's a long story," she said happily. She obviously had some complicated psychological theory about it. I wallowed deeper in the chair, nursed the wine in my coffee cup, and waited. James Blood Ulmer was on guitar now, making a sound like a litter of piglets being tickled.

"I've got time," I told her. I loved to hear Margot talk sex and psychology. Her theories were like dirty fairy tales for big kids, with the moral built right into the middle. But as it turned out, I didn't have time. Beck clomped up the stairs and banged on the door.

"Open!"

"No," I said, with feeling. Margot let him in, cutting knife in hand.

"Peace pipe," Beck told her, guiding the knife to the side. "Me powwow giant white squaw ray long fish over cold waters."

He had another stock tip for you, from his brother at Kidder Peabody.

"She's not home yet," Margot said.

"Go away," I said.

"Never."

He threw his leather saddlebag at me, the one he used all the time, though it weighed more than whatever he put in it. He'd bought it one Sunday at Les Puces for an undisclosed sum and thought it was authentic Polish cavalry, circa '38. I knew it was Andalusian contemporary and that he'd been handsomely ripped off by a Frenchman posing as a gypsy. I batted the bag down.

"Where have you been?"

"Working," he said.

This was secret agent talk for sleeping the afternoon away. I'd finished the worst of the cleaning the week before. Then I'd bought materials to begin repairing the walls, which needed to be patched before I painted them. Beck, in the meantime, had finished the beers of Belgium and started on those of Holland. It wasn't as if he'd been idle.

"How's it hanging, Sweet Cheeks?" he said.

He walked up behind Margot and didn't goose her, it was slower than that. He massaged her ass affectionately for a moment with both hands, grunting to himself in a boarish way. He could do that, just as he could say anything.

"Zubir's got a sister. Did I tell you?"

"You told us, Beck," I said. "You tell us every night."

"Zohra doesn't play an instrument, but she's part of the band now. She comes to all our rehearsals just to see me."

Margot rolled her eyes. Beck had found the bass player, Zubir, on the bulletin board at Beaubourg. There were lots of musicians' cards up, he'd told us, but most were the whinings of pathetic basement rock stars. There in the middle of all the rubbish was a message neatly printed in English — *M. Zubir Derouiche, bass acoustic. In research of the bebop experience.*

"Why didn't you show this morning? Zubir and I waited for you."

"My J-O-B," Margot said. "Remember? I told you about those."

"I'll show you the charts. We set 'Y.A.T.A.G.'"

Beck, Margot, and Zubir played together all fall. They needed a drummer, and the trio, christened the Tone Wizards in time for the first of their Thursday gigs at the Tahonga, would have been a quartet. Instead they stayed a threesome, Beck played with his West Indian big band, and Margot and Zubir started gigging as a duet at Le Cambridge and Twenty-One King Opéra. Everyone grew artistically and got paid once in a while.

"Red stuff?" Beck said.

"You were bringing it. I left you a note."

Beck weakly slapped his forehead.

"I am aweary," he said in brogue.

I dragged myself upright and held out a palm. This was the way all our disagreements were resolved — Beck's money, my time. Before I was out the door, he had usurped the chair and was contentedly listening to Margot's voice and the sounds of saxes and cooking. I understood him and almost forgave him his interruption, but couldn't quite until I ran smack into you on the landing.

"Bonk," you said. You leaned down from the heights of your boots and kissed my cheek.

I led you back down the stairwell, across the courtyard, and through the gate.

"Wine," I told you, as if the word alone justified not letting you say hello to Margot. The cool print of your kiss melted from my cheek in the October breeze. In the shop on Rue Duret you asked advice in French good enough not only to formulate questions but to understand answers. I had a standing directive from Beck about how much to spend. We would drink three bottles in descending order of value as we lost the power of discrimination. You chose a fifty-franc Domaine de Villemajou, a white Muscadet for half that, and a vin du pays du Var for twelve francs and sous. The man wrapped our bottles in pieces of white paper so they wouldn't catch cold. I suppose that was his reasoning. He didn't offer us anything as useful as a bag.

It had been a long day. Ballet was becoming more painful, just when I thought it couldn't possibly. Beck's dormant existence appealed to me, as did your double career as an actress and Parisian intellectual. You'd spent your morning on Boulevard Raspail at a seminar on Napoleon's legal, political, and social impact, and how France wouldn't have come out looking at all French if it wasn't for him. Then you'd gone to your acting workshop with the enthusiastic but brutally honest Monsieur Jano Hanbowski, Polish dissident playwright-director. He taught drama disguised as dialectics, or was it the other way around? Now you looked culturally aware and refreshed, and I was jealous of your rich interior life. It made me wish I'd been less premed at Syracuse, but I'd graduated and it was too late. No matter how much money I made, no matter what kind of physical shape I kept myself in, I would spend my days becoming less and less sophisticated, until I died an unexamined death. That was when you started laughing.

"I'm thinking," you explained, "about the guys on the green motorcycles."

"What?"

"Who suck up dog shit."

"On cycles."

"You don't know," you said, "what I mean."

You held open the door for me and I maneuvered through with the bottles.

"They ride down the sidewalk. They wear green overalls with *DES TROTTOIRS NETS* on the back."

We walked into the last rays of sunlight.

"They wear white helmets," you tried again. "They hold metal vacuum cleaners down over the poop."

Then your sight memory entertained you on a different level and you couldn't talk at all. So much for your intellectual life, I thought. We stopped beside a bucket of chamomile bouquets at the florist's. I tried to zero in on what you'd seen, but my new powers worked better on your childhood than on temporally proximate occurrences. Your eyes squeezed shut. You hugged yourself and bobbed in place.

"They wear rubber boots," you said. "They rev their engines. Water shoots out."

You looked volumes at me.

"They push a button. That vacuums it back up."

"Right."

"It's like a rug shampooer. Except for sidewalks."

Tears rolled down your face and right off your chin. You wrapped your arms tighter around yourself and bent over until your nose was between your knees.

"Why not use a shovel?" I asked.

You stood up holding your breath and started forward. I took rapid baby steps to match your pace. When we stopped next, it was in front of Giorgio's, where a yellow belt cost a lot, I remember that. You wiped your eyes with the hand that wasn't clutching my arm. Then you started taking full steps and I held on to the bottles for dear life. We zoomed across Avenue de Malakoff and through into Berlioz. I still don't know how you managed to see through your laughter and catch that bottle, the Villemajou of course, when it finally slipped its wrapper and headed for the stone. But you did, and so it was the two of us who landed on the cobbles, side by side, under the linden tree, in love.

Partisans

Nanterre Ville was a sixteen-minute RER ride from Châtelet. We walked out of the station into a blaze of sun, then made our way past the Monoprix and the moss-caulked walls that hid all but the red-tiled roofs of the houses.

"You need not be anxious," Paola told me at the bus stop. "You will be of sufficient quality."

"I'm not concerned. I am a man, and modern dance is my preferred form."

She spoke her formal French translated from Italian. I translated this into English in my mind, thought of an answer in English, and then outputed it to her in French, so that she could start processing it back into Italian. The result of all this was a satellite time-lag in our communication that made me feel precise and logical, and at the same time as if both of us had a mild cognitive impairment.

"Do not overestimate your opportunity," Paola said. "Catherine anticipates a humble posture."

"I must be noticed."

"Yes, but you are not an invited soloist."

Paola had taken me under her wing in ballet class that very first day. She praised me whenever I kept up, and consoled me when I fell behind and took a tongue-lashing from Madame Lafontaine. The second week I'd come to class looking bewildered. Paola wondered whether I was ill. I confessed to her that I'd fallen in love with two women the night before. From that day on we were each other's confidants.

"Conform yourself to the group," she told me now. "Control your arms. Maintain your chin level."

"I'll try to remember."

We waited for the 159 bus to the Palais des Sports. I had a problem with wild arm movement, when I became too excited about what my feet were doing. I also tended to look at the floor about twenty feet in front of me, a vestigial track habit.

Paola was in love with a dancer, Joseph, in the modern company for which I was about to audition. In a way it was Joseph's audition, too. I'd promised to tell Paola if I thought he was worthy of her. Her brothers were in far Verona and couldn't advise her.

The bus took us from old Nanterre to new. We passed the concrete Crèche Municipale, then the black tower of the Hôtel du Département, finally the Salvador Allende parking structure. The bus turned off Avenue Joliet Curie and we jumped down opposite the Théâtre des Amandiers. It was hotter than ever. Paola led me up across a soccer field to what looked like a miniature airport. We made our way to the basement, where Paola chatted in Italian with a blue-garbed *femme de ménage*. We went further into the dark, cool complex. Paola led me through a gym and a moldy weight room, then down a corridor from the end of which came music and the improbable sound of a choreographer shouting out counts. She squeezed my wrist as we peeked into the studio.

The dancers stopped working. A scrawny woman with buckteeth stepped over to a cheap boom box and switched it off.

"You're early," she accused, advancing on us with long, unselfconscious strides. Paola introduced me, and Catherine Bilgère repeated my name in the French way, *Don*. Her pale eyes were surrounded by tiny wrinkles, and her arms were long for her body. The others nodded their greetings without conviction. They were waiting to see if I was going to be just another one-day wonder before they exerted themselves. All except Joseph.

"Hi," he said in a broad American accent, shaking my hand.

I told him I'd heard a lot about him. He said hi again, and that's when I knew he didn't speak English. A tall woman with striking eyes walked past me. I knew from my glimpse of rehearsal that she was the best mover there. The others hadn't been too intimidating, especially broad-shouldered Joseph. He looked like a rugby player whose girlfriend had recently dragged him to dance class. He pulled Paola away. They stood talking and touching hands.

The last two women in the company left the studio without a word to me. I thought they were snobs but found out later that they had desperately wanted a smoke. Catherine asked me where I'd studied, in whose companies I'd worked, where I'd performed. I only lied a little. I named Trisha Brown and Robert Kovitch, then a couple of fledgling New York choreographers she couldn't possibly have heard of. She nodded with the same solemnity at each name. The truth was Brown and Kovitch had been handsomely bribed to come upstate and set their pieces on DanceWorks, the Syracuse company. I made it sound as if I'd studied with them in the city. Bilgère wasn't fooled any more than I was. I saw that she didn't know much about the New York dance scene, and she could tell I wasn't part of it.

I went off to change. The empty locker room was big enough to hold two soccer teams. I pulled on my tawny tights and white muscle shirt, then checked myself out in the mirror at the end of my row of lockers. My hair was longer than usual. I had good pectoral definition, a dangerous gleam in my eyes, and hungry, shadowed cheeks. I was audition-ready.

The fake rehearsal went quickly. I pretended not to follow anyone so Catherine would think I was memorizing what she showed us. The others pretended not to watch me, and after twenty minutes we were all moving so fast they weren't anymore. They knew everything Catherine threw at us, while I had to hustle just to stay on the right foot. I had to impress this choreographer. I knew from Paola she was not eager to add anyone to her payroll.

The studio was airless. Our sweat created treacherous puddles on the yellow wood. I tried to anticipate the movement, overdancing each phrase to show Catherine what an eager recruit I was. We took a two-minute break. I pulled off my shirt and wiped my face with it. Joseph walked up to me and slapped me on the back.

"Shit," he said in a flat midwestern drawl. He knew two English words. *"Fait chaud, non?"*

I left the shirt off just to stay cool, but when we started dancing again I could see that this had been a wise decision. Half naked, I proved I wasn't shy and indicated that I was willing to prostitute myself in whatever ways Catherine Bilgère might have in mind. I watched her watch me and thought, *Yes*.

Then we stopped. The stillness was broken only by the sound of six dancers breathing. Drops of sweat hit the floor. Joseph and the three women I didn't know were all smiles now. I was one of them. We sank to the floor. The oldest of the group, a woman with sad eyes and a slow clown's smile, was beside me. She said her name was Anne, and asked me what I was doing in France. I told her I worked for the CIA, on a project called Bohemia. We were cold war counterrevolutionaries. She looked puzzled.

Dominique, the beautiful one, slid across the floor to Joseph. She straddled him, her long hair grazing his back, and massaged him with her full weight. Paola gazed calmly into space as if she weren't furious. I was still explaining to Anne about Bohemia's goals when the others dragged her out of the room toward lunch. Catherine looked at her notes, then at me, then back at her notes again.

"I am sorry. I will not take you," she announced.

"Je —"

I reached into the air. Paola and Joseph appeared in the doorway. Paola had been waiting to encourage or console me, as always. Now she went to Catherine and began whispering while I tried to collect myself. Had the woman really decided not to take me, after I'd auditioned so hard? I couldn't quite imagine that.

Paola and Catherine spoke on. Joseph gave me a thumbs-up sign and nodded as if everything were fine. Catherine's voice rose above an angry whisper from time to time on the word *non*. I heard my name. I gathered that the person attached to it had insufficient talent and training for the position to which he aspired. This was reasonable, but in my mind it had nothing to do with my obvious place in the group now eating lunch. I belonged with those dancers. I'd earned their respect with sweat and derring-do. Why didn't Catherine understand that this was more important than a little technique or movement memory? Those skills would come with time and experience. What I had to offer was the American get-up-and-go spirit. Her company, her country, needed me.

She turned her long-armed body toward me and squinted with forty-year-old eyes. Paola raised her eyebrows in my direction.

"*Madame,*" I began, "*je sais que vous êtes pressée.*"

My French mobilized itself for the emergency like a ragged army of partisans.

"*Je serais reconnaissant si vous pouviez me donner un moment. Je voudrais vous dire combien j'ai envie de travailler avec vous.*"

I was suddenly able to speak. This was the linguistic equivalent of an eighty-year-old woman heaving a Volkswagen off her grandchild.

"*J'ai beaucoup de respect pour ce que vous faites ici. Je voudrais continuer mon audition cet après-midi.*"

She was bewildered. Audition more? I had to keep talking. I brought up a second wave of French, small, hasty words. I said I admired her work. She represented a new vision. I had danced with many choreographers, I said, and listed a few more Greenwich Village gurus who'd commuted up to Syracuse when their NEA money dried up. But I'd never felt so compelled to dedicate myself to another's work. Catherine represented a unique synthesis of European and American dance forms. In short, I wanted her to give me another chance, because I just couldn't imagine dancing anywhere else.

Paola's face held a mixture of disbelief and pride. I'd come up out of the trenches firing rock-salt bullets with an accuracy born of despair. Catherine still looked puzzled, but I could see her coming slowly around to this new point of view. She was not a minor choreographer in a suburban Paris gymnasium, supervising a half-dozen poorly trained postadolescents. She was an undiscovered genius of the first rank.

She shook her head to clear it. That was when I knew I was still in trouble. I started to speak, but Catherine shot me down with a short burst of French and a rapid shaking of her head. Did I not understand? Was it not clear that I could go home now? Had I not noticed that she herself was exhausted and wished to have a cup of coffee before afternoon rehearsal?

I looked at the floor. I'd lost the battle, but I'd also lost the war. That was when the third, indigenous assault surprised all three of us. Joseph came at Catherine from behind, with the full power of his native tongue. He was sick and tired of doing all the men's parts, all the lifting. At the very least Catherine could give me a chance, since I was a friend of Paola's and had come all the way out here on this miserable day.

Catherine threw up her hands and stormed out of the room. How could she argue with people who simply didn't listen?

I sat around all afternoon. The next day she let me dance for an entire half-hour. The third day I worked most of the afternoon, and Friday she grudgingly gave me corrections along with the others. Monday I became a full company member, earning nearly two hundred dollars a month.

There is no such thing as defeat.

Horse Thief

"We do our necessaries in a bucket," Beck said. "But it's home."

I stood aside as he showed you and Margot around our place with a proprietary sweep of his arm.

"This here's the master bedroom, also the living and dining room. This here's the morning room or kitchenette. Our original plans called for a mirrored gallery leading to a suite of twelve interconnected chambers, each representing a geologic phenomenon — the ice floe room, the delta basin room, and so forth. But then the peasants came at us from below, and the king and church from above, and, well, what with one thing and another, we decided to make do with what we call an efficiency."

It was mid-October, and the apartment was finally presentable. I'd scraped the dirt out of the floor and started patching the north wall, where the water pipes had sweated for years before they were disconnected. Germaine arrived with uncanny consistency whenever I started working. It was as if the walls of the whole building were connected to her fingertips by silken webs. She insisted on overseeing whatever I did. By the time I could risk pointing out to her that I wasn't likely to steal from myself and that there was nothing valuable of the Villeneuves' in the place, I understood that she was upstairs for the pleasure of our talks. I provided an excuse for her to leave her lonely post at the front door, where, officially, she was supposed to stay unless she was watching a contractor or a repairman at work. I soon came to depend on Germaine's company. She saved me from the loneliness to which Beck, buying his way out of the renovation, abandoned me.

"Now here's how the water closet works," Beck said as the four of us crowded into the bathroom. "You light this candle, then close the door and hunker down over this bucket. You pour the results into this pipe, which one day will connect with a toilet, if that elegant French son of a bitch Claude Villeneuve ever gets around to commissioning one."

My trowel and putty knife stood neatly in the corner. I turned to them as if they were guests who had arrived before you and Margot and were being neglected. I longed to describe to you the work I'd done and was planning to do, so that you both could admire my rugged simplicity and manliness. But Beck wouldn't give me a chance.

"Then you button up and carry this spanking clean water bucket, not to be confused with the necessaries bucket, into the morning room. Pardon me, ladies. You use this here wrench to turn on the water, you fill up your water bucket, and you carry it back to deluge the pipe, thus. Hopefully, when you take this handy flashlight and with it probe the depths, you find that your offering has been drawn toward the origin of all things. If not, repeat the watering procedure, then seal the pipe with this ornate Florentine mini-manhole cover. That contains the noxious airs."

Beck was an inch taller than your five-ten, which gave him nearly a foot on Margot. Because of his girth, I tended to forget his height. He placed the bowl, with its bright floral pattern and yellow rim, over the pipe. Beck had discovered it among Claude's dishes. He was proud of every detail of his makeshift john, but never dreamed we'd have to use it for eight months. From one week to the next we were sure that Claude would hire a plumber to install a toilet.

"We'd been on the train, then in a cab. I was like to bust. Dan warned me that if I opened the water main, we'd have ourselves a fountain."

He indicated the six copper pipes ending in midair in the bathroom. These would eventually connect to the sink, bath, and bidet. The piping winked elegantly in the shadows, like modern sculpture.

"I believed him, but nature will out. Luckily, the bathroom pipes are on a different main from the kitchen. I offered songs of praise to my patron deity, Ogg."

Beck kept up the talking while I went back to the cooking. You and Margot wandered around our room like parents on visitors' day at a summer camp, marveling at how well your boys had gotten on without you.

"Where do you shower?" Margot asked.

"Leprechaun showers with the others after leprechaun class," Beck said. "I mortify the flesh."

"You don't shower," Margot said.

"The life of the body no longer concerns me. I live only for the indescribably divine, majestic, and ever-changing celestial music, which blows in a ceaseless cosmic symphony through my waking dreams. When I get around to it, there is the charity bathhouse at Oberkampf."

Beck got around to it every third or fourth day. Two would have been optimal. It was my flesh he mortified, especially when he missed his Sunday evening deadline. After that the public bath closed until Thursday at noon, a bureaucratic absurdity remarkable even for France. To aggravate the situation further, Beck had a habit of mixing up all his clean and dirty clothes. He claimed he did it on purpose, that the clean garments drew filth from the soiled ones and rendered his entire wardrobe clean enough to be worn again. Germaine said he was *sauvage*.

You joined me in the kitchenette.

"Reminds me of the old barn," you said.

"At Logs."

Your haircut was particularly bad that night. I remember noticing how short and square it was in front, how it stuck out behind your ears, and how none of that mattered. I couldn't stop looking at you.

"In Gorham, where Grams and Gramps live," you said.
"Well, Gramps is dead, and Grams lives in Lincoln now."

You were scanning *Louons Maintenant les Grands Hommes,*
the French version of James Agee and Walker Evans' book
on Alabama in the Depression. You said this was to help you
imaginatively capture a role in a play set in Poland in 1814. You
held up pictures for me to admire as I cooked on the double
hotplate. Black sharecroppers and white sharecroppers, stick
thin, stood by clapboard shacks or carried hoes along dusty
roads. A few fat white folk, with mottled complexions and tiny
ears, peered out from shadowed porches, or from inside bar-
ber shops. Little did I know, that October night in Paris, that
three years later I'd be doing physicals on these southerners'
ill-nourished bodies.

I seasoned my tomato sauce. You explained to me that the
Stanislavsky method was misunderstood, that it had nothing to
do with becoming a street person to play a street person or a
bank robber to play a bank robber. You said it was about finding in oneself psychological landmarks upon which to execute
a particular "emotion memory." I still didn't understand why,
in order to play a pregnant landowner's daughter in Poland,
you had to familiarize yourself with Alabama, but I liked listening to you and having you close to my stirring arm. Meanwhile, Beck had cornered Margot in the loft. He was com-
plaining in a loud voice that it was my bed.

"The bastard conned me. You have to keep an eye on Daniel. He's harmless enough until you get between him and something he wants."

I tried to listen to both you and Beck. In your play, you were
about to give your child away to a servant girl. You were too
young to have your chances for a good marriage jeopardized.
The only way you could approach your role was to remember
the time when you didn't qualify for the hunter-jumper cham-
pionship in Madison Square Garden. At Andover, you'd had
special permission to spend every afternoon for two years
riding Titania, your mischievous seven-year-old thoroughbred
mare. Before you returned to school for dinner you sang her

Pretenders songs while you groomed her, and late at night you cleaned and saddle-soaped her Hermès saddle and martingale, her bridle and stirrup leathers, until the leather shone like iron but was as supple as old rope. Your dorm room was filled with trophies and ribbons, and you rode and jumped damn well in Devon and Ox Ridge. But still you came up seventeen points short for the Medal-Maclay, and that was the end of your career. The sense of giving everything and still failing was what counted now for your character preparation.

Beck was lying about how I'd demanded the loft bed. The only route to it was a jump from the small refrigerator. Beck could get there all right, but had trouble descending. That was why he went out and bought himself a cot.

"Dan had me over a barrel. He said if I didn't concede the decent bed, he wouldn't do the renovations. He's a devil child, there's no question about it. Don't let that face of his fool you. Did you know his grandfather was a horse thief? The whole family's crooked as a bent nail. Back in Deutschland, they were the Shoenfeld Gang."

My great-grandfather Rudolph was the horse thief. There was no gang.

"I'm just not sure I can give up that baby," you were telling me.

When you talked about acting, you became even taller and more handsome. You leaned your weight on one hip and squinted with thoughts.

"I try to want the fashionable balls and the well-off neighboring landowner. I try to see Father's stern expression at table, but none of that's very persuasive."

"Danny rules me at every level," Beck was saying. "Knowing that doesn't mean I can stop him. It's classic codependency."

"As for the balls, I have to wear whalebone corsets, I can't eat a thing, and I can't ask anyone to dance. I'm even supposed to refuse most of the boys who ask me. Frankly, I'd rather be home suckling my sweetie."

Your eyes were off in social history land. I flicked a piece of pasta at the wall. It stuck, but I had no idea what that meant so I pulled it off and tasted it. It needed another minute. I took the sauce off the heat and maneuvered the pot lid into place to serve as a pasta strainer.

"For all I know he has a hairball, and his stern expression at the dinner table doesn't have squat to do with Svetlana."

"Svetlana?"

"My darling. I'll never give her up. I don't care what they say."

I poured the water off.

"But you have to, don't you?" I asked. "I thought in the play you marry the neighboring landowner, and your maid raises the girl."

You looked at me as if I were simple.

"The first thing you have to understand," you said, "is that character process has nothing to do with what happens."

"Short bastard," Beck pronounced. For a second I was sure he meant me. "Regular bastard's the same two hundred fifty grams," he added, breaking off the heel. "But not so round."

I sat across from you and Margot on two paint cans topped by a board. Margot sat in your lap, and you sat on the two plastic crates I'd found by the garbage bins behind the Rue d'Aligre market the week before. The meal was poor in comparison to what it would have been at your place. The bastard was crusty, and the second and third bottles of wine were of first-bottle quality, since you'd brought them. But the salad was undistinguished, and my tomato sauce balanced right on the edge of inedible. I'd managed to crush one more potent dried pepper into it than I'd meant to.

"Christ, Dan! Not again. What is this, Thai marinara?"

Beck gripped his throat. You and Margot politely chewed, eyes watering.

"I'm sorry. I tasted it along the way. I don't know what happened."

"I do," Beck said. "Bou blew in your ear and you loosed a handful of those peppers. Why did you ever buy those things, anyway?"

"They were pretty. They only cost four francs."

"They've cost me two weeks of groceries."

This was only a minor exaggeration. Margot was as dark and composed as a Persian cat. You whispered something in her ear and she smiled.

"I think it's delicious," you said, eating ambidextrously with your right hand, your left on Margot's knee.

"I think you're very kind," I answered.

"And I," Beck said, "think you're both full of shit. Did I tell you that Zohra wants me to modernize her?"

"You told us," one of us said.

"Not this part. Zubir thinks it's okay for her to come out of the house and hang with us at rehearsals. Margot's trying to get her to look people in the eye. But today Zohra informed me that she's chosen me, personally, to modernize her."

I watched you and Margot and tried to learn everything about you. I was a booby hatchling imprinting your parent forms on my visual cortex. I was instinctively drawn into the twig-and-seaweed circle of your intimacy. Beck was my rival hatchling, but we didn't know that yet. That night it was still all warm sand and heat-retentive tail feathers.

"Truthfully, the whole modern-woman business is Zohra's idea. She was telling me today, over a cup of that unbearably sweet mint tea —"

"Is that what you two were whispering about?"

"Indeed. She wants to learn how to converse without giggling, how to smile without hiding her teeth, how to walk next to me and not behind me."

"But you love all that," Margot said.

"I know. I didn't have the heart to tell her."

"You modernize her the way you'd like to," Margot said, "Zubir's going to take a scimitar to you."

All four of us forgot how hot the tomato sauce was. We paused in our meal only to pant and drink jars of water. I memorized Margot's voice patterns — her airy whistles, her clicks, especially her low hoots. She lifted her jar, sky-pointed, and cooled her parched throat with a long swallow. Then she settled deeper in the shadow of your wings.

"Don't be ridiculous. Zubir hasn't got a scimitar."

"Bet his dad does," Margot said.

The two of you floated off down the stairs at eleven, Margot's arm not around your waist but around your ass. While I did the dishes, Beck harangued me, just as he had at the end of long mornings at Hôpital Forcilles. There we'd performed the traditional gofer job of new lab workers, examining and describing the feces samples, then potting them for overnight baking. First thing each morning the previous day's set was sorted and weighed, but by then the shit was just dry powder. We processed the wet batches the nurses sent down just after ten.

The hospital had once been a resort spa. From the lab, Beck and I looked out on a sloping lawn and an oval flower garden. Beyond that was a patch of woods with a clearing for a ping-pong table and wide paths along which visitors and patients took slow walks. On both sides of the lab's entrance, white trellises supported tangled rosebushes. We faintly smelled the roses on our way in at eight o'clock, when the blooms, squeezed tight, were sparkling with dew. But we didn't appreciate the scene until twelve-thirty or so, when we'd finished our seventy to eighty pots, run the fans, and were on our way out to lunch.

On those summer mornings, the subject of Beck's lectures was often how I should have a higher opinion of myself and apply to the best medical schools. We were both obsessed with med school, and spent all our free time drawing up lists and daydreaming. Beck said I couldn't get into a top school if I didn't apply, and that I couldn't afford to sabotage myself by ruling out even one of them. I tried to explain that I wasn't going to apply to the first-ranked schools because I wasn't brilliant and couldn't possibly get in. Never having been in my position, Beck couldn't accept my attitude.

That night in October after you and Margot left, Beck once

again advised me. He wasn't talking about med schools this time.

"You like the girls, don't you, Dan?"

"Yes."

"You find them both pleasant to look upon. Their conversation soothes you. Their caresses delight you."

I nodded, wondering where he was heading. The dishwater splashed into the bucket under the sink with its three-quarters-full sound. I picked up the wrench and shut off the flow, then switched the full bucket with the reserve bucket, which fit under the sink's drain right where a trashcan would have gone in an ordinary home.

"They like you too."

"They do?"

"They think you're cute," Beck said. "But keep your wits about you."

I carried the bucket to the bathroom, lifted the bowl, and poured the water away. The wash echoed up as if from a well in a fairy tale.

"Wits?"

"All," he said, "is not what it seems."

I put the spare bucket upside down by the sink. It doubled as a stool for sitting on while peeling vegetables or rinsing clothes in the other bucket. Then I opened the water up to a trickle.

"Could you be a little more specific?"

"Perhaps you've noticed Margot looking a little edgy."

I rinsed spoons, but said nothing.

"As if permanently on the rag," Beck added. "Twitchy."

Apparently we weren't talking about the same woman. My Margot was all downy underfeathers and radiant energy. She was a call that purred and warbled, that rose exactly when I thought it would fall, and that I knew I would now recognize if its notes were hidden among a thousand others.

"She's not pleased," Beck observed, "when you and Bou are off together."

I hadn't ever seen Margot when I was off with you. I'd always imagined her contentedly cooking, drinking white wine, and listening to Beck. If Beck wasn't around, I assumed she read psychology, or one of the lesbian thrillers her friend Rachel sent her every few weeks. At the moment she was working on *Straight Shooter* by Blaise Newcastle.

"I might be wrong," Beck said, "but I think our friends are coming up against the three-year itch."

He spoke with authority. I scrubbed the saucepan until it was clean. Then I rinsed it, and it turned out it wasn't clean.

"Perfectly natural. Happens to straight folk too. A couple goes through the book of love. They learn just how well they fit together, how they weather storms in their airtight love capsule. Then they get restless, or rather one of them gets restless. Best is if both get restless, or neither."

"Isn't it seven years?"

"It was," Beck said. "Loaf of bread was a dime, now it's a buck forty-nine."

"I don't follow."

"Could be you don't. I don't think the ladies know yet themselves. I'm just saying keep your eyes open and don't let yourself get recruited, Dan, if you don't want to fight for the flag."

He patted me on the shoulder like a wise uncle, then left me alone with the dishes. I had an idea what he was talking about. I was supposed to leave you and Margot alone. But all I wanted was to be near you, and to know you.

"Trust me," Beck called from his cot. "It's the itch."

I did trust him, Bou.

You just spooked me again. It's nearly three in the morning. Charity Hospital sails through the New Orleans night like an old Mississippi steamboat. The lights from Gravier through the window are as pale and white as moonlight off brackish water. Where are you? I feel you nearby, but you don't show yourself.

I heard about you from the wee ones just after nine this evening. I was standing next to Jennifer Sandler in Well Baby on the northwest corner of the building. There were these three newborns howling at the moon like little wolves. Their mouths were turned inside out with the effort, and the noise they made was so loud it made my eardrums wobble. *Bou! Bou!* they called.

It suddenly occurred to me they were telling me you were pregnant. What else could creatures five hours old have to report? You're not pregnant, engaged, married, or a mother, are you? You catch my drift. *Bou's fine,* Margot wrote in her Rosh Hashanah note last month. That doesn't mean *Bou's pregnant.* If you were pregnant, either she wouldn't have mentioned you at all or she would have written, *Call me. I want to talk to you about Bou. Don't worry, she's fine.* That would mean you're engaged or pregnant.

Jennifer Sandler is two calendar years, three professional years older than me. She and Tim Clinton supervise me and Joel Nash. Clinton's friendly enough, but Jennifer's the real teacher. She's not impatient and she doesn't get carried away with her explanations. When I ask a question, she doesn't lecture me for twenty minutes about details I'll never remember anyway. She and I walk around the nursery when Delivery's quiet, even though it's not our turf. Jennifer's thinking about doing a perinatal fellowship when she's done with OB/GYN.

Tonight Grant is back from Miami, where he gave yet another paper on risk factors for recurrence of gestational diabetes. He's nationally known in his field, which only partially accounts for his making everyone else here feel so ignorant. With him back on the ward and my fellow subintern, Steve Tsintolas, sucking up to him, Jennifer and I managed to steal ten minutes to run down to the nursery. I knew Steve would handle anything that came along without even telling me about it. He thinks the more patients he treats that the rest of us don't, the more points he gets.

Jennifer and I reached the northeast wing and started toward Nursery Four, where the tiny ones live — the feeders and growers, as the nurses call them. But I pulled her to the Tulane side of Well Baby. I couldn't help it. I love to loiter in the healthy nursery, which looks like a giant laundromat, except that all the rolling baskets have babies in them. I started bothering a female Rodriguez. As a rule I don't pick up new ones. They're a temperamental bunch, and if they're not crying it's best to leave them be. If they are crying, they're much too loud to hold. I let them lie on their pads and just palm them around the belly or back, whichever presents itself. They feel like flannel-wrapped basketballs.

I palmed the Rodriguez girl too hard and set her off. Her cry triggered two other younger people, and soon it sounded like a police raid on Nursery One. Nadine Croft, who's been the Well Baby nurse since before I was one myself, stayed right where she was in her chair, hating me.

"Good work," Jennifer yelled. With a motion of her head, she indicated that I'd observed the well infants enough for now.

But I couldn't move. I just stood, listening to the pack.

The last time you spooked me was in May when, by some miracle, I came home early from the hospital. I was microwaving my dinner. As always, I was wondering why Dana and I had broken up, why I both did and didn't miss her, and why I couldn't shake myself out of the horrible state of mind I'd been in ever since. I live at the stately Deerfield development in Terrytown, an adult community offering "the services of tomorrow with the grace of yesterday." What a joke. The place is a collection of McHouses next to a shopping center. My two rooms are just as I found them when I moved down from Poughkeepsie three years ago. I tell everybody I'm going to move across the river to town or at least furnish my place, but I don't. I stay and don't buy a thing, content with my deck furniture in the living room, my bed and dresser in the bedroom. I've put no work whatsoever into the place and don't intend to. I just take my loan check and pay my bills. I never dry-wall, paint, wire, resurface, light, or plumb, as I so carefully did that dwelling of Beck's and mine on Rue Roubo.

That afternoon the TV was on. When I looked up from my microwave burritos, ELIZABETH PHILIPS floated across the screen. You had snuck up on me, just to answer my question about what was wrong with my life. Obviously it was not that Dana was gone, but that you hadn't arrived. I gasped and pressed my palm to my forehead, like a bad soap actor.

When I recovered, the credits were over. *TV Guide* told me only that you had been in one of two Vaclav Havel plays on A&E. I don't know which play was yours, or if you had a cameo or were the star. The one time the plays were on again, I carefully programmed my VCR to record them, then left for the hospital without putting a tape in. I know — I didn't really want to see you, or I wouldn't have botched the recording.

My first year here, Mike Lewitt was my anatomy partner. His sister Tracy knew someone who knew you at Juilliard. Tracy's a cellist, but her best friend was in the drama program. She told Tracy, who told Mike, who told me, that you spent a lot of your weekends out of town. You were seeing another actress at Juilliard, but she definitely wasn't the only one in your life.

That was the last news I've had of you. Mike's sister came

down to visit last fall and told me that her friend had left Juilliard and moved to Los Angeles. She's waiting to be discovered and in the meantime has made a L'eggs commercial. You've stayed in theater work in New York, the way you always said you would for at least five years. I like to think of you at a rehearsal somewhere, out-Streeping everybody with your historical knowledge and accent wizardry. Someday you'll be a famous actress, then a director. Margot is too wise to tell me anything about your personal life in her yearly notes, but I know I'll hear about you again soon from unexpected sources. You'll float up in front of me when I least expect it, the way you did last May. Or you'll call to me, loud and clear, from the quivering, O-shaped mouths of babes.

Spackle Dialogue

Beck studied for MCATs and drank beer. It was Italian beers that week, so he had a Raffo or a Poretti. While he worked, he watched that Grundig portable he'd rented with Grandma Beckett's latest check. He'd just picked it up at Locatel one afternoon, the way I might have stopped on my way home for an umbrella or three pairs of socks. That's the way Grandma Beckett would have wanted it. She didn't mess around with care packages or letters. She sent little notes and big checks, and the one phone chat I had with her lasted less than a minute.

Beck's Grandma Whitney was another grandmother altogether. She sent long letters once a month, and every six weeks or so she sent those heavenly packages. Once when Beck wasn't home, she and I talked for twenty-five minutes. She asked where my people came from. I said Poughkeepsie and she told me she'd been to Vassar to visit her cousin. She made it sound like this had been the week before, but Beck assured me it was in the '30s. We talked about the glories of the Catskills for a while, then she asked my family name in case she knew my people. I told her we were the Shoenfelds and that Mother had been a Blumenthal of Morristown, New Jersey. Without missing a beat Grandma Whitney said she had lots of Jewish friends. Once, she told me, she'd been to Grossinger's, and she loved mahjong. I told her I loved her care packages, and let slip that I especially appreciated the HoHos. We got extras from then on.

Now Beck studied and watched a Coupe d'Europe match between Toulouse and Naples on Grandma Beckett's TV. I spackled the south wall.

"Black is dominant over white, rough coat is dominant over smooth," Beck said. "A purebred white rough-coat male is mated to a purebred black smooth female. Their offspring are (a) all white with rough coats, (b) all white with smooth coats, (c) all black with smooth coats, (d) all agouti, or (e) all black with rough coats."

"D."

"How, might I inquire, did you know that?"

"That's a little complicated. What's agouti?"

Rain had fallen off and on all morning. It was on now, and water poured down the window in long, scalloped rivulets. I thought about the fifth floor of Bird Library, where I always studied at Syracuse. My chair by the window looked down at the frozen sugar and Norway maples in front of Lyman, and in March, when the wind blew the melting snow off the roof, water poured past my study window just as it did now. I'd sit in my neon orange chair for hours, watching the twisting transparent stream and working chem problem sets with a boredom hard-on.

"What kind of animal was that?"

Beck ignored me.

"You have at your disposal benzene, bromine, nitric acid, and sulfuric acid. If you wish to produce m-bromonitrobenzene, you should (a) nitrate the benzene and then brominate, (b) brominate the benzene and then nitrate, (c) perform either (a) or (b), which work equally well, (d) forget it, because you cannot obtain the desired product with these materials, or (e) mix all except the sulfuric acid."

I vaguely recalled something about nitro groups. Nitration had to come first or else it had to come last. I was pleased I'd located the crux of the problem.

"A," Beck said when I'd stalled too long.

"Right. But do you know *why?*"

He flipped the page. The rain accompanied my spackling. I

lifted the tray and scooped up a glob, studying the secrets in the wall. With short strokes I buried them, one by one, forever.

"Characteristics that are common to the arthropod, mollusk, echinoderm, and chordate lines are (a) coelom and a parietal eye, (b) endoskeleton and coelom, (c) segmentation and a coelom, (d) compound eye and segmentation, or (e) endoskeleton and a parietal eye."

"Segmentation and a coelom."

Finally he'd given me some biology I could get my hands around. I was so pleased I blew each of the next three physics and chem questions. Beck forgot nothing and repeated nothing, and all the time he followed the soccer game. He knew the players' names, as if it were the Mets against the Sox, and despite the beer and the TV I knew he'd never forget a single detail of what he reviewed. Margot wrote me that in the end he scored a cool six fourteens and a thirteen, and was disappointed.

Events occurred in Naples. Beck looked up from the book.

"*Maradona!*" he shouted, along with an estimated seventy thousand Italians.

"Who?"

"Diego Maradona. Argentine two-way midfielder. Pelé's legitimate heir."

He swallowed chem, bio, and soccer all together in great drafts. He was an information machine. Even in jazz he found more data — industry rankings, record labels, dates of historic gigs. It must have been hard to be Beck. I wonder if it's gotten easier.

He studied. Naples nearly scored. He and the Italians roared. *"Attacca! Attacca!"*

In the south there was sunshine and jubilation. In the shadowed north, the French waited for their chance. The sky through our window was an unburnished silver, closer in spirit to the gloom of Toulouse than to the Italian lightness of heart. Beck, the traitor, hummed and cheerfully squeezed his hands between his thighs.

At four Germaine went for bread, waddling on her bad feet

across Roubo and on past the furniture refinisher's shop. I knew she'd have spent the afternoon with me if Beck hadn't been there. She thought he was making fun of her whenever he spoke in his offhand way. She didn't realize he was like that with everybody except doctors. I asked Beck if he believed in true love.

"Sorry, Dan. I thought you asked me if I believe in true love."

"I did."

That slowed him down for a minute.

"Do you mean love at first sight?" he asked.

"That's part of it."

"What's the rest of it?"

"That there's one person for you and only one. That you two are forever. That you've always known each other, even though —"

"I get it," Beck said. "No. I don't believe there's only one person, and I don't think anything that has to do with being human is forever."

For a while he was silent, but I knew he was still mulling over true love because of the way he ignored his beer. There was a thoughtful look on his face when he wasn't scanning the books or watching the game. I also noticed that each time I smoothed in a nail hole, I felt lighter. It was as if I had that much less to remember. Still, part of me never stopped worrying about what I was erasing. I tried to reassure myself that history remains, even when it's spackled under. Germaine said each life leaves a myriad of traces. She called them *gifts* and said that one day, when I was not afraid, I would see them.

"You don't believe in it?" Beck asked.

"What?" I wanted to make him say it.

"True *luv*."

He pronounced it funny so he wouldn't be embarrassed. I wondered why he didn't want to say *love* normally.

"I don't know. I used to."

Suspense built in Naples. Beck's eyes went south for a while, and when they returned I asked him the real question, the one I had been saving while I spackled in an archipelago of secrets.

"Do you love Bou and Margot?"

"Both of them?" he asked.

"Yeah."

"Do you mean like *luv* love?"

"Yes."

I knew I'd gotten his full attention then. He pushed his Lehninger across the card table. I erased a plaintive split in the plaster that appeared and disappeared and finally, by the window, dove deep into time.

"Dan."

"Hm."

"It's traditional to fall in love with one person at a go."

I shrugged. I knew this. It had always been my habit to fall in love with only one at a time. I tended to pick women who were inaccessible — too attractive, too far away. I knew how to do it right.

"It's just"— Beck looked troubled —"simpler. The logistics, the medical"— he waved his hand —"considerations."

"But you know them. They're . . ."

Now it was my turn to search for words. I didn't find them, so I pointed my putty knife at him instead and brought the rounded blade flat against my left palm. I felt the wide-open expression of a village idiot on my face. On the television Maradona did something heroic, but Beck neither chanted nor clapped. He did look at the screen for a minute, but I could see he was preoccupied with the idea of a roommate who was in true love with both of his other two best friends in Paris.

"I knew you had a crush on them. We discussed that."

He retrieved his Lehninger and ran his fingers over the diagram of the hexose monophosphate shunt.

"I suggest you go out with one of the dancers in that ballet class. There are about fifty of them, aren't there?"

I nodded that fifty was a reasonable estimate, then shook my head. None of the dancers was Margot or you, Bou. Certainly none of them was both of you. Beck leafed through his book and I knew my problem was under consideration, along with the shunt and the soccer game.

"At first," he said calmly during the fifteen-minute midgame break, "I thought you were going after Margot. Especially when I surprised you two during that little massage of yours, when Bou and I went for pizza but forgot money. Then, for a week or two, I decided it was Bou, the way you two kept disappearing together and coming back all winded. But that was before I realized your relationship is based solely on stupid jokes. Then I decided you were after both women or neither. I hoped neither but thought it prudent to warn you not to give too freely of yourself, lest you become a player in a game from which you will ultimately be excluded. I did that after you fixed us that little snack with the chili peppers."

He paused, drank a quarter of his beer, and then actually closed both his books. That made me nervous, so I filled another hole with the knife.

"Now you're telling me you want something to happen. I anticipated this."

He spoke with a solemn, coach-faced-with-personnel-change look on his face. It was as if he had just been called in by the Italians to make a substitution decision.

"They're no different from us, Dan. You have a notion that you can create a new order of love with Bou and Margot. Forget that."

He enunciated his words carefully, as if I were a little slow.

"Margot may talk as if she's above jealousy, private property, and all the rest of it. She'll feed you that depth-psychological, feminist palaver until the cows come home. She'll prove to you your father is your mother, your cock is a semiautomatic weapon, and *The Honeymooners* is the most dangerous piece of propaganda ever aired. But just remember, at the end of the day our little utopians pull off their panties one leg at a time, same as us."

Germaine turned the corner from Faubourg St.-Antoine and

shuffled, like a white pigeon, down the sidewalk. She'd bought milk from the *crémerie* across Rue de Chaligny, as well as her usual *pain complet*.

"You mess with that pristine relationship of theirs, you try to turn it into a New Age, Parisian love threesome, and you'll find out quick that you've been living in Never-Never Land."

I stayed by the window in the soft light. Beck had gone further, or less far, than I had. He thought something might happen besides what was already in place. But I was floating between you and Margot, where I could hear both your voices. You saw yourselves in me, and I found myself in you. While we were living, our lives would weave a shining braid, two bright energy streams and a third, fainter one, winding in and out. After we were dead, our gifts would remain invisibly joined forever, crisscrossing cracks buried in a white wall.

I just wondered if Beck was coming with us.

"Tell me this," he said. "You wouldn't want to hurt either of the women's feelings, would you?"

"No."

He still spoke in his coaching voice. I didn't mind that he talked down to me. He understood a lot of things I didn't. But this time I thought he was the one who hadn't kept up.

"Don't you think it would hurt Bou if you were too close to Margot? Or Margot if you were with Bou?"

I considered this, spackler dangling.

"No."

Beck sighed. For a minute he watched the game as if it might offer some insight. A call was disputed. I spackled. An Italian was carried off the field. Toulouse scored. The Italians and Beck sat in stunned silence. He looked at me as I was running my hands over the area I had just completed, brushing the smooth surface with my fingertips.

"Let's look at it from another perspective, Dan. You're content with the way things are right now. All four of us together."

"Yes."

"Good," he said cautiously. It was as if he were thinking

about sending me in to replace the injured man. Though I was a rookie on his bench, I had just told him that yes, I had played striker. This gave him something to work with.

"There would be no reason, then," he said deliberately, "for you to complicate our mutual relations by, for instance, becoming physically intimate with one or both of the women."

"No."

I studied the wall. I could start painting as soon as the spackle hardened and I completed the last sanding. In his letter, Dad had told me to give the spackle seventy-two hours. Otherwise it would absorb paint and leave dull spots in the gloss.

"What do you say, kid?"

"You're right."

I didn't know what more Beck wanted from me. How could I tell him that three of us were exactly where we were meant to be?

I ran my fingertips over the section of plaster I had just spackled. It was a frozen ocean of love.

First Breath

"Joseph has asked my hand in marriage," Paola said.

"He has what?"

"Yesterday at Tati. I was trying on a new pair of walking shoes because mine have developed holes. He was weaving my laces so slowly I chided him. He asked me if I would become his wife."

"Very nice," I said, picturing sturdy Joseph on one knee. "The amorous salesman."

"Don't be comical. This is a matter of importance."

There was a deep calm in those minutes before ballet. Paola and I lay on the floor, polished a rich brown by leather slippers and pine rosin, in the fragile morning light that came through the windows. The radiators clicked and pinged in the corners of the long room, the warmth spilling across to us.

"Joseph is hurrying himself," I said cautiously.

"He is an older man."

Paola herself was twenty-two, but I could never think of her as my age. She had lived with her parents and brothers in Verona until she'd come to Paris the previous spring, and that made her young. But she'd started dancing full-time when she was fourteen, and in Verona had been teaching ballet to children for three years. That made her a working woman, not a college girl.

"He declared that he will marry me one day, but that he knows I am not prepared. He will demand me again when he believes I am more favorably prejudiced."

She waited for my opinion, but I held back. I had little insight into Paola's expectations for life. I knew Joseph less well, but understood him better. At twenty-eight, he thought he was an old bachelor who had sown his wild oats. The year before he had been accepted for his DUG at Paris Dauphine, but he had taken time off to dance. Soon he'd go back and finish the degree, marry, and settle down. Paola had led me to understand that she was a virgin and would remain so until her wedding night. I didn't know how that affected her thinking, or Joseph's.

"How shall I respond to him?" she asked.

"How did you respond to him?"

"I assured him that I loved him," Paola said, "and that I believed the sincerity of his intentions."

"Good. He ought to be satisfied for the moment."

"He was delirious," Paola reported. "He rose and danced a great circle about the store."

Five minutes later, Nicole plunked down beside us. Every weekday morning, Paola, Nicole, and I took ballet. Most afternoons we commuted out to Nanterre together for rehearsal with the Compagnie Catherine Bilgère. After two months of this routine, the two women were as familiar to me as if I'd grown up across the breakfast table from them. Nicole was usually so irritable in a seventeen-year-old way that when she came out from under her cloud, she was irresistible. Now she gave us each a kiss and began her meditation, a silly look on her face as she chanted her mantra. Her cheeks and the skin above her eyebrows were marked with tiny pimples.

Mademoiselle Rose passed along the mirrored wall. She settled at the piano, lifted, and settled again. Without warning she lit into a minor scale, then dropped her hands to her lap. Her eyes wandered unsteadily over the room as if following the flight of a moth.

Madame Lafontaine rushed into the studio, her heels striking the wood like castanets. A moment later the overhead lights erased the shadows. I hurried behind Paola to the barre. Madame whispered to Rose. The first breath of Mom's favorite invention filled the sunlight.

Rose played a lot of Bach I recognized and a lot of other music I didn't. I loved to sneak up on her after the barre and name the pieces. Mom and I had played a Bach tunes game before I could talk. She sang the beginning and I sang the end. We used to describe to each other what the songs were about. There were lots of different kinds, but the ones I remember best were the running songs and the flying songs.

When I was a teenager, I played name that tune for real with Dad. He took it way too seriously, as if we were having a putting match on the back lawn. He knew everything, so I'd only give him a bar or two. We even played name that conductor, trying to guess which recordings were which. By the time I'd finished high school, I knew my way around Mom's collection almost as well as he did.

At first Rose wrinkled up her nose and stuck out her mustache when I crept up on her with a guess. I've never known how to approach a blind person, and in French I was worse. I wasn't going to say *Je viens* or *C'est moi* every time I wanted to name a sarabande. By November, I noticed Rose was playing more Bach. She started choosing bits I had to search for. The piano stuff was easy, but she threw in her own arrangements of violin and cello works and tunes from orchestral suites. She loved it when I guessed wrong.

"Take that in," Madame Lafontaine said. "This is not a go-go room."

She was suddenly behind me at the barre, her forefinger jabbing at my coccyx. She passed me and adjusted Paola's shoulders with a gentle touch.

"*Arrêtez, arrêtez,*" Madame said a minute later, cutting Rose off. "Perhaps you are all ready to dance now?"

Rose lowered her chin and reintroduced the exercise. I held in my stomach, the tip of my spine tingling. Five minutes later, Madame grabbed my arm and twisted until the skin burned.

"Why are you here?" she demanded.

The question has always been a tough one for me, even when I'm not trying to sustain a *développé*.

"If you want to sleep, go home," she told me, and clacked off.

I thought about this. I hadn't known I was asleep, but by Madame's standards I'd probably been awake for only an instant now and again during the whole course of my life.

I never really told you how bad it was. I didn't tell anybody. In the early fall, Madame's attacks brought tears to my eyes. Then came the third Wednesday in October. During the adagio, I lost my balance and spoiled the effect of a whole line of dancers. Madame stopped the music, stalked up to me, and shook me by the shoulders. The others laughed nervously. She threatened me with immediate expulsion. After class, she called me over for a conference. While the others pretended to file out, Madame made me promise to work *ten times harder*. I was lazy and had no training. Her second husband had been an undisciplined American dancer like myself and had never gotten anywhere, just as I never would. Men, she said, had no notion of sacrifice.

After that I was careful not to let her hear me speak. I knew the unpleasant associations my accent had for her. But her corrections no longer brought tears to my eyes.

"Around on eight. Extend to *attitude* and hold. *Fondu* on three to *passé,* four. Arms to first, third. Over *penché.*"

Madame choreographed with gestures of her fingers and head. Mireille, her long-time protégée and now a corps dancer at the Opéra ballet, flanked her on the right like a bodyguard. She converted Madame's sketches into movement the rest of us could follow. Paola stood in the second row on the piano side, and I hid behind her. What Paola did, I did. By the time Madame switched the lines and I stood in front, I could bluff my way through the adagio.

But I couldn't hide behind Paola in the fast, intricate *petit allegro.* The *assemblés, brisés,* and *entrechat-quatres* were like so many riddles I had to solve in midair. Inevitably, I fell behind and had to step quickly to the back of the room, out of the path of the other dancers. I tried to tell myself that I was not inherently slow or uncoordinated. It was simply that these women had learned all that footwork while I was busy playing sports. If the tables were turned and we were required by Madame to tackle or evade one another, I'd be at a great advantage.

The two other men, Marc and Thierry, were far better than they had any right to be. Marc had been with Roland Petit's company and had retired only the year before, in his mid-thirties, to live a more civilized life with his boyfriend, Gilles. Thierry had been on his way to a solid ballet career before he gave it up for law. Now he made it to class a few mornings a week, but when his beeper sounded from his dance bag under the piano, he skulked off like a fugitive.

Paola always told me I could master the *petit allegro* if I just took it one step at a time. "Learn one step each day," she would whisper to me as I stood in the back of the room, eyes on the floor. I didn't believe her until the second Monday in December. That day the *petit allegro* was as easy as they come. The first part of it was a set of *coupé, assemblé, pas de bourrées,* with only a *sissonne, changement* for spice. I recognized the piece Rose was playing but couldn't pin it down. That was what made me forget myself and dance the first half through. I was in midair when I realized Rose was improvising her own variation of the courante from the D-minor partita for unaccompanied violin. Madame immediately decided the music was wrong and Rose played another piece, not Bach. I couldn't get through the *petit allegro* again that day, but once had been enough. I remembered the sensation of traveling through space in a stately fashion while my feet did all my thinking for me.

From that day on, as soon as class ended, Paola worked on her step and I worked on mine. Once I had it, I'd tiptoe to the dressing room, holding it carefully. When I was dressed I walked it to the elevator and out of the building, then to rehearsal, where I took it out and played with it during breaks. At five-thirty I brought it to your house, and at eleven-thirty, when Beck and I left, I trotted it home.

The métro was empty at that hour. I danced against the tug of the train and of my street clothes. Beck read *France Football* at the other end of the car. He never had to work at trombone the way I did at ballet, but I could tell he respected me for plodding along.

In bed, my feet would have one last go at that day's move. They'd dream it, with little twitches, before I fell asleep.

Soup

"Let's split another one," I said to Margot. "I'll buy."

I ordered the *café crème* from the waiter in the black vest and bow tie, and settled deeper into the red plush. I relished the whole of the Brasserie Scossa — the marble tables with scrolled iron bases, the fluted columns and arched mirrors behind the bar, the brass-leafed chandeliers, and the thick brass curtain rods at the level of my collarbone, which held a mesh curtain tautly in place along the length of the Rue de Sontay window. But I especially admired the shell that enclosed the front and sides of the restaurant. The steel had been disguised as oak inlay, lighter and darker rectangular woods meticulously detailed with the whorls and spots of natural grain. At my pace, just the panels beside our table would have taken a week.

"What time will Bou get up?"

"One," Margot said. "Maybe two."

The coffee came. We allowed ourselves to finish our brioche. Spending money with Margot was an entirely different pleasure from spending money with you or Beck. In the shakily caffeinated calm of Saturday morning, Margot and I could taste the francs we swallowed one by one.

"She only took Napoleon because it meets Tuesdays and Thursdays before theater," Margot said. "That means she can sleep in the other days."

"All five?"

"She has workshop on Friday, but that's in the afternoon."

I seldom saw Margot before dusk. I felt a breathy excitement high in my chest, as if I'd swallowed a little pillow. I wondered if she knew how much it had meant to me when she'd suggested that we two meet for breakfast and leave the sleepyheads at home.

"Bou says you don't want her to do the séance."

"She's projecting," Margot said easily. "I didn't say that."

I learned more than one new vocabulary that year. *Projecting* was a Margot word that meant putting your thoughts or feelings inside someone else. When dead people sent their thoughts and feelings into us, Germaine called it *union*.

"I'm just worried Bou will expect too much."

"Germaine will be there to chaperon."

"You're terrible," she said, and drank a little more than her share of the coffee. I nibbled a little more than my share of the brioche.

"It's Beck's fault," I said.

It was true that Beck had started it. At our Thanksgiving dinner he'd noticed that whenever you talked about Nathan, you turned the same shade of rose as when Margot nibbled your neck. Then he pointed out that you hadn't laughed when he'd made the remark about how if he had a sister like you, he'd be a father of two by now and they'd be sharing one body. That was when he guessed that you and Nathan had fooled around, which I suppose you'd told Margot years before. She'd served that perfect pie with the apples in it still crunchy and the caramel glaze, and tried to diffuse the situation with a lot of statistics about how brothers and sisters almost always play doctor. But it was clear from your face that you'd done more than let Nathan watch you pee. Naturally Beck wouldn't let the subject drop until you hit him just over the eye with a chestnut. In March, when you and I rode double on the carousel at the Pont d'Iéna and you finally told me what you and Nathan had done, I couldn't believe how innocent it was.

"What was yours like?"

I'd had my séance the week before.

"All right," I told her. "The chicken was overcooked." I wasn't sure how far I should go.

"Seriously. Was it worthwhile?"

"Germaine told me that my mother's soul might be too nebular for direct contact. We were in search of the matrix of energy she'd left behind."

"Good," Margot said. I knew she'd like that part.

"We ate the chicken, which, as I said, had been on the fire a little too long. I told Germaine all the things I'd wanted to tell Mom."

"Compensatory surrogate."

"Yeah? Every once in a while Germaine told me what Mom thought."

"What she thought?"

"I guess Germaine could sort of hear her," I hedged. "She set a place for her. You know what it's like when you cook for somebody and they don't show. She was probably just pretending."

"She talked?"

"Who? Mom?"

"Germaine. Yes, your mother. Whoever."

Since Margot was prepsychoanalyst, Germaine's medium activities were a little too close for comfort. Margot was quick to translate whatever Germaine did into her own language.

"While she was serving seconds, Germaine started laughing. She said Mom thought my glasses made me look like an accountant."

I'd had my contacts in all day for ballet and then rehearsal, so I'd worn my glasses to the séance. I didn't want to see ghosts unless they were there, and after wearing my hard lenses for twelve hours, I might well have decided that Abraham Lincoln was across the table, gnawing on a thigh bone.

"Wait a minute. You said your mother's spirit was too nebulous for direct contact."

"Soul. Nebular."

"Whatever. Now you're saying she doesn't like your glasses?"

"Germaine warned me that Mom might not fully enter her earth field. She doesn't tell me everything. She knows I'm skeptical, so she protects herself —"

"Countertransference," Margot whispered, a charm.

"— by giving me only part of the story. I bet Mom was there."

"You don't actually believe —"

"Not for me. For Germaine."

I was countertransferring now. Mom's always there for me, not in any scary way, but just around. Germaine helped me understand Mom's presence in a new way, just as she helped you later, in January. I don't think Margot ever understood Germaine's work. Margot doesn't know what it is to live without someone you love and need. I hope she never will.

Dad would understand. Once, when I was in high school, I found Brenda crying in the breakfast niche. Brenda was divorced and worked in the office at Beth-El. She'd always been Mrs. Krantz to me, just the tall, square-shouldered woman who was always calling Mom about "volunteering" to help with some temple activity or other. But a year after Mom died, Brenda and Dad started going out. I had to learn to think of her as a person outside of temple. That morning, when I was in tenth grade, I was on my way to the basement to lift before school when I found Brenda crying. I asked her what was the matter. She finally admitted she'd heard Dad talking to Mom in the shower, the way he does. I think it was the first time she realized he was still thinking about Mom all the time. I told her not to worry, that Dad just missed Mom.

I know your mother would appreciate Germaine. I remember you told me she talks to Nathan every night while she takes off her makeup, even if she calls it praying.

"I couldn't see her," I told Margot. "But Mom was there for Germaine. Germaine answered my questions, and even told me things I hadn't asked about."

"Such as?"

"Such as that Mom watches me sometimes."

Margot looked worried. I told her about the way Mom and I danced in the living room to *West Side Story* and *Hair* when I was little. Mom never ran with me, because I started running when she was already in her chair. By then I'd decided dancing was only for the girls in my elementary school who took ballet at Rutherford's. I was ten, and my workout was eight laps around the park on Alda Drive with the Stork brothers, Larry and Jeff. They wanted to be Joe Namath and I wanted to be Abebe Bikila, the Ethiopian who won the 1960 Olympics in Rome barefoot. I'd come jogging home in my leather Adidas, which weighed about four pounds each back then, before foam, and Mom would be in the front window watching me. I told Margot that Germaine said that Mom's still near me when I dance — not always, just sometimes — and that that's why it feels so good.

"Your mother can see you," Margot said.

"Sure. Well, not see, exactly."

"She's with you," Margot said, and took my hand.

Mom was thirty-four when she died. She looked like Margot except she was taller, her eyes were green, and she didn't have Margot's pointiness. Margot's cheeks and ears point up, so she always looks like she's about to fly away. Mom just stayed right where she was. My favorite picture of her is the one I had up next to the window at Rue Roubo, where she's lying in the sand next to her sister, Esther. Do you remember how dark they are with their summer tans? Margot looked like that against the red plush of the Scossa.

"I told her about you," I said. "And Beck and Bou. I told her I hadn't had friends like you all since I was a kid."

Margot squeezed my fingers.

"I told her about my job at the hospital, and about the dance company. I said I feel like my life has just begun."

"I know," Margot said.

"She wants to meet you."

"Germaine?"

"Mom. Germaine says Mom wants to get to know all of you."

Margot looked at the table. I hadn't meant to put her on the spot.

"Doesn't she know me already?" she said finally. "I thought spirits knew everything."

I knew by the way she said *spirits* that Margot was picturing Casper the Friendly Ghost. Germaine never talked about spirits. She talked about souls.

"They only know what we tell them." I tried to assume a distanced tone. "Germaine says they respect us. They're not powerful. Their energies are like radio waves, too weak to be heard if we don't consciously draw them in."

A smile flickered across Margot's face. I didn't mind. She was nervous.

"So you felt good about the dinner, overall," she said.

"Definitely."

I should have left it there. If I had, Margot would have been much more open to your visit with Nathan.

"She loved the soup. Carrots, chickpeas, zucchini. Very spicy. Mom likes good —" I caught myself. "She liked good soup."

Margot sank back on her bench.

We walked Avenue Victor Hugo to the Bois, beneath a sky the color of the inside of a shoebox. Margot wore that mountain of a black-and-white sweater she'd knitted for you. It looked like glued-together gravel and reached her knees. A dozen men were playing *pétanque* at the Square Alexandre Premier. None of them was more than five feet tall, all smoked pipes and wore baggy pants, and all stopped their game to follow our progress with unfriendly, golfers' stares. I felt like I was caddying an afternoon round for Dad, Ben Letzger, and Roger Morris out at McCann, and we were going through a bunch of businessmen who couldn't find their way out of the thirteenth hole sand traps because of the highballs they'd had with lunch at Christo's.

"I didn't decide to be gay," Margot was saying. "I fell in love with Laurie."

We walked among four even rows of denuded maples, alongside a lake that had walls instead of shore. Moored in the middle were supple white rowboats, their varnished interiors golden with sun.

"Were you scared?"

"No."

She looked contented now that we weren't talking about Germaine. I was the one feeling a little shaky.

"I lost a few friends," Margot said. "I made new ones."

"But you said when you told your parents, your dad was —"

"They were both surprised. But then they saw that nothing terrible was going to happen, that they weren't going to lose me."

"Don't you think," I asked cautiously, "that you reach an age when you're stuck being straight or gay?"

We left the maples and entered a triangular cluster of larches. The park was laid out like a specimen room, and that was reassuring. Not that what we were talking about was new to me. Even before Paris, I imagined that one day I would be with a man. It just hadn't happened. Margot explained that this was called latency. I'd always thought of it as a form of procrastination, and felt hesitantly guilty about it.

"Do we have that much choice?" I asked. "We think we do, but maybe we don't."

In the Bois I mostly talked about you. You weren't there and I didn't want to talk about me. I was afraid Margot would tell me what I already knew, that what it came down to was that I was a coward. Gay men shared a world I'd seen the shores of, and I was afraid of going there. I thought that new world would crumble away beneath my feet as soon as I reached it, and that at the same moment I'd find out I couldn't get back to where I'd started.

"Beck says Bou can be with men, but she won't love them the way she loves you."

"He says what?"

"He just says he thinks you two are . . ."

I made a loose V-shape with my arms and tried to collect my thoughts. We crossed beneath a winterized white willow, its bare branches trailing in the dark lake.

". . . mostly gay."

"As in confined to gayness," Margot said. "Straight is open country, gay is reservation land."

Had Beck meant that? I didn't think so, yet I'd managed to insult all three of my friends at once. We hiked away from the walled shore and down the Allée des Dames. We left it on what started as a horse path but opened out into an oak forest. Three-pronged trunks rose forty-five feet out of pools of ivy, then turned snaky and rose another twenty feet. At the top they leaned southwest, as if trying to catch a peek of the distant Seine. Margot was silent. I summoned the courage to talk about myself again, so I could stop insulting everybody.

"I'm attracted to men sometimes," I said faintly.

Even leafless, the trees halved the daylight. The ferns and maple saplings soaked up what was left, shadowing the flattened leaves, sodden branches, and nearly weightless, wormholed acorn cups beneath our feet. I clutched Margot's arm and felt the way she must have when I'd told her about the soup.

"I am," I said, "but I don't do anything."

"Why?"

"I'm afraid."

She waited.

"I think if I were a woman it would be different. Women just drift along for years, ready to be gay or straight, waiting to see what happens. There was this dancer, Alison, at Syracuse, who —"

"Look, Dan."

Margot stopped dead in her tracks. *Now I've done it*, I thought. *I've shown my true colors, and Margot won't trust me anymore.* I started talking again.

"She was gay but she had this boyfriend. Then for a while she was straight, but she was still spending weekends at the co-op where —"

"Look!" she said, pointing. I realized she didn't care why I thought women had it easier. I just thought women were allowed to occupy neutral ground in a way that men couldn't, or wouldn't. But Margot had stopped because of the condoms. There were two in front of us and three to the right of the path, like flattened, faded balloons left over from a summer party.

"*Capotes anglaises,*" I whispered.

"What?"

"English caps."

But dangling from the saplings, they looked like sagging Christmas ornaments. I didn't care. I'd fallen into a deeper confusion.

"Where were we?" Margot said. "You were telling me that since you're a boy, you've had to make up your mind about everything already."

"That's not what I meant."

"What, then?" she asked gently. She rubbed my cold hands in hers.

"Just that if I were with a man, I wouldn't be serious."

"You might be," she said. "Or you might not."

She put her arm around my waist and gave me a comforting squeeze. We talked our way through the last of the oaks and Margot led me to understand that there was actually nothing she expected me to say, or do. She was herself. I was me. I would lead my own life any way I chose. That was a friendly and sensible point of view, and I started to breathe easier.

We headed toward the hippodrome on a path that turned muddy. We skirted one puddle only to find our way blocked by a longer one.

"How do you do it?" I heard myself asking, now that I was free not to. I towed Margot across the wet grass.

"Do what?"

"Start. I mean, I know how with a woman," I said. "But with a man . . ." I shook my head vaguely.

"You know how?" Margot asked, delighted. We pulled up short beneath a Scotch pine, whose branches created a permeable ceiling of needles overhead.

"A woman," I started to explain. "She'll . . ." I held my hands together, then turned the palms out.

"Just opens right up?" Margot asked, smiling. "Like a flower?"

Beyond her, in the distance, were the fences and box hedges of the track.

"It's hard to describe," I said, squinting and trying to be serious. I started to cup my hands again.

"Forget your damn hands. Show me."

I didn't stop to think. I pulled her close and kissed her like a sixth-grader. Her smiling lips were parting, so I skipped a few grades and kept kissing her. She stopped smiling. Our bodies shaped themselves together, and my hands walked off without my permission down the back of Margot's endless sweater. They reached the bottom and slid up inside the hot curve of her back. Margot pressed herself closer against me. Her breath and my breath came tumbling out together. We stayed there for a moment, mostly still.

"I see," she managed, "what you mean."

We separated and walked unsteadily on, holding each other up now.

"You want to know how," she said.

Beyond the Allée des Dames, the deserted hippodrome looked like a quarter of Yankee stadium cut out, dipped in white paint, and dropped into a cow pasture. Beyond a fence and a line of low hedges, a ragged chevron of potential horses thudded invisibly past.

She turned me by the shoulder. I thought she was going to demonstrate on me this time. I tried to look casual, as if it would be just another experiment when she took me in her arms.

"Have you ever been on a rider mower?" she asked instead. I shook my head.

"Bou's dad has one. It cruises. All you do is steer once in a while."

She lifted my hand to her face. She rolled my thumb, studying the carpometacarpal joint. When she looked up, her mono brow was suspended high above her eyes. Suddenly I could see where she was heading.

"So you just," I said, "let yourself —"

"Yes."

We walked to the edge of the track and leaned on the fence. We waited for the racing season.

Last week I spent Halloween at Joel Nash's toy-size house on Lapeyrouse Street. He said his sister Sally was bringing her two boys over to trick-or-treat, and he wanted to take them around the neighborhood but didn't want to leave his sister alone in the house. Could I come over and spend the evening with them? I told him definitely yes, then tried to hide my pleasure so he wouldn't know how much I was looking forward to being with people.

Sally and I took the first shift, handing granola bars and raisins out the front door while Joel took her boys out. Sally's three years younger than Joel, but looks and acts older. She has the same wavy blond hair, and her elbows bend too far back just the way his do. Her boys have normal elbows.

She told me life begins again when you have your first kid, that whoever you were before is just plain gone. She didn't sound particularly happy about it, but when Clay and Josh came back after forty minutes, she acted as if she hadn't seen them in six weeks. She squeezed little Josh so hard he involuntarily squealed, like a rubber duck. Then she took the boys out, leaving me with Joel. Joel did slow back-falls to show how scared he was when neighbor kids showed up at his door. Then he just sat there, fanning himself and catching his breath. The little ones loved it and so did the moms. The dads weren't sure.

I took the boys out on their last run. We worked a couple blocks along North Dorgenois, then started down North Rocheblave Street under the high-tension lines. The eight-year-old, Clay, had stripmined all the neighbors nearer by. Every hour since six, he'd returned to Uncle Joel's to empty his pillowcase into a dry aquarium and to decide what block to raid next. He was a store-bought Ninja Turtle and his little brother, Josh, who's six, was a scary piece of chicken liver. Josh wore dark red facepaint and a brown smock. He had a big sheet of white styrofoam on his back, and plastic wrap, with a weight-and-price sticker, around his front. Sally majored in design in Baton Rouge and had worked out the packaging details, but the original concept of being liver was Josh's.

He didn't give a hoot how much candy he ended up with. He said candy's bad for you and so is meat. Sure enough, it turned out that, earlier in the evening, Uncle Joel had indoctrinated Josh about the wonders of raw vegetables and yeast by-products. By nine he was staggering, then riding on my back wherever his mercenary brother led us. Clay knew that the neighbors wanted to get rid of their candy, since the night was almost over. He asked for seconds and thirds, and palmed more candy corn than anyone who made the mistake of opening his door could believe.

I thought of you, of the Boutique which turned into a money-maker just when all the church ladies were convinced it was make-believe. I thought of you, too, because I had a little guy riding on my back and was chasing his brother's five-and-dime carapace down the street under an electric hum. I felt alive, and not alone, for the first time in four months.

I'm falling in love with you all over again, but I shouldn't write about that. I have that tight feeling in my chest whenever I think about you. I'd forgotten how that hurts.

I'm going to write to Beck for a while. Eighteen nights have passed since I started my first letter, and tonight the computer, which advises me periodically, is telling me it's time I open a new directory. It was really the computer's idea that I write to you in the first place. I turned it on and it told me to start writing about Renee Gilbert's C-section delivery of little Jordan. The next day the computer gave me its second shove. It was way after midnight when I booted up to tell you about my first ballet class with the humorless Madame Lafontaine. By mistake I chose *CASE* from the initial menu instead of *CHART*, the format I'd used the first night. *CASE* looked right, so I stayed with it. After an hour, I simply couldn't imagine Paris in any other graphics mode.

CASE, the computer revealed to me, is where memory lives. *CASE*'s layout is just spacious enough to accommodate the avenues and balconies, the windswept skies and wine-drinking nights, of Paris. But I returned to *CHART* a few days later when I wanted to tell you about the outlet-forceps delivery of Judy's girl. *CHART*, with its compact, businesslike font and split screen designed for quick notes about meds, vital signs, diet, is just like this hospital. At a glance, *CHART* is efficient and impersonal, but once you get inside, it's as alive and moody as Charity. *CHART* contains in its split self both Charity's panting hours of quiet and her sudden, frenzied hours of birth.

For two and a half weeks now I've come to this room to string tiny green lights across this monitor's black sky. In the mornings I store the sparks in the hard drive and go home for twelve or twenty-four hours, then I return here to call the sparks back into the midnight screen. The first two weeks I was sure I was engaged in a constructive therapy, that I was transferring heat from my weary brain and fibrillating heart into this metal box. I planned to fall out of love with you while my personal computer fell head over heels. Eventually, I reasoned, the PC's tiny clock speed would double, while my big one would slow to a more moderate rhythm. But that hasn't been the clinical outcome at all, and during the last week I realized my condition was actually deteriorating. I performed a few diagnostic tests and found, as I suspected, that this computer is as imperturbably slow as the first night I told it about you. As for myself, I need you more every time I see you, and I see you more clearly each time I type your name. In the mornings, I wander lost in love out Charity's front door with a fever that's burning just a fraction of a degree hotter than it was the evening before. I need new medicine.

That's why I'm going to write to Beck for a while. Beck will make this heat-shunt therapy operate the way it was intended to. He'll be like a cool bath, startling at first, but soothing for a patient right on the edge of spontaneous combustion. Before I leave for my ER rotation in seven weeks, I'll print out *BOU.DOC* along with whatever ends up in *BECK.DOC*. Then I'll send the whole packet to each of you, yours on the wide, green-striped computer paper that's waiting in this box under the table, Beck's in a more compact, and higher velocity, medium.

I miss you already. It's as if I've had you by my side these nights. I wonder when I'll really see you again, if only for a few hours. I'd better not worry about that right now. Tomorrow I'll start sending such high-voltage sparks out of my fingertips into this reluctantly amorous keyboard that soon fireworks will shoot right out the top of Charity and up into the Louisiana stratosphere. One night you'll look out your window in Manhattan and see a faint glimmer on the other side of Trenton, Philadelphia, and Amtrak points south. Follow those sparks to their source, Bou. I'm right here. In the meanwhile, my Beckian bath will diffuse the heat that has started a part of me dangerously smoldering, just below the loose V-neck of my scrubs. I've got to temper that place, before I start a fire that neither I nor all the jangling red engines in New Orleans would have a lover's prayer of putting out.

BECK.DOC

Yes, Beck, I'm writing to you. I know you think I'm a nut, but I forthwith make the unilateral decision to get back in touch with you. You can't very well refuse me, because Margot casually included your INTERNET address at Mass. General in a P.S. to her last note. She tells me you are in the first year of a surgery residency, subspecialty orthopedics. Congratulations on this post, by the way, the latest but by no means the brightest feather in what will, I'm sure, be a long and brilliant cap. In January, when I leave OB, I'll carry my disk over to my friend Todd Perroy's molecular chem lab in the med school, plug into his monster computer, and loose *BECK.DOC*, along with *BOU.DOC*, in your direction. One dreary Boston morning, not too far in the future, you'll come in to work and log on to check lab results on one of your victims. You see you have mail. *How nice*, you say to yourself. *I wonder who it's from.* You call it up and there I am in your face, a couple hundred thousand bytes of me, enough to gladden even your hoary heart. You see, I'm back. I refuse to be surgically excised from your life, the way I was that May day four-plus years ago.

What exactly am I up to? I give varied accounts. Kate McIlroy came in twenty minutes ago, smelling of that dark floral scent she wears. She set beside me a cup of the fine coffee that comes from the video instruction room for new mothers next to the nurseries, and which is seldom to be had after ten o'clock. Kate and I have become friends just this last month. We both believe we can tell immediately when the other one needs coffee or gossip. I find her or she finds me. Yesterday I chased her down in the middle of a delivery to give her doctor-nurse dope on Matt Richards and Mary Breyer. Today she came with coffee and follow-up.

"He just took her out to lunch," she said.

"I told you."

"Richards is a damn dog," Kate said. She's New Orleans Irish from the Channel, and has a pristine Bronx accent. *Deam dowag*, she said. She claims half her neighborhood talks like that.

"Their cars are side by side in the LaSalle lot," I reported. Matt has a mint-condition '73 Karmann Ghia I would trade my eyeteeth for. Mary, poor woman, has a '91 Escort.

"That jerk," Kate said. "He only broke up with Margery in Prenatal on Labor Day."

Joik, she said, *Mahjree*. Kate's forty-three but looks fifteen. She's about Margot's height, with pink skin and one of those always-smiling faces. It looks like she's smiling until she smiles, and then you realize she wasn't smiling.

"How's the letter?"

"Finished," I told her. "I'm writing a new one."

She shook her head and wandered off. She never tries to read what's on the screen, but she's about the only one who doesn't. The whole staff of the tenth floor now knows about my tapping. Tim Clinton, the third-year resident who has taken this Tuesday off to float up and down the Mississippi in a miserable outboard he carries pictures of, with a thermos of coffee, a fishing pole, and a ridiculous Huck Finn hat — Clinton has broadcast far and wide that I am not to be disturbed when I'm in here.

"Don't bother Shoenfeld," he told everybody yesterday. "He's in love. Let's us tend to the fanny wiping."

The whole day staff immediately crowded into Conference, and I had no recourse except to turn the brightness knob on the monitor to black. I felt like a schoolboy hiding a note. They all wanted to know what I was writing. A letter, I told them, a long letter to someone they don't know. That satisfied all except Steve Tsintolas, who came right back five minutes later.

"You're not writing a letter."

He spoke with such confidence that I knew at once I had to lie to him. No, I admitted.

"You getting a paper out of this?"

He's nothing if not direct. I glanced at a stack of *Obstetrics and Gynecology* that had been on the floor since I arrived.

"I'm looking at efficacy of ritodrine in preterm labor."

"What have you come up with?"

"Just taking notes," I said.

He was visibly shaken by the idea that I'm researching a paper at night while he's busy stealing all my clinical experience from me. *Good luck,* he told me in that slippery voice of his. He doesn't know how much luck I need. I'll have to pick up the pace if you and Bou are going to get this as a slightly late Christmas present.

I have no doubt he'll sneak in here and try to read my research notes. He's not going to get very far, though, unless he has Lagachian powers. To access my CASEs and CHARTs each night, I must type my secret code, LOVE. Then I hit the Enter key, with its little arrow pointing back to the Paris past. And you know what? Every night I fall right back in again.

But I'm not traveling to Paris this afternoon. I'm taking you to Chevy Chase.

It's been six months now since Dana and I broke up. That means that in a parallel universe, in which we stayed together and I proposed to her on schedule, we'll be married this spring on the Rowes' back lawn in Maryland. See us, Beck, standing side by side? Dad and Brenda are seated on the folding chairs behind us. Beside them are Gramma Sarah and Grampa Walter, down from Morristown, and Mom's sister, Esther, up from Sarasota. Both Esther and Gramma Sarah are thinking how much Mom would have loved to have seen this day. I'm thinking how much Esther, who teaches high school math, looks like Mom. Beside her sits Oma Leah, who flew in from San Diego carrying the ketubah that she now holds on her lap. She made it herself, writing out the marriage formula in stately calligrapher's Hebrew on her own handmade paper. A row back is Tante Trude, from Utica, with her husband, Felix, the pharmacist, who everyone says gives discounts to his old customers even though he's hopelessly in debt to the people further down his row, namely Onkel Fritz, the tax man, and his wife, Judy, in close but never peaceful proximity to Onkel John, the cardiologist, and Tante Clara, registered nurse and maker of the world's best Linzertorte. The two couples have just argued all the way from Schenectady about whether the route Fritz chose was as fast as the one John wanted him to take. Behind them are Tante Trude's daughters, Lise and Ellen, and her son, Maurice, all from Utica, beside John and Clara's son, Curt, and daughter, Mina, flanked by the older grandchildren, Tessa, Michael, and Little Trude. Lise and Mina are holding their new babies, Abe and Naomi. That makes three generations of Ernst and Heinrich Shoenfeld's descendants, all staring across the aisle at Dana's family like trigger-happy Hatfields ready to mix it up at the first sign of trouble.

In the home pews sit Dana's mother, Sandra, in a designer gown that makes her daughter the bride appear underdressed, beside Dana's older brothers, Greg, the internist from Silver Spring, and Jerry, the middle boy, an exec at Procter & Gamble in Cincinnati. The second row is filled with Dana's dad's North Carolina medical clan, with enough specialties between them to run their own Mayo Clinic right there in the research triangle, and all their children except the youngest who, as flower girl, is the only one at the wedding having any fun. The rest of that side of the caterer's tent is bursting with Sandra's family, mostly Mazda-dealing Leitners from Rockville, the women with the parched faces of aging models, their car dealer husbands tall, slick, and irritable, and all of them glaring across the aisle at the Shoenfelds like so many McCoys ready to go toe-to-toe at the least provocation.

In the midst of this armed camp stand Dana and I. My soon-to-be father-in-law, Harry, gives me an encouraging nod, and together the three of us face Rabbi Lyle Fishman, to whom Sandra introduced me with unbearable solemnity after her cousin's son Tommy's bar mitzvah at Temple Ohr Kodesh last fall. The rabbi talks about illness and death and the hard times, as if that were the whole point. Dana and I stand beneath the chupah, ignoring him as best we can. We look deep into each other's eyes and say *I do* and *I do*. I stomp on the velvet-wrapped glass, which crunches in a promising way, and we are joined.

After we're married, in that other dimension, Dana and I see each other about once a month. We take turns flying between New Orleans and Philadelphia, where she's in her neuro residency. After a year of this, I move up there with her. That's assuming that I can make up my mind what residency to apply for, and that come April I'm sought-after enough to match in Dana's vicinity. I admit this is unlikely in any universe.

But it doesn't matter, because none of this is going to happen. Instead, Dana and I are now *friends*. I talked to her just last night and we forgot for a while that we had broken up, that we won't see each other soon, and that when we do, it won't be like before. She was telling me how much her feet hurt after rounding all afternoon. I told her I'd massage them if I were there, and she sighed into the phone. Then we both woke up and realized what was happening.

The conversation became very dry. Dana said she's tired of diagnosing everything from adrenoleukodystrophy to myasthenia gravis and then not being able to treat anything. She says she went into neuro because she thought psych would be too frustrating, that in psych she'd just hang out in a city hospital somewhere, handing out pills to a bunch of disturbed outpatients who really need to be in-house and in therapy. Now she's wondering if neuro isn't going to be just as frustrating as psych would have been. The diagnostics are fascinating, she says, but the therapies are so limited.

Why, you might ask, did Dana and I spend the last twenty minutes of our hour talking about the distance between diagnosis and treatment in late-twentieth-century neuro? Safe ground, I reply. What we didn't talk about was how much we miss each other. Dana didn't tell me that she's still furious at me. I didn't admit that even though I keep her picture in my car, where I see it much more often than if it were by my bed, I do like living alone. We didn't talk about any of that.

The only time we broached these subjects was one Saturday last May, when Dana told me she didn't know how to be with me anymore. She couldn't stand my silence, my distance. I said I loved her but I had to be alone. It wasn't that I was nervous about the idea of our getting engaged. It was worse than that. I wasn't nervous enough. She said she was worried about me. We ended up making love instead of fighting, but it was the end.

Now we're locked into the let's-be-friends posture. We tried the silence-is-best strategy for almost two months. That was when I started having my nightmares. Did I mention the nightmares? In the worst of them Dana's mother and the car boys are chasing me across their dealership out of Hungerford Road in Rockville, Maryland. Dana's grandfather Saul is by Sandra's side. He's wearing his Texas hat, and his eyes are as flat as a fish's. *You signed the plan,* he says, and as he plods across the lot toward me he waves the payment schedule I signed three years ago when I put fourteen hundred down on my Corolla.

Our pact of silence didn't last. Dana and I missed each other too much. We met my first year, Dana's second. She helped me, or rather made me, study, locking me in my room and lending me all her old notes, then quizzing me into battle form for my upper-extremities-and-chest exam. She was mad at me all the time in January and she couldn't figure out why, until she realized it was because she was in love with me and didn't know if she wanted to be. We went out for three years, except for one summer when Dana broke up with me, took up with her college boyfriend, Russell W. Rothstein, J.D., and then decided I was the one after all. In the back of her mind she thinks I'm getting even with her now for that summer, which did take a lot out of me. She thinks that when I've made her suffer enough, I'll want her back. She hasn't said any of this, but I know she believes it. I also know she hasn't decided whether she'll accept me or not. That depends on how long I make her wait, and whom she meets in the meantime.

Last May we decided to play it this way. I'm the troubled guy whose mother died when he was eleven and who even now can't sustain a loving relationship. Bou, about whom I talked Dana's ear off that first year, isn't even a real woman. She's just a fantasy I use in my adolescent weakness to ward off the realities of an intimacy I can't handle, because I'm so afraid I'll lose another mother. This theory, which may be true — I guess I'd be the last to know — is useful to both of us. You can see that it gets me off the hook. My breaking off the relationship is now not something I chose to do but a failing I couldn't help. Dana doesn't have to feel rejected. She fell victim to my troubled psyche. This allows her to behave compassionately toward me. Her only real mistake was to have believed her love could change sad me into a healthy plant.

Last summer was the worst. In the middle of June, I almost killed myself studying for my surgery final. Then it was all over and I had ten whole days to breathe before I started the first block of my fourth-year rotations. That was the first time I'd stopped working since Dana and I said goodbye. All at once I started thinking about Paris again. I'd never stopped thinking about Paris, but last June was when I started thinking about nothing else. It wasn't until I sat down in front of the computer up here three weeks ago that I decided to write to Bou. If I hadn't broken up with Dana, I probably never would have written a word. Now I'm engaged to this computer instead of to Dana. That's a thought.

Help me, advise me, like you did in the old days. Why didn't I propose to Dana? She's almost as bright as you are. She's very sexy and sweet, she knows how to cook cookbook food without cookbooks, and she's going to be a wonderful mother. Okay, she wears silly outfits that are coordinated from top to bottom, no component of which can ever be worn independently, but that's Sandra's influence. It's true, too, that she called me the same pet name she calls her father, a name I won't trouble you with, and that this irritated me more than I might have believed possible. Granted, too, I generally know exactly what Dana is going to say about any given movie. She wouldn't let me help her cook, and that took a lot of the deliciousness out of the dishes she made. If I insisted on cooking something, she'd just let me do it alone.

But are these impediments to a marriage of true minds? I'm sure Dana has a list four or five times this long of what's wrong with me. Aren't all our petty complaints overshadowed by passion, trust, simple good friendship?

No. I hear your voice resounding through the still Tuesday afternoon air. You come in loud and clear as always. I didn't dote on Dana, you say. I loved her, yes, but I disrespected her in some ways, and I did not sufficiently dote. I knew last April that you would have raised these objections. I could hear a Beck deep in my consciousness saying, *Fine, young Dan. Marry a woman you aren't wild about, and whose name is yours with an a added to it. Settle in a suburb somewhere, have 2.3 kids, drive a Mazda 626LX with all the wrong options you got a deal on from your gangster in-laws. Turn into Dana's father, be another* — no, I won't burden you with the nickname Dr. Harry Rowe and I share.

The point is that even though I haven't talked to you in more than four years, and even though you still blame me for wrecking our four-cornered friendship in Paris, I'm still listening to you. Thanks for the advice. I'll come screw up your almost-engagement sometime.

We haven't been out of touch, after all. That's why I found my fingers typing your green name onto the screen when I knew I shouldn't type Bou's any longer. It's just like old times, isn't it? Me talking to you about Bou, and another woman.

Fish and Spit

"So he wasn't really a horse thief."

"No. It's just that the horses belonged to other people."

I was telling Bou about the last member of my family who I knew had ridden horses well. I mean Great-Grandfather Rudolph.

"He was a horse repo man," Bou said hopefully. No one had ever put it that way.

It was the middle of December, Thursday of the week before our trip to Chamonix, and Bou was one sick little camper. We thought we might have to call off the trip until her bronchitis cleared. She spent three days on the chaise in the living room, under Margot's quilt. I told her as much of the Saint Rudolph story as I knew.

It seems Rudolph had lent one of his mounts to Cousin Otto in Deggendorf, whom everyone still talks about as a no-good. Otto neglected to return the animal, so Rudolph had no choice but to go fetch it. Soon a neighbor came to Rudolph for help. The man's son had married the daughter of a farmer from a neighboring town. The farmer wouldn't give the impoverished couple their promised dowry. One moonless night in the 1890s, Rudolph agreed to ride with his neighbor to the farm of the father-in-law. When they arrived, he handed the neighbor his bridle, and the man rode off toward home, leading Great-Grandfather's horse behind him. Rudolph then strolled to the stable of the ungenerous farmer and collected the finest of the man's mounts, which he rode bareback into the Bohemian forest. He emerged at dawn with a horse that had undergone the turn-of-the-century equivalent of a hundred-twenty-dollar Earl Scheib paint job.

"You can't paint horses," Bou said.

"Well, Rudolph did something to him. Then he sold him and took the newlyweds the cash."

"So he wasn't really stealing."

"No. He was righting wrongs."

I wasn't entirely kidding. I'll never know the truth, because I have only Dad and Oma Leah to rely on. The way they talk, Rudolph was a Bohemian Robin Hood.

Bou still looked uncomfortable. She changed the subject before I could raise the philosophical question of what was worse about having a horse-thief great-grandfather than a couple of murdering, land-thief ones.

"What do you think of our Wizards?" she asked instead.

I'd attended your jam session in Maisons-Laffittes on Monday, and despite your talk, you'd behaved like a gentleman. You made polite conversation with Zubir's sixteen-year-old sister, Zohra, and you drank only two beers and perhaps a half-dozen glasses of mint tea. Madame Derouiche stayed out of sight in the kitchen, along with Zubir's older sister.

"Margot," I said. "Margot's . . ."

But there were no words for the Sax Machine. I got off the chaise to strut up and down the Berlioz living room, demonstrating the way Margot had covered Zubir's small house. I pretended to blow, all bent over, my shoulders hunched, face twisted with concentration. I did the shimmying, hip-shaking bob that Margot used to squeeze the last sweet drops of sound out.

"Yes," Bou said, coughing and laughing. "Yes."

I climbed back onto the chaise.

"The first time I saw Margot play," she told me when she could, "I nearly wet myself. That woman makes me completely, all-over crazy."

"She is a sax demon."

"She's a raisin," Bou said. "That's what she is."

We played cards all afternoon. Bou's cheeks were flushed, her eyes teared, and I knew her muscles ached because she kept massaging her upper arms. She said she felt fine and didn't want me to leave. She taught me how to play war, beggar-your-neighbor, and go fish, and right in the middle of our fifth go fish game, she told me as much about how Nathan died as she ever did in one sitting. She started by explaining what happened three years later.

"I had a breakdown," she said, "freshman year. I didn't hallucinate or anything. I just stopped working and didn't go to meals or leave my room. At all."

She frowned faintly, as if remembering a bad headache. She wasn't dramatic about it.

"Eights," I said.

"Go fish."

"That's when you and Margot met?"

"Twos."

I gave her my two twos.

"At a party," she told me. "I was making gum wrapper chains. Sevens."

The cold had given her a sexy, wraparound voice.

"Go fish."

"It was strictly a gum-wrapper-chain party as far as I was concerned."

"Sixes."

"Go fish."

"Shit." I had three. "Were you gay?"

"I was trying to be, but I hadn't done anything."

"You shouldn't whisper," I said. "That's the worst thing. I'll make tea as soon as I win."

"Fours."

She didn't tell me the whole story of how Nathan died until January. We played go fish and she talked about how she and Margot had gotten together. All she said about Nathan was that her brothers had been surfing at Squibnocket Point at

Martha's Vineyard when Nathan's board had caught him in the head and he'd gone under. Jason didn't see that Nathan was down for nearly ten minutes. Bou didn't tell me until February that Nathan hadn't died right away. Jason managed to resuscitate him, but too late. Nathan's pupils were fixed and dilated. He didn't die for two days.

But Bou didn't explain all that to me the week she was laid up. She also didn't tell me that she'd gone out with Nathan's best friend, Bruce, when she was a senior at Andover. She just said she'd spent a month in-patient at Yale–New Haven freshman year, and that I should be grateful for what Mom and I had.

"You said goodbye to her."

"Yes," I said, because it's true. I started the week Mom stopped using the wheelchair and stayed in bed, even though she hated to be inside when the sun was out. Dr. Letzger came that Thursday morning as always, and left without changing her prescription. Dad drove off to his office without remembering to kiss me goodbye. I climbed up on Mom's bed and just lay there. She put her hand in my hair. We didn't talk, but we were saying goodbye.

I didn't win any games but I made tea anyway, and we drank it and started playing gin. Bou discarded fast and remembered every card, or most of them. I lost at gin, too, and tried not to let my feet stray up between Bou's legs under Margot's quilt.

"Who were you with at school?" she asked after a while.

"I was alone," I said. "Almost."

"Another jack. Really?"

There was a funny smell in the place. It wasn't Bou, though it was partly her flu sweat. The leaky radiator steamed up the window and made the air as heavy as if we were in a greenhouse.

"Syracuse was a lonely place," I said. "Snow, wind, chemistry." I thought that covered it.

"Gin," Bou said. "Eleven cards, two runs, four aces. What have you got? What about dates?"

She wrote down the new score. I was down 137 points and we'd only been playing for half an hour.

"I didn't much. There were always women around I wanted to meet, but it never worked out."

"What didn't?"

I shrugged, dealt.

"That's what I could never figure out. I kept picking the wrong ones. There was this physics grad student, Bev, in my Limón class. We went out twice but then she gave me a let's-be-friends talk."

Bou listened. I played the part of the shy lonely-heart. There was no harm in behaving the way she expected me to. She was sick, after all. I had to be nice to her. All right, so I was a calculating dog. That's what you're thinking, Beck, and perhaps you're right in a thoroughly cynical way. But I thought I was playing cards and talking more or less truthfully about myself and about Bou and Margot, the way I always did.

"What was it like for you two?"

"You want to hear it, don't you?" Bou said. "It turns you on."

"I'm just curious."

She shifted under the quilt, hiding her cards from me. Somehow my right foot ended up in a very warm place for a moment.

"It was nice. Margot was sweet. She brought me African violets. They were fuzzy and beautiful, and I promptly killed them."

I filled in the gaps later. When she met Margot she was seventeen, the age Nathan had been when he died. Her first semester, she stayed in her room when she didn't have classes to go to. Then she met Margot and started seeing the town with her. They always left campus. That was key. Then Bou went home for Christmas, and in the spring she got worse and checked into Yale–New Haven, and afterwards was sent home for two weeks. She came back at the end of April and she and Margot became more serious about each other. Bou managed to get her course work done with Margot typing all night for her a couple times. She started intensive therapy and took a class with this actress at Yale Rep, Sammy Topkiss, who'd been performing Shakespeare since she was a teenager. Bou says that knowing this woman, seeing how hard she worked and how satisfying theater was for her, helped her as much as the therapy. I know you've heard all this, but I doubt you've ever put it together chronologically the way I finally did.

"When did you first sleep together?" I asked.

"My, you are nasty. I'm telling you about the champagne and violets, and all you want to hear about is the action."

She was forgetting about the game. I could tell by the way she discarded that she wasn't noticing the cards.

"You're right."

"Okay," Bou said. "Three weeks after she —"

"She what?"

I dropped a queen. One more eight or four of diamonds and I'd gin.

"— three weeks after she told me she was in love with me," Bou said, "we did it."

"Wait a minute. She told you she loved you? Just like that?"

"She wrote me a poem, but I knew."

So did I, though I couldn't possibly. Everything about Margot and Bou was as familiar to me as if I had been there from their first kiss. When Bou recited Margot's poem, I could have spoken it right along with her. It was full of clichés but was wildly romantic anyway, because Margot had written it for Bou in October, when they were first in love. Then Bou gave me my four and I could barely let her recite the rest of the poem, which was only about twenty seconds long, before I threw down my cards.

"That's really pretty," I said. "The ace is high."

"I don't have a thing."

I picked up fifty-three points. It was my deal. I took my time, savoring my gin. I knew I might not get another one, and I was right.

"Was it awkward?" I asked, shuffling grandly.

"I wasn't any good. Margot had to teach me everything."

That made us both blush. Girl talk, that's what it was. Bragging, telling secrets, listening to decent rock on *radio libre* instead of that outer-space jazz of Margot's for a change. Bou talked more than I did because she had more to tell. All I could offer in return was Rebecca stories, and Rebecca and I, as you never hesitated to inform me, were about as exciting as warm milk on a summer afternoon. Bou's Margot stories had a lot more to them. Hers were about love, mourning, loyalty, the problems of the rich dating the middle class, the terror and wonder of coming out. Mine was about puppy love and the sorority girl who left me for — I know it's stupid — a football player named Cliff. What can I say? I've led a corny life.

Bou beat me at casino. She sat on the kitchen floor under the quilt and beat me at superball-peanut jacks, which as you may not recall was jacks played with a superball and peanuts. Finally we climbed back onto the chaise and I beat her at my game, spit.

"Ready?" I asked, knowing she wasn't. It was about five o'clock. The light through the window was the color of wet slate.

"Yes."

We sat Indian style.

"Go."

We threw down cards, building runs in short, frenzied bursts.

"Only one hand," I reminded her, when I probably could have beaten her if she'd used both.

"Shit. I forgot."

"Don't worry. Jack, queen, king, ace, two."

"Spit!" she croaked, and grabbed the smaller pile.

"Good."

I pretended to be proud that she was learning. But that round was an exception. She caught on fast, but not fast enough. I dropped my last card and symbolically slapped the nonexistent pile.

"Wipe that grin off your face," she said.

I guess I didn't because she attacked me, pushed me back on top of the blankets and tickled me hard. The odorous air enveloped us. I didn't fight her because she was too strong. Instead I just tightened up all my muscles and let her work on me until she wore herself out — standard antitickle maneuver.

"I thought," I said when she was done, "you were sick."

"I am. Now you are too. You've got cooties for sure." She sat back and pouted, her cheeks red. "You're not very ticklish," she complained, and coughed.

"Nope."

She lay back and I fell sideways in her direction until my head was on her crossed legs and I was looking up away from her. I wasn't worried about catching the flu. Bou's hot hand touched my forehead, my nose.

"When did you first do it?" she asked, leaning over me. Her breath smelled like tea and peppermints.

"All the way?"

"Yeah."

I drew my legs up under the quilt. I don't know why. It was so hot under there it made my skin itch. Behind my back, Bou was like a radiator.

"College."

"Really?"

"No. I was thirteen. Dad took me to his brothel in the city. What do you think?"

"With Rebecca?"

"No."

"Who?" Bou asked. I looked past the dining room table while Bou focused that curiosity of hers on me.

"Jane."

"Who's Jane?"

"You Jane. Me Boy."

"Seriously."

"A girl," I said. "A woman."

It was quiet for a while. I wondered if Bou had dozed off. Her breathing against my back was as steady as the heat she generated.

"Did you love her?"

I shrugged. You, Margot, and Zubir were off rehearsing, and the apartment was very empty. Whenever I was there at that hour, it was with Margot or you and Margot, waiting for Bou to get back from her acting class. But Bou was right behind me, and you and Margot were in Maisons-Laffittes.

"What was it like?"

"Disappointing," I said. I'd forgotten what I was talking about, but I knew that whatever it was, it had been disappointing. Then Bou shifted behind me and I remembered. Jane.

"Not all I thought it would be," I said.

The daylight had faded. There was just the faintest glow on the ceiling. It was as if we were under water and the ceiling was where the air started. I told Bou that when I lost my virginity at college, I was already debauched because of how imaginatively my girlfriend Amy Kessler and I had been trying to avoid regular sex during our last two years of high school. It was my fault. Amy wanted to go all the way as early as homecoming junior year, but we didn't. Instead we did everything else we could think of.

What disturbed me was I'd told Margot about Amy when we'd gone out to Chez Thang after your jam session, and you'd gone off to your Caribbean gig. That had been three days ago, but Bou hadn't heard my stupid story from Margot. I realized for the first time that it was possible to say something to just Bou or just Margot. They didn't automatically share every experience in their lives. I remember breathing the steamy jungle air of the apartment and thinking, not without disappointment, that the two of them were separate people.

"Did she know it was the first time for —"

"Yes," I said. "We pretended it was very meaningful, but it wasn't. I just wanted to get back to my dorm. I had a calculus midterm to study for."

I couldn't understand why Bou was interested in my first time. I thought it was just good manners. I'd asked about her and Margot, and now, to be polite, she was inquiring about me and Jane.

"Was that bad, that she was more experienced than you were?"

"I don't know. The whole night was bad. I should have slept with Amy in her basement after homecoming junior year."

Bou liked that. The chaise rocked with an underwater sway.

"Amy wanted to, but I didn't. Then she changed her mind and it stayed changed for most of twelfth grade. That was when I wanted to. Then when she wanted to again after prom, I didn't, because I was about to go off to college and didn't want to be committed."

Bou thumped me gently on the back with both fists. I could tell the story pretty well because I'd practiced on Margot over our swallow's-nest soup, scallops in black bean sauce, and ginger pudding. I thought that was the end of it — my little tale, the daylight, both were pretty well played out. But I was wrong.

"Do you wish you'd been with someone else who hadn't done it yet?"

I wondered for a second why Bou wouldn't let the story end. I was exhausted by all the card games I couldn't win and the one game, spit, I couldn't lose.

"Not really. Jane's being experienced was the only good thing about it. At least I didn't have to worry about her."

"What she expected?"

"Sleeping with me wasn't that big a deal to her."

"But she loved you."

Bou's arm was like a hot-water bottle on my shoulder. I kept wanting to get up and open a window, or get a glass of water, but I just lay there. Across from me, the fireplace was a dark hole. The last flicker of daylight had left the ceiling.

"I don't think she loved me."

Bou took this in. You wouldn't have noticed anything unusual about her questions. Well, you might have. You don't miss much. But I just lay there and wondered when I should go home, and why.

"Did you love her?"

I sighed.

"Bou," I said, "it wasn't like you and Margot. Jane was just this woman in my writing class who liked James Bond movies. She wrote an essay about how James Bond was a modern-day dragon-slayer. We went to *Goldfinger* at the Watson Complex, then we slept together. After that I hardly saw her."

"Oh," Bou said, and took her arm off me.

"I'm sorry. I didn't mean to snap at you. There just isn't any more to tell. I doubt I was much fun for her."

"Oh," Bou said again.

And that, Beck, was that.

No Man

We pulled out the seats in the train compartment to make three short beds, side by side. By the time we passed Lyon we'd finished the second, medium-quality bottle of wine and started on the third, el cheapo bottle. Outside the thick window the town rocked by, dimly lit in a French way, as if the fifty-cycle-per-second current of Europe wasn't quite up to our sixty-cycle North American brand. The four of us cozied down into what Margot said was a dog pile.

"Like Three Dog Night," she said. You immediately began to sing in your most melancholy voice.

"One is the loneliest numbah that you'll evah do. . ."

Do? I thought.

"When it's cold, the Eskimos let one dog into the igloo," Margot placidly explained. "When it's really cold, they let two in, and when there's a blizzard, they let three in. That's why they call it a three dog night."

That made sense to me. I was so grateful for the information that I gave Margot, who was nestled against my shoulder, a kiss.

"Two can be as bad as one," you crooned.

"But where," Bou asked distinctly, "do you get *dog pile* from *three dog night*?"

Wine made Bou a hair-splitter. While I found it easier to accept ambiguities such as, for instance, the presence of Margot's hand in my right pocket and the way I kept finding reasons to kiss her cheek and the edges of her lips, Bou had turned into a stickler for accuracy. As she reached the third bottle, she needed to get to the heart of every question.

"Because the dogs," Margot explained, "pile on top of them."

"No, no," Bou said. "I understand about the *number* of dogs. What I want to know is why they're in a *pile*."

"*Three,*" you began, "*is the . . .*"

You trailed off. There is no three. You were on the window side of Bou, and I was on the door side of Margot. A bottle appeared in front of me, and I had just raised it and begun to suckle when the door slid open.

"*Billets, s'il vous plaît.*"

I swallowed hard and rolled right, pressing the bottle into Margot's hand, which was no longer in my pocket.

"Bou," I said. "Bou."

Her brow, in the light from the corridor, was still furrowed over the folk idiom "three dog night." She emerged from her linguistic reverie only after I told her again that we needed the tickets. She searched for them in her pack while the conductor stood punching little geometrical holes in the air. Finally the man did his job and shut the door of our igloo. You pulled down the window shade and switched on the blue light.

"Beck, don't," Bou said.

"But I *luv* you."

Your voice in the compartment was full of mournful longing. Bou sighed. Margot and I settled in, her hand not in my pocket this time but low on my belly. The train rocked along past Culoz and Aix-les-Bains, Bonneville and Cluses.

"Neo-cuckoo clock," you declared the architecture of Chamonix as we emerged onto the Avenue de la Gare, dizzy and smelly, at dawn. The Alps lorded it over us like geologic bullies.

"I've seen pictures of this," you told us. "Brian came here last year with Girlfriend of the Week."

"What's your brother like, Beck?" one of us asked.

"Like me."

"Is he fat?"

"The Becketts have big bones," you said, as always.

You never did tell us anything substantive about Brian. It was only by listening hard that I realized how often you were thinking about Claire and Si, and especially Brian. You couldn't quite disguise your admiration for his high-speed lifestyle and his dramatic rise at Kidder Peabody. He was to Wall Street what you were to medicine, an *enfant terrible,* except that he wore dark suits and worked out at his club every morning at dawn.

We made our way to the cabin one of Poppa's clients had lent Bou for the week. It turned out to be a three-bedroom chalet built of darkened timbers under a steep slate roof and set down on its own little hill above Les Moussoux.

"The Morrels have only been here twice in ten years," Bou boasted. "Poppa found it for them."

In the middle of the living room was a sunken fireplace under a gleaming copper hood.

"What exactly is a tax write-off?" I asked. It bothered me that if you were rich enough, then spending money on houses you never saw, businesses that failed immediately, and the arts was actually a way of turning a profit.

"Poppa will tell you all about it when you visit," Bou said. "He explains it to me every time I'm home. He'll also tell you why a recession is different from a depression, and why the deficit is so serious."

You said tax write-offs were one of the great paradoxes, like Zeno's tortoise outdistancing Achilles. The mystery was revealed only to those of fair skin, who attended private schools the names of which are pronounced differently than they're spelled.

We changed and trudged back to the ski shop by the Brévent *télécabines* in town. Ski boots turned out to work pretty well as *pointe* shoes, as long as I didn't rise above a half-toe. I did an interpretive dance for you, Margot, and Bou. The Norwegian teen fitting your boots spoke an English so colloquial it was spooky. "Hey, check out your friend," he said as I *pas-de-bourréed* forward, making falling snowflakes with my hands.

"Winter," I told you, jiggling my fingers and executing a character pirouette to one knee.

"I don't know the boy," Margot said. "Do you?"

"Just follow me," Bou told us. She disappeared in a puff of snow, then reappeared on the mountain below us. "Turn," she said, suffering from the illusion that we were near her. "Turn here. Here."

Then she vanished for the day. You had skied once before, but neither Margot nor I had.

"That was helpful," you said. "No, we don't need to take the beginner's class. Bou will be our teacher. She used to teach kids in New Hampshire."

Standing at the top of La Parsa chairlift in your dark-green paratrooper suit, stuffed with sweaters on top but lined only with long underwear on the bottom, you resembled a length of rock-anchored kelp. Beside you in her jeans and baby-blue down jacket, Margot could have been any Syracuse student, male or female, between November and March.

"She'll come back," Margot said.

"I hope she brings body bags," you said, but we managed without her. All right, it was a disaster. I guess I'm remembering days five and six, when we could turn to both sides and the swelling had gone down in your knee. That first day, when Margot could only turn right and I could only go straight, we probably shouldn't have gone up the Piste du Col Cornu for our second run. But through the snow swirl of time, I don't remember minding that I had to hurl myself to the ground just before I ran into people or things. And you were doing well enough yourself until you broadsided that Lufthansa woman and tweaked your medial collateral ligament. So you spent the rest of the day on the deck of the Planpraz restaurant, drinking Cardinals and looking across at Mont Blanc, and you ended up a little glum. It wasn't the end of the world.

Margot and I skied and played in the snow, and didn't find

Bou until four o'clock. The day wasn't cold by upstate standards. The peaks stopped looking so vicious after I realized that they were made up of fields of snow where people went, and rocky parts over which only birds flew. I'd never wanted to ski in New York. Dad thought it a freezing sport that lacked all the dignity of golf, and the dancers at Syracuse said one fall and I'd never dance again. But I knew if I tried I'd like it, and that was the real reason I hadn't gone on any of the cheap introductory ski weekends that were advertised on the bulletin boards in Goldstein. In France I couldn't resist, especially when it meant six nights in a row with Bou and Margot.

The four of us never bothered to choose bedrooms, just unpacked wherever our knapsacks fell and mostly slept in the master chamber under two of those oceanic duvets. We shared the king-size bed in different threesomes every night except for the last one, when you fell immovably asleep in the middle of it, Margot slept at your feet like one of aged King David's virgins, and Bou and I curled up together in front of the honeycomb embers of the last expensive log. The other nights it just didn't matter who was the one too tired to want company, the one who went off to sleep alone in the quiet rooms. We took turns being too tired. Margot and Bou didn't mind the lack of privacy. I imagined they made love in that bathtub with the hand-held sprayer and the view of Les Grands Montets, high above the tree line.

What did we eat besides those huge chunks of the fondue cheeses we bought that first night, and those four-hundred-gram chocolate bars? I remember cold Emmental and Comté for lunch on the mountain, at night fondue, then grilled cheese sandwiches, omelets with the Fribourg, and those Venus navel pastas with grated Beaufort. After every meal we washed the cheese down with rows of chocolate dipped in tea, just in case there was an open artery somewhere we'd missed.

We had six days, but in my mind now it's all one long day we spent together in a constellation superior to our Parisian one. You were with us. You were still the grumpy, parental figure you had established for yourself in the fall, but by the middle of the week it wasn't Bou, Margot, and me fooling around with you watching and judging us. Instead it was the four of us dragging groceries up that damn road, the four of us doing dishes in the middle of the night, when our legs felt like lead and our eyes burned and teared from all that wind and sun. There was nothing we didn't share. We were together, not a gay couple and two guys, not two roommates and a couple, but four friends who could go — who knew where? — into the future.

I believed that, I admit. I didn't think it through, but I felt the possibilities. And I imagine, even now, that you believed in us too.

"It's my Christmas present," Bou explained.

She was taking us out to dinner at the Hôtel Albert Premier. Bou didn't carry a purse, just a couple credit cards in the pocket of her gray silk blouse. I don't know which was sexier, the oblong cards or the round shadows of her nipples.

"I thought coming to Chamonix was your Christmas present," I said.

"I thought the CD player was your Christmas present," you said.

You were still sore because in an early Christmas card from Mam, the same letter with the *Times* clipping, Bou had received instructions to purchase for herself a CD player and some CDs. This she had promptly done, comparison shopping for an entire fifteen minutes at FNAC Les Halles before hauling off an eight-hundred-dollar Aiwa rack flanked by two powerful speakers. She was supposed to wait to open the card on Christmas morning, which we'd spent in the chalet breakfasting on chocolate crêpes and singing carols and two-day-early Hanukkah songs around the scrawny yule log. But Bou claimed she hadn't seen DON'T OPEN TILL CHRISTMAS in red magic marker on the back of the envelope. Deferred gratification was not one of her strengths.

"The CD player was for the first day," she said. "Coming up here was for the third day. Didn't anybody ever tell you people about the twelve days?"

"A toast," you said. "To not having to ski tomorrow."

Skiers' robotic boots and padded knees paraded past the window, their heads invisible in the restaurant's curtains. They were on their way home from happy hour at the pubs.

"To not having to fall down," you added. "Then get up, then fall down again."

"To no more purple bruises on my ass," Margot said.

I squeezed her hand on the white cloth and looked at the ring her father had made for her with his dental tools. The opal in its gold setting had a faintly crownish look to it, but I could see it had been crafted with fatherly love. Margot's hand was small and hot. It took all my concentration not to crush it.

"Oh, one more thing," you said, glass raised. "Here's to not having to pray that you can keep from pissing yourself while you peel off uncountable layers of clothing in a hot bathroom, after waiting four hours in arctic cold."

"Bottoms up," Bou agreed.

The champagne was icy. Bou's lips widened and her eyes narrowed as she tipped, then lowered, the flute. I wondered what she looked like after she came.

"Is that what she looks like after she comes?" I asked Margot. That's the way it was all week. I just said what I was thinking, did what I wanted, the way you always do. For that one week I could get away with it, too.

"More like this," Margot said, and slumped against me in her chair.

"Fuck you," Bou said distinctly. "Both of you."

She drained her glass, set it down, and reached for the bottle in the bucket with both hands.

"Let's sit on the rock," Bou said.

We gazed toward it. It didn't look far, but it was distinctly higher than we were. After making our way up to the chalet

126

from town, we didn't have much altitude change left in us. You, especially, were wheezing the way a fat person does after a stiff half-hour climb on top of a bottle of champagne, a *ravioli d'homard à la crème d'ortie,* and a few tastes of my *terrines de foies d'oie au kiwi,* your chateaubriand grilled *feu de bois* and served *à la béarnaise,* with a side of *buisson d'asperges aux quatre sauces,* namely Chantilly, *verte,* mousseline, and *maltaise,* followed by the salad of that frizzy lettuce with wood strawberries and pine nuts and then, naturally, the indispensable rolling selection of about forty cheeses and *truffes au chocolat,* chased with espresso and cognac.

"Let's lie down and die," you suggested alternatively.

It was too late. Bou had marched off up the road with Margot, her hiking boots crunching the frozen snow. A car coughed to life in front of one of the chalets and bore down the road toward us, its headlights searching the darkness predatorially. Margot and Bou stepped into a driveway. You and I clung like spiders to the boulders that lined the road, while the magnificent black Citroën Prestige Turbo CM avalanched past, nose to the snow.

"Goddamn, that was close," you roared. "Let's go home!"

It wasn't clear whether you meant New Canaan or the chalet, which was only thirty yards downhill. In either case it didn't matter. Bou was up ahead singing a marching song about how her pants were heavy, her boots were tight, and her tits were swinging from left to right. She advanced toward the rock which was silhouetted against the starry sky, Margot tucked under her left arm like a football. You kept walking but cursed Bou, the mountain, and French civil engineers.

"Why are we following that madwoman? Who designed this cowpath of death? Why are we up in this wasteland in the middle of winter?"

You panted and leaned into the hill.

"I ask you, man, what kind of road is this? No doubt these rocks are intended to kill us and the people in the cars before any of us can damage the priceless snowfields."

You ranted on while I dreamt my way back to our second night in Chamonix, when I had come close to milting on either Bou's or Margot's smooth hip, I didn't know. It wasn't so much dying on French soil that I minded as dying before I found out. I knew the scarf that I'd tugged from Bou's or Margot's neck was a dream accessory, because neither of them wore silk scarves to bed. I was fairly sure I'd imagined the fluttering of wings that woke me up. What I still wondered was whether I'd dreamt the whole experience.

"Hold on a minute," you gasped. You bent over, clutching your side.

I stood by in tactful silence until you had wheezed your way down to idling speed. We climbed again.

Bou's boulder turned out to be another ten minutes, straight up. Margot was still trying to scale it when we reached its base.

"I don't know about this," she said.

"Give me your hand," Bou told her.

"I can't. I'm using them."

"Just reach out with your foot. There's a crack."

Margot made it, and we started up after her. The boulder was tricky with numb hands and a swollen belly, but once I was past the spot where Margot had stalled I decided that climbing the rock was, like most of Bou's ideas, worth it. We lay on our backs on the rough summit. The fabric of bright and dim stars enclosed us. Across the valley was the rocky tower of the Aiguille du Midi. It was so huge it looked close. Bou wept steadily.

"I'm so happy," she said. She often wept when she was sad, too.

"Wrap your leg over mine," Margot ordered me.

That night we dog-piled against the wind in earnest. I ended up mostly on top of Margot, facing south and up.

"Do you think we'll ever come back here?" Bou asked. Snot and tears shone in the moonlight on her cheeks and upper lip.

"Not without ropes," you told her. Your head was lodged firmly in her armpit.

"Gosh, I don't know," I said. "We have to. Don't you think?"

"Yes, I do," Bou said in a trembly voice.

For a while no one talked. I closed my eyes and heard cowbells, but when I was skiing I hadn't run into any cows. I imagined they were down in the valley, wherever cows winter.

"Even if we don't come back," Margot said, "we'll never forget this time."

"Don't hand out that wide-eyed shit," you said. "Are we going to come back up here or not? Bou's asking a question."

Who was this speaking? Surely it wasn't you, Beck. You weren't changing the subject, and you weren't making a joke of it. That was how I could tell that you felt pretty much the same way the rest of us did.

"I was trying," Margot said, "to answer her."

"You were trying to pacify her."

If I could have read the spray of stars surrounding us, I would have known that in a year, when we might have come back to these mountains, we would instead be leading separate lives. Only Bou and Margot would be together. You and I would be on our way to futures as far apart as the most distant corners of our galaxy.

"I just meant," Margot said, "that we'll remember each other. We'll think of each other."

"I know what you meant and it's bullshit."

I'd have kicked you except that I couldn't move my limbs. Didn't you see you were hurting her? She was offering us her vision of what we might take with us. You wouldn't let her.

"I don't want your fatalistic 'At least we had this moment, you're always with me in my thoughts,' not quite mystical, crystal-waving swill," you roared.

The stars backed away from you.

"I have no use for sentimental, Girl Scout friendship badge, yearbook-signing, blood sister, voodoo karma ca-ca."

Bou stopped sniffling and just let herself run. I think I would have hated you, if I hadn't realized how much you loved us all.

"I want us to come back," you said, with an awkward trombone break in your voice. "Not in our minds, not in another life. I want us," you repeated, "to come back."

The stars crept cautiously nearer.

"Can't you understand? To be together again, that's all I'm saying. Bou wants that too."

"Okay," Margot said. "Okay."

"Or not leave," you shouted.

"Yes," Margot said.

The next morning we got up at five and packed. At seven we took the day train, which was nothing like the night train. It was crowded because while we'd been in Chamonix, the Europeans had arrived thinking they had some right to the place. Now significant numbers of them were leaving again.

Bou talked to a Belgian fellow who sold raw plastic all over France. You read *Fig-Eco.* Margot and I argued about med school and managed to get ourselves all worked up about philosophies of curriculum. I was against rote learning, since it takes me approximately six weeks to memorize my new phone number every time I move. Margot believed that medical students should be given some idea of where and how to find the information they'll need as specialists rather than forced to identify every piece of gristle in the anatomy book. You wouldn't think that she and I could have debated a topic, all the way back to Paris, about which we so obviously agreed. But in those days we were so anxious about our medical educations, we could have gone on arguing nonsense all the way to Oslo.

At two in the afternoon the Gare de Lyon was crowded. New Year's was still two days off, but the Parisians were everywhere, like fire ants. We lugged our packs through the station to the métro tunnels. Margot and Bou took the Pont de Neuilly line home. We waved goodbye as their rubber-wheeled car carried them off, and I felt as if I'd never see them again. It turned out to be eight days before I did.

On New Year's Eve, you had a Caribbean gig, Bou and Margot went to a party at Margot's boss's house, and I had dinner with Paola at Joseph's. When we all finally got together that next Tuesday, Chamonix was fixed in the past. Our week there floated, luminous and intact, like an island in the sky we had visited together, or like that little island the size of two tennis courts below Mount Desert off the coast of Maine, which Bou said her Uncle Will had bought and officially renamed No Man. Chamonix was already that far away.

Over the next weeks we all settled back into our routines. The quality of fourness stayed with us, but slowly we turned back into two twos. We forgot about the long feather-pillow nights, about the blinding days of sun we'd known in that high place.

Tremor

"Complete the word," Margot ordered through the microphone.

I sat in her lead-lined box, like a sarcophagus with a porthole, and stared at the screen on the other side of the glass. It said *SERR?* and I realized the word I was supposed to complete was *SERRÉ.* Now my only problem was to find the damn *É* on the French keyboard in my lap. Margot and her boss, Docteur Maupin, sat on the other side of my standing casket. I wore what looked and felt like a heavy catcher's mask flipped back on my head. This mask held six miniature thermoses full of liquid helium, within which loops of wire registered tiny changes in the electromagnetic field generated by my brain.

POM?E appeared and I duly typed in the *M,* figuring I must have the idiot-level program if I was getting words that easy. I then wondered what sort of magnetic frequencies feeling like an idiot generated. Twenty minutes later I was out of there, my responses recorded on beautiful color software from Palo Alto that made my thoughts look seismographic. Have you noticed that a lot of California programming, even the stuff my dad uses to do his taxes, has an earthquaky feel to it? I studied my brain map and saw what looked to be about a five-point-seven on the Richter scale. I asked when the disturbance had occurred. Sure enough, it was right when I'd gotten *POMME* and decided I must have the low-normal protocol.

"You were attentive," Margot said.

"Was I unusual?"

I didn't like her wielding a powerful diagnostic tool over me. I wasn't so paranoid I refused to be a rodent the way you did, but I was curious about what she'd seen.

"I can't say yet," she told me.

"Give it to me straight. What's the initial diagnosis?"

She sighed, put down her menu, and looked at me.

"DAP."

I dutifully asked what DAP was.

"Dancer Attention Profile. A slowing of the higher functions, a tendency to gaze into pools of still water for extended periods."

"Ouch," I said.

I was used to that kind of treatment only from you. Margot was annoyed with me, and I had no idea why. We were having the lunch that all the rats received after running the maze, and that was the reason Margot and I had concluded it was worth my leaving ballet early. We'd been to the restaurant once in the fall, but today Margot had brought four of those thirty-six-franc *ticket restaurant* coupons with her. Two meal tickets were my cheese. Margot had saved up the other two, but even with four we were going to have to kick in a few francs.

"Aren't I allowed to ask?" I asked.

"Can we order?" Margot answered in an unfamiliar voice. I hadn't even looked at the menu.

"You mean *commitment?*"

Margot pretended to cough and drank some water.

"The C word," she said.

"I'm sorry. I didn't realize it was like that."

"Not for me," Margot told me. "For Bou."

Mam in Lincoln and Miriam in Newton had simultaneously forwarded forms about housing at Yale for Bou and Margot's last year. I didn't see what the problem was. Obviously Bou and Margot would live together in Saybrook, the way they had since sophomore year. As seniors they could get a couple of excellent rooms, even a fireplace for show. That was how Margot saw it and, after she explained it to me, how I did too, but Bou wasn't sure.

"She's afraid she's too dependent on me."

"The D word," I said.

Bou was right, and Margot and I both knew it. Margot had been taking care of Bou since they'd started up freshman year, when she'd coaxed Bou far enough out of her depression to get her through her course work and into therapy. I'd seen Bou pull Margot out of the dumps more than once in Paris, but those were *petits dumps,* not *grands dumps.* Bou really couldn't make it without Margot. They had both told me that. Bou's last serious collapse had been at Martha's Vineyard after their sophomore year. Bou hadn't dared spend a summer on the island since Nathan had drowned, but she and Margot decided it was time for her to try a July out there. She was all right until the actual anniversary of Nathan's death, on the ninth. Then she went to bed and didn't get up for two days, not to eat, not even to go to the bathroom. Neither Jason nor her parents once mentioned that Bou wasn't at the table. Only Mam had gone to her room to see her. Bou wouldn't talk. Margot took a baking pan upstairs to use as a bedpan.

"She thinks we should live with other people," Margot whispered now. I'd never seen her like this.

"You mean in a suite?"

Margot studied the copper cassoulets and the paintings of vineyards that hung on the walls.

"No," she said finally. "She wants to live with Kim and Robin. I've told you about them. Kim's from Atlanta. Robin's the one who wants to be president."

"I remember."

"Bou wants to live off-campus with them. She thinks I should stay in Saybrook with Yolanda from Jazz Ensemble."

"Well?"

"I don't want to."

"So how are we going to change her mind?"

Margot cheered up slightly. I was about to offer to come live with her myself — with Margot, I mean.

"Hypnosis wouldn't work," she said. "Bou's about as receptive to suggestion as that pâté."

"We could tickle her."

"I'll do her back," Margot said, because right between Bou's shoulder blades, where her skin is invisibly rough, there's a spot where she can't stand to be tickled.

We ate and pretended we'd solved Margot's little problem. I was as frightened as if I'd heard my parents fighting behind their bedroom door, which I had once. It wasn't my parents, it was Dad and Brenda. I was going to be bar mitzvahed in seven weeks and I still wouldn't call Brenda anything except Mrs. Krantz, though she and Dad had been together for a year and a half. I went to the bathroom and saw the crack of light under their door. I heard her telling Dad he should *ask* me to call her Brenda. Dad said that I could call her whatever I felt like, that it was natural I didn't want a new mother. *Oh, so that's what this is about,* Mrs. Krantz said. *It's not that you don't want to ask your son to call me by my given name. It's that we're not going to get married.* They were both quiet for a while. Finally Dad said no, he didn't know if they would get married.

The next day, and every day after that when I didn't forget, I called Brenda Brenda. I stopped seeing her long face in profile, her nose and chin jutting out, as if she were an emperor inscribed on a coin. Instead I started looking at her from the front, and I noticed how her eyes crinkled up when she laughed, and how white her teeth were. I started talking to her about school and track, and even, sometimes, about Mom. She began to take me with her when she went grocery shopping, Wednesdays, at Adams.

"When did Robin decide to go for president?" I asked, determined to keep Margot from gloomy thoughts.

"Her mother decided for her, right after her dad took off. I think Robin was seven."

"That's right," I said. "Her mom told her, 'Don't make the same mistake I did. Don't live for a man. Be president.'"

"Robin's serious about it. She won't take a whiff of pot. She has positions on everything."

"I have positions," I said, taking Margot's *quenelles de brochet* from the waiter and setting the plate in front of her. "I'm just not sure I agree with them."

"She was all by herself," Margot told me. "It was a crew party. Half the women were straight, and almost all the men."

"Wait. What about the gum wrappers? I don't get that."

We walked beneath the riveted belly of the elevated tracks, where the outdoor market stretched from Rue Daniel Stern to Rue du Commerce. The market was closing, the vendors all packing their goods and breaking down their long tables. We reached the corner where in the fall the health department had sequestered a very thin Indian man and his tropical birds. Now all that remained of the bird seller's colony of toucans, barbets, touracos, and birds of paradise was the guano of nostalgia, speckling the asphalt beneath a waterlogged January sky.

"You know," Margot said. "Gum-wrapper chains. Didn't girls in your school make those?"

"My babysitter, Polly Spagnolo, made one as long as her driveway. Mom and I saved our wrappers for her. But why were you all doing it at Yale? Is it a gay symbol now or something?"

Margot laughed, startling three pigeons, one with white head and tail feathers, who immediately parachuted back down in front of us again and bounced along on their hind toes like wind-up toys. *There are still birds here,* they were telling us. *We may not be tropical wonders, but we're on the job.*

"It was just a stupid idea for a party. Like a toga party, or a beach party in the middle of winter. Nobody but Bou took it seriously. She went out and bought twenty packs of Wrigley's because she didn't have any wrappers. She had a bag of gum in her pack for months."

"And you sat down and talked to her."

"She was lonely," Margot said, leading me up Boulevard de Grenelle. "The whole women's first novice crew was chugging beer and carrying on, not even noticing little Bou on the couch. She had this wrapper chain in her lap, maybe six inches long."

I'd never heard Bou referred to as little before, but then I'd never seen her next to the women's first novice crew.

"What did you say to her?"

"I said I wanted to borrow her Armatrading tapes."

"You never listen to Armatrading."

"True," Margot admitted.

"No, I mean what did you say first? When you sat down."

We hustled up Rue Cambronne alongside the office and hotel complexes. Margot's spirits had rallied after lunch. I had the feeling that the rooming question would resolve itself within the week. Margot had just been having an off day. Now I wanted to remind her of just how much she and Bou had behind them. I was trying to be a good historian.

"I don't remember what I said."

"You do, too."

"All right, I do."

I was the one who loved Bou and Margot best. I made them feel sure of themselves. That had been my role since the night I'd met them. Now, for the first time, I had to work at it.

"I said I knew her from somewhere," Margot told me, checking her watch and tugging me toward Rue de Vaugirard. "She started listing all the preppy schools and riding academies where we might have met."

"You never rode a horse in your life."

"I didn't mention that."

Margot picked up the pace, throwing her tough new ski legs out in front of her. With her earrings on, in her charcoal corduroys and long coat, she looked like a doctor.

"Then you just dragged her off?"

"No," Margot said. "We stayed for hours. I was with Laurie."

"You were?"

"She rowed crew with Bou's roommate, Alexandra. That's why we were all there."

"Oh."

I felt illuminated and at the same time lost. It was a bewildered, intelligent feeling that I thought must be generating miniature magnetic storms all around the invisible catcher's mask I hadn't been able to shake.

"But I thought you and Bou fell in love right after that?"

"We did," Margot said.

I knew that Bou and Margot had gotten together within a couple days of that party, but that they hadn't slept together for almost a month. Bou had told me all about it while whipping the pants off me at gin.

"You must have broken up with Laurie pretty fast," I said.

We turned alongside the colonial Hôpital St.-Jacques. I waited for her to tell me that she and Laurie had broken up slowly, but somehow in under three days. Then I knew Margot wasn't going to say that, because that wasn't what had happened.

"You stayed with Laurie."

"Yup," Margot said, but nothing more. She showed her badge to the guard at the institute. I pointed to the tricolor visitor's sticker on my breast.

"Sounds like a situation," I said.

"It was."

We slowed in the courtyard. Margot glanced one last time at her watch. In front of us, a bronze boy fought a rabid part-bulldog. The kid wielded what looked like a snake stick with a thick leather catch strap. In muzzling the frothing beast, he'd lost one of his bronze shoes. I waited for Margot to draw a conclusion, offer a caution, or simply summarize exactly what sort of situation she and Bou had found themselves in. But she didn't. She just stared at the poor mad animal.

"Well," I said. "Thanks again for the cheese."

I leaned and kissed her.

"Listen," she told me. "I'm sorry I'm such a pill today. I didn't sleep much."

"I had fun."

"You did not."

She pulled me down and we kissed again. Then she hurried across the white gravel toward the Bâtiment Fernbach, bearing away my struggling heart.

Real Life

We stood outside Café de la Plage, looking through the glass to where couples sat drinking beer. The place didn't look like a nightclub, and we wouldn't pay the whopping cover until the doorman assured us that you and the rest of the Orchestre Antillais were already hard at work downstairs. Poor as they were, the dancers made a collection to pay my eighty francs, and I let them. My birthday dinner had just set me back two weeks.

"Is it that I will at last have the opportunity to encounter the women you love?" Paola asked while Joseph counted out bills.

"Perhaps the tall one," I told her.

I knew Bou might show up around midnight. Jano Hanbowski was having his monthly showcase, and even though she wasn't performing, Bou had to watch. Margot was playing late with Zubir at Le Cambridge. She'd wished me a happy twenty-third when I called her in the afternoon for cooking instructions. She said she had a present for me but hadn't finished it yet.

We made our way into the bar and down the spiral staircase. Below was a stone-and-mortar cave. Two rooms were connected by an arched doorway, over which was set a green emergency *Sortie* sign pointing further in. A waist-up passage cut through the same four-foot wall the doorway traversed. We could hear your orchestra but couldn't see you until we filed through the archway. On the other side was a remarkably wide dance floor, at one end of which you and fourteen or so West

Indians were crowded onto a sectioned platform. You sported your parrot shirt, maroon-dyed OshKoshes, and army boots. Your horn jutted up above the rest of the band almost to the ceiling. As soon as you saw me, you motioned me forward. I was flattered until I realized it was Paola and Dominique you were after.

You knelt and introduced yourself to them, kissing Paola four times, then attaching yourself to Dominique like a jawless lamprey, until her boyfriend, Didier, pried you loose.

"Glad to meet you," you shouted, pumping his hand. He led Dominique away.

"Fetch me a couple Kronenbourgs, buddy. Wait," you said. "Meet the boys."

The bone player to your right was nearly your width. He reached down and lifted me to my tiptoes with his right arm. In a voice like a washtub bass he asked my name, then told me he was Nestor, from Port-au-Prince. Your other neighbor, who looked like me with dreadlocks and the most bloodshot eyes I'd ever seen, offered a gentle caress of a handclasp. I knew this must be Julien, the source of the kick-ass hash. The three of you stood to play. I went for your beer.

You stood out, I admit, and not only because you were the only white guy in the ensemble. Bathed in light, your body slimmed by our dance-floor perspective, you looked almost elegant. You swayed and blasted at the sky. Your cheeks swelled into wide embouchure smiles that made you look like a Buddha in overalls.

We found a table on the other side of the arch. The dancers bought me a sundae bowl of rum and other liquors with a pink umbrella floating on top. In a way I was hoping Bou wouldn't make it to the club. I hadn't seen her in nearly two weeks, not since before my rodent get-together with Margot the week before. I thought it might be just as well if I spent my birthday with the dancers. Bou should work out her rooming plans with Margot. Then we four could have dinner together as always.

Dominique unwound herself from Didier and led me from

the table. Her walk drew the eyes of everyone we passed on the way to the dance floor. To be Dominique's escort was a nice birthday present all by itself. Soon the other dancers joined us and made a little island of white folk with you, our patron saint.

I don't know exactly when Bou showed up. The dancers and I had been going at it for some time. We did things with our hips that we hadn't learned in ballet class. When the ambient temperature reached midsummer tropical, Dominique side-knotted her shirt. A dozen men set down their drinks, and a dozen women sat up straighter and adjusted their shoulders. Nicole and Anne knotted off their blouses too, and their bellies gleamed in the flashing lights. You and your pals beat and blew a reggae symphony. I danced with my eyes closed so I could hear better.

When I opened them, Bou was standing in front of the stage and you were kneeling to kiss her. I danced over.

"Hello, stranger!" she yelled. Paola sambaed up, met Bou, and dragged us both to the middle of the floor. Your number ended and you and the other Rastafarians mopped your faces and searched frantically for your beers. We wandered back to our table, where someone handed me another drink, with a blue umbrella in it this time.

I introduced Paola, Dominique, Didier, Joseph, Nicole, Anne, and her husband, Patrick, and wondered how much of our fertility ritual Bou had just witnessed. I hoped she'd seen us when I was deep in my voodoo trance. Half the dancers lit up cigarettes from Didier's pack, and all of them tried to talk to Bou at once. Your band started a slow jam. I took Paola's hand.

"She is marvelous," Paola said as we negotiated the tunnel. I told her the other one was, too.

We danced right through the next songs. Anne and Patrick came out, then Bou with Joseph, who was talking a blue streak in Bou's ear. She smiled and held his hands while she danced. You and your buddies played another slow one. Joseph and

Bou showed no signs of leaving the floor, just pulled closer to continue their conversation. Paola headed for the table, and I left for the men's room feeling what toward anyone but Bou might have been jealousy. When I came out of the bathroom, she was there.

"How come I never see you anymore?"

I shrugged. I'd decided not to talk to Bou about her problems with Margot.

"You too busy for us now?"

"Yes," I said. "I'm booked."

The absurd was safe ground. We sat down at a table at the bottom of the staircase. A model *QE II* dangled above our heads. On the wall behind Bou was a palm tree in three neon tubes — blue sand, pink trunk, green fronds. We could hear each other there without yelling as loudly as on the dance floor.

"Margot scares our friends away."

"She's pretty scary."

"I keep telling her I want to see you guys. She just wants us to be alone."

"She loves you," I said without thinking. This was not the tone I'd meant to take. Who did I think I was, a marriage counselor?

"I miss you," Bou said.

I was looking into her eyes. She lifted her chin at me in a thoughtful way.

"I want us to stay close," she said.

I realized that my lips were pursed and that I wasn't breathing. I unpursed them, leaned against the back of my chair, and took a breath. She said something else. I leaned forward.

"What?"

"I don't like having to pretend that you're just somebody I know. Another acquaintance."

I sat in the racket in my own little silence. The square table, the smoky club, was just the right setting for words I'd never thought of speaking to Bou. But suddenly there they were in my mind. I used other words.

"She's worried," I called across to her. "She's afraid you don't want to live with her next year."

"I don't."

I pretended I couldn't hear her. I wanted her never to have started saying what she was about to say.

"I said I don't. We've been together for three years. We've got to stop clinging to each other."

"Not clinging. Holding on."

"You have no idea what it's like," Bou said, not shouting now because she had the shoulder of my shirt in her hand, I was looking between her breasts, and she was warming my left ear with her words. "She says she wants us to have our own lives, but then she wants to know every thought in my head. She wants to cook everything I eat. She says we should get out more, but she doesn't want to see anyone except you and Beck."

She shook her head.

"Now she's worried that I'm going to hurt you," she said. "That's what she keeps telling me. She says I shouldn't be so close to you, because you'll . . ."

She stopped. My ear waited.

"Me and Beck?"

"You. She thinks I'm leading you on. She thinks you'll . . ."

"What?"

"Fall in love with me."

I nodded thoughtfully, as if a difficult theoretical position had just been advanced, one that I was familiar with but that still required some working through. I studied the tiled floor, a rippling trompe-l'oeil pattern in baby blue and white.

"Don't worry about it. Margot's nuts."

Bou let go of my shoulder and ruffled my hair. I was a boy with a crush and I hadn't even known it. Margot was worried about me because she knew I was dreaming about Bou, when all the time I thought I was dreaming about Bou and Margot.

"Do you know what she calls you?"

"Do I want to?" It was an honest question. I did, but suspected it was a bad idea.

"Bamboy."

"What?"

"Like Bambi. She says you stare at me just like little Bambi."

"Why doesn't she call me Bambi?"

Bou didn't hear me. Bamboy wasn't too bad. I was expecting worse, but Bamboy was enough to save me. I was a fool, but I didn't mind that. You might say I was used to that. All that mattered was that this wasn't serious, my talk with Bou at the table in the smoky nightclub. It was just an unusual chat, after which Margot and Bou would be together as always. Even if Margot was right and I did have more of a crush on Bou that week, the wheel always turned. Next week before ballet Paola would ask me who I was thinking of, and I'd say Margot.

"I don't know what's going to happen," Bou called across the table. We were both shaking our heads now, though about what I wasn't sure. Obviously, as soon as the two of them sent in those housing forms, the four of us could resume our old life. So what if I was the baby of the group, with crushes so obvious that only I didn't know about them? That was harmless, and it was all over now. Bou gazed past my right shoulder, then looked at me.

"I can't stop thinking about you," she said.

I felt the words before I heard them. I thought if I spoke I might orient myself.

"I told Margot," I said, "that you two were going to be fine." I said this to remind myself of what I knew as much as for any other reason. I recognized that my statement was not quite up to date.

"I keep thinking about Chamonix."

"I told her," I went on saying, as if Bou were talking about an unrelated situation, "that I knew you two would always be together."

I said all that. Bou just shook her head.

"It's not that simple."

I pulled back and looked up at her. I'd never been involved in a conversation like that one. We were speaking, if I wasn't mistaken, about love, and the two of us. The whole situation bore a striking resemblance to what I'd long thought of as *real life*.

"We almost broke up," Bou said. "We're still together, but we don't sleep together these days. I mean we sleep in the same bed, but we don't do anything. We might break up when we leave Paris."

I looked at her. I waited for her to start laughing, punch me in the arm, and pull me to the dance floor. *I really had you going, didn't I?* she'd say.

"I want to be with you," she said instead. "Not with Margot and Beck. Just us."

She took my hand, which was lying between us on the table. "We should talk," I said, "like this."

I was still a little behind. She pulled me across the narrow table and hugged me awkwardly, as if we were distant relations at a wedding. I heard the hungry wail of your horn. You were soloing. I was going to tell Bou so we could go watch and listen, but I didn't have the chance.

"Do you love me?" she asked, warming my other ear now.

"Yes. But — "

She kissed me hard, as they say in novels.

I have exactly twelve minutes. I've been playing with the new ones. There are five of them this morning. Monica Jorgenson, the nurse who alternates with Nadine Croft in Well Baby, looks on with contentment as I march past her. Monica is temperamentally Nadine's opposite. She likes it when young almost-doctors come to play with her healthies. The babies sense her sunny presence and don't cry at the least excuse.

"Beautiful morning," I say to Monica, though I haven't set foot outside the hospital in twenty hours.

"Lovely," she answers in her gentle voice. All the babies sigh and settle.

I tamper with a male Kramer and a female Compton, both still wet behind the ears. Softly I whack the pad beside Kramer, and he throws up his arms and grimaces, his Moro reflex transforming him into a petulant old man. Compton, Girl, offers me her left hand with easy confidence. She's like a Sig Ep boy at Syracuse, setting his elbow on Chuck's bar for an arm wrestle. I place a forefinger in her palm. Her fist closes on it like a Venus' flytrap. Carefully I hoist her 3,267 grams almost off the foam by the strength of that palmar grasp.

"Strong," Monica says.

"Amazing."

Compton and Kramer have been out of the womb for eight hours. In less than six months they'll cast aside these instincts like the habits of an earlier primate existence they choose to forget. No more *startle*, no more *grasp*. Standing

147

there, I realize that's how we fall in love. A thump comes through the ground and suddenly someone is there. Our eyes widen, then narrow. We throw our arms and legs out for balance, draw breath, wait. We feel something warm press right into the middle of us. It's frightening, it's wonderful. We grab on for dear life. Nothing will shake us off.

We only fall in love one time, Beck. All the way in love, with no holding back, no pretending. Then we lose the gift. We love again, but never with the same terror and wonder as we did that first time, before we knew how.

Blue Train

Bou kissed me hard. Then she said things in my ear over the music. I was so close to her that she was an area into which I disappeared whenever I kissed her back. You were far away onstage, your solo finished. Margot was at her gig. Nicole approached, then walked quickly away. Was it because Bou and I were together? Bou and Margot had broken up, in a way. Bou and I could touch now, though *now* had followed *then* pretty fast, was almost part of *then*. Still, I thought the new situation should be clear to anyone who saw us together. Why did Nicole hurry off? At last Bou and I untangled ourselves from the table and stood.

"What are we going to tell Margot?" I asked, as if remembering an important detail about a trip at the very last minute.

"Nothing, for now."

I wondered about this but Bou was sure, and I thought she understood everything better than I did. Margot was safe, playing alongside steady Zubir at Le Cambridge in the seventeenth. Margot didn't need Bou right now, so I led her to the dance floor and found a few of my friends in motion. I noticed for the first time in minutes how tall Bou was. When we came together, my head fit against her shoulder as it hadn't when we clinched across the table. That put Margot right between her breasts, or even on the underside of them.

"Comfortable."

"What?"

"Comfortable," I shouted.

"I'm not wearing any."

The music was loud. That was all right. I wasn't sure my thoughts were in any condition to be shared. I remembered having started a third bowl of punch before I'd gone to the bathroom. The umbrella had been either yellow or orange. Perhaps the conversation Bou and I had just carried on at the bottom of the spiral staircase had been a misunderstanding. Bou had spoken virtually inside my ear. Still, she might not have said that she was in love with me and wanted to be with me. The statement didn't square with other empirical observations I had made in the past, such as that Bou lived with Margot and was gay. I decided, as I watched her hair rising to and falling away from her ears in Caribbean time, to put the whole question of what she had said on hold. Whatever it was, it would keep.

We were diplomatic with my friends. We'd neglected them while we were alone together. Now I danced with Anne, then with Nicole. We were all together in a herd, but the mood had changed. Bou and I were making a gracious sacrifice to dance with the others, and they felt it. Paola did, at least.

"Where were you?"

"I was with Bou."

Paola held me at arm's length and studied me. Had Nicole told her about the kisses she'd stumbled upon? Yes, I nodded to Paola, with Bou. Was there a problem? Why was Paola turning her merciless Veronese eyes on me? Couldn't she trust me, just once? Obviously this was not the time for one of our usual talks. I was simply delivering the news. A great weight lifted from me when Paola released my arms, prematurely as it turned out.

"How can you be together with her?" she shouted, pulling me back.

"She is no longer," I yelled, "with Margot."

I danced away from her. This explained everything. Why was Paola still glaring at me like my fourth-grade teacher, Mr. Kittridge, when I told him that St. Louis was a state? Her eyes asked what that meant, that Bou was no longer with Margot. I danced evasively and repeated key formulas inside my head — *Falling in love, Don't sleep together, Can't stop thinking about you.* The music you and the others played had taken on a steady, noonday-in-the-marketplace feeling. That and the phrases in my head were all I needed. *We don't do anything,* Bou had said. I especially relied on that one.

But how could I explain the new situation to Paola? She reached out and again pulled my head down to her. Why was everybody always pulling on my head?

"What exactly," she shouted, "do you propose to do?"

"I will come to know Bou better," I returned. "We will then decide what we intend."

That covered it. Even Paola couldn't argue with a statement that indirect. While she and I looked accusations and defenses at each other, you and the boys blew, plucked, and banged. You knew nothing and nodded in tranquillity between thunderous, water-buffalo riffs. After a while Paola pointed and I saw you waving me over.

"Where have you been?" you shouted. "I need beer."

"With Bou."

"Kanterbräu Golds," you said.

Bou came up behind me while I waited at the bar.

"Let's get out of here."

"Now?"

I was still the host. My friends had come to celebrate my twenty-third birthday.

"It's two in the morning," Bou told me. "They'll leave soon anyway."

We were selfish. No one was going to stop us. Joseph looked at me with new respect when I said I was leaving.

"You are sleepy?"

He punched my arm. The others avoided my eyes, except for Paola, who stared at me.

"I must walk my friend to the métro," I shouted to Dominique.

All the time, I was wondering why Bou and I were leaving. The club wasn't closing for three hours, but the dancers were fading fast. We could have waited. We must have liked our

151

new game already. What we did wasn't even deceit, just bad manners.

Across the room Bou flashed me a guilty smile. I brought you your beers and you paid me.

"I'm walking Bou to the métro. She's not feeling well."

"Isn't that a shame."

You took the mouthpiece off your trombone and lobbed a chamber of spit onto the gray rag by your foot. Most of it hit the rag.

"Feeling low, is she? Well, she's looking fine."

You studied me, kneeling.

"I guess what she needs," you said, "is a birthday boy like you to make her feel better, even if she ends up looking a little worse."

You'd known since October. Margot had known for at least a week or two. Why did everybody know except me? You'd been telling me that something like this was going to happen since you and I had made our first appearance at Berlioz. I hadn't listened to you. I wasn't about to start now, next to the stage of Café de la Plage, with Bou waiting for me by the stone tunnel.

"I'll see you at home," I said.

I waved goodbye to Julien and Nestor. Bou waved to you and you lowered your bone, then lifted it partway, as if raising a flag to half mast.

"Do they make the soup from little turtles or big turtles?"

"I don't know," Bou said. "They have gold spoons. I remember that."

She dipped her *beignet abricot* in the little plastic coffee cup. We were sitting inside the revolving doors to Le Train Bleu, the restaurant that slumbered above the floor of the Gare de Lyon. We'd passed the spot only a month before, filing off the platform from the Chamonix day train.

"I thought kids didn't like to eat animals."

"I ate bunny in Vienna," Bou said. "I loved snails."

"What about" — I hesitated — "horsies?"

"Mam had the good sense to lie to me about that," Bou said quietly.

With only its night lights on, the center room of the restaurant was golden and dusky. Above, in a fresco framed in gilt, a naked woman was being traded to a man in a hunting cap for a giant sack marked PLM. The woman's companion, dressed in a toga and wearing an olive-leaf garland, had just spilled a horn of plenty. The fruits tumbled toward us through a summer sky.

"They told me the stores with the horses' heads outside were saddlemakers. Mam said there were so many saddlemakers because all the kings in the olden days rode horses, and everyone who went along with them had to ride, too. I saw lots of paintings in the Louvre of fancy people fighting on horseback, so I believed her."

Bou had been five when her parents had taken all three children on an eight-week tour of Europe. She didn't know what she remembered and what she'd heard later, when her family told stories about that summer. Trish, their Irish-born nanny from the South End, had come along, as had Phunt, fuzzy then, and with the power of sight.

"You remember the Louvre?"

"I remember a smelly man sketching the Venus de Milo. Trish went out to meet him at night, and Mam said she should be careful, or she'd end up washing out paintbrushes with a baby on each hip."

The aerodynamic TGV trains nosed toward us, their segmented orange tails snaking along the platforms.

"I wondered how she'd hold the babies and still wash brushes. She and Mam had a big argument on the balcony while I was having my nap."

On the floor to our left, in front of the exchange windows, a group of men sat talking and smoking. Above the silent or dieseling trains, the black schedule board announced departures for Briançon, Nîmes, Bourg-St.-Maurice, Milan, and Montereau.

"What happened to the Boutique?"

153

"I was five. Boutique Mademoiselle and Boutique Mademoiselle Upstairs closed just before I turned four."

"You don't say," I said, kissing her so deeply I forgot where I was. The first time had been when we'd left La Plage. On the street a light rain was falling, and under the droplets we stumbled into each other again and again, going nowhere, trying to find parts that kept slipping away.

Wait, Bou had said. *Wait.* But we couldn't. The best we could manage was to get partway down Rue Trousseau, so that when the dancers came out of the club they wouldn't trip over us. We spent some time against the window of Alcooliques Anonymes on the west side of the street, then walked the Passage de la Main d'Or in search of a bench, which we finally located beside a locked park on Rue Baudelaire. That was when we forgot we were in public in midwinter, forgot it was our first date, and forgot to stop. Bou's sighs turned into long almost-words.

"Close," she said finally. She pressed her back against the bench and shut her eyes. When she opened them, she saw the police station across the street.

"You'd better put yourself away," she told me. "We'll get locked up."

"You took me out. You put me away," I answered.

Bou molded me into the configuration of a sixty-pound hunting bow at full draw, then zipped me. We rose from our bench, our bottoms wet from the wood, and wandered south looking for an empty bed. Either there were none or they were hidden behind the walls of buildings. We breathed the wet air and read Bou's watch. It was two-fifty, we were chilly, and Margot was worried. All at once we both knew that. We decided to call her, but there were no phones. We started thinking, if you want to call it that.

Margot and Zubir's gig might well last until four, so Margot wasn't home yet. We had decided not to tell her about us, for now anyway. When Bou got home she'd explain that after my party, she and I had gone to the Latin Quarter for coffee.

That sounded reasonable and we felt practical again, not like betrayers.

Paris was small in the fog. We hiked through it. From Boulevard Diderot we saw the square clocktower of the Gare de Lyon. We climbed the steps from street level toward the purple neon SNCF sign. When we got closer, we read the art nouveau lettering, LE TRAIN BLEU, painted on the arched station windows. We wandered inside and bought our *beignets* and coffee from a man who drove a tiny purple snack vehicle called a Module Borneo. Then we mounted the iron staircase to the closed restaurant, which Bou said was her favorite in all the world. The revolving door was locked in place, and that made the left side of it where we settled by far the most comfortable spot we'd found all night. We were all but hidden from view there. It was warm.

"I had a clearance sale. Mam's friends were at the house planning how to get the bus to the march in Washington to remember Martin Luther King."

I was having a hard time keeping up. I wasn't kissing Bou now but I was looking at her, and that interfered with listening.

"Mam told the church women it was important not to stop the momentum, even though Martin Luther King had been dead for two whole years. I wasn't sure that people stayed dead. I thought Mam wanted Martin Luther King to come back to life and find his work proceeding under her direction. She kept talking about 'the movement,' and I wasn't sure whether she meant Martin Luther King's movement, which had stopped but not forever as far as I was concerned, or the push for reform, which was losing ground to the conservative reaction which set in after the Civil Rights Act of 1968."

"Bou?"

"I also thought Mam and Reverend White and the others were going to give up their seats on the bus to the Negro people from TV, and then stand up all the way home from Washington, the way Jason had to stand up on the way back from Lincoln Day Camp so the girls could sit down. Jason and

I didn't think that was fair. I'd heard about the Negroes on the buses in Alabama."

"Wait a minute. When did you find out about the horses?"

"Crossing to Dover. Nathan was mad because he threw up on the ferry and I didn't. It was windy and we were on the top deck. I asked him if he was feeling better and if he wanted a drink of water. He thought I was making fun of him. He said, *Remember the saddlemaker stores in Paris? Well, really they kill horses in there, and people eat them like hamburgers.* I pushed him as hard as I could, and he fell against the rail and cracked his top front tooth."

"No."

"It wasn't a permanent tooth. I didn't mean to."

My head expanded and shrank in a steady way. High above us, the ceiling of the train station was a vast divided skylight of milky glass, backed by soot and darkness. The surface of it was opaque, fragile, and precious, like the inside of an enormous Fabergé egg. I could happily have spent the night there, talking and making limited love to Bou. She assured me that one of her cards would be accepted, and that at noon we could brunch at the restaurant. Just inside the revolving door, on a three-tiered table topped by a golden cock, the menu promised Sevruga caviar, brill soufflé with forest mushrooms, smoked Norwegian salmon in the "façon Charles Barrier," and duck crêpes with wild honey sauce. We could afford whatever we wanted, Bou said. After all, it was my birthday.

"I still don't understand about Emily's hats."

"I sold them off. I opened the Boutique under the table, the way I did every week for Mam's bridge game. The only difference was that instead of invisible money, I took cash. There were so many people over, not just the usual seven for bridge, all these church ladies. I got the idea of using real money because Mam was collecting checks to charter the bus to Washington. She put them in her red sewing box."

A street cleaner, forest green topped by a spinning cherry, appeared from a street side of the station and glided up

Track H. It looked like a Zamboni rink surfacer, but left behind a soapy trail instead of dark ice.

"Kathy Pritchett from the bridge club told the others about the Boutique. Everyone thought it was adorable except Mam, who wanted to get on with the meeting."

"Kathy Pritchett's the one who named you Bou."

"She was Mam's bridge partner. She and Mam spoke French when they didn't want the others to understand. First Kathy called me *la petite propriétaire de la Boutique Mademoiselle.* Then everybody called me Bou."

According to the ornate poster on the wall below, the *couchettes*-only Train Bleu had left the Gare de Lyon at nine forty-five. Now it was nearly at Marseille, where it made a maintenance stop at five-thirty before traveling the Côte d'Azur to Vintimille.

"Kathy gave me a ten-dollar bill and told me not to lose my 'little treasure.' Soon I'd sold every hat I had, including Aunt Emily's April Fool's hat, a ridiculous turquoise-and-fuchsia bibi with a black satin bird's nest. Then I went out to watch Kill Crow, and on the way I buried the treasure behind Eddie's house."

"Eddie?"

"Poppa's black lab. He loved Poppa best, but I was his second favorite until Nathan made him love him more than me by giving him people food, which was bad for him. Poppa built him his own Cape Cod doghouse with cedar shingles, and trained him at Sandy Pond after church on Sundays."

The *beignets* and coffee were long gone. I didn't care. I lay my head on Bou's shoulder.

"Jason killed a crow once. Nathan never killed any, but he bruised them pretty bad. The trick was to stun them long enough for Eddie to retrieve them. Then we'd put them in the trashcan and listen to them try to fly."

A half-dozen Eurailpass gypsies slept beside the escalators. They were our age, and they used the edges of their packs as pillows.

"After Mam finished organizing the bus, the ladies came to find me and get their money. They were all wearing Aunt Emily's hats, and they surprised us right after Nathan nailed a little crow right in the head with his WristRocket. It flew away before Eddie could retrieve it, but the committee said we were cruel to shoot birds with pieces of Pepsi bottle. I said they could keep the hats. Mam said, *What about Aunt Emily?* I said the hats were mine, and I'd sold them."

Two national policemen led a Doberman along the end of the tracks.

"The ladies wanted their money back, especially Lorraine Pembroke, who Mam said might not be able to play doubles with her at Concord Club anymore because her husband had been involved in irregularities. Mam finally gave Lorraine ten dollars for the mauve Melusine with the charcoal silk rouleau. Then she handed out all the rest of the cash she had in the house. When Poppa got home, he came straight to my room to explain why I had to give Mam the money back. I said I'd informed everyone in advance that this was going to be a real sale and that the money was going to be mine forever. He decided he couldn't really argue with that, so I got to keep the hundred and seventy dollars.

"Fair's fair," I said.

"Until Andover I pinned my bankbook under my picture of First Secretary, the colt of Secretariat and Number Twenty-four. I wanted to buy him from Jack Nankivil so I could jump him. First Secretary was half Appaloosa, but he still cost thirty-five thousand bucks, so I knew I had to save up."

"Number Twenty-four?"

"The test mare Secretariat first covered," Bou said, "who proved he could sire."

We nestled together under the arrivals board inside Bou's coat, which still smelled of smoke from the club.

"Let's take a train," Bou said.

Soon, I thought, the Train Bleu would be on its way to little Juan-les-Pins, and then the principality of Monaco.

"An under-the-ocean train," Bou said.

"A submatrain."

Behind Bou, an ordinary orange train putted toward the darkness at the station's mouth. I pressed against her, against the closed newsstand.

"A never late, never early train," she said.

"Goes only where you've never been train."

I touched her here and there. Then I was spinning through the air. When I landed, Bou pressed me against the wall with her long self.

"Only stops," she whispered, "where you want to go."

Golden Chalice

"I find it very, very easy to be true. I find myself alone when each day is through. Yes, I'll admit that I'm a fool for you."

My head wasn't through the door yet, it was nearly five in the morning, I had just walked twenty blocks in the rain, and you were singing Johnny Cash. I dripped while you stared upside-down at me from your cot. Your mouth worked redly.

"Because you're mine," you sang, dwelling on the low note like an ex-con, *"I cut the twine."*

You flipped, seal fashion, up into the air and over onto your belly. Little red men squared off glove-to-glove on your boxered bottom. I hopped, tugging at my wet Reebok.

"I did have a good time," I said when the shoe released me. "Nice of you to ask."

I hopped some more. You reached a hand, palm upward, my way, then looked right toward an invisible third party. *"Transfixed upon her golden chalice, he lost his heart, but found his balance."*

I dropped the second shoe, crouched, and waited for my dizziness to pass.

"Was it *true luv?*" you asked. "Or just a little birthday present?"

I sidestepped the rented sander and made my way to the bathroom. My tube socks left humid paisley marks on the floor.

"You must be very proud," you said, when I remained silent. I used the bucket for half an hour or so. You kept at me through the open door.

"I can't help you now, you know that. You've ruined more or less everything."

You spoke with a steady momentum that meant you weren't as drunk as I'd thought you were.

"What about Margot? You remember Margot. The short one with the heart-shaped ass, whose woman you just ran off with."

With my bladder back to its rest dimensions, I didn't feel lighter so much as less endangered.

"You and Bou go hobbling into the night like a couple of dogs in season. Leave me to take care of your friends. I don't mind."

I stepped out of the bathroom. That week I'd finished the third sanding. The floor gave up an infinite quantity of fine dust, just as Dad warned me it would in his letter.

"Why didn't you just go to a hotel? Hell, Dan, you can be her fancy boy."

Why didn't we go to a hotel? I thought.

"There's one question I do have. Is it 'cause she's queer that Bou thinks she can jump you and it doesn't even count? No demerits, maybe even a Nature Discovery badge? Or is it because she's about to come into a portfolio the size of the Boston yellow pages?"

Your overuse of the rhetorical question was typical of mid-level inebriation.

"Well, you've shown your colors. Two-timing Kraut horse thief, just like your great-grampa. Rip off other people's chattel in the middle of the night. Ride into the woods with hot goods between your legs."

You were my own red-faced conscience, that part of myself I'd been ignoring with little difficulty.

"I thought you wanted us all to be friends. Correct me if I'm wrong, Dan, but didn't you and Margot just do lunch? Didn't you promise her you wanted only the best for her and Bou?"

I leaned against the loft. The dishes from my birthday dinner with the dancers were piled on the table, scattered on the floor. Glasses, ranged along the windowsill, winked a dozen greetings. Empty wine and cider bottles waved hello from the floor. Had it been this same night that Paola and Joseph, Anne and her Patrick, Nicole and I, had eaten our feast? Was I still in the first twenty-four hours of my twenty-fourth year? I was having a hard time with time.

"Let's face it, Dan. Your balls won this round hands down. Whatever reptilian bundle you use for brain was dismissed after supper. Come midnight, Sir Tallywhacker walked off with the door prize."

The only cleaning up you had done was your trombone. It was arranged in parts on top of your saddlebag, like a murder weapon from which telltale fingerprints had been buffed.

"Adorable, that's what you are. A genuine Don Juanberg."

You were up off the cot now. Beside your pillow, a French *Penthouse* lay open to Mademoiselle Décembre, who wore a Santa Claus cap. You fiddled with your Marantz Superscope, and soon Curtis Fuller seconded everything you said on his trombone. I wrapped up the remains of the *Saint-Nectaire* and the *coeur de Bray*.

"Bou's the one who did it, is that your defense, Danny? Not your fault when a wicked girl drags you into the night. What's a boy to do?"

"I'd love some help," I said, trying to find room in the minifridge for the cheeses.

"I don't buy it, buddy. You knew exactly what you wanted. Don't try to pull that innocent Poughkeepsie boy routine on me."

I wasn't exactly tired. That had come and gone a few hours back. Now everything looked overexposed — the white napkins too white, the glass of the glasses too blue. Sweat tickled my upper lip, but my feet were numb.

"She coming over for a little nightcap? Hey, Casanovsky! I'm talking to you! She running over to Margot's to pick up the diaphragm?"

You apparently felt that Bou and I had acted hastily and inconsiderately. I wondered about this while I followed the rules and did the glasses first. They took a long time. Then I started on the plates and silverware. I ran out of drying space, so I wiped the wood dust from a section of floor by the radiator in the main room, spread my bath towel on it, and ranged the wet dishes on the towel. The accumulation of clean, wet things was a comfort.

When I looked up, you were yakking. Had you been carrying on all that time? I didn't think so, but then I couldn't remember not hearing your voice. Ever.

"A love larger than life. A passion unbound by human law."

Grachan Moncur III was your chorus now, the honk of his horn just quieter than that of your head. I wished I could throw you into the soapy water with the pans. You would come out cleaner and quieter.

"The real Hollywood stuff. You and Bou not ordinary working people. Your rules not ours. Yours a hunger that —"

I handed you the pot I'd steamed the mussels in. I wondered what time you'd stopped speaking in questions. You were sobering up, which took the form of brief declaratives. I stripped the aluminum foil off the colander. Margot had taught me that the device would keep the mussels above the boiling water. That had been some time back, in another country. I'd talked to Margot on the phone while I chopped onions.

"An unquenchable thirst. Longing without bourn. A tender fury —"

"Dry."

But you just stood there, emptying yourself of wind, holding the dripping pot in your hands. Finally I took it from you. There was nowhere to set it, no room on my bath towel, none on the table or beside the stove, and no part of the floor without sawdust. The third sanding, with the fine-grain paper on the power drum, had left the floor powdery smooth.

"A month was too long to wait. Even a day, or an hour. You had to have her now."

I screamed "*Shut up!*" in my ridiculous adolescent voice, which surfaces when I'm angry. I stood there, my clenched fist in midair, eyes burning.

"Just tell me why, Dan." You ignored my fist, but you

couldn't quite hide your satisfaction at having reached me. "Don't you realize what's going to happen now?"

You took the pot from me and held it in the air beside you.

"We talking desire that can't be snuffed? Candle burning at both ends?"

For a minute I almost thought about what you were saying. Why had Bou and I gone off together?

"You didn't drink one of those poisonous island milkshakes?"

In answer I pulled three umbrellas of tissue and balsam from my pocket. They were badly crushed. The pink, blue, and yellow dyes had run together. I set them carefully next to the salt and pepper shakers for drying.

"Three? Danny, you don't drink. Did you forget? No wonder Bou led you right up the spiral stairs by your dingus. You wouldn't have slowed down if someone had been at the top, pointing a gun at you."

Your tone was almost kindly, suddenly. I had meant to do something next. I studied the area around me for clues. You set the wet pot on the floor. It rolled to a stop, picking up an orange mustache of dust. That wasn't what I'd meant to do.

"What exactly did Bou say? What news made you decide all of a sudden, tonight, that it was copacetic for you two to make time?"

You raised a hand to your nonexistent mustache. Stroking it, you paced back and forth in front of the window, pivoting in front of the little city of clean dishes. You looked like a pasty-faced Sherlock Holmes in camouflage pants and a Wynton Marsalis T-shirt. Someone had dressed you.

"She persuaded you," you said, "that she's free. Why? Because she and Margot aren't lovers. Not exactly lovers."

I should mop the floor, I thought. That was next. But when the floor dried, the dust would be there again. Dad had written that I'd have to surface the floor once just to keep the powder under. *Smoke dust,* he called it.

"Bou explained to you that even though she and Margot live

together, they have — what, Dan? — an open relationship. Am I warm? An understanding of sorts."

I was glad to hear the sound of your voice. I wasn't alone. I wanted to ask you questions, but there wasn't time. I had work to do.

"So theoretically you two could jam. She and Margot are really just buddies. Come on, Dan. A little help here. Lift your right paw for yes."

I suddenly remembered that I had been about to scour the hotplates. An enormous calm settled over me. In the kitchen I rinsed the rusted steel wool and went to work. Margot's recipe for the rabbit, with Manzanilla and chanterelles in the cream sauce, had been a success. I loved Margot.

"If you don't mind my saying so, you really are a randy upstate schmuck."

I didn't mind. You were standing close beside me and your tone was still gentle, though your words were not so friendly. I knew you were going to help me with whatever it was. It wasn't in the kitchen, I was sure of that. You would find it, and do whatever was required.

"Wait, I've got it. Bou and Margot had a spat. Bou told you she and Margot aren't sweethearts this week. They're just good friends who spend twenty-three hours a day together, speak in riddles, and are miserable without the sight of each other."

Your voice became quiet.

"Dan, you didn't buy that malarkey, did you? You do know that restless women have been handing out that we're-not-really-lovers line to eager peckerheads like yourself since ancient times."

You put your arm around my waist. I kept scrubbing.

"Yes," you said sadly, "you believed her. You lapped up every sweet word she dropped as if it were Eve's own precious, lotus-flower funk."

You patted my hip and strolled out of the kitchen.

"Ah, well. *Plus ça change . . .*"

I finished the burners. You kept talking, and I listened while

I swept the floor and started mopping. I did the kitchen, then worked my way toward the loft from the windows. You paused for breath and I seized the chance to ask you please to stand somewhere else. Your feet left the floor, heading up. That surprised me. I saw that smoke dust had turned the bottoms of your blue-and-green argyles a rusty orange. I looked overhead and there you were, hanging in the air. Then you rotated onto your back and tumbled downward, bouncing to a complete stop on top of Mademoiselle Décembre. An unfamiliar roar filled my head. I dropped the mop, pressed my hands to my ears, and backed to the window. Silence.

I turned to the west. The clay chimney pots across Rue Roubo shone pink, as if they'd just been lifted from a kiln. Far beyond, across the city, two women slept in a curved embrace. You shifted and I heard a crumpling noise. I walked over, eased the magazine from beneath you, and set it down. Mickey Mouse, on your dangling wrist, pointed one yellow glove at seven, the other at four. I placed your arm on the cot beside you and realized that now everything, and everyone, was where it was supposed to be. Only I hadn't been put away. I climbed to the loft and lay there, very still, with my eyes wide open.

Tango

"Come now, children. This time with feeling."

Catherine spoke in what she supposed was a pleasantly teasing tone. The studio's heat didn't kick on until the late afternoon, and it was the coldest week of the year. We wore everything we had, staggering through our parts like mummies in layers of wool and cotton. The recorded music echoed through the room.

"Please, people. Think about what the piece means," Catherine shouted.

I did, but didn't come up with much. We were working on the finale again. In another ten weeks the whole performance had to be polished so we could take it on the road to Le Mans, Angers, Limoges, St.-Étienne, Besançon, Nancy, and Metz.

"More strength in the torso, Anne. Carve the space with your chest."

"Carve the space with your ass, bitch," Anne whispered, passing me.

I walked over to Nicole.

"Be careful," she told me. "My back."

A backache today. Yesterday it had been a bruised heel. A few days before she had been able to turn only on her right leg. None of this would have bothered me more than her ailments had all year, except that now I was choreographically joined to her for seven out of forty minutes.

You are Siamese twins who love the tango, Catherine had told us in our initial instructions. *You would ignore each other, except for the bond between you.*

Catherine had attached our heads. This was the sort of notion she came up with all the time.

"Don't rush the counts," Nicole said as we started.

Our hair ground together like sand rubbed between two fingers. The first life approached, and I reached my thumbs around her ribs to hoist her.

"*Mer-de!*" she said inside my head as she rolled across my back. Through our crania, her voice was both distant and penetrating.

Nicole and I had an ongoing argument about whose fault it was that nothing we did ever worked. I often told her, as diplomatically as I could, that she was a skittish seventeen-year-old brat who never did the same thing twice running. She, in turn, never hesitated to inform me that I wasn't man enough to get the job done, whatever it was, and that my hesitant partnering always hurt her.

The music stopped.

"Dan! Where are you?" Catherine sang mockingly. She pretended she couldn't find me, though I stood in front of her. This was her way of saying that I, or rather we, weren't where we were supposed to be.

"I know you are here," Catherine crooned. "I have an intuition."

Naturally, Nicole had made the two of us botch our *chaîné* turns across the stage, foreheads pressed tightly together. Catherine walked up to us.

"Either you two get yourselves out onstage on measure nineteen," she said, "or I cut your part out."

I nodded; Nicole scowled at the floor. The whole company had to repeat the section, and we were tired. This pressure was more effective than Catherine's threats.

"I'm going to throw you," I warned Nicole as we took our places. "When you hit the floor, start spinning."

She was too surprised to answer. Music poured from the little box. Catherine's musicians, who looked like a troupe of electrified minstrels, had come to our rehearsal two weeks before to record the tape for us. There were six of them under the direction of Monsieur Lussier, composer. They traded off electric piano, lute, electric violin, jew's harp, electric bass, accordion, and an assortment of other toys. Their piece, called *Condition Postmoderne,* had been written for Catherine's dance of the same name. It was unlistenable.

The company began its marionette fits and starts. On measure eighteen-point-eight or so, I jettisoned Nicole upward. She pivoted slowly in the air above me. Perhaps, I thought as I watched her eyeballs float past, she'd been right after all. Perhaps I hadn't been strong enough.

"What happened?" Dominique asked during our break. "You were on time."

It was true. Even Catherine had been forced to yield the greatest of compliments — no comment.

"Nicole and I needed to get to know each other," I told Dominique.

"Come on," she said, offering me a stick of Hollywood. "What did you do to her?"

"I lifted her."

"So cool," Dominique said.

She pronounced *cool* in the French way, which made it sound like a brand-new piece of slang. I stood beside her, chewing chlorophyll-flavored gum and thinking yes, it was true. That first week I was with Bou, whether I was dancing or just walking down the street, I felt cool.

"Tell me, Dom," I said, leaning back against the wall. "What does a woman most want from a man?"

"One secret thing?"

She looked at me from under her sheet of black hair. All I was worrying about was a present for Valentine's Day, still two weeks off.

"You're in love," she said, with a little pout.

"Answer my question."

I'd never flirted with any woman nearly as breathtaking as

Dominique before. It was like the time I'd sprinted against Mike Morris, who went on to the '84 Olympic trials. Freshman year, he and I crouched side by side in the starting blocks in Manley Fieldhouse. For one millisecond, when the gun popped and all down the line the runners flew into the air, I was as fast as the fastest boy in the state. Then he was gone.

"A woman wants only to be remembered," Dominique said.

Paola passed with her towel and her bottle of Vittelloise. I'd hardly talked to her since the party. In the minutes before ballet, we were shy with each other. I had disappointed her. She didn't know what to say.

"Just to be remembered?"

"Not for a week or a year," Dominique said. "Always."

She was serious. I'd been making small talk during our break, which I usually spent with Paola and Joseph.

"By the men who have loved her?"

"One man," Dominique said. She lifted her left foot and tugged at the tape on her second toe.

"I imagine you have one," I said, still trying to be playful.

"Yes." She released her foot and settled closer to me against the wall. She was as solemn as at first, and I stopped trying not to be.

"You're always in his thoughts."

"He loved me first," Dominique said.

I looked at her fine feet, with their proud arches and gentle toes.

"Before you loved him?"

"I was his first lover," she explained.

Down the hallway a team of soccer players, fifteen-year-olds in Elf jerseys, emerged from the locker room and jogged into the gym.

"Not Didier."

"No," she said.

"You left this man?"

"He loved me too much. I couldn't breathe."

"But you said —"

"I love him. I always will."

Catherine emerged from the bathroom. The company was exhausted. She knew that the longer she waited before starting rehearsal again, the less we'd be willing to work. But she still hesitated to herd us back to the studio because of how much we would hate her.

"Do you see him?" I asked, my eyes holding Dominique's long-lashed ones.

"Listen, kids," Catherine called, much less loudly than usual. "Back to the factory. Only one more hour."

"Does Didier —"

"He knows nothing," Dominique said. She pushed herself from the wall and gave me her familiar coquettish smile. But her eyes were still somber. She passed so close to me her hair trailed on my arm. I wanted to stop her, to ask her again whether she saw this man who loved her too much. But she filed into the studio with the others.

Down the corridor in the gym, the soccer coach shouted a command I couldn't make out. The feet of thirty boys drummed the wooden floor.

Yesterday I covered for Mike Lewitt in perinatal. He took a day for me last month when I had the flu. As soon as visiting hours started at eleven, Renee Gilbert came to the preemie nursery to see Jordan. She didn't leave until nearly four, and was sitting beside his isolette when he played his trick. The resp monitor went off and Renee jumped up so fast she dropped her coffee. She touched Jordan on the shoulder and he started breathing again, the way he always does. He had a pleased smile on his cupid's lips because he'd fooled Mommy.

Renee looks like the painted bust of Queen Nefertiti that was in the library at Vassar Road Elementary. She has a long, forward-tilting neck, and her hair sweeps back off her high forehead like a headdress. It's been five weeks now since her Jordan was delivered by C-section at twenty-nine weeks. He started at around 1,030g and just broke 1,460g. He stops breathing every once in a while to remind us of his original due date. Last week he was a touch anemic, so they put his peripheral IV back in and gave him a transfusion. But overall, both he and his next-door neighbor, Lisa Norton, a 1,395g thirty-five-day-old, born at twenty-nine weeks and 970g, are doing fine.

I came up to see them on Jordan's first, Lisa's second day, when they were intubated and had umbilical art caths in for bloods and IVs in their hands. I walked by on day two/three and found them wearing matching white eye bands under the UV lamps. Their bilis were both around eight, but by five days the jaundice had cleared and they were just a black boy and a white girl again. Jordan's fourth day, the attending, Woodley, wrote the IV-plus-PO order on both of them. Jan Webster, the head nurse, started their feeds slow, at 2cc every two hours, increasing 1cc every other. She told me yesterday it's the only safe way to handle those little bellies. By the end of the week both kids were up to full tube feeds.

But they still don't know how to nipple, and they forget to breathe every now and then. Yesterday afternoon after Renee left, in the half-hour Webster spent teaching me, Jordan and Lisa each took one respiratory break. When Lisa's monitor went off, Webster stood and rubbed her lower back. Lisa started taking deep breaths again. Jordan's isolette was right beside Webster's chair, so when his alarm sounded she just swung her sterile gloves' fingers lightly across his face, as if challenging him to face life. He started breathing immediately. Many babies need a good backrub or foot tickle, Webster said, but Jordan only needs a touch on the nose.

I keep thinking about that flying island in *Gulliver's Travels*. You're familiar with the book, I'm sure, along with every other book I've ever read. The citizens of the floating island were philosophers, and each had a servant called a flapper, whose job was to tap his thinker on the head every few minutes with an inflated pig's bladder on a stick. What I've realized is that we're the flappers for the preemies. Without us, the little citizens drift off into philosophical speculation. I know, because whenever I remind one of them to keep the lungs pumping, he or she looks at me with such irritation.

But Renee still panics every time Jordan plays his trick on her. Yesterday I showed her Jordan's chart and explained to her that while she'd been at work all the previous afternoon at the family garage, Jordan had taken two breaks, one roughly every four hours. Was he going to die of crib death? No, I assured her, he was not. But until he had no apnea episodes for a full five days, he would need to be monitored. Then he would start breathing reliably on his own.

That's when I started exaggerating. I didn't lie, I just wanted to make apnea less frightening. There was still panic in Renee's eyes. I wanted to make her feel secure. One minute I was talking sensibly about lung development, and the next I was way up in a cloud kingdom where babies born early, whose mothers truly love them, never die.

Jordan fell asleep. His lips were wet and sugary. His fingers stirred, his tiny fingernails sparkling like seed pearls. Renee watched him, her head tilted in a royal way.

Bou Rising

Bou let herself in with her new key, undressed, and jumped into the loft.

"Faker," she said.

It was true. I'd been up for hours. Still, our bodies were shaky and tender. It was only our third time together. You were sleeping off that wedding dance in Rouen.

"Consider yourself fortunate. I don't commute for just anybody."

I considered myself fortunate. I'd imagined Bou with me every night since we'd been together. Now she swayed above me like a tree, her knees flanking me, her breasts out of reach. She swooped and kissed me, then placed me against her.

"We welcome you," I said, hard in a tentative, morning way.

"Thank you. And thank you, First Consul."

She was referring to the eventual Emperor Napoleon. Our second get-together had been an evening affair, during which she'd christened mine Napoleon and hers Josephine. We'd been talking about her seminar and also about how like a young Bonaparte mine was, with his sleepless nights and imperial moods. He would conquer the known world and still feel himself to be lacking, Bou said, while her Josephine was as ambitious as he was in her own Paris empire. No matter what circles opened to her, Josephine would never stop feeling like the little Creole. That was why she was driven to futile acts of infidelity when Napoleon, whom she loved more than anyone on earth, was off conquering Milan, and then again when he was in Egypt whipping the Mamelukes, with no fleet to carry him home.

"Go," I told her.

Bou had the most solemn look on her face. I wanted to try again. This time my weight would not bear down on her, not even lightly. We'd tried to make love that way twice and had stalled both times, once because I stopped myself and once because Bou stopped me. These failures surprised me because in between we'd accomplished all sorts of trickier maneuvers. What Bou and I did was so much more interesting than what I was used to with Rebecca, really with anyone since Amy in high school.

"What are you looking at?"

"You," I said.

She was gentle all at once. She drummed briefly on my chest with her fists, and when she'd finished she pressed her palms flat and settled over me.

"Oh God," she said.

I knew all at once that she wasn't just a three-years virgin. She was a virgin.

"Ow," she said, descending. I attempted a dignified retreat. "No," she said.

With a poised, equestrian motion, she rose and then fell a vertical inch. I held my breath. She leaned over from a great height. Her lips found my shoulder. She moved minutely forward and down. The beginning was over.

The blue sheets I'd hung as curtains were filled with sunlight. Bou and I ate our salad, sitting side by side on the cot. I'd cut vegetables into the wooden bowl at midnight. Perhaps I'd been spending too much time with Germaine. I'd been persuaded that if I combined the gifts of the earth correctly, Bou and I would be successful in bed. The Belgian endive and capers especially, but also the spinach, red pepper, and baby corn — all had properties beyond the nutritive.

"Why didn't you tell me?"

"I thought you knew," Bou said.

I held out a white leaf on my fork. Tears filled her eyes.

"I'm sorry," she said. "I don't know why I'm . . ."

I hushed her, but wondered about her tears. When I'd lost my virginity, I'd been dry-eyed with disappointment. I'd felt as if I'd been tricked, mostly by myself. Now I remembered how soon Jane and I had broken up after our first days together.

"Do you love me?"

"Of course, crazy man," Bou told me. Her tears were gone. She composed herself. "You're wonderful," she said. "I'm sorry I'm such a klutz."

"Bou, don't —"

"You're awfully nice. I'm no fun. I'll be better next time."

She'd never felt closer to me, she said. Our morning together had been perfect. I interrupted her. I said I knew that wasn't true. I wanted to tell her that later, though she couldn't possibly believe it now, making love to a man would be all she'd been waiting for.

"I know it wasn't great," I said instead. I wanted to tell her that what this morning had been a whisper of pleasure inside her would grow stronger when she knew how to listen for it. But she interrupted me this time.

"Did I tell you I'm going to see kabuki with Pascal? His brother in Japan says this troupe that's coming is legendary. The performance lasts eight hours —"

"Bou, don't worry. I'll show you —"

"Shh," she said, hushing me. She held me and I let her comfort me. She said that she liked what we'd done, but that it hurt a little and she wasn't sure she was doing it right. I told her she was, and that soon it wouldn't. Then I tried to act as if I weren't afraid.

"Do you still respect me?" I asked.

She threw her legs across me, her thighs cool on mine, and leaned back on a tangle of checkered pants and bowling shirts.

"You mean now that I've had my way with you?"

"You're not going to break up with me and His Glorious Person?" I pulled her to me. She played with my nipples.

"Let's do it again," she whispered in my ear.

"What about your salad?" I asked. I still had faith in the salad.

"I want to do it," she breathed, "different ways."

I was more afraid than ever. After we'd spent a few weeks in bed, what more would I have to offer her? I remembered that mothers used to advise daughters not to go to bed with boys, no matter what they promised. Suddenly I understood this, though my mother hadn't been around when I reached dating age, I wasn't her daughter, and I thought not having sex before getting married was about as impractical an idea as any I'd ever come across. Still, how wise those old-fashioned mothers were, I thought. How silly their careless daughters.

Bou stood, took me under the arms, and hoisted me to my feet.

"Promise," I said, "you'll be gentle."

"You goof. Climb."

"Will you marry us?"

Bou lifted me up onto the mini-fridge and patted my behind. I vaulted into the sheets and lay back, worrying, as Bou rose.

Logs

"Tell me how it's gonna be, George," I said, as always.

"We'll go to the big farm, Lennie. You'll be happy there."

Bou and I were at the brasserie on the corner of Sèvres and Raspail. I'd hustled straight over from ballet to meet her beneath the out-of-control rubber plant, just inside the doors of the EHESS, after her morning seminar. Now we shared a salad, not a magic one but a large niçoise with pink tuna that didn't like to break apart, hard-boiled eggs, anchovies, tomatoes, olives, and rice. We also split a salmon quiche with a crust cooked slightly past brown.

"Will I get to hold the wabbits?" I asked.

"In a minute. We're not up to the rabbits."

Outside the café, tiny snowflakes colored the world and slowed its turning. Bou's coat was across her lap. I squeezed close beside her at the corner table and found my way under the folds of damp suede. If anyone cared to notice, it looked like we were holding hands.

"Oh, Lennie."

"Nice wabbit."

I pressed her and tried to imagine what was going on behind whichever color panties she was wearing that day.

"Tell me about the farm."

"I'll finish my courses in May," Bou answered distractedly. "But I won't have my papers done, so I'll take incompletes, and finish in June."

In the afternoon, she had her acting class on the Île St.-

Louis. By now Bou knew that Monsieur Hanbowski was no substitute for her mentor at Yale, Sammy Topkiss, who'd been performing Shakespeare since she had run away to London at age twelve, and who was teaching Bou everything about life, everything. But Hanbowski wasn't bad.

"Tell me about the horsies."

Bou looked to the far side of Boulevard Raspail.

"We'll leave Paris. You'll go home to Poughkeepsie and see your daddy, and I'll go to Lincoln, where Poppa will be in his study reading market reports and planning his next move. Mam will be upstairs writing a paper on Piaget that was due at U. Mass. a year and a half ago. Mam and I will work on our papers together, except that she'll have to stop to go to Filene's to buy presents for my cousin Julia's bridal shower and for the wedding. Also new dresses, so that Aunt Bess and all the New Hampshire cousins will see that she's not a fuddy-duddy church lady."

"The horsies," I urged, pressing the back of my hand up and in until Bou's eyes widened and she pressed her lips into a little line.

"Then," she said with a sudden breath, "we meet at Logs."

"Why's the farm Logs?"

"Oh, Lennie, you remember. Remember," she said again, her eyelids fluttering. "Logs isn't really Logs, but an Algonquian word that sounds like *logs*. The settlers thought the Penna-cooks were saying, 'Here, take all the logs you want. Clear the forest, build farms, plant potatoes, give us nasty European diseases and shoot at us —'"

"George?"

"So the settlers called the place Logs, even though it was probably Lauggs or Lawgus or Laushgus, or something much more interesting but harder to say than Logs. The native word probably meant 'untroubled place where people live in harmony with each other and the forest and only engage in limited warfare with a strict set of moral and strategic parameters, freely observed by all —'"

"The horsies."

"Right, right," she said, because I'd found something. I wasn't sure what. "Right," she told me forcefully. "I'll introduce you to the horsies. They'll be your special friends because they're as big as you are, Lennie. I'll let you ride Casey because he's gentle and —"

"Sweet as he can be."

"— the gentle, sweet one."

Bou came to a complete stop. I didn't, and her lips parted as if the word *one* had stumped her. Her gaze rested on the weeping birch, which the French call a *bouleau pleureur,* at the edge of the Square Boucicaut. Next to our table, snowflakes danced off the glass and melted as soon as they touched the sidewalk.

"So tender," Bou said, her voice unfamiliar. "Horses," she reminded herself, brow furrowed.

The waiter was beside us, asking if we had everything we needed. Bou's hand clamped mine, her eyes not moving from where they were fixed, thirty yards away in the birch. I suddenly saw the other people eating lunch in the brasserie. One was a woman in her fifties who had just finished the plate of the day, which was duck, and eaten all the bread in her basket. Now she poured water from an oblong Pastis 21 carafe, buffed white with use, and pulled a tablet of writing paper closer to her hand. The waiter's hair rose in an alternating gray-and-white brush from his forehead. He stood with the neatly balanced stance of a flamenco dancer.

"More wine?" I asked Bou. No, she answered politely. I assured the man we were fine. He disappeared as he had come, in a gliding instant.

"Bou," I said, tentatively beginning again with the now familiar prelude. "You're not just telling me all this because I want you to."

"You mean because you need to hear the same story over and over again, like one of Mam's three-year-olds at Saint Anne's preschool?"

"It's all true, isn't it? About the farm, and how we're going there this summer?"

"There isn't a word of it," Bou said, straddling minutely forward against my fingers, "that isn't true."

"The horsies."

"Casey doesn't mind letting city slickers, who don't know jack about riding, grab him with their knees and poke him with their tennis shoes —"

"I know jack."

"— tug on his bridle, fall on his ears, toss around on his hips, and jerk his girth first to one side, then the other —"

"I won't jerk Casey's girth."

"— city slickers who are rude to him in ways that are more annoying to a sweet old gelding than you could ever imagine, ride around on him. He won't try to scrape you off on trees or go the opposite of where you want him to go. He won't speed down hills when you're off your trot, so you bruise your butt. He won't do any of the things Titania would do to a silly city fella like you."

"I'm Lennie. I'm not a city fella. I'm a developmentally handicapped southwestern fieldworker."

"At night we'll sleep in Gramps' bed. He won't mind 'cause he's gone now —"

"He'll haunt me."

Abruptly, Bou pulled my hand away, drew it to her lips, and kissed it. She shaped the words *I love you* and placed my hand on the table, like one who has outlived his usefulness.

"We'll sleep," she said alertly, "in the big mahogany fourposter under the silk canopy that Nathan used to pretend was the *Santa Maria*'s sail."

"Wait a minute."

"I'm allowed to put new elements in," Bou said. "Only a three-year-old would object to a new element in a formulaic narrative. You're not a three-year-old, Dan."

"Lennie. There's no *Santa Maria* in the story."

"There is now. Nathan said the canopy was the sail and he

was Christopher Columbus. I was one of the other captains. What were their names?"

"You're asking me? I'm Lennie. Besides, my grandparents—"

"Came from Bavaria in 1922 and lost everything in the crash as soon as they arrived. I know, you're a tough immigrant kid and I'm a spoiled New England girl who doesn't realize what the world is. I still thought you might know the names of the other captains."

"Nineteen twenty-seven. Didn't they sink?"

"Columbus did. He hopped to the little *Niña* when his *Santa Maria* was foundering."

"Let's get back to the real story."

But Bou was crying. Three tears, two on one side, one on the other, unmistakably trickled down.

"Bou."

"I'm okay. I was just remembering the way Nathan used to convince me to continue west."

"What?"

"I didn't believe we were ever going to get to India. I thought the world was flat and we were going to fall off, so I wanted to turn back. Columbus convinced me to go on by making me smell his feet."

"He did not."

"Nathan had the stinkiest feet of any boy you ever heard of. The rest of him was fine, but his feet smelled like Fritos."

"Bou, I'm trying to eat." I indicated our quiche.

"Exactly like Fritos," she said.

The three tears had traveled all the way to her chin now. I dried the tracks.

"Be that as it may," I said, "they didn't have Fritos on Columbus' voyage. And Columbus definitely didn't convince his sailors to go on looking for India by making them smell his feet."

"No."

Bou smiled and ate a few bites. Beyond the glass, the snow turned the sidewalk the color of raw wool.

"But Nathan did," she said.

I waited while a car sped north up Raspail with an aggressive European whine.

"The bed," I whispered. Bou looked at me.

"Grams won't mind us sleeping in her bed, because she's got an electric bed now at Brookhaven home, where Mam can look after her."

"Not much, she won't. She and Gramps will put a hoodoo on me, and Napoleon will lose his strategic brilliance."

"An adjustable bed of her own so she doesn't need the canopy anymore, especially since Gramps is in heaven reading Revelations."

"Excuse me?"

"I told you about that. In the morning I'll show you how to milk the cow."

"Hold on a minute. Revelations?"

"Yes."

"I thought you were two. How do you know what he was reading?"

"I'm the one who found him. What do you think? Mam told me last year. I don't know how she got me to church in the first place. I just remember sitting in the exact center of the middle pew next to Jason and feeling deeply lesbian. The reading was all about the army of horses with lion heads and the storm of fire and blood. Mam leaned over from behind me and said, *Albert read that the day he died.* I thought she just meant the *day* he died. So I listened to Reverend White try to find a benign and reassuring interpretation of Revelations, the way he did with every scary part of the Bible before he moved on."

"How did he die?"

"He's in Dallas," Bou said. "After the service I asked Mam what she meant about Gramps reading about the seventh seal and all that. She said the hundred-and-thirty-year-old Bible I used to think God himself had written with a tiny pen was on Gramps' knees when he had his heart attack."

"Damn."

"When I was two I kept asking all these questions. *Was Gramps making a beebee, Mam? Was he finished, Mam? How did he know he was dead, Mam?* She knew I'd overheard someone at the funeral saying that Gramps had been on the toilet. She decided she'd better spell it all out for me before my potty training turned wild. But she didn't tell me about Revelations until last spring."

"I can understand that."

"Yes."

"Am I going to meet all these people, Bou?"

"They're dead."

"Not Nathan and Albert. I mean Mam and Poppa, Jason and Grams, Titania and Casey and —"

"Of course, you silly boy. Why do you think I'm telling you all about them?"

"Because I force you to. Because I make you tell me about Lincoln and Gorham so that you'll get used to the idea of being with me in America."

"You do coerce me," Bou said. "But that's common, I understand, for boys your age. You believe that hearing a thing over and over again makes it more true."

"Yes. And it is true, isn't it?"

"I just said it was."

"Say it again."

"You'll meet them in June, the whole carnival. It's not fair. All I get to meet is Brenda and your dad, and they're normal."

"Your dad's normal."

"Yes," Bou said. "But he and Jason are the only two in the bunch who aren't colorful. That's counting cousins."

"Dad leads a life of quiet desperation."

"Looking in people's ears and up their noses? Playing golf, having bloody marys while Brenda cooks, and seeing the same two couples four nights a week? Making your lawn look like a green crew-cut?"

"Underneath, he's lost."

"Pretty far underneath," Bou said.

I'd shown her Dad's last letter, which had described one of his more exciting Friday evenings. Instead of golfing away the afternoon at McCann, taking Brenda to Banta's for dinner, and then slipping into Beth-El right after the *L'cha Dodi* to sit with Ben and Didi Letzger and Roger and Gloria Morris, he and Brenda had celebrated her forty-eighth at Le Pavillon out on Salt Point Turnpike. They didn't get back to synagogue until halfway through the *Sh'mon Esrei*, and everyone, including Rabbi Zimet, turned to watch them walk up the side aisle. I could tell Dad was pleased with the commotion he and Brenda had caused. Most of the folks Dad's age still regarded Brenda as a gay divorcée. After all, she and Dad had only been steadies for ten years.

"There must be something you haven't told me about him," Bou said. "A hidden vice."

"He eats a lot of pickled herring."

As if in response to this, Bou and I quickly divided up the last bite of quiche.

"I thought you sold Jemima."

I hurried her. I knew if she didn't finish, I'd be restless all day. She kidded me about needing to hear the story through, but it was true.

"Jemima lives in Shelburne now," Bou said. "I'll show you how to milk Lucille."

"The cow next door."

Bou helped a gnarled man get up the curb of Rue du Sabot.

"The half-a-mile down Durand Road at the Castles' farm cow," Bou said, rejoining me. "Then we'll go for a long ride. If it's hot, we'll take the horses to the pond. Casey, that crazy horse, can eat all the dandelions he wants while Titania nibbles sweet clover. We'll skinny-dip and have a picnic, and then ride all afternoon."

She breathed deliberate actress-style breaths in order to manage the talking and walking.

"Will we be alone?"

"We'll be all alone. If it's warm enough, we can screw on the swimming beach."

"After we swim and make love and have our picnic, we'll ride five miles on Pelvis Trail —"

"Prentice. One slow mile. You'll trot if you're lucky. Only if you have a decent seat, and don't grab onto poor Casey's neck like a baby opossum the first time he tries to canter."

"I have a decent seat."

"We'll see," Bou said. "When we're done, I'll show you how to groom him —"

"And Titania. I take off their saddles and do their hoofs. I give them feed —"

"Whoa. The rub rag. First, the rub rag. Then the brushes. Just Casey. Titania would kill you dead."

"And then the pick."

"You lean against Casey to support him. You run your hand down the back of his leg below the knee. Give him a good squeeze, and say, 'Casey, I'm going to pick out your near fore-hoof.' Then you lift it up."

"Do I feel stupid?"

"Not as stupid as if he spooks because he doesn't know where you are, steps on you, then turns to see why you're yelling and tears the top off your toes."

We circled two little boys who wore backpacks on their chests.

"At night we'll see the movie," I said, glancing at Bou's watch. In my rush I'd forgotten I was Lennie.

"There's only one movie playing at the Princess in Berlin. We'll see it even if we've already seen it and it's bad, because we always see the movie. Then we'll come back and make a campfire —"

"In the Old Fireplace," I added.

"The Old Stone Ring, where you can still find arrowheads. We'll lie on horse blankets and look for shooters."

She slowed in front of the Librairie Historique J. Clavreuil. I pulled her away.

"You'll think you see a shooting star," she said. "But you're a city slicker. It's an airplane. I see a shooter but you miss it, because you're looking in the wrong sky."

"There's only one sky, Bou."

We were in the turmoil of Boulevard St.-Michel.

"We make love," she said, "then we fall asleep. We wake up at three —"

"I see the correct stars in your eyes."

"— at three in the morning with cold dew on our faces," Bou said. "It feels sticky even though it's just water."

I paused before a row of gleaming black pumps with gold tips in the Bally window. Bou led me away, past the lousy restaurants on Rue St.-Séverin, then beneath the scaly- and smooth-necked gargoyles poking three feet out the side of the *église*. All was quiet when we reached Rue Galande, and for a moment neither of us could pull the other away from the collection of trusses, orthopedic braces, and custom bras inside the Établissement Brunet.

"Is all this really going to happen?"

"Dan, don't start that stuff now. We'll sleep in the sticky dew. In the morning I'll make wheatcakes and applesauce."

We hurried off, barely glancing at the full-size viola da gambas and the thumb-size harps and battle drums in the window of J. P. Luthier's.

"With apples from the apple tree behind the barn."

"The new barn," Bou corrected.

"And real maple syrup from the Tightlips' maples."

"The Tipples' maples."

"Yes."

It was over. We'd made it. Each time we walked from Napoleon to acting and Bou told me about Logs, the story took longer and felt better. We crossed the Pont de l'Archevêché and hiked away from the flying-buttressed hindquarters of Notre Dame to the Île St.-Louis. I wondered how long the telling would take next time, and when that would be, and how good it would feel.

"Thursday night?" I asked, as we reached the crumbling courtyard of the École Florent.

"After rehearsal," Bou said.

I tugged her hands downward and she leaned closer. It would be two days before I'd see her again. No snow fell. From the crooked stairwell to the theater came a burst of laughter. We smiled as if we knew what was funny.

"They're starting," I whispered.

Bou turned and ran to her friends.

Jordan's in the NICU. I walked by the nurseries this morning and he and Lisa were gone. Jan Webster told me that Lisa died at two this morning. *Necrotizing enterocolitis,* her chart says. On Friday both babies were fine. Lisa hadn't even had an apneic episode in a day. She was feeding well. On Saturday she had small residuals after feeds and her abdominal girth was up two centimeters, and Jan was worried because she hadn't stooled in thirty-six hours. Woodley, the attending, thought her belly was soft, but Jan says she could feel a few loops of bowel. She told Woodley to slow down, but he went ahead with the feeds.

I just looked at the films from radiology. Yesterday there was all this free air up under Lisa's liver. They had had her on increased fluids and antibiotics, and reintubated her when her resp rate hit a hundred. They started her on dopamine when her pressure dropped and she wasn't peeing. Surgery hadn't even been called when those films came back at eleven. At one they took her upstairs. The surgeons took out three sections of bowel. She died just after two this morning — severe acidosis and sepsis.

Now Jordan's trying to follow her. It's like the two of them are linked. I just read his chart. Apnea frequency went to every ten minutes yesterday afternoon. Webster was out of town for Thanksgiving, and a new nurse was looking after him. She assumed Woodley knew about it. When Webster got back last night she heard grunting respiration at seventy-five. Jordan was gray. This morning he's barely moving. *Reversion to the*

190

fetal state, Spellman called it when I was in there. Jordan's working lungs on the films are the size of a butterfly. His head and neck shudder when he breathes.

I can't watch, Beck. One problem leads to the next. Jordan probably got the staph infection from the peripheral line they gave him for the transfusion. Now he's got sepsis and pneumonia. His chest is mostly white on the films. Renee spent the day in the hall outside NICU. I kept passing her. We never spoke. I wanted to say something but couldn't. I remembered what I'd told her, and now there's nothing to say. When Spellman came out of NICU at three, Renee's husband and girl were there with her. Spellman told them that Jordan was not improving. They listened while Renee wrote everything Spellman said in her daughter's Little Mermaid coloring book. When she couldn't keep up, she asked Spellman to repeat the medical terms. Finally I stepped by her husband to help her. She looked up. If she remembered me, it was just as another young doctor.

Renee's husband is so muscular he's humpbacked. Marcy, who's five, swung from one of his arms as if it were a rope swing. As he listened, a sound rose from deep in his chest. It took me a few minutes to realize that this meant he understood, not that he didn't. His hair, razored close to his scalp, is white on the sides. He has a downward-curved nose like an owl's beak.

"The baby is on a respirator," Spellman told them, looking as uncomfortable as always. He said *the baby,* never *Jordan.* "He was having a hard time breathing on his own, so we had to reintubate him."

Jennifer says that Spellman is an excellent pediatrician but too shy to deal with adults. He did the best he could. Renee asked about the intravenous line in Jordan's scalp. Spellman explained about the danger of dehydration and the need for antibiotics. When he was finished, Mr. Gilbert asked what his boy's chances were.

"Not good," Spellman said.

They waited for a statistic. When none came, Mr. Gilbert

made the questioning sound in his throat twice. Renee held her pen above the coloring book, her eyes blinking.

Jennifer was down in the NICU explaining to Renee that she's the obstetrics resident. It was perfectly all right that Renee had her paged, but Dr. Spellman was the specialist. Renee said she'd already talked to Dr. Spellman, but remembered Jennifer from her C-section. Jennifer took her arm and walked her up and down the hall. She asked Renee questions about Jordan. I fetched his chart and Jennifer scanned it. Renee was a different woman from the one who had quietly listened to Spellman. She waited impatiently for Jennifer to finish, then bombarded her with questions of her own. Her husband stood beside her, with Marcy asleep on his shoulder.

No, Jennifer told her, no one had done anything wrong. Premature infants are always at risk for infections. She described the way the staph had made its way into the baby's blood and from there to his lungs. She talked about Jordan's acidosis and how Spellman was trying to increase blood pressure to keep up Jordan's urine output. Her descriptions were more technical than Spellman's, but Renee could follow them. She asked when they would know if Jordan was going to be all right. Jennifer took Renee's shoulders in her hands and put her head close to the smaller woman's. It could be a few days before he was in the clear, Jennifer said. If his blood pressure could not be stabilized, he might not make it through the night.

Jordan's in the land of the living. At two this morning his fingers were stirring, and his eyes followed creatures on the ceiling above me that I couldn't see.

It's been the longest thirty-six hours I can remember. It's
morning again now, but when I came in to work — what is it,
twenty hours ago? — I headed for the NICU. Renee was waiting for me. Turns out Jennifer had given Renee her home number, and Renee had called. Jennifer wasn't coming in but told
Renee that I was, and that I'd explain things to her. Spellman
had increased the dopamine from ten to fifteen mcg/k/min.
Before I arrived, Renee asked Spellman what this meant, and
all he told her was that they would have to wait and see. That
really scared her. Was her baby getting worse? I told her I
didn't know.

I went in, read the chart, and talked to Spellman. It was the
reversal of our positions from last month, when I did my rotation with him. This time it was me interrogating him. Was the
0.5cc/kg/hr increase in urine significant? Why did the films of
the lung look as clouded as before if the infection was clearing
up? He said the urine was promising and that the lungs would
X-ray white for days after the infection was under control.
Then he asked me if I had looked at the new admissions in
Labor and Delivery — in other words, didn't I have any work
to do? I'd managed to exhaust his patience in less than ten
minutes, a task made easier by his postcall fatigue and all the
worrying he'd already done.

When I came out of the NICU, Renee hit me with questions as fast as if I were Jennifer herself. I said Jordan was very sick, but there were encouraging signs. I explained that the increase in the dopamine was an ordinary dosage adjustment and shouldn't worry her. It was too early to tell, I told her as gently as I could, whether Jordan was better. We would have to wait.

He wasn't better. When I checked at eleven after rounds, his O_2 sat was down to seventy. At two he was down to sixty-five. Renee sat weeping outside the door. Her pastor was with her, but not Mr. Gilbert. I ran back between deliveries all afternoon. At six, Jordan's sat came up, then his pressure. At ten Spellman started to wean him off the ventilator. I was there just before midnight when he came out and told Renee and Mr. Gilbert that Jordan was out of danger for the moment.

Mr. Gilbert made that sound deep in his chest. Renee thanked Spellman, then thanked him again, turned away, and wept, her hands hanging by her sides. I floated down the hall and up the two flights of stairs to Delivery with a feeling I've had only once before. It was at the end of a master class with Zhang Chunhua, premier dancer from the Peking Opera company, at Syracuse. He'd had us hold our legs in high second position for ten-minute, then fifteen-minute intervals. It was a form of Chinese ballet training he wanted the members of DanceWorks to experience. The next day none of us could walk. But at the end of that class, when we let go of our feet, our legs floated. Huang called it hummingbird exercise.

I'm coming down now, but I can still feel that lift, a faint, airy laughter up under my solar plexus. Tomorrow Jordan will move to the step-down unit. He'll stay on the antibiotics for a couple weeks. Renee will come visit each day. Then he'll travel back to Nursery Four, to be with the other feeders and growers. I'll come see him early in the morning. In a month he'll bust right out of Charity and ride home, with his parents and a score or two of seraphim watching over him. His big sister Marcy will look out for him at home in Chalmette. He'll grow.

One day, when my Corolla's transmission gives its final thump, I'll tow the car to the Gilbert garage. There I'll find Jordan playing in his sister's old crib in the office, where Queen Nefertiti works on the books beneath the car calendars and the Valvoline, STP, and Champion decals. Beyond a plane of glass stands Mr. Gilbert with his huge hands and owl face. His voice echoes off the oily floor, off the lint- and grease-covered I-beams overhead.

I step to the crib and look into Jordan's eyes. At once he rises. I rise with him and we float, like a pair of hummingbirds, out of the office into the garage, then up above the men at work. They step out from beneath the mighty steel horses. Beside the glistening columns of the hydraulic jacks and the tables loaded with tools, the mechanics gaze in wonder. They clutch torque wrenches, round planetary gears. Jordan, high above them, extends his hands. His brown fingers with their pearly tips curl into a horn of plenty. He burps a baby blessing over the world.

Amen.

Norma Jean

Bou was late. The minutes stretched themselves out. I wrote to Marvin Druger, my favorite bio professor, asking him for a recommendation, but even med school scheming couldn't distract me. That gives you some idea how impatient I was. Our neighbors were coming home, the elevator was wheezing up and down, and footsteps were climbing the stairs, but not Bou's. I left my bed unmade, the sheets in the loft thrown back for her. Daylight faded from the walls.

I wrote to Dad for instructions about track lighting, did my lunch dishes, screwed the covers on the electric outlets I'd bought to replace Claude's old scratched ones. I looked over some chemistry for as long as I could stand it — about ten minutes. A pair of pigeons stood guard on the metal crest of the building across Rue Roubo. A lamp came on behind the lace curtain of a window. Still no Bou.

Monsieur Remier, our building's only pianist, arrived. I opened the door to hear him play a few miscellaneous pieces, then his usual first two minutes of the Italian Concerto before he got his hands all tangled up. It cheered me to hear him attempt the runs, even though I was tempted to knock on his door and ask him please to take a day off from work and learn the rest of the first movement, or just skip it and learn the second, which was much more his speed.

Another half-hour passed and time turned bitter. I clumped down the five flights of stairs and knocked at Germaine's door.

"Daniel."

Her eyes fixed me. The left eye held me steady while the right one kept wobbling outward. After a few seconds of this, my eyebrows seemed to tip diagonally, while my nose grew longer and turned to the side. I felt like a multiperspective portrait of myself that Picasso had just finished painting.

"You are waiting, little one?"

I nodded.

"Come, take a tea. You must not stand in the dark."

I left Germaine's door ajar so that Bou couldn't sneak by. A biography of John F. Kennedy lay on the business end of Germaine's table, its pages held apart by a small wrought-iron monkey's paw. Germaine pulled the book to her and read aloud about the link between Joe Kennedy, the Irish Republican Army, and the Bay of Pigs. It turned out the attempted invasion had nothing to do with Castro or communism. Jack simply wanted to get even with a few gentlemen of Havana who had double-crossed Joe during Prohibition, when the old man was moving molasses into Canada. Irish Republican Army hit men did the dirty work while Navy ran interference. Once the scores were settled, the president called everybody out.

Germaine read in a journalistic tone. When she'd finished, she asked if I was familiar with the Kennedys. I hadn't met anyone in the family, I told her, but I knew a bit about them. Was I aware that Jack was clairvoyant? No, I said, I hadn't known that.

"Jack foresaw his death. In a letter to Mama Rose, he told her he dreamt that a man would shoot him 'from a high place.'"

She squinted at the diabolical accuracy of the premonition.

"Jack never calls Marilyn Marilyn," she continued. "He calls her Norma Jean. Marilyn is like Monsieur le President, he tells her, a title for the public."

She rose and poured tea into one of the two cups warming on the pilot light of her stove. She looked prettier than usual, but I couldn't figure out why. She had on her everyday dress, support stockings, work shoes. Then I noticed her hair. She had dyed it a more reddish brown than before and turned it carefully under, from her temples to the nape of her neck.

"You are beautiful this evening," I told her.

She patted the side of her head and quickly sat down.

"Jack loves Norma Jean more than he cares for Jacqueline. Norma Jean understands him. Jack has always hungered for pleasure and for games. He and Norma Jean play, how do you say, Skwabble and upskosh."

I wondered about the present tense and the upskosh. I asked, and Germaine sprang to her feet once more. She hopped and jumped a set of invisibly chalked squares alongside her bookcases, then returned to the table.

"Jack and Norma Jean are together now," she said, out of breath. "They have what they always wanted, peace and time alone. There is no tranquillity when one is in the cinema or the government."

Germaine often used the present tense when referring to the dead. Her husband, Edouard, who died of his second coronary occlusion in '53, never lets her dry-mop or clean a window without his companionship.

"When Norma Jean gave birth to Jack's daughter, he hid her from the CIA in an underground sanctuary in Dakota North. Jack's double, a young actor whose face had been altered, attended to affairs of state while Jack traveled to see Norma Jean. Jack named his daughter Petite Norma Jean."

Germaine blinked at me, and only then did I notice the eyeliner that cleared the corners of her eyes to end in sharp, rising points.

"Petite Norma Jean was raised by the Carmelite sisters in Rhode Island. Today she is married to the sultan of Brunei, whose fortune is one hundred seventy-five billion francs."

I nodded. It all sounded plausible enough. Young Norma Jean had probably gone to Princeton en route to Brunei.

The front door opened. I strained forward as if tied to my chair. A tall figure stood in the gloom.

198

"Bou?"

Monsieur Touzet punched the hall light. He scanned his mail without a glance our way, then stepped to the elevator.

"What time was she to come?"

I weakly held up six fingers. Germaine frowned. I was not wise to depend on Bou. Despite my prying, Germaine hadn't told me much about Bou's contact with Nathan at the luncheon séance. But the next morning she had drawn me into the corner behind the stairs and, mop in hand, had warned me that Bou would always be a danger to me. *She is a wild horse,* Germaine had said. Only her brother could calm her. For everyone else she would always be an innocent menace. I must look out for myself, even though I loved her.

The door clanked shut in the entranceway. Again I peered into the twilight. A boot on a short rope was dragged into view. The light came on. No, it was Madame Baranger's dachshund, with strings of fur the same shade as Germaine's coiffure. Madame Baranger spoke a high-pitched stream of doggy talk to the animal. Germaine's nose wrinkled with disgust.

"Jump up, little potato!" Madame Baranger sang as the elevator door screeched open. I inhaled the steam that rose from the golden infusion flecked with yellow buds and black stems, my favorite of Germaine's teas.

"You are not well, Daniel," she said. "What have you eaten today?"

I was silent. I'd once made the mistake of revealing to Germaine the contents of one of Grandma Whitney's airdrops. She hadn't liked the look of Froot Loops, and was deeply troubled by the concept of spray cheese.

"I've elaborated your birth map," she announced, as casually as if she were beginning another chapter of the Norma Jeans' lives. She lifted the cutting board from where it was balanced against the wall. I drew a startled breath. My chart, etched with circles and lines and shaded in a rainbow of colors, was pinned to the board like an enormous tropical butterfly.

"Saturn dominates your nativity," Germaine briskly began.

"There is a grand trine of our moon and Pluto in Virgo. The principal conjunction is in the Sixth House of the Journey, not in the Fourth House of Awakening, as one might expect. Of twelve factors, seven are receptive. Elements of iron, calcium, and live carbon predominate."

"What does this mean?"

I pointed to a ladder that turned while curving in on itself until it formed a runged Möbius strip. Germaine frowned at my interruption.

"We will talk about the manifestations later," she told me. "First, know your determinants."

With a carefully manicured finger, she touched the vertex of an angle drawn between two planet symbols. But my eye followed a row of spheres containing flowers, doll furniture, and baby snakes, which advanced along the bottom of the page. These grew fainter as they proceeded with a shadowy phase effect I recognized from the work of John Romita, greatest of the Marvel illustrators.

"Like all form weavers, you are man and woman. We know this already from your hands. Your attributes merely confirm the placement of Mars in Scorpio."

We do? I thought.

"As Aquarius, you are drawn into being by the Pole of Moisture. Your Star Father is Ea, he who pours water from two vessels. That is why you are your mother's first and only son."

She whirled the board ninety degrees and slapped down the metal hand as if to say, *Just look at the facts.*

"You are feminine in your bearing. Stellium is on the ascendant. In your desire for stasis, you are masculine. Capricornian Saturn is within your apposite sky."

In my life I've had more than enough of these feminine-in-your-bearing remarks. I'd been hearing them since sixth grade, when Sean Drennan kindly pointed out to everyone in shouting range that when I played bombardment, I dodged with my arms and fingers held to the sides like wings.

"Your refractions rise between Mars and Pluto. Against time you struggle with bone and sinew. Note the close biseptile aspect to Neptune, which is singleton."

She pointed to a boring symbol on the edge of her faint chart. I looked right past it to the rowboat fighting against a deep whirlpool, which flushed violet and amber. The corner of the boat farthest from the suction was held in a monkey hand, much like the metal pointer. Its wrist was grafted to the roots of a swamp tree, itself anchored in the Gorgonzola surface of Saturn's largest moon.

"Will I marry?"

She frowned. My impression was that she wasn't sure whether I should settle down or not. She also wasn't going to let me change the subject.

"You cannot enter time through the mirror," she said.

The mirror was set in the side of a cucumber, and did look too far from my refractions for convenient time access.

"Open the window to enter the river. Gula is the God of Streams, from whose finger-ends all water flows. Yet because Libra is ascendant, you will always seek solitude."

The window had an eastern exposure. A crocodile was enjoying his own rocky planet there.

"Venus in Pisces counters Jupiter in Leo. You find rest only in motion."

"Will I always be with Bou?"

I noticed that mundane questions had a useful impact on the discussion. They brought Germaine back into the room with me.

"I've looked briefly at your synasty, but have not drawn in Bou's indications."

She tapped the board quickly in six places with the metal paw, as if she were in a stellar locker room showing her half-backs and ends what was expected of them.

"Bou's Jupiter is sesquiquadrate to your own."

She pointed out an invisible planet's position on the chart. "And?"

Instead of answering, Germaine lifted the metal hand once more. With a gentle brushing motion, she indicated a south-southeastern axis. Along the faint lines, her drawings, and even the atmospheres of the planets and stars, pulled asymptotically into a tunnel of graduated density.

"Gula is also called Hapi, who is Ea. When tenderness and violence mate, love is awakened."

The metal paw circled the darkest region along the axis, about two thirds of the way out. Germaine's paw paused there beside a spin-blade lawn mower cropping a clump of onion grass. This didn't help at all.

"Childbirth and healing are of Ea."

The paw ran due north along a flurry of lines. A pair of fish chased a hook with an angel sitting inside it, knees flexed, wings in takeoff position. Germaine raised the paw as the door in the vestibule opened. I didn't care who was out there. I wanted Germaine to tell me about the hand mower and childbirth. She pursed her lips.

"Bou," she said.

I stood and stepped into the hallway.

"You're two hours late."

"I'm sorry. I was caught in the —"

I punched the light button.

"You might say good evening to Germaine," I told her.

"Somebody's in a mood. *Bonsoir, Madame.*"

"Good evening, my dear."

Germaine and Bou embraced. I looked past them to where the chart lay on the table under the lamp with the magnifying glass. The onionskin rose and fell in the draft from the vestibule.

"You slept poorly last night," Germaine said, grasping Bou's arms above the elbow.

Bou said she'd read until four o'clock, and told Germaine how pretty she looked. I asked Germaine if we could return to the chat.

"This is not the moment," Germaine said. "Tomorrow."

She waved us away from her door. Bou stepped closer and leaned to kiss Germaine goodbye, as if they'd spent the day together instead of forty-five seconds. Germaine smiled so hard her thickened lashes stuck together. She waved us away once more, and closed her door.

Sock Diary

You were sitting in judgment, in the broken-bottomed cane chair, when I came home from ballet.

"Is Margot all right?"

"What the hell is it to you?"

It was everything. When I'd called Berlioz the previous night, Margot had told me in a quiet voice that it wasn't a good time for her or Bou right now. She hadn't called me a traitor, or said that she never wanted to see me again. It wasn't until I heard her blow her nose that I realized she was crying.

Why hadn't Bou told Margot about us from the beginning? It wasn't as if the two of them had never discussed sleeping with other people. And if Bou didn't want to tell Margot, why did she write down everything we did in her diary and then leave it where Margot would be sure to find it? Five years have not solved that mystery.

"Beck. How is she?"

"She's whipped. I told her straight to her face. You may be a woman, I said, but Bou's got you whipped good. Otherwise you'd throw that lovely companion of yours right out on the *trottoir*."

I emptied my knapsack on the floor, sorted out clean clothes, and repacked. I had rehearsal at two. I knew if I waited, you'd tell me what had happened.

"Of course she didn't pay me any mind. Throwing Bou out would be way too simple for Margot. Instead, she wants to learn from all this. She talks about 'overdetermined anxieties.'

She talks about the 'process of denial.' The girl's a shameless thinker."

I pushed past you to the kitchen. The water in February was so cold it burned my hands and face.

"What exactly is she denying? That you've been slipping it to Bou for two weeks? That you've been over to dinner three times, talking sweet to her while you wrecked her home?"

I tried not to listen.

"You want to know how Margot is? She wants to know how you are. That's how she is."

I stood in front of you. What you saw in my eyes must have warned you to ease off. You spoke more quietly.

"She knew right away you'd sent me over while you went off to twinkle school. She said it was very thoughtful. I don't know which of you two is creepier. She told me it's healthy for Bou to reach out to another lover, especially a man. That's you, by the way. She says it shows Bou has achieved a new stage of acceptance in her mourning for Nathan."

You went to the window. Suddenly you were shouting again.

"Nathan! That little prick's been dead for seven years! Now he's Bou's excuse to get laid by the first pair of pants she happens across in Paris. Margot, I said, you ought to horsewhip Bou and come after Dan with a straight razor."

The floor beneath your sandals gleamed. The first coat of polyurethane hadn't given it much gloss, but had trapped the dust. I'd mopped on the second coat with lamb's wool, and that had brought up an ordinary shine. But the third coat, which I'd squeegeed on after burnishing the surface with the power wheel, had transformed our little apartment into a frozen lake. I couldn't help but admire the way the polymer gave back the daylight.

"I just don't get it," you were saying. "Bou jumps your bones and no one has a word to say against her. Margot worries about you. You thank Margot for her concern, and manage to convince yourself you care about her relationship with Bou. If you did, you'd tell Bou you weren't going to see her anymore, and that would be the end of it. But you're not going to do that, are you, Danny?"

I didn't look up.

"Of course not. So please, please don't ask me how Margot is. She's very well, thank you, except that she doesn't sleep, bakes all day but never eats, and doesn't seem to be able to stop weeping."

You shuffled to the bathroom. I slid down the wall next to the window.

"She says you shouldn't come over anymore."

You gave a little snort over the bucket. My heart sank. This was it, then, the moment I'd been dreading since I'd put down the phone the night before.

"For a couple weeks."

"What?"

I wondered if I'd missed something. You were talking in the midst of your other activities.

"Until she and Bou have made a few decisions. I told her that if I were her, I'd never let you darken my door again."

"Thanks."

"But Margot feels guilty about not having you over for breakfast this morning. She honestly thinks she has no right to treat you differently than she did the night before last. Remember? When you two were so cozy over the dishes?"

I did remember.

"I'm supposed to tell you that she thinks you should take a few days to consider what's best for you. She's afraid you're too wrapped up in Bou."

You emerged from the shadows, pulling up your shorts.

"Margot was telling me that since your mother died, you've been searching for a stable love object, whatever that is. She implied that Bou was probably not one of them."

You were planted directly in front of me. You wore your green army socks with your sandals. You rocked forward and back, toes fanning.

"Frankly, I'm a little tired of all five of you — I mean you,

Margot, and Bou, and now your mom and Bou's demanding little surfer. It's been complicated enough this month, trying to decide which of you is bumping which, without Margot tossing a couple stiffs into the equation."

Above the socks, your shins were covered with curly orange hairs. Your knees, level with my eyes, resembled the red, wrinkled foreheads of fat twins.

"That's what you and Bou talked about the first time you did it, isn't it? That you need each other because you've both lost so much. That no one else truly understands."

I stood, my fists finding their way closed. To my surprise, you backed off a whole step. I crossed the room, climbed to the loft, and lay back. I shut my eyes and tried to remember what I was doing. Beneath the deception of the last two weeks was a morally defensible position. I needed to find it again. I could, if only I could recognize one or two landmarks.

Bou and I were a couple, I reminded myself. That was where I always started. Margot and Bou were best friends. It wasn't my place to tell Margot that I was with Bou. That was between the two of them. I had to respect Bou's ideas about their relationship. That was why I hadn't said anything to Margot. I reconstructed this fragile chain of logic, but couldn't help noticing that in this view of things, I'd done absolutely nothing wrong. That struck even me as suspect.

What had changed? On Sunday, Margot had done the laundry. That was all I knew for sure. She'd taken the straw hamper from the corner of the bathroom, emptied it into the two-wheeled folding cart, then clunked down the steps and pushed her way to the tiny laundromat on Boulevard Flandrin. She'd sat on the plastic bench she and I had shared one Sunday in October, but this time she was alone. She'd read her newest thriller, Shawn West's *A Real Lady Killer,* while opposite her the week's clothes soaked and spun. The book was about Detective Donna Knight and her pursuit of the mad coed-slasher of peaceful Boise, Idaho. Margot had been almost halfway through it on Saturday when you and I were over for dinner.

I'd skimmed past her bookmark as I sat in the window chair. So I knew that when Margot read at the laundromat, Knight's manhunt had ended with the impotent murderer falling nineteen floors down the elevator shaft of the West One Bank building. Then, in the privacy of Knight's well-heated and unrealistically accommodating Trans Am, the detective and the frisky, lambda-wearing sorority girl, Angela, had consummated a passion that had been smoldering ever since they'd met in Tom Grainey's Sporting Pub two hundred pages earlier. The last sigh of pleasure escaped Angela's lips just as Margot and Bou's clothes stopped warmly tumbling. Margot folded only the pants and button shirts, then put the rest of the clothes in her Printemps shopping bags in the cart and hurried home before the wrinkles could set.

She'd made top speed beside the tall apartment buildings of Boulevard Flandrin, past Université Paris Dauphine and the elegant façades of the embassies on Avenue Foch. At home she had lugged the cart up the stairs, then shaken and quickly folded the clothes on the dining room table. In the bedroom she'd thrown her socks into the right top bureau drawer and Bou's into the left. That was when she saw the diary in its familiar spot. What had made her take it out and open it? Perhaps she often read the little book with its battered, malachite-print cover, and had never found any secrets before. Perhaps yesterday had been the first time she'd explored its pages.

"They don't necessarily like you. Bou loves you, but her heart belongs to Margot. Margot sympathizes with you, but she wishes you weren't around. *Capisce?*"

I leaned over the edge of the loft and found your face. It was redder than usual because you were angrier than usual, and your body, from my perspective, was foreshortened. The impotent coed-slasher probably looked a lot like you as he made his last desperate grab at Knight's kicking feet.

"These women live together in an intimacy you can't shake a stick at. They don't need you. Do you hear me, Dan?"

I did. I knew that despite, or because of, what you were

saying, you were probably the only one left in Paris who still had my best interests at heart.

"Every night before they go to sleep, our two lovebirds moisturize each other from head to toe, neglecting neither nook nor cranny. Bou probably hasn't mentioned that, has she?"

I started to speak, but you cut me off.

"Who cares whether they're lovers this week? They pluck each other's eyebrows, Dan. They buff the bottoms of each other's feet. The point you don't seem capable of grasping is that they're very close."

You were trying to help me. I reminded myself of that.

"Why do you suppose Bou left that diary out? She wanted Margot to read it. You do understand that much."

My eyes were tired.

"Dan. I'm asking you a question."

"I don't know."

"You don't know?"

You heaved yourself up onto the refrigerator and pushed me to the other side of the loft. Then you beached.

"Well, let me tell you," you shouted, as if you were further from me now, instead of closer. "Since you don't know."

You were trying to save me.

"Bou put that diary in Margot's hands. She opened it to the right page."

You wore your violin boxers. Above them, your belly was as white as if it had never seen sun.

"She wanted Margot to know about the night you left your birthday party. She told Margot that you two couldn't get it on when you first tried."

I stared straight at the ceiling, which was lower than usual.

"Yes, Dan, we all know. Bou made sure of that. She gave the diary to Margot, and this morning Margot handed it to me. Don't you see how overripe this is getting? Your big date, your ups and downs, are in the public domain."

I looked to you in mute appeal.

"It's not romantic, Dan. It's not elegant, tricky, or sexy. Don't you see that you're just a life experience for Bou? Her first boy, and what better place than Paris."

You reached out a hand and grasped my shoulder. There were tears in my eyes. I had to get my contacts out.

"I know this hurts, buddy. But you've got to cut loose from this one."

You'd never spoken so kindly. It was as if you were coaxing a cat from a tree.

"I wish" — my voice caught in my throat — "Bou wouldn't tell everybody everything."

"I'll bet you do." Your hand squeezed my shoulder encouragingly.

"We did have problems at first. I thought maybe she was just sleeping with me to —"

"She was."

"No, Beck. It's not like that. We're going to live together in New Hampshire next summer. I'll study for MCATs up there."

You were silent. I wondered what else Bou had told you.

"Did the diary say anything about . . ."

I couldn't say it. You just raised one eyebrow.

". . . about whether she likes being with a man?" I whispered.

You shook your head.

"You won't tell Bou —"

"No."

"Sometimes I think she wishes I was —"

"A woman."

"Maybe," I said, glancing at you. "It's how she holds me."

"Your tits?"

"Not only. She holds my leg like, like —"

You swung yourself across me and took my thigh between yours.

"She told you?" I asked.

You dropped my leg and flopped onto your back.

"You can always tell what a woman's used to," you said reflectively. "At first she makes it with you just the way she's been making it with Fred, or whoever preceded you. That's what I call the burden of history."

You took a breath and settled deeper into my pillow.

"Soon the pair of you discover your own favorite perversions, that is, if you're worth a damn. The longer your research-and-development phase lasts, the deeper in love you fall. If you're repeating yourselves after a week, you were meant to be friends. If you're still inventing new moves after four or five months, you may be what we call lovers. Not that sex is the most important thing, mind you. It's the only thing."

I propped myself on my elbow.

"Now there's a dark side to all this," you continued. "If you two break up and your gal goes off with Ned, or whoever succeeds you, she'll require him to maintain the traditions you two have established. You're history now. You're Ned's burden, his Fred. In practical terms, this means he's nibbling your ex's little toe while he keeps one finger in her left ear. He's tied himself in a sailor's knot under your old dining room table, he's getting rug burns on his elbows and cramps in his scalp, and he's wondering if his unit will bend that direction."

You held your hands up, illustrating your ideas with abstract gestures.

"You'll never see the woman again, and you're leading a life of solitary misery, but at least you haven't been forgotten. Your legacy endures. It's not much use to you, granted, but there's no point in dwelling on that."

As you spoke, I felt a pleasant distance from my own problems. I wondered why I couldn't be more like you, sensible and decent. You weren't messing around with anyone's girlfriend. You were writing to Valerie.

"Bou will call. Don't worry. She's just lying low for a few days."

I didn't think I'd ever see her again.

"She'll be here before the weekend. I guaran-damn-tee it."

"I know what you think I should do, Beck."

"No. You haven't the faintest idea. I haven't told you yet.

Now listen carefully. I may be wrong. You and Bou may be the debutante couple of the decade. You may get hitched in Lincoln next June with a rabbi and a preacher in attendance, with your people filling up all the Motel 6's for a hundred miles around, and all Bou's polo-Pilgrim, yacht-club yahoos jetting into Boston for the big day. Could be society page stuff, Elizabeth Anne Philips, daughter of Cynthia and Richard Philips, to wed Daniel Mordechai Shoenfeld, son of David and Carol —"

"My middle name's Henry."

"Could be all this will come to pass, but I'm afraid my money's still on the short girl. My sense is that you should be making a plan. I'm not asking you to break up with Bou now. I know you're hormonally incapable of it. I say take two, three weeks. No, take a whole month. Stay up late every night writing poems to Bou and thinking up new events for those afternoon gymkhanas of yours. Give her a Parisian winter she'll never forget. Store up memories of your own, so that when you're a gnarly geezer, crawling after your walker in some space-age retirement community in the year 2050, you'll recall with a frisson of geriatric delight the Paris moonlight of impetuous youth."

You climbed ponderously from the loft, groaning as your feet stretched for the fridge.

"Do it right," you said, your head level with me. "Because when March comes, I want you to bite the bullet and tell her goodbye."

You wanted us to decide this together. That way, you thought I'd have a chance.

"You kiss her and walk away, just like in the moving pictures. The beauty of it is that the very next day, you and I trot over to Berlioz for dinner. You can love both Bou and Margot again in an innocent fashion, like last month. Remember last month, Dan? It was when you weren't sneaking around feeling like stink dirt all the time."

I did remember last month, vaguely. I opened my mouth to speak, but you reached up and placed your hand over it.

"Think about med school, the bigger picture," you said. "Ask yourself what it is you want from life."

You lifted your hand away and fell to your cot.

We were never closer than that day. I knew you'd stand by me, even if I couldn't do all that you were asking of me. And you did. That's why I'm still grateful to you. It's also why I haven't forgiven you.

Ned and Fred

Margot and I met above the Opéra métro. She looked dignified and powerful, and not at all as if she'd been crying for a week.

"You're not starving, I hope," she said, as businesslike as she'd been on the phone Tuesday. She'd called to tell me to meet her before she and Zubir played their evening session at Club Twenty-One. I was to dress nicely and meet her at seven-thirty, she said, and hung up.

"We'll have dinner late," she told me now, handing me her soprano case and keeping the alto.

For twenty minutes I'd been standing, lightheaded, looking up at the angel on the corner of the opera house roof. She was a heavyweight angel, twice the size of her two companions, who rested their backs against her legs. I'd looked and wondered how I could explain myself, what I had done. Now Margot was in front of me in her jazz woman pants and jacket, her fake pearl necklace and Bou's real pearl earrings, and I was no closer to an answer.

"How's the lab?" I asked lightly.

She looked at me to see if I was kidding. What she saw on my face must have convinced her to go along with the charade for a moment.

"We mapped your dipoles."

I discovered in those weeks that I easily hid what I was feeling or not feeling.

"And?"

"We determined that French isn't your mother tongue."

"Science. Are there no limits to her wonders?"

The Café de la Paix and the Grain de Café floated like space stations in the gloom, their glassed fronts full of oxygen. I wanted to lie down inside one of them where no one could touch me. Margot reached out and took my arm.

"Why?" she asked.

"I —"

"Forget Bou."

I hadn't said anything about Bou yet. Margot pulled me forward past the people heading our way and the closed banks and airline offices. If we slowed down for a minute, I thought, I'd know the words.

"I trusted you," Margot said.

I didn't feel guilty, because I didn't exist. Nothing I did or had done mattered. This was my secret, and I hoarded it.

"I thought you cared about me."

She waited for me to speak. But I was realizing that for three weeks, since Bou and I had been together, I hadn't given Margot a thought. I'd been worrying about another woman, one who looked like Margot and lived with Bou. She suffered and I felt sorry for her, but she wasn't Margot.

"You came into my home," Margot said, and stopped. She wept, her eyes wide open, there in the middle of the sidewalk. People passed us on both sides.

"I didn't mean to," I said. "I wanted to tell you."

"When?"

The faces of strangers approaching us were lit up by a low street lamp.

"Damn you. What are you looking at?"

She bolted off, dabbing at her eyes with her free hand. I tried to make my mouth work, and my legs, but I advanced after her only sluggishly.

"I wanted to call you that night, after we left La Plage." I shaped each word deliberately, as if my lips were numb with cold. Margot drew further off.

"Bou said she'd talk to you," I weakly called. "When I was with her, I couldn't think. I couldn't tell her what we should do."

"I know."

I wasn't sure Margot had spoken. The sound drifted back to me. I leaned heavily toward it.

"When the four of us were together," I said, "I pretended it was like before."

"I remember that," Margot said. I heard her that time.

"I decided to tell you myself the first time we came over. I was going to stay after Beck left. I thought you and I could talk. Then I'd tell Bou that —"

She turned and I bumped into her.

"I'm sorry," I said.

Her eyes collected me as I descended, pound by pound, into gravity.

"I'm sorry."

"I knew this was coming," she told me. "You have a right to ask, now that I've read that damned diary. But you realize Bou set us up."

It was after eleven. We were in a restaurant on the corner of Bouloi and Coquillière. The exterior was lacquered wood, the interior stucco and frame, like a Tudor house turned inside out. I told Margot what you'd said, that Bou had laid the diary out for her. But Margot hadn't found the diary in the sock drawer when she did the laundry. Bou had left it, *by mistake,* in Margot's knitting basket.

"Bou told me that you two weren't —"

"We're not," Margot said sharply.

"I thought that meant —"

"Listen. Bou and I have been together for a long time. I know you don't believe me, but at first we were a lot like you two are now."

She was right, I didn't believe her. I didn't think any couple had ever been like Bou and me. Margot realized how full of myself I was. That only made her try harder to protect me.

"You're dizzy. Bou has this look I haven't seen in a while. I've known for a month you two were in love. I just didn't think you'd sleep together. The way you acted when you and Beck came over made me think —"

"I'm sorry."

"You keep saying that," Margot said. "You acted like a first-class shit."

She couldn't talk for a minute. She drank some wine.

"Laurie is the reason you and I are here talking," she said quietly.

I stopped trying to swallow a bite and instead tried to look at Margot, but I couldn't do that either.

"When Bou and I started up, I didn't bring her over for *dinner*. I didn't bring Bou into *our house*. But I went behind Laurie's back."

"But Bou said —"

"Shut up. When Laurie broke up with me, she didn't cut me off. She could have walked away and never talked to me or Bou again, but she didn't. That's why you and I are here."

"Beck said —"

"Leave Beck out of this," she said, stabbing a few fusilli.

For three hours I'd watched her play, bobbing up and down beside Zubir, who stood motionless behind his double bass. I loved watching her so much that I'd gradually forgotten I'd wronged her, and lost her. I'd managed to persuade myself that she and I could go back to being just as we had been. But that wasn't true. She would always be wounded, and I'd always be the one who had wounded her.

"I wanted," I said, "to keep her secret. So that I'd have her more —"

"To yourself."

"I thought if no one knew about us, she'd be more mine."

"I remember," Margot said.

I was sure she was thinking about when she and Bou started up, but she didn't talk about that. Instead, she told me things I couldn't understand. She thought I knew the ways lovemaking changes over time, how much better it gets, and also how it can become a struggle. I didn't know. I'd never lived with a woman for more than two months. I thought sex was either good or bad, and stayed exactly the same forever.

"We were getting stuck," Margot told me as she finished her fusilli and started on my saltimbocca. "Study, fool around, get ready for bed, make love, sleep, get up and go to class and work, come home, fool around. We decided to slow down."

It had been Margot's idea, just a few weeks before Chamonix. She suggested to Bou they just slow down for a while. Sex was getting in their way. Did that mean they were going to be with other people? They didn't rule it out. They agreed there would be no secrets.

"I just want Bou," Margot said. "I don't know why." She almost smiled, but then didn't. I sipped my water and wondered what she was thinking.

"I had a brief sluttish period. Just a few months. I wanted to fool around with every woman I was attracted to. I thought monogamy went with being straight."

She shook her head at her foolishness. I tried to look as if I weren't surprised.

"What about Bou?"

"Bou," she said, pushing my empty plate away. "Bou always wanted to be with a guy on the side."

I felt cold. It was as if Margot had said Bou had always collected luna moths, and I'd just noticed the yellow circles on my hind wings.

"Then I'm —"

"I thought so. That's why I was pissed at her when I read that diary. I told her she had no right to use you." She drank my water. "But she isn't," she said. "She's serious about you."

"She is?"

Margot frowned. I must have looked too happy.

"Yes."

Margot was hurt by our lies. She was furious, and jealous, the way anyone would be. But Bou loved me, and Margot accepted that. And those are two things you'll never begin to fathom, Beck.

Margot ate all but two spoonfuls of the zabaglione we ordered. She said that she and Bou had been talking, and that she didn't know whether they were going to stay together after they left Paris. She wished I'd had better sense than to get involved with Bou now, but she knew I hadn't planned to be with Bou. It had happened. She'd try to let me come back to Berlioz in a few weeks, once she and Bou had spent time alone. She wouldn't make any promises. If it was too painful, I'd just have to stay away. That was the choice I'd made.

"This is for you," she said.

We were standing in the tunnel of the Palais Royal métro. She took a package from her purse. I held it to the light and saw, beneath a red bow, rows of brainwaves mapped in snaky lines on graph paper. Inside the package was a luxurious pair of midnight-blue leg warmers. The wool was compactly woven, with plenty of stretch to it. I could wear the warmers over my knees to the tops of my thighs, or roll them down to double-heat my calves on cold mornings.

"They're exactly what I need," I said.

I forgot everything again. I hugged her, breathed through her dark hair, and remembered. I wondered what I was doing, if I had ever decided to do it, and whether I could stop. Margot pushed me away.

"I'll see you in a few weeks," she said, squeezing my hand. She walked beyond the turn in the shopping tunnel.

"Wait," I called after her. "What am I doing?"

She came back. She didn't look surprised.

"You're with Bou. I thought we'd covered that." She walked away again.

"You knew this would happen," I shouted.

She came back more slowly.

"You're a lot like me," she said quietly, and shrugged. "We're in Paris." She disappeared around the wall.

"What's going to happen now?" I asked.

She came back very slowly this time.

"Now?"

"Next month. Next year."

She took a deep breath and studied the sea-green shards of the mosaic floor.

"We're all going to be tired," she said.

Before she could start walking, I stopped her.

"Wait."

"What?" she asked, irritated now. The sound of a departing train came from the tracks.

"I love you."

"I know," she said. "That's the other reason I'm here. It's not the same."

"Why?"

She leaned against the wall.

"For one thing, I'm gay," she told me, tilting her head.

I thought about this.

"But Bou's —"

"Bou," she said, "is curious."

She turned and just kept walking.

I need to take a four-day rest cure in my apartment, with the blinds drawn and about ten movies stacked up on the VCR. I need to turn off the brain for a while, the way Dave shut down Hal in *2001*. I'll leave only enough intelligence to order pizza, transfer beer from floor to fridge, and operate the remotes. I think I'll make reservations now for the beginning of January, when I'll have a few days of limbo before I start Emergency.

This time first year I was performing in the legendary Giacobbe Academy *Nutcracker*. I was Prince, which entailed mastering the Battle of the Mice solo and the Land of Sweets duet. My Marie was Stacey Berman, a sixteen-year-old with the fastest feet I've ever seen. Diane Nichols, my ballet teacher and artistic director of the Christmas gala, drafted me at the last minute when she realized that none of her current crop of boys could begin to partner Stacey.

The *Nutcracker* was a real ball-buster, coming as it did on the eve of my head-and-neck final. Even though Diane puts on only a thirty-five-minute abridgement of the Balanchine, I was completely befuddled by performance night. I'd been studying for an hour in the dressing room, surrounded by a couple dozen overstimulated five-year-old girls, who played kissing tag with me as tree. Their mothers tried to keep them from wearing themselves out before they went onstage to surround Herr Drosselmeyer for the Gift of the Nutcracker scene. I just kept right on studying. My exam was in twelve hours.

I stepped into the footlights to go up against the Mouse, still chock full of anatomy. I couldn't quite decide whether to dance a circle of Willis around the Mouse's optic chiasm or to execute a set of military *coupé-jetés* between the beast and the innocent high school child. The *Picayune* reviewer described my performance as "breathless," but I believe she intended "breathtaking." I passed the final, too. My only worry is that someday I'll be performing brain surgery and I'll confidently announce that I'm ready to expose the Sugar Plum Fairy.

Next week all I have to do is cheer on my high school friends. Linda Simmonds, a high school junior and a Giacobbe classmate of mine, will try to fill Stacey's pointe shoes. Senior Rob Vasquez, last year's Mouse, has been upgraded to Prince. Linda's mother, Sharon, and I will watch the two dance their duet in front of the forty-foot painted Christmas tree. I fill in for Linda's father, who's probably only a few years older than me, wherever he is.

I don't want to scare you, but you should realize that I talk to you all the time. I hold entire conversations with you when I'm driving home or out running. I consult you here, when I'm ready to store these CHARTs and CASEs. I don't say out loud, *Well, Beck, what patient name shall we store this one under?* But I come up with names I wouldn't have thought of myself. That's how I know you're nearby.

It's not the same as when Germaine talks to the dead. I'm very glad you're alive. I even think we should get together from time to time, during the years in which we both number among the living. In March I've got a week off, and I'm coming up to Philadelphia to see Dana. I hope by then she and I will be able to spend a weekend at her place without acting as if we never knew each other well, or tearing off each other's clothes and making frantic love for twelve hours. We managed to combine these two elements during our one less-than-conclusive attempt at a friendly visit last August.

This weekend will be both better and worse, I imagine. A new boyfriend would change everything, naturally, but given the hours Dana's working at U. of Penn., she's no more likely to meet a man who doesn't have a debilitating neurologic disorder than I am to meet a woman who isn't having another man's baby. After I see her, I'd like to come up to Boston to hang out with you for a few days or nights, whichever you're off.

What do you think? Margot would have told me if you were married. Whenever she sends me her annual New Year's note, she mentions "life-cycle events" as Feinberg, the new rabbi in Poughkeepsie, calls them. With her usual tact, Margot avoids telling me what she knows about Bou's love life or her own, which may or may not be in part the same subject. She also leaves out any mention of having spent time with you. She did tell me that you and Val broke up when Val stayed in China that extra year. I was sorry about that. And she does inform me of your honors as they accrue, the Henry Christian Award you won fourth year, your spanking new residency at Mass. Gen. I toasted you that night with a glass of ginger ale. *To Sir Beck,* I said to the air. *My wise and faithful friend.*

In Boston we can hit the town, overeat, drink cold ones, and stare mournfully at women whose breasts are widely separated. Now I'm off to cruise my stretch of corridor. I must be sure that nobody here at Two-Lane, the Highway of Health as we call it, needs a hand from a friendly man in green. But first I must bid you a temporary *au revoir.*

I'm going to write to Margot for a while. I'm into this pen-palism deep enough now that I'll definitely INTERNET this whole sucker to you as I planned, the *BOU* and *BECK* directories together, and a *MARGOT.DOC* too, which is what I'm thinking I should start tomorrow. Then I'll print out two copies of all three *DOC*s and send them to Bou, via Mam in Lincoln, and direct to Margot in Los Angeles. Now that I hope to see you before too long, I don't feel like I have to write to you anymore.

Besides, I owe Margot a letter, and while I admit that what I've got here is a fairly extreme solution to that problem, I do think I should catch her up. I decided weeks ago that I'd send her what I've been writing to you and Bou. But yesterday in the shower, I realized I want to write to her in person for a while. Frankly, I'm tired of hearing you talk back to me. You tell me I never knew what the hell was going on in Paris and that I still don't. I find I'm spending too much energy proving to you that you're wrong, and showing you all that you were too thick-headed and loud-mouthed five years ago to notice yourself. That's wearing me out.

Margot doesn't doubt me. She never has. I need to hear her believing me as I go along. She's one of the few people I've met in this world who doesn't think, deep down, that she knows in advance what a person is going to say.

Look at it this way. You're driving a mountain road at night in that Audi 5000S you said your dad was going to give you. You're on a weekend trip to the Adirondacks in pursuit of a woman you met for five minutes at a friend-of-a-friend's house-warming party two years ago, a woman who made the mistake of saying she hoped she'd see you again. As you drive along, you're listening to my broadcast, which is coming to you direct from here on the tenth floor of Charity. You take a hairpin turn. Your headlights sweep past the guardrail, out over a forest of red spruces, sugar maples, and yellow birches, and my voice disappears. You press the search button on the radio. The signal-finder hunts, but all it comes up with is what my dad calls moon music. Blips, clicks, and hissings — a porpoise talk show, a Martian traffic update. I'm still broadcasting, though I sense that I've lost my target audience. My words are out there looking for a listener. They don't find you in the Northeast, so they head out West. Soon I feel the crisp *zing* of a new contact. I've connected with the living soul of Margot Deborah Levi, in Santa Monica.

You take another turn. Suddenly you tune me in again, but I'm talking to Margot now. You turn up the volume to compensate. Meanwhile, in the back of my mind, I know you're still out there somewhere, with the radio on.

MARGOT.DOC

Last week I was sleeping up on the thirteenth floor when I heard Joel return from a delivery. It must have been an exciting one, because he decided to take a three o'clock shower to wash it off. The water sounded far away. Then I woke up. Something was wrong. The water had been on for too long. I jumped from the bunk and pushed into the bathroom. Joel had slipped, knocked himself out, drowned.

No. The meat-, egg-, and milkless Seeker was asleep, leaning against the wall like a horse dozing next to a tree in a pasture. I recognized his state of being. I'm asleep now, upright in this chair. In my dream I see the four of us lying side by side on a night train. St.-Gervais in an hour, Chamonix two hours off. Blue light seeps from the bulb above the window. I sit up and find I'm the only one awake. Beck's knees are drawn up beneath him. He softly butts the wall with his head, in time with the rocking train. Bou rides him bareback, her arm hugging his chest. I curl around you, Margot, warming you from three directions.

Come visit. Stay with me in my crummy apartment in Terry-town, a little-known vacation getaway. We'll lie around on the floor, snuggle, and catch up. I want to hear about Reesa. What does the woman look like? Is she Jewish? You'll tell me every-thing, won't you, if I promise I won't fall in love with her?

I figure she must have bucks. From your notes it's clear that you two live in places loan babies like you and me can't afford. You wrote last time that you're within sight of the beach in

227

Santa Monica. How do you do that on twenty-three hundred a month before taxes, med school loans, and car payments? You said Reesa works as a free-lance editor for a publishing house in Boston. That doesn't sound lucrative. Your house in Ann Arbor had a hot tub and a music room. How does this work? I suspect *unearned income.* Where do you find these rich girls?

If we manage to get up off my carpet, I'll show you New Orleans. We'll dine at Crêpe Nanou, where Dana and I took each other for our birthdays, our two anniversaries, and to celebrate her neuro match at Penn. Come in the spring, in crawdaddy season, and we'll go to Pampy's to hear a little jazz, then sup before midnight at Frankie and Johnny's on juicy little crustaceans in cayenne, onions, and garlic, with smoked sausage and potatoes along for the ride. We'll wash them down with a pitcher or two of Abita Amber, and, fingers stinky, lips burning with pepper, we'll drive the Corolla cautiously across the Mississippi River Bridge.

You'll rest your head on my shoulder. With your hoarse voice leading, we'll sing "These Foolish Things," "Od Lo Ahavti Dai," "Night and Day," and "Yerushalayim Shel Zahav." By the light of the moon, we'll cross the muddy waters to reach Terrytown, Jewel of the Delta. At my place we'll settle once more to the welcoming floor, this time with blankets and pillows.

I'll be ready to hear about Bou then. You see, it will have been months since I'll have finished writing these letters and mailed/INTERNETed them to the three of you. I'll have survived my Emergency rotation and will be working reasonable hours in Medicine. I'll have chosen a residency, and my life will stretch out in front of me like a well-maintained fairway. I'll be ready, by morning, to ask you a few questions. Not jealous ones, such as when did you last see Bou, is her hair long or short, and did she ask about me? Well, I will ask those. But then I'll ask the important questions, the ones that won't frighten me anymore. When dawn comes we'll be lying together in a sleepy torpor, my head on your belly so I can listen to the noises there, the way I did at Berlioz. Sunlight will stream through my living room window.

I'll ask if you still think about Bou all the time the way I do. I'll ask if you weren't once afraid that you'd never love another woman as much as you love Bou. I'll ask what you think happens to love that isn't accepted. And then I'll ask once again, Margot, why you never abandoned me.

Sacred Grove

"Beck," I said. "What are you doing here?"

"I am the spirit of this grove, preserver of the sanctity of the lesbian home. I forbid you, in the name of Hector Berlioz and Alice B. Toklas, to brush your nasty satyr's hooves upon the smooth roots of this place."

I put the spare key back under the vase in the hall. Beck was curled on the sofa in your living room writing on a legal pad. He was wearing a pair of baggy yellow culottes and one of his own white V-necks, against which his tits plumply hung. He held an ordinary Berlioz Heineken in his left hand. His trombone sat beside him like a metal person, slide up.

"At the risk of repeating myself," I asked, "what are you doing here?"

"I'm supposed to meet Bou."

"No, Beck. I'm meeting Bou."

"Oh, right! You're Lothario. I'm Pan. So confusing at times."

"Are you high?"

Beck's eyes indicated the floor, then the ceiling.

"Aren't you rehearsing with Zubir?"

"Go home. Your spark is feeble in these parts. I am now Smokey the Bear and I say unto you, light no wicked campfires beneath these blessèd trees."

"I told you I'm meeting —"

"You are a malefactor."

I knew exactly what he was talking about. It was late February. My exile had ended the week before. You'd let me come over for dinner two nights the previous week. Now Bou and I were taking advantage of your trip to Reims with Docteur Maupin for the afternoon neuro meeting to meet at Berlioz. It was not proper. Beck glared at me.

"Bou will be here in half an hour," I said lamely. "Margot won't even be back in the city until eight-thirty."

I'd arrived early, with my chem book for the wait.

"You want to run into Margot, don't you?"

"Bou's coming from school, I'm coming from Nanterre. This is the logical place to meet."

He sucked his beer empty, leaned, and rolled the green bottle across the floor toward the fireplace. He lifted another one from beside the chaise and opened it.

"Let me ask you something, hombre to hombre. Don't back away from this, Dan. I just want to pose you a question." He smiled bitterly. "In the abstract."

"Only if you tell me why you're wearing Bou's clothes."

"What, pray tell, would have happened if Margot had come home early today, instead of me?"

"I'd be chatting with her."

Beck stared morosely up at me. I sat down in the window chair. On the floor next to it was Beck's warm hash pipe. I thought he was a little more articulate than the three bottles near the grate could account for.

"Margot and I both love Bou," I said. "We have —"

"What you have is a time-share agreement. I, for one, won't stand for it." He gulped, wiped his mouth. "Do you think that just because you're in Paris, you can do whatever pops into your heads? Leave me out of it for a minute. Do you think that playful Ogg and his consorts are going to put up with all this ambiguous fornication?"

The culottes he wore carried the shape of Bou's hips. It was as if her bottom half were supporting Beck's torso.

"When was the last time," he asked, "that you ever heard about three people happily boffing each other in any combination? Do you really think that just because Margot reads all that psychology, she wants you pawing her friend? Leaving aside the questionable taste of your doing it in *her own bed.*"

I looked out the window. Beck sat up and laughed, his head back, his breasts shaking. His pad was beside him now, and his trombone bounced up and down in his lap like a child.

"Yes, yes, fine," he said. "You both love Bou, and she loves the pair of you. And we're in dark old Europe, where complicated arrangements make puritanical, corporate-American, dingleberry types — of which I'm not sure I'm not one, by the way — want to hide in unadorned churches, leaving only to go work sixty-one-hour weeks in the fallow fields of God's visible approbation."

He took a breath. I picked up the pipe and sniffed it.

"Europe," he said, "in which such clandestine arrangements have been carried out in shadowed parks, in gondolas sliding through stagnant canals, in slatted, sunlit pagodas beneath honey-blossomed pear trees, in the cool marble archways of the silken rich, even in simple flats and ordinary houses, ever since the Renaissance. All right, fine, I gotcha."

He swallowed a quantity.

"And two of you are Jews, who don't accept Christian notions of abstinence and denial. Recently ex-European Jews who tend, with lumbering collective consciousness, toward the German Romantic, Freudian quest for mind-body union. As Margot would have it, a healthy libido just barely constrained by the reality principle, ego in the service of the id and so forth. With the tolerant God of King David hanging out far overhead, letting the Lion of Judah lie down with Bathsheba, so long as he dances in the spirit of contrite worship in the streets when he gets around to it. *I did it Yah-way,* as Old Blue Eyes might put it."

"Letter to Val?" I asked. I knew he was writing that week's installment of *Letters to Valerie.* But just to annoy him, and to remind him that I was lucky and he was lonely, I walked over and picked up his pad. I read a sentence of such explicit pornography that I dropped the yellow pages and backed away.

He could have had the decency to turn the pad over. I'd given him plenty of warning.

"And then there's Bou," Beck said, pleased with the success of his trap. "Who knows what our handsome princess is into? Only one thing's for sure. She's determined to kiss old New England goodbye, to bury our plain-dressing, sensually impoverished wilderness behind her. That's why she became a harlot of the floodlights, and that's why she's here in forbidden Rome."

He swiveled, lifted his legs onto the chaise, and lay his head back against the raised side. He rolled his eyes up to the ceiling, until all I could see was white.

"You're just a corollary in her conquest of the Old World," he murmured. "Any dusthead can see that her one enduring goal is to make those see-nothing, think-nothing parents of hers notice her — notice anything, really, besides the death of their precious son, which was apparently the last event that raised the dinner conversation in Lincoln above the level of small talk at the church crafts fair."

"You wanted to ask me something?"

"True. I was just reminding myself why Bou is here, and what she could possibly see in you."

He heaved his belly into the air and adjusted Bou's culottes.

"No offense," he said as he oscillated to a stop. "But when I met you this summer, I thought you were just an upstate scholar-athlete type who had traded in his cleats for spandex but somehow neglected to become gay. Now here you are, official mascot of the Yale Lesbians Overseas. Figure that."

"You figure it."

"I'm trying. It's the blue boy factor that's key. That's what I keep coming back to. You've got an ingenuous, virgin-popper diligence about you that Bou was snookered by. She thought it meant she could have it all, *something soft and something hard,* as Dr. Seuss might say. She knew you'd be the gentle sort, and then love her for the rest of your days."

I cracked open my Huey.

"You don't know what I'm talking about," Beck said.

"No."

"Are you ever going to forget Bou?"

"No."

"That's what I'm talking about."

I had known, roughly. Beck meant I was for Bou what Dominique's guy was for her, the man who would never forget her, even for a minute. I was Bou's what-every-woman-wants. But I thought Dominique was wrong. Women are like men. They don't want to be remembered by someone they've left behind. They want to be remembered by someone who's in the next room, and who sneaks up behind them every five minutes to kiss them on the ear while they're reading. And Bou had you for that.

"The immediate question is this," Beck said. "What if the recently unveiled beauty of my heart, Zohra — whom I hope will greet me in Allah's paradise when I perish doing battle with adulterous Jews, inverted Christian whores, Kleinian polygamists, and other assorted infidels — what if last night my odalisque Zohra had convinced Margot as well as Zubir and myself to sample a few of the industrial-strength *merguez* of which she was so proud?"

Outside the window glass, the motionless vineyard ivy blanketed the fieldstone in a deep winter green. Below, the stones of the courtyard were a cool blue.

"Why then, this afternoon," Beck was telling someone, "with a contrite phone call to boss lady Maupin, Margot would have turned around on the way to the train, taken a cab home, and scrambled for the jakes. And say that occurred in —"

"So that's why you're wearing the outfit."

I smiled nervously. Beck paid me no mind. He studied his Mickey watch like a NASA mission control leader.

"Leaving Bou forty-seven minutes for elitist tardiness, and figuring it would take the two of you about thirty seconds to have what passes for a conversation before you ripped her clothes off and buried your —"

"Hey," I said.

"Figure fifty-one minutes from where we sit now to where the two of you are . . ." He gestured down the hall with his head. "Then Margot would have interrupted the proceedings at about three forty-six."

He sighted at me down the neck of his beer bottle as if it were a precision instrument.

"So my question, Daniel, is simply this. What would you two libertines have done? Or was that the idea all along? You *want* to force Margot to kick you out of here permanently. You don't think you've done enough damage already."

He looked at me with sullen, porcine eyes.

"We're going out."

"You're damn right you are," he told me. Then he rolled his bottle into the middle of the hearth and blew powerful trombone blasts that shook the candelabra. My plans to spend time alone with Bou at Berlioz were not postponed, but canceled.

She splashed down three minutes, eight seconds ahead of schedule.

Rosalyn Darby is asleep in Prenatal, her girl's face hidden by her belly. Ten hours of hard work and now nothing. She's going to have to start all over again. Her aunt is in the east corridor. Visiting hours ended three hours ago, but no one can get the woman either to go sit in one of the blue seats down in Family Waiting and watch the hanging TV or to go home.

"I told Rosalyn it wasn't her time. She wouldn't listen."

Rosalyn's aunt is tall and gaunt, with a long face that hooks outward at the chin. She cradles a big Bible in the crook of her arm.

"Rosalyn, I said, you listen to me. You won't have that baby till the middle of next week."

"Visiting hours —"

"She said she had the pains. Pete got out the truck and said if I didn't want to come, I could walk."

Pete stands at the end of the hall reading *People* and pretending he doesn't know his aunt-in-law, whom Kate christened Nightmare this afternoon.

"I knew she wasn't going to do a thing," Rosalyn's aunt says.

"How?" I ask, despite myself. I'm hoping for the sort of folk wisdom that makes its way into the *New England Journal* ev ery few years.

"She isn't due for nineteen days. That's your counting. By my counting she's got thirteen, but then I know when Pete had his days off and you all don't. Then in our family we're always early with our firsts. That's why I told Rosalyn next week."

What she says about the nineteen days is true. That's why we decided not to augment the labor.

"Rosalyn's a strong girl," she says. "I've been looking after her. She'll make it."

I try to hide my disappointment. I was hoping for a sample of hillbilly medicine, like Rosalyn wasn't going to deliver today because the toadstools under the back porch weren't leaning southeast.

"She'll stay overnight. Then if —"

"Her pains are gone."

She says *pay-ins*. Rosalyn's last pain was three hours ago. I explain that we're not going to release a woman who's been in labor for ten hours, especially not in the middle of the night. She and Pete might as well go home, I say. I excuse myself and walk away.

"Pete can't drive back in tomorrow," Nightmare yells after me. "Let me take her now."

Her voice has a white Louisiana twang. I turn around and explain the situation once more. Nightmare looks at me as if I'm too stupid to realize that her niece is not going to have a baby. I look at her and realize that Rosalyn, down the hall under that belly of hers, has the same high forehead and long nose as her aunt, but doesn't have the upturned chin or the voice. Nightmare might have looked like Rosalyn once.

"Come on, Pete," she says when I'm done speechifying.

Reluctantly, he closes his magazine. Nightmare takes his arm and the two of them walk toward the central elevator bank.

I'd only been at Tulane for a month when Dana and I met. It was at a tag football game at Riley Center, second-years against first-years. Dana was one of the organizers and she took it seriously. I ended up blocking across from her for a while, and discovered she had a pair of killer elbows. That's all I remember about her from that day.

Two weeks later, when I ran screaming from my anatomy book to Fat Harry's, Dana was there with Michelle Janowitz from my study group. They were in a booth next to Mike Lewitt from my class and a couple second-years. The second-years were all talking about how impossible the path exam had been, and Dana was silent because she'd just aced it. She got up to play one of those machines with the miniature crane that drops down to grab prizes. It has to hit the plastic capsules with the prizes in them just right or it won't pick them up. Dana became obsessed with a giant fly key ring. She spent three bucks in quarters and almost had it twice, but ended up with a pair of miniature handcuffs that even today are locked to my rearview mirror. I cheered her on. Then she and I left together. I was just going to walk her home, but we ended up hiking all the way up Marengo and General Pershing to Galvez. It was one of those spooky New Orleans nights when the leaves of the live oaks, veiled in Spanish moss, blink like a thousand shiny eyes. We talked and talked. Dana and her mother had just had an even bigger fight than usual, and she'd — well, I don't need to explain all that. I just wanted you to know how she and I started up, so I could tell you how we ended. That's the part that still worries me.

It was last October at the Winn Dixie on Claiborne. Dana had just flown in from a long weekend in Maryland. I'd been up all night studying for a peds midterm. I picked her up at the airport, and on the way to her apartment we stopped for groceries. Next to the lettuces I saw a broccoflower. I pointed it out to Dana and we agreed it looked awful, but we had to buy one anyway. Then I started to envision other hybrids. Cross an eggplant with a kiwi, create a kiwegg. Cross a turnip and a watermelon, call it a turnomelon.

The next thing I knew I was laughing the way I did when I was sleep-deprived and suddenly with Dana after having been alone for days. Dana was as bad as I was. She came over with two kinds of grapes, looking silly and lovely with that crooked smile of hers. She asked me what was the matter. I was on the floor, clutching my broccoflower. I told her about the other hybrids. She came up with rutamangoes and butteryams. Next thing I knew we were both on the linoleum next to the cantaloupes.

238

I had the hiccups. I sat holding Dana's hand and waiting for them to pass. She shook silently. She sneezes silently too, though she does the right sneezing motion. It's as if the soundtrack is missing. She tried to stand but only managed to crawl a few feet. Luckily, it was eleven o'clock and there weren't many shoppers. I stood and helped Dana up, hiccupping while she silently opened and closed her mouth. We pushed the cart out of produce, through checkout, and to the car. Then we were all right.

Over dinner we talked about next year — this year, that is. Our idea was that I'd do an immunology research block for a chunk of the spring, up in Philadelphia or wherever Dana ended up. That way we wouldn't be apart for more than a few months. I lay beside her that night, thinking. I was too tired and jittery to sleep.

Dana and I had never made it past the joking stage in our wedding talks. After we'd gone to the wedding of one of her high school friends at this incredibly tacky marriage factory in Beltsville, Maryland, we'd decided that we were going to get married in the same place. We'd invite two hundred and fifty people, and our theme colors for the twelve bridesmaids would be lime and banana. That was the kind of planning we had done. But as I lay with my arm under the pillow under Dana's head last fall, I decided we should get serious. It was time.

In March Dana matched at Penn, her first choice. She was as unsure as I was about when we should get formally engaged. Each of us was waiting for the other to be decisive. Then, one Sunday at the end of April, Dana was having her weekly talk on the phone with her parents — first her mother, then her father, because the two of them can't stand to be on the phone with each other. I lay beside her, half listening. Suddenly I remembered hiccupping on the floor of the Winn Dixie, and Bou was there with me, not Dana.

I know that isn't clear. I lay beside Dana listening to her talk to her father about the addition he's building on their beach house in Ocean City, and I realized I couldn't marry her. To explain why, I'd have to tell you about the trips we took to Poughkeepsie and Chevy Chase to meet all the parents.

But not now, because I've got to go. Twenty minutes ago, Grant walked by and gave me a looking-over. I think he's beginning to wonder about me. For a few weeks I fooled myself into believing that he thought I was a promising, or at least a competent, medical student. I don't try to out-doctor the world, like Steve Tsintolas, but Grant has seen me do decent work. I imagine he's forgotten all that now.

Yesterday we had just finished a delivery when Grant was called down to Emergency by the first-year resident. He asked me if I wanted to come along. I said sure, and knew right away I was going to regret it. The admission turned out to be a woman who had rushed to the hospital in labor but had only made it as far as the ER before she delivered. Grant and I arrived in time to see the term baby come out looking flat, with a bad resp effort. Grant asked if I wanted to practice passing an infant resp tube, a rhetorical question.

I advanced the blade of the laryngoscope, then eased it back, picking up the epiglottis. I could see the vocal cords, but you know how anterior the airway is on those little guys, Margot. I asked one of the many gawking paramedics to give me some cricoid pressure on the cartilage, but I ended up bruising the poor baby before I could pass the tube.

The procedure only took me a minute, and Grant was ready to take over if I couldn't do it. Still, the one time I have the most trouble all month, there are seven people watching. The whole ER staff helped by getting in my light. Grant stood beside me, saying nothing. *The baby's fine, Dan,* would have been nice. At the very least, the man could stand to learn a new facial expression. But when I looked up, he just grimaced at me.

I'd better go see to my damaged reputation. I don't think there's anything to do, but I'd better wander the ward anyway. I'm worried that Grant's going to report me to Dean Fulginiti and have my ass thrown out of the program. I'll try to get back to you before dawn.

Ruth's House

Bou banged on the door of Anne and Patrick's apartment. She fell against me when I pulled the latch. It was April, and the next morning I was leaving for the two-week trip with the company.

"Are you excited?" Bou asked. She wandered into the living room, which opened into the bedroom on one end and on the other squeezed down toward the kitchen.

"Art," I told her, "must reach the little people."

"How little?"

"Elementary school," I admitted.

Anne and Patrick's place was high above Rue du Faubourg St.-Martin. I was housesitting, or rather dog-sitting, for one day so that Anne and Patrick could visit her brother on the way to Le Mans for our first concert. I'd leave in the morning. Patrick would drop off Anne and return in the afternoon. It was complicated, but worth it to me because it meant a night with Bou.

While we ate dinner, we talked about everything but the Mediterranean beaches where you two were taking Beck for vacation. Afterwards we took Nikki, the gray terrier who cocked his head in a way that made him look intelligent, for his walk. He peed in front of Établissement Bazin Imprimerie in the courtyard, then sat by a cast-iron fountain talking to an orange cat with high white boots. Back upstairs we ran a bath, the smell of Anne's lavender crystals filling the long apartment. The water heater fired up in the kitchen. The pipes rattled in the hall.

I knew you were on my side, Margot. You wanted me to have my one night with Bou. I needed, you said, to know what living with her was really like. We undressed like an ordinary couple before a weeknight's rest. Bou washed her underwear and socks while I took out my lenses. I wondered if this was what it would be like if we lived together in the summer. After our bath, Bou wrapped herself in Anne's beige towel and fell into bed. I rinsed out the tub with the nozzle.

"What are we going to do?"

"Not what you want to do," she said.

Nikki stood at the foot of the bed. With his outsized jaw and curly gray coat, he looked like a cross between a wolf and a lamb. He studied Bou with counterfeit intelligence.

"You want us to plan the rest of our lives right now," she said, "before we go to sleep."

She was right, naturally. I kissed her and wondered how to overcome her resistance to planning.

"When you visit me, Dad, and Brenda next year," I began, "we'll have to sneak around. I'll put you in the guest room. At midnight I'll drop from my window to the ground and then climb onto the garage and in through your window. In the morning I'll go the other way."

"Why not use the stairs?"

"Okay."

What I really wanted to talk about was where I was going to stay with her at Yale. She'd sent in the forms giving up her spot in Saybrook so that she could live with Kim and Robin. But I knew she was thinking about changing her mind. If she lived with you, I wondered how she and I could be together, even for a night.

"What about when I visit you?" I asked casually.

"We'll see."

"Maybe we could stay at Robin and Kim's, if you're not living there. Or —"

She kissed me with those deep kisses of hers. She held my face in her hands and looked into my eyes.

"You want to know what's going to happen," she said. "I can't tell you."

I didn't care if she ever told me anything again, as long as she kept looking at me like that.

"I can't imagine not being with Margot," she said. "And now there's you."

She wrapped one of her legs around mine and ran her flexed foot up and down my calf while she talked. It was as if her foot repeated everything her voice said.

"I know it's not easy," she told me. But it was easy now. She held me again and her eyes looked right into me. "At school," she said, "all our gay friends always told me there's no such thing as bi. They said I just wasn't willing to accept that I was gay yet. My straight friends told me the same thing, except they said my being gay was a stage I was going through or a game I was playing. Nobody I knew said I might be both except Margot, which is ironic because she's sure she's gay. That's why I believed her."

I pulled Bou's head to my shoulder, looked up at Anne and Patrick's ceiling, and wondered what all this had to do with where she and I were going to sleep when I visited in the fall.

"I know I want to live with you," Bou said. Nikki was beside her now, and she scratched his wolf head, as if to convince him. "I always pictured my dream guy as a cross between my father and Cyrus Killian, who I went to junior high with. When I left for Andover, I was sure I was going to run into my guy in a language class. That's why I kept starting and dropping languages. He didn't turn up in Russian, Chinese, or Spanish. I never guessed I'd meet him in France, and that he wouldn't look like Cyrus or Poppa at all. He'd be you."

Her foot repeated all that up and down my leg.

"Margot and I used to talk about having kids at the same time. We were going to find someone we loved to get us both pregnant so we'd have half-brothers or sisters, or a half-brother and a half-sister. We picked names, and Margot even chose our house in Santa Fe. It belongs to this woman, Ruth, Margot's Bubbi Shel's best friend."

This was all news to me. I wondered, with a sinking feeling, what other plans I knew nothing about.

"Margot visited Ruth with Shel when she was a girl. Ruth's a painter, and used to teach art at St. John's. She lived on a kibbutz in Israel in the fifties, and in Mexico. She looks just like Hedy Lamarr."

I wondered why you'd never told me about Ruth.

"Her house is adobe, with old, carved doors. It's on this hill looking down on the town. There's a vegetable garden in back. Ruth says Margot's her granddaughter. She sends Margot birthday presents every year, even though Margot's only seen her twice since Bubbi Shel died. Last fall Margot wrote and asked if she could buy Ruth's house someday. You know how Margot is. She's in debt and she hasn't even started med school. Here she is trying to buy a house two thousand miles away that she's only seen four times in her life."

Nikki wandered off, not quite sharp enough to notice that he'd been in a state of bliss right where he was.

"Margot and I had all these plans when we were sopho-mores," Bou said, as if that had been a decade rather than a year before. "Now we argue about everything. She hates the way I leave my stuff all over the apartment. I can't stand the way she's always judging me, trying to get me to cook, or at least identify spices in things."

I told Bou you only wanted her to be more sure of herself.

"I knew you'd take her side," Bou said. "You two always agree about everything. I don't want to sound like Beck, but do you think it's because you're Jewish? Do you all have a secret agreement that you'll understand each other, even if you've never met?"

Yes, I thought.

"Maybe you and Margot should get together and plan my life," Bou said, "and just leave me out of the discussion al-together. Better yet, maybe you should plan your own life together."

But you and I wanted to be with Bou, whose feet could talk,

and whose arms could pick us right up off the ground. I kissed her hair and gave her a one-armed squeeze until my triceps quivered.

"I know I'm lucky," Bou said after a while, "but sometimes I wish I was alone. I never had a boyfriend or a girlfriend until I was sixteen. I think I'm best at being alone. If I was, I could just sleep and act, and eat whatever the hell I want."

We slept with the reading lamp on. In the night, Bou lay her head on my chest and stretched one giant leg across my two. I stayed still for as long as I could. It hurt, but I didn't mind. When I finally slid her leg off, she stirred.

"Bou."

She opened her eyes.

"All four of us can be together," I said, "when we get back home."

She looked at me from far away. I wondered if she knew where she was.

"Four?"

"You, me, Margot, and Beck," I said. "But I'll be the father. The one you and Margot were going to look for."

"Aren't you sweet," she said, and put my hand in the damp place beneath her breast.

"We'll have a boy and a girl. Beck will be their uncle."

"Beck?" she asked.

"Uncle Beck. He and Margot can play jazz in the basement."

Bou laughed. I couldn't tell if she had woken up.

"That way, they won't wake the babies upstairs."

"Oh," Bou said. She drew my head to the triangle of her collarbone.

"But I'll be the dad, not Beck."

"Sure, sweetie." She touched my head softly.

"Tell Margot," I said.

"Margot."

"That I'll be the father."

"You'll be the father," she said.

"You mean it?"

"Absol*uuu*tely."

Her voice was so quiet I wondered if she was thinking about what she was saying. I decided to test her.

"Whose father?"

"The father," she murmured, "knows where the keys are."

"Hm?"

I propped myself up. Bou was smiling a secret smile.

"Keys?" I asked.

Bou didn't answer. Slowly her lips stopped smiling. I lay down.

Damn, I thought. If only Germaine were there. She'd have known all about the keys.

Country

The next morning I waited like a spy on the prearranged corner of Avenue du Trône by the large traffic circle of La Nation. Above the closed video arcade and Snack Burger stand, the undersides of the new locust leaves were pale green. In the middle of the circle, a bronze giantess hesitantly started into second arabesque while balancing on a giant bowling ball. Below her, a naked woman and a man wearing only bronze trousers were forever beckoning to an invisible multitude to come see if the giantess could pull it off.

A sound like a harmonica played with a bellows came from Avenue de Taillebourg. I turned and found Joseph's cousin's twenty-year-old *Deux Chevaux*, with bug-eye headlights, circular scrollwork overlapping the front and back doors, and a peel-back top. It made the noise again.

"*Buon giorno,*" Paola said when I reached her.

The car was the purple-blue color of ditto ink. I leaned sideways into its hinged window to kiss Paola's cheek. Joseph, in his John Lennon sunglasses and sailor's cap, stared straight ahead. I lifted the back door handle, which looked like the head of a Ping putter, and before I was settled into the back seat, Joseph hit the gas. He headed for the Brasserie Puechavy on the other side of the circle, and for an instant we almost drove inside the place, its mirrored columns winking, its lampshades nodding behind dark glass. Paola's hair ballooned over the headrest and I gathered it in my hands as we swerved and rattled east toward the *périphérique*.

I slept, my head on my arm on the window frame, my teeth clenched. When I woke, we were pulling off the queer French highway with its two neat, icing-smooth lanes in each direction. An Arche restaurant spanned the road.

"How was your reunion?" Paola asked when we'd parked. She meant my night with Bou, but didn't want to be vulgar.

"Quiet."

I had explained to her that Bou and I were going to be like an ordinary couple for one night.

"She prepared your dinner?"

"Naturally. I read the newspaper. Afterwards, she cleaned up. I took a brandy and cigar."

Paola frowned. All year she waited for me to tell her that I had decided to leave you and Bou alone. She thought that her combination of patience and disapproval would wear me down.

We climbed to the cafeteria. Directly below, virile cars flew past both sides of an endless, flawlessly groomed euonymus hedge.

"This is a garden, not a highway," I told Paola, steering her by an arm into the food line. "Do the roads in Italy —"

No, she assured me, there were no such highways in Italy. Only a country like France could lavish so many francs on its citizens. I realized that, as usual when Paola and I were together, we were ignoring Joseph. He looked more approachable without his sunglasses, so I rose on my toes and kissed him on the cheek. He wiped the kiss away and stepped back from us again. We waited for him at the cashier with our trays of coffee and *pains aux raisins*. It was barely seven o'clock.

"The afternoon Catherine gave us costumes," Paola told me.

I'd asked when she and Joseph had started up. Beside her, Joseph looked at the table.

"I put my costume on without difficulty and was waiting for Catherine to examine it," Paola said.

"No," Joseph said. "It was the next week." He leaned his

248

chair back to look through the window at the scant flow of traffic below the restaurant.

"We began together after that rehearsal," Paola continued. "I said I would sew his costume and he said he could not allow me to engage myself in such a project."

Almost none of the costumes Catherine handed out had fit, Paola said. But Catherine pretended they were fine because she didn't want to pay to have them altered. Joseph's unitard was much too small.

"He looked ridiculous," Paola said.

"She admired my body."

"I observed that he was helpless. I decided that I would at least open the waist of his costume. That was the beginning."

"That was nothing."

Paola raised her dark eyebrows ominously.

"Not the real beginning," Joseph corrected himself. "The real beginning was after the next rehearsal. On the way home."

"Yes. In the métro."

They agreed on something. I didn't know quite what. Their eyes met in a way that excluded both me and my questions.

"What happened," I asked, "in the métro?"

"We realized we had been looking for each other ever since we could remember," Paola said, and took a deep breath that brought her bosom against the table edge.

"We kissed," Joseph said. And then, as if to clarify, he looked at me and said, "We kissed."

He swallowed hard, his Adam's apple pulsing down, then rising back into place. He placed his hand carefully on Paola's far shoulder.

I tried to formulate the phrase "That must have been some kiss" in French. Then I realized I didn't want to say that, or anything at all.

I jerked the *Deux Chevaux* around the parking lot to the highway, getting the feel of the light clutch. Soon I rattled along the right lane, the steering wheel shimmying in my hands, the walls

249

of the toy car popping and flexing like baking pans coming to heat in an oven. All the traffic blew by us. Paola took a nap in the back seat. Beside me, Joseph looked like the Marlboro man. He gazed out at the sky, his shoulders high above the bench seat, his brown hair brushing the cloth roof.

We were on tour. That felt good, despite how sleepy I was. My head was full of speeds roughly converted into miles per hour. I loved driving the little 2CV6 Spécial, with its gearshift sticking straight out of the dashboard about ten inches above the hand brake and its speedometer the size of a large watch face. Joseph pointed at the northbound highway and grunted. All I saw was a truck, with decals of soccer teams on the doors. He told me it was a Mercedes and what model. He told me what its engine could pull, its maximum speed on a flat road and on a climb, loaded and unloaded, and then he listed obscure statistics about cylinder pressure. His father was a trucker.

"*Tu connais Hank Williams?*" He pronounced the name *Honk*. Yes, I said, assuming he meant Junior. And Tanya Tucker? Sure, I told him. He said his father listened to Honk and Tonya in his truck all the time. Did his father speak English? Not a word, Joseph said. All their lives, his parents had lived in the port of Le Havre. In his thirties, his father had taken to wearing cowboy boots and a Stetson. Joseph explained this to me without smiling. The topic of his father was a solemn one.

"Do you resemble him?"

Joseph nodded.

"What does he drive?"

Joseph searched the passing trucks for a few minutes until he found one in the same phylum. He listed its features at high speed. His father's rig was contracted to a shipyard. Usually he carried containers full of industrial ceramics from Le Havre to Spain, then returned with produce. When Joseph was a boy, he had traveled with him. He had his own bunk to sleep in. There was a cooler of cheese, bread, wine, and apples, and a thermos of coffee. His father had carved a high seat for him out of styrofoam. Later Joseph had trained to be a driver himself.

"I was engaged," he said. He meant engaged to a trucking company.

Joseph had never said so much to me at one time. He kept talking. He had planned to live in Le Havre, in a second, small house his father had built. He was engaged — to a woman, he meant this time, since he said *fiancé,* not *engagé.* His whole future lay before him.

"But you left Le Havre."

"She left me," he said. "I came to Paris and studied accounting at Assas."

"When did you start to dance?"

"A friend brought me to her rehearsal. The man in the company didn't arrive. I took his place for an hour. They said I was stronger than he was."

That was the whole story. He said no more about the woman in Le Havre. Paola woke.

"I want to curl up on your belly."

"Pascal and I did all right," Bou told me. "The class liked us more than Hanbowski."

She spoke in the loud voice that meant you were right there in the room.

"I want to drink champagne from your navel. We performed brilliantly tonight. Le Mans will never be the same."

"I'm glad it went well," Bou told me.

"Joseph and I have a little room under the eaves. I have a teeny bed. We'd hardly fit."

"Sure, I'll tell her. Dan says hi. They had their first show and it went well. Margot says congratulations."

"I thought about you all night."

"Yeah, we're packing right now. Really early in the morning."

"I love you madly."

"You drive carefully too," Bou said.

Our debut had been in the municipal theater of Le Mans, for an adult audience. The piece had gone over well. Now we were celebrating in a pub on Rue des Jacobins across from the theater. The phone was at one end of a zinc bar, at the other end of which was an old pinball machine with tinny bells instead of electronic gongs. On it, a muscular cavewoman in a leopard-skin one-piece defended herself with a wooden club against a screaming man-ape. Four short men stood drinking short beers between the machine and me, and glaring at Paola, Catherine, and Dominique with a mixture of resentment and desire.

"I'll come find you," I told Bou.

"No. I haven't even looked at a map."

"I'll sneak up behind you on the beach and give you a hickey."

"Yeah. I have to go, too."

"The kind that looks like it hurts but doesn't."

"Bye now."

She hung up, a little panicked. I was pleased with myself. I could almost never startle her. Only occasionally, when I was out with Beck somewhere, drinking. I had been just about to ask her to put you on.

It was that first performance that made me feel so free. After floating through the lights in the finale, I didn't see any reason why I couldn't call Bou, tell her about the bed in which I had missed her the previous night, and then talk to you about the trip you were about to take. Anything seemed possible, even likely. I called back.

"It's me."

"I know," Bou said. "I'm still packing."

"May I please speak to Margot?"

During those two weeks on the road, I came close to having everything I wanted. I was with Bou and I was your intimate again. Our last dinner together at Rue Roubo had been almost like old times. Beck had forgiven me. Before I'd left, he'd offered me pocket money for emergencies, which I'd gladly accepted. I could tell he wished I was coming with you three to the South.

"Hi, Dan," you said. "We're kind of busy."

"I wish I was there. How are you?"

"I can't wait to get out of here."

"Once you leave Paris," I told you, "it gets very French."

"So I've heard. Listen, I've got to go."

"What did you have for dinner?"

"Borscht."

"With bread?"

"No, with eggrolls. Dan, we're packing."

"Have a good time," I said. "I miss you."

I imagined the Côte d'Azur would be like Chamonix, only warmer and offering a more balanced diet.

"Bou says you rocked the house tonight."

"We did," I said.

"Don't be surprised if it's not like that every night."

"Why?"

"Because it might not be," you said. "It's never the same twice."

"So what do I do?"

"Dance."

The next day we paid our toll and left the highway, driving east toward Angers through greening fields. The road was bordered by poplars like whiskbrooms turned upside down and stuck into the brick-colored soil. Joseph pulled over to ask a teenage couple for directions to the Centre Socio-Culturel. They told us it was by the stadium, then stood arm in arm staring after us as we drove off.

We parked beside a cemetery. The stones looked like pools of water. High above them a mackerel sky traveled steadily southward. Paola and Joseph walked an *allée* of cropped ailanthus, their branches ending in tar-blackened fists from which large new leaves stubbornly sprouted. I trailed behind.

The Centre Socio-Culturel, at the end of a street of gingerbread houses, looked like the Greyhound station in Binghamton. Inside its belly Catherine stood alone on a narrow stage, calling out directions to the lighting man.

"Mark that one number three."

We climbed backstage. Dominique and Anne were changing in the wings.

"Too much," Catherine shouted, holding her notebook up into the blue light. "Down a notch."

She performed her lonely solo, stepping from one place to the next.

There were hundreds of kids. A white-haired man shepherded one group, then hurried back to the entrance to fetch another. We peeked from the curtain's edge. Would these fourth- and fifth-graders appreciate Catherine's *Condition Postmoderne?* Would they understand that the piece dealt with the forces that shaped their lives? That looked unlikely.

The musicians plunked and honked in the pit. The stage manager hustled back and forth, giving us annoyed looks. We stretched and stole glimpses of the mob. Joseph came to remind me of a change in the timing of a series of hops we did opposite each other. He was sinister in the backstage dusk, his cheekbones sharpened by rouge and shadow, his painted lips gleaming. My feet were stone cold on the plastic flooring, but sweated steadily anyway.

"Five minutes!" the stage manager shouted, making us all jump. I rubbed my hands as if I had just set off on a cold night without gloves. Catherine cornered us with last-minute discouragement.

"Dan, don't look at the floor. Nicole, hold in that belly of yours."

Catherine would have ordered a surgical tuck for Nicole if the state would have paid for it. Nicole's belly bothered her just less than my forward-thrusting neck, and just more than Dominique's habit of licking her lips in midair, which I admired. Having distributed ugliness all around, our director shook her legs one at a time, then briskly massaged her thighs.

I turned away and completed my own ritual as I peered past the curtain.

The children knelt in their seats, waving to each other. They weren't going to notice us, so it made little difference how we performed. This was reassuring. The white-haired teacher shouted for quiet. A woman in a red skirt made threatening motions in front of some very young ones. The other teachers, scattered throughout the theater, had given up.

Suddenly the stage manager was right beside us, hissing like an enraged puff adder. We turned to him and he pointed at his watch. Nicole, trembling, took her place beside me in the wings. The backstage lights faded. I turned to wish Nicole good luck, but didn't. She looked curare-stricken. Instead, I stood beside her, sweating and shivering. The house lights came down.

I couldn't see the kids, who fell silent. Then came a long *ooo* sound, and a storm of giggling. The teachers called for quiet as Monsieur Lussier's musicians started in with their atonal hooting. The curtain opened on Joseph and Catherine, posed in the rusty haze of the footlights. Catherine hung from Joseph's neck by both arms, her tiny bottom tucked up against his right hip. The stunned children were silent again.

I crossed the stage, counting so loudly in my head that I was sure it was audible. Paola came from the opposite side to meet me. As if it had all been planned, I took her hand and lifted her with my other hand by the underside of her leg. She was weightless. I turned to face the audience, but couldn't see past the first ten rows. The children there were attentive. I directed my movements over their heads.

Paola and I exited toward Nicole, who watched us with terror. The kids were waking up after the initial shock of seeing all those grownups dressed in their underwear. Paola and I reached the safety of the wings, and Nicole steered herself on-stage in broken puppet movements. Her arms flailed, her short red hair flopped back and forth. The kids in the front rows turned in their seats to talk about Catherine Bilgère's work.

We made our entrances during the first dozen measures of

the Morning Prayer section, until the stage was covered with us. Joseph and I executed our leaps over the twisting forms of Paola and Anne. The kids pointed and jeered. We danced on, throwing ourselves into our knee spins and running slides.

Then we slowed down, rejoining Paola and Nicole for the careful unison work that supported Catherine's duet with Dominique. Their duet, Catherine had explained, was about the difficulty of intimacy in a world governed by mechanical time. Our efforts were met by a chorus of raspberries and provocative French *uu* and *eu* sounds. A carton of apple juice landed downstage right, and a pool spread from it. The counts finally said we could leave, and I followed Anne's glistening back toward the wings.

As I entered the offstage darkness, I wondered if this modern dancing was all it was cracked up to be. I thought about what you'd said, that every performance of the same piece was different. It turns out that every half-performance is different. After intermission, the kids were used to us and we were used to them. They started laughing in the funny places and being quiet in other places. And when Nicole and I came flying out of the wings, head-to-head, in tango, the little monsters sat right up and watched.

Happy Medium

"We've got to talk," Beck said solemnly, wearing his dolphin boxers.

"Now?"

"It's about Bou."

"She told me."

It was May and we were all back in Paris. I had a strange orphaned feeling that came with not having rehearsal after nearly two months of steady work.

"She thought she was pregnant," Beck said. "We went to the clinic in Fréjus."

I eased up the knob and the track lights cast cylindrical beams down the north and south walls. I seldom had the chance to see my lights operate against the semidarkness of the slatted blinds. I'd had to buy adjustable beds with tightening screws for the tracks, because the ceiling was so uneven. I'd already mounted both sets and gotten them wired in when I noticed the gaps between the tracks and the plaster. I'd unwired them, taken them down, and started over. It had never occurred to me just to leave the damn things dangling while I redrilled.

"We tried to call you in Besancon," Beck told me with a pained look on his face. "You weren't there."

"We stayed with Catherine's friends, not at the hotel. Saved her some money."

I walked to the window and cranked the blinds. Beck raised

his elbow, covered his eyes, and bared his teeth, like Dracula. It was a few minutes after one. I turned off my lights.

Beck woke up in a funny mood sometimes. I always tried to reassure him that the world was more or less as he'd left it the night before. Now I opened the windows, leaned out, and drew the air into my lungs, feeling privileged, as always after ballet. But Beck had not had class. He was almost naked and entirely unhappy with whatever fantasies had haunted his long sleep.

"You hungry?"

He sat back down on his cot, opened his mouth to answer, then just smacked his lips several times, like a toothless old man. His eyes were puffy and his unshaven cheeks had a fungal fuzz on them. Too much sleep was not good for Beck. It gave him time to think.

"We didn't go to the clinic at first. Bou was afraid to know."

"You were terrific. I don't know what she would have done without you."

"I thought we should come back to Paris," Beck said. "Margot didn't want to."

Bou and Beck had driven to the clinic in Fréjus, where she had had the pregnancy test. That was definitely the right way to proceed, except that the rural clinic's five-hundred-franc test was probably no more reliable than the hundred-thirty-franc drugstore kits Bou and I had used twice already.

"I kept trying to call you."

"Bou needed you," I said.

I sorted out the edible from the too-far-gone lettuce. On the rooftops across the street, the chimneypots glowed. Beck was melancholy, but stirring now. He mumbled to himself as he searched through one of his piles of dirty and clean clothes. I came out of the kitchen to find him tucking his Maytag shirt into his sherbet-green polyester pants.

"Margot called you a dildo." He spoke mildly, without looking up.

"Did she?"

I set down my glass of water, sidled up around behind him, and slipped a headlock on him.

"Also a turkey baster."

"Nice," I said. "What did you say?"

I tightened my hold. His face, from my oblique angle, stretched into what I knew was a grin.

"She suggested that it would be just like you to knock Bou up as a means of reducing her to the status of a bearer of live young."

I choked him a little.

"Oh?"

"She said . . . you wanted . . . to make Bou . . . bear sons . . . in your image."

He elbowed me, and I gasped and lost my grip. The truth is Bou and I were careful, but she kept thinking she was pregnant anyway. The first month we were both completely panicked for five days. The second month I wasn't nearly as worried, and the third month I was a little curious. Why did Bou think she was pregnant all the time? She followed her pills' lilac-to-cinnamon wheel with religious devotion.

"Margot says the ancient prohibition against graven images . . . is compensated for by the . . . patriarchal subjugation of women . . . to the father-son mirror."

"No shit." I had a good grip again.

"Bou is little . . . more to you than a pacifier. Upon which you . . . project . . . your primitive fears and desires."

His voice came out slightly duckish.

"She said that?" I let go of him.

"No, I made that last bit up."

"Not bad," I told him as I pretended to walk away. Then I turned and caught him in the jejunum. He made a carp face and doubled over. I yelled in his ear.

"Did you defend me?"

"Don't ever," he whispered, "hit me."

"I don't think you did. I'm gone two weeks and you let Margot reduce me to a turkey baster."

"Don't ever do that again." He played with his sandals.

"She fills Bou's head with psychodoodoo," I went on, quoting Beck to Beck. "You tell Bou she's pregnant so you can hold her hand and whatever else you can reach."

His head sank a little lower. He was having trouble with his sandals. They were custom-made by a New Haven craftsman who hadn't realized how pudgy Beck's feet were.

"But she isn't pregnant. You all lie on the beach all day eating drippy Brie sandwiches and drinking liters of the cheapest white wine you can find. That makes Bou feel poorly." I could see Beck as a Maytag dishwasher repairman on a suburban kitchen floor, studying a warped water propeller. "Don't you know Germaine told her to ease off the cheese and wine?" I asked.

"I thought the Happy Medium," Beck muttered, "told her to eat lizards and abuse the dead."

He sat back, fully awake now, as I'd hoped he would be. I pretended not to notice.

"But your nasty plans didn't work out. True love conquers all."

I rinsed the lettuce, shuttling the water bucket to the drainage pipe in the bathroom. I thought about plumbing. I was done with the electrical fiddling by then and didn't know what to do next except mess with the pipes and fixtures. That scared me. Dad assured me in his letters that I'd be fine, but I kept writing him for more information.

Beck scowled contentedly. He'd just needed to wake up and acknowledge all the slander he'd heaped on me during his trip south. He'd felt bad about not sticking up for me. I was pleased he worried about such a minor disloyalty as name-calling. While I lunched, he breakfasted on Alsatian beef jerky and a bottle of Japanese Tokura. We'd completed our world tour of beers with a case of Tahitian Hinano and one of Thai Singha Lager. Now we drank whatever Beck wanted, and his tastes remained exotic. One day he brought home some Schlitz from a country called Milwaukee. I sat on the crates, looking past his mop of hair out the window and relishing the bits of Roquefort in my salad.

Beck felt all right, but then he didn't again. He wore the saddest expression. A sliver of beef fell from his cracker to his beer.

"What's wrong now?" I shouted.

It didn't work this time. He just fished in his beer with my spoon.

"I think," he said, "I should tell you something."

He stood and set his beer on the windowsill. One by one, he erased drops of condensation from the brown glass. He looked lonely and old.

"Bou's going to break up with me," I said quietly, scaring myself. Beck looked up and opened his mouth.

"She told you that being with me," I bravely continued, "was a mistake."

Beck shook his head. I'd spent only one afternoon with Bou since we'd all been back. She'd been gloomy and quiet, and I hadn't been able to reach her.

"That's not it," Beck said.

"Margot," I said, suddenly sure. You and Bou were over your winter troubles. Bou knew what it was like to be with a man. Now she just wanted to be with you again.

"There's no room for you," Beck said. "There's no room for anybody. Believe me."

He grabbed his Tokura and fell back into his chair. His green pants protruded through the broken cane. He closed his eyes and pressed the bottle to his forehead. I left him alone for a minute, then leaned over and patted him on the shoulder.

"You didn't have much fun, did you?" I asked.

"Nope."

"Margot and Bou had a week of love by the sea, left you on your own. I should've been there. You and I could've cheered each other up."

He didn't answer. He didn't need to. I understood why Bou

had been so distant, and why Beck, remembering the trip, looked the way he did.

"Bou made me promise —" he said weakly.

"Don't worry," I interrupted. "I knew anyway. I won't tell her you said anything."

He winced. *Poor guy,* I thought. Then I looked out into the sunshine of the day and forgot all about him, Margot. I was thinking about you, me, and Bou.

Rosalyn gazes down at her daughter. She doesn't look up when I come into Postpartum, any more than she notices her aunt badgering her from the chair by the bed.

"Don't make her suck if she don't want to, honey. She'll come to it."

Rosalyn offers the nipple and waits. After a minute, the girl baby suckles with the monkey skill of the newborn. Rosalyn's eyes close. Her husband, Pete, stands with his arms crossed, staring out the window.

Nightmare was very much present in the delivery room this afternoon. The nurses remembered her from last week and groaned when she turned up again. She talked to an expectant husband, who told her that he was allowed in Delivery but wasn't going to go in because he feared the sight of blood. Nightmare came straight to me and said that if a man could be in the delivery room, she was sure a woman could. I explained to her that she wasn't the husband. She countered that Pete didn't want to watch, and that she was a healer. She took a laminated card, like a fake driver's license, out of her purse — Miss Candace Bettina Preston, Deaconess of the Mount Gillian Baptist Church in Arcola. She isn't a midwife. Mostly, she told me, the Lord makes use of her in cases of arthritis.

Joel came in to assist at the last minute.

"I can't hear a thing," he said quietly.

Together we found the fetal heartbeat, right where it should have been, a steady 110 low in the curve of Rosalyn's belly. Joel helped me place the external monitor. Once the ocean noises were coming steadily through the little speaker, we all calmed down. Then Joel had to go cover another delivery down the hall. He is getting better, there's no question about it.

Rosalyn worked hard. The delivery was squeaky tight. It had only been seventeen years since her own head had made the same journey. Nightmare's relentless praying didn't help anybody's concentration. If I had known she was going to call out *Lend us your strength, Lord* in time with her niece's groans, I wouldn't have let her in. But she isn't a Jehovah's Witness — Rosalyn signed the general consent form, which allows us to do transfusions. Her aunt can pray right in my ear with that paper signed.

"Just breathe for me now," I told Rosalyn.

She'd been working hard for about forty minutes. She looked at me, eyes fluttering, sweat popping on her forehead.

"You stay," she said.

The birth itself was fast. There had been three-plus meconium. Jennifer came in but she let me lead, the way she has the last couple weeks. I asked Rosalyn to stop pushing when the baby's head cleared.

"What are you doing?" Nightmare said, crowding the table. Jennifer, who hadn't dealt with her yet, shoved her back out of the way with one hip and went in with the suction. The shove was hard enough to make Nightmare grab a stirrup to catch her balance. She muttered something about a girl doing a woman's job. The scene was fast degenerating into your basic delivery room farce. She stepped closer, but not as close as she had before, and demanded again to know what was going on.

"There was poop in the water," I told her through my mask.

"There's nothing wrong with a little baby —"

"We like to clear the nose and throat before the baby takes its first breath."

Jennifer nodded that she was ready. I took my place and leaned over the table.

"Rosalyn. We're going to have this baby now."

I took on a calm, purposeful expression, and to my surprise, we did have this baby now. It was a girl. Kate clamped the cord, I cut it, and Jennifer took the baby. I cleaned Rosalyn up and waited for the placenta. Kate shouted out minutes. Jennifer returned the Apgars, which were fine.

"How you feeling, darlin'?" Nightmare asked Rosalyn. Rosalyn didn't answer. Jennifer showed her the newborn, and Rosalyn looked at the baby without the least interest. She waved a hand in the direction of her aunt.

"Here's your little girl," I said, when Nightmare was holding the baby.

"I wanted a boy," Rosalyn said flatly.

Her aunt traced the contours of the baby's face with her long fingers. In order to get her healer's license, she apparently hadn't learned about mother-child bonding in the first minutes of life. But then neither had Nadine Croft, who works Fridays and came from Nursery to get the girl. For a minute she and Nightmare fought crone to crone. Soon Croft prevailed.

"Watch you don't switch her with nobody," Nightmare called after her.

Nadine didn't even slow down.

Jennifer washed up and took off. Kate and I waited, but the placenta didn't descend. Rosalyn's uterus felt loose from outside. She was bleeding, a steady trickle. I sent for Jennifer and asked Kate to put an urgent order in at the blood bank, just in case.

"What's going on?" Nightmare demanded. I told her to sit down, and pointed to the chair across the room. Bill, one of the day nurses, came in and said he was to assist. Jennifer wasn't available unless I had a problem, even if I did have a problem. There was a crash C-section in OR, and Grant needed her.

"You're waiting on the afterbirth," Nightmare told me. She had never sat down.

Yes, I said. I explained to her that we were going to massage Rosalyn to try to detach the placenta.

"How old are you?"

I told her I was twenty-seven. Her frown deepened.

"If you have to go inside, you know where to go?"

I said I did.

"You just slip that sack off. Like —"

Rosalyn's aunt pushed her hand inside the sleeve of my gown. She pressed hard against my arm. I nodded, suddenly grateful for her presence.

Bill talked to Rosalyn while he massaged her. I asked Rosalyn's aunt why, since she knew so much midwifery, she hadn't delivered the baby at home.

"I never intended her to come," she answered bluntly. She nodded in the direction of the girl, whose eyes were closed. The hospital had been Rosalyn's idea.

When I reached for Rosalyn, she opened her tired eyes and looked me over, as if it were midnight and I'd just asked her for one more dance. Then she closed her eyes again, her lips tightening as I touched her.

It had been forty minutes since the delivery. With my left hand I pressed on her uterus, which had partially contracted down. Through her belly it felt like a catcher's mitt with a hardball in the middle of it. My right hand found its way up and inside. Rosalyn groaned.

"You'll be all right, honey," her aunt said from behind me. I didn't know which one of us she was talking to.

I had the whole placental mass in my hand. What was difficult, as usual, was just to wait. I held there, the uterus contracted around my hand like a big fist around my little fist. Miss Preston didn't understand.

"What you waiting for?"

I told her in a whisper. Suddenly she was beside the table, pushing Bill out of the way and holding a plastic bin over Rosalyn's face.

"Just what —" Bill said.

"Hush," she dismissed him. "Rosalyn, honey. Blow now. Fill this up."

266

Rosalyn blew. I felt a deep contraction, but nothing more. Rosalyn looked from her aunt to me. Why, her eyes asked, was I letting her aunt take charge, when she had come all the way to the hospital to have a real doctor?

"You're not trying," her aunt said. "Blow hard now."

Rosalyn looked trapped. She drew a breath, then drove it all the way out, her eyes rolling up. She blacked out.

"Bill, get that thing off —"

Then I felt my hand inside Rosalyn, the hand I had all but forgotten about, start to move. The membranes released, not all at once the way I had imagined, but in stages.

"It's coming," I said. Rosalyn's aunt lifted the bin from Rosalyn's pale face. The girl opened her eyes. I noticed for the first time the dozens of umbilical-cord blood-tubes scattered over the table and floor. It occurred to me only then that Miss Preston hadn't been carrying an empty bin of her own.

"I'll get the mess," she said.

She stooped to pick up one or two of the tubes. Rosalyn's uterus softened around my knuckles.

Nearly five now. This has been an interesting night. Jennifer keeps dropping by. The first time, at nine yesterday evening, I'm sure she's Kate bringing me either coffee or gossip, and I don't look up from the screen until she's right next to me. Jennifer says hi and disappears. The second time, at ten something, I'm still tapping away, writing about Rosalyn. I jump up to go work, but Jennifer tells me there's nothing to do. She's just come by to say hi again. She sits down and asks point-blank what I'm working on all the time. She knows I told everybody it's a letter, but she's heard rumors. One is that I'm doing a research project. Another is that I'm writing a report on conditions in the hospital for someone high up in the med school. She wants to know the truth.

I agree to tell her, if she'll admit she's been listening to Steve Tsintolas. Next week Joel and I are going to work our butts off with the skeleton crew for Christmas. I'm a Hebrew, and Joel's a Baptist turned Hindu whose sister and parents are going to Pensacola for the week, so he and I both volunteered to spend Christmas Day in Maternity. That means Jennifer and Steve will both be off, and therefore have had their shifts together this week.

She admits she's been talking to Steve about all my computer time. Then she surprises me by saying he's the one who guessed I was writing a report on OB for the med school brass. Creative of Tsintolas to try to turn Jennifer against me and at the same time not to give me credit for the research he thinks I'm doing.

I really am writing a letter, I tell her. Actually three letters — one to a woman I was in love with for a long time, one to my best friend who I hated for a few years, and one to a woman who was my other best friend, who I was kind of in love with, and who was the lover of the woman I was very in love with. That quiets her down. I keep my eyes on the window across the room, embarrassed to have said so much to someone I hardly know.

Jennifer tells me I did a good job with Rosalyn and her aunt. Bill told Grant how I'd handled things, and Grant said he wished I weren't leaving in two weeks. That's high praise from him, she says. Usually he can't wait to get rid of his fourth-years. That cheers me up. I thought he was ready to file a complaint about me after that ER fiasco.

Jennifer gets up to leave and says she'll only bother me if anything interesting happens. That was an hour and a half ago. After twenty minutes, Kate comes in with coffee and says she wants to gossip about me tonight. I say great, what don't I know? She says Pam says Jennifer's been hanging around with me. I say I know that, and Kate says did I know that last week Jennifer told Pam that her boyfriend out West had just broken up with her? No, I admit, but what about it? I say I'm just glad Jennifer doesn't believe the lies Steve's been handing her, that I was spying for the med school deans. Kate says Steve Tsintolas is a snake, even if he is a hard worker and good-looking. I never thought he was good-looking.

Then we talk about Kate's big pre-Christmas date with this physical therapist she met at traffic school. He's divorced like Kate, and has two kids, too. He and Kate went to Toys R Us and put big bucks on their cards. Then they went to Schwegmann's to shop for their Christmas dinners. Kate says the date was the most fun she's had since she doesn't know when. Then Pam calls her and she takes off.

I'm just closing my eyes, with my head on the table next to the keyboard, when Kate's footsteps come back. I look up and it's Jennifer. She says she's sorry for waking me, she just came by to ask me to come to her house for dinner next week. I say I'd love to. Neither of us knows what to say next. After a minute, Jennifer says the letter I'm writing sounds like a good idea. Maybe she should write one, too. Her boyfriend in Seattle just broke up with her, and she's a little confused. I say I'm sorry and pretend I don't know. She sits down and starts telling me about him. He's a chemical engineer at U. Wash. Before she gets very far, we're both called down the hall to Delivery.

I've got to hurry now. Wednesday, Tim Clinton rolled Monopoly dice to figure out who gets night duty on New Year's Eve. He claims that as me, he threw a six and a five. Low numbers were off, so I'm on. If he'd asked, I could have saved him the trouble. I don't mind working as long as I get computer time. I only have two weeks. I could use more than that. I'm off from the second through the fourth. Then I begin in ER, fondly referred to here as the New Orleans Gun & Knife Club. On Saturday nights there's one trauma team on knife wounds and another on gunshots. That's how many come in. We have to make sure the people who tried to kill each other in Desire Project and down on Rampart Street don't end up in Recovery together. If they do, they get right up and go for each other, tubes and all. There's no computer down in ER for me to play with, and I won't have any time anyway. So it's now or never.

I don't know for sure, but I feel like I'm getting somewhere. I've started sleeping again. I miss watching late-night movies, but I find that sleep improves my mood. I was beginning to make three ballet classes a week before the studio closed for *Nutcracker* rehearsals. Now I've even got a date. I suppose it's more like a work meeting than a date, but you never can tell. Am I jumping the gun? Jennifer only asked me to dinner, after all, a friendly gesture toward a colleague at the end of his sub-internship. She probably invites everybody over at the end of their stint. Kate will know.

Love Letter

Germaine's footsteps approached the door.

"Dan?" she called.

"Come in."

But she wouldn't, so I opened the door for her. There was Bou, Germaine as small beside her as a child.

"Fooled you," Bou said, propelling Germaine into the room. I cleared my books from the table and offered Germaine the chair.

"I asked Madame to come up and bother you," Bou said, which was at most half an explanation. Germaine's attitude was plainly visible in her eyes. A visit was all very well, but not on a morning when there was work to be done. And one should not simply be pulled along, an uninvited guest. There was no pleasure in such a proceeding, and no respect.

"You've seen Nathan," Germaine said to Bou five minutes later.

"I dreamt about him last night," Bou said in wonder. "He was cleaning Poppa's gun."

"What was he wearing? He was naked," Germaine answered when Bou hesitated. "Which?"

Again Bou caught her breath.

"The gun," Germaine said impatiently.

"The Weatherby."

"For birds." Germaine nodded, as if she'd guessed as much.

"Tonight he visits again. You will find him downcast. Do not be troubled."

She finished her tea and rose. She turned to Bou from the doorway.

"Put *serviettes hygiéniques* in your bag tomorrow." With her good eye Germaine indicated Bou's canvas sack. "You will menstruate heavily at dusk."

She left, her work shoes shuffling to the stairwell. Bou turned to me.

"How did she know he was naked?"

"You looked funny when she asked what he was wearing."

Bou gazed out the window, lost in admiration. *Heavily?* I thought. I cleared the table. Bou pensively finished off the marshmallows from Grandma Whitney's shipment, then came to the kitchen and kissed me. Her lips were sticky and sweet. I held back.

"Where were you last night?" I asked, reminding myself to stay angry. She was supposed to have come for dinner but didn't appear, and didn't even call until I'd been waiting an hour. I knew her surprise visit was an apology, and it occurred to me that Bou had brought Germaine upstairs to forestall this moment.

"I'm sorry," she said. "I was going to call, but I forgot. Pascal had a party for his brother who's just back from Japan. He's been teaching there for two years and —"

"Forgot?"

"That's awful, isn't it? I don't know what's wrong with me these days. I'm sorry. I won't do it again."

"Bou, I cooked."

The *choucroute garnie* I'd prepared had been fast and easy, and I had to work hard to keep an edge on my voice. Bou was more upset than I wanted her to be.

"I know you made something scrumptious. I was starving. Pascal only had noodle soup with seaweed. We didn't even get that until midnight. His brother turned out to be sort of Japanese. He's French, but he's just finished his military service over there. When he speaks he hardly moves his mouth at all. Pascal says it will wear off now that he's home. I meant to call you as soon as I got there. We played Shogi, this game. Ariane, Pascal's girlfriend, wouldn't get off the phone."

"It's all right."

Bou kept apologizing, tears in her eyes, as she stripped off her T-shirt, pointy shoes, socks, and drawstring pants. She climbed the refrigerator toward the loft in her panties. She was in a terrible state, as she had been the only other time I'd seen her since we'd all been back home.

"Bou."

I was as dressed as when she'd arrived.

"You poor baby. Let me help you."

She climbed back down and pulled my shirt over my head. But that wasn't what I'd meant. It was chilly in the studio, and I didn't necessarily want to lose the shirt. Madame Lafontaine was teaching a week of master classes in Geneva, and I was enjoying a warm, dry morning at home. I was going to be half-naked and sweaty all afternoon at Nanterre, where rehearsals had just started again.

"Are you all right?" I asked.

"I think so."

She knelt and removed my slippers and tube socks, lifting my feet one at a time. She pulled my pants down by the legs and, standing, picked me up and sat me on the fridge. I climbed to the loft and she followed.

"Why are you so nervous these days?"

"I don't know. It's all so new."

I lay down beside her.

"I'm not your only lover," I said, absolutely as casually as I could. "That must be strange."

Bou pulled me to her. She kissed my face all over. I felt foolish and small, like a kitten getting cleaned.

"Yes," she said. "But not bad."

I talked against the kisses.

"Please tell me," I said, "why you're so upset."

"Oh, you know."

She moved against me with a little sigh. But I didn't know. All I knew was that she was very confused.

"You shouldn't try so hard to please everybody," I told her. "We'll take care of ourselves."

She kissed me gratefully again.

"Please," she said, and we made love as always. But somehow it wasn't right.

"I'm sorry," I said. "I thought —"

"No, that's good."

I tried.

"That's nice," Bou said finally, which meant stop.

She stared up at the ceiling. I lay beside her, resting my head on her arm. I wished we hadn't climbed to the loft. Why couldn't we have just stayed below and talked? I asked her what had happened in St.-Raphaël. I thought if she told me about it herself, she might stop feeling like you and I were having a tug-of-war over her. I wanted her to know we could go on just the way we were.

"Beck told you," she said.

"Yes. But you didn't."

"Are you sure you want to hear it? You'll be jealous, you know. Anyway, it's over now."

"It is?" For the first time in forty minutes I must have looked cheerful and not just sympathetic.

"Didn't Beck explain that?"

"How would he know?" I asked.

Bou laughed as if I'd made a little joke. But how would Beck know whether you and Bou were lovers, Margot, now that we were all back in Paris? Beck didn't have any more idea than I did.

"He knows it's over," Bou said, cradling me in her arms, "because I told him it was over."

That didn't make a lot of sense. I was going to ask why she didn't just tell me, instead of telling Beck to tell me. In a way I was disappointed. I'd come to accept, during the long week since I'd woken Beck, that you and Bou were madly in love again. I knew you wouldn't take Bou away from me. But I also liked the thought that she'd been unhappy because she wasn't mine alone. I felt both ways at once. It was like being an intelligent, open person and at the same time an old-fashioned moron.

We made love again. This time we focused more on me. I was being rewarded, but for what I wasn't sure. I only knew that Bou was pleased with me.

"After a long siege of Mantua and the exhausting armistice negotiations with Pope Pius VI," Bou said, "Napoleon was on his way to Josephine, who had finally dawdled her way to Milan."

"Don't stop," I said.

"*J'arrive*, he wrote to her from Crema," Bou said. "*Ne te lave pas*."

"I don't get it. Stop."

"Silly," she said, not stopping. "He'd separated the Austrian and Sardinian armies and taken Turin. He and his wife — that's all she was then — had spent exactly one married night together in Paris before he'd left for Nice back in 'ninety-six. And they weren't really married. It wasn't until the coronation that they got the paperwork right."

I squirmed and tried to think.

"What's a Napoleon complex?"

"A sense of inferiority due to a perceived lack of physical or social stature, compensated for by a will to dominate. This is completely different."

"Completely."

"This is the young Napoleon's desire to possess the older Josephine outside of time."

"How often did women," I said, evading her briefly, "how often did they wash back then, anyway? Didn't they just put on perfume?"

"Goof. That was Queen Elizabeth, about two hundred years earlier. She bathed once a month. Sometimes, when Sir Walter Raleigh was in town between plagues, she'd skip a month."

"Romantic fool."

"When Josephine was a kid in Martinique," Bou lecture-demonstrated, "she swam in the sea every morning with her father watching over her. At Malmaison a servant kept her bath hot from dawn until she woke. Three attendants scrubbed her with lemon pulp and rosewater. They soaked her hair in milk and rubbed it with liquor of ambergris. Until the afternoon, she wore a vermilion turban."

"She was clean," I managed.

"He immediately grasps the heart of the matter," Bou said.

To be Bou's lover was enough for me. I didn't need to be the only one, or to be more than what I was. I could have lived like that for years, being with her sometimes, thinking about her sometimes.

Brother Enemy

"I know she's home," I told Paola and Joseph. "Her paper's due tomorrow morning."

"Is the apartment far?" Joseph asked.

We'd seen the *tarif réduit* show at Cinéma George V, and I was feeling left out. I wanted to visit Bou so it would be four of us, two couples, if only for a few minutes. Joseph wanted to say a quick goodnight and whisk Paola away.

"It's a fine evening for a walk," Paola said, settling the matter.

We crossed the Champs-Elysées and circled on Rue de Presbourg. We passed the crystal façade of the restaurant Sir Winston Churchill.

"Dan," Paola said. "Select a jewel for Bou. I will choose one of my own."

She pulled Joseph and me to the window of Tresoro on Victor Hugo. But the velvet finger stands held no rings, and the hollowed sea stones, no diamond brooches.

"Pick two," Joseph said to Paola, giving me a nudge.

"You see? She's expecting me."

I pointed above Rue Berlioz to the dim shadows cast by the candelabrum.

"Come up in five minutes," I told Paola and Joseph as I crossed the courtyard.

I knew Bou was working at the high desk with its broken roll-top, the outsized French typewriter humming away like a little generator. The spare key was under the vase in the hall. Beyond the door, Coltrane was playing, an unusual choice for Bou. I knew you were at Zubir and Zohra's for dinner.

The typewriter on the desk wasn't humming. I tiptoed down the hall, deciding I'd kiss Bou awake from her nap. I could picture her smiling sleepily up. Then I thought, *No, she'll be frightened.* In fairy tales, the princess opens her eyes and falls in love with the handsome prince who wakes her. In real life, women scream while their hearts and lungs race in fight-or-flight adrenaline response. I decided I'd quietly call to her from the bedroom door, which was a crack open.

A candle burned in the brass holder. Beck, in his propeller boxers, leaned from the foot of the futon to reach a box of those florentines from the Chocolatier Tanty. For a split second I wondered whether he was going to bring a few home or was planning to finish them off. Bou was flipping through an Italian *Vogue,* a wineglass on the table beside her. Jason's blue flannel shirt didn't look big on her.

"What," she said.

"It's okay," I said.

Beck pushed himself up and pivoted to adjust the volume of Bou's Christmas stereo.

"What," Bou said again.

I opened the door further and nodded to her, meaning *It's okay* again. Frowning, Beck raised a florentine to his lips, but didn't bite it. He looked like a sea lion, lazily rousing himself to defend or abandon his rocky shore. A smaller male had approached, but Beck wasn't at all interested in getting up. He pursed his lips, trying to summon the energy to explain the situation in which he found himself. He unpursed his lips and lowered the cookie.

"It's okay."

"What."

We were suspended there, me saying *It's okay,* Bou answering *What,* Beck raising and lowering the florentine. I wished, with my words, to indicate that nobody needed to take any specific action. But was Bou's *What* part of a question or of an answer? *What* what? I wanted to ask her. But there was no time.

I retraced my steps. It was as if I'd found a bomb somewhere in the apartment, but failed to disarm it. I negotiated the ironing board in the hallway, perimetered the living room where Bou wasn't writing her paper. It wasn't until I gently shut the apartment door behind me that I realized I was walking high on the balls of my feet, as if I'd just finished the hundred meters and was waiting for my calf and thigh muscles to stop trying to wing me off the gravel.

Paola and Joseph were necking on the landing below. I took Paola's arm and led her back down to the ground floor. There was the bomb, we must evacuate, I would explain later. That was my attitude. I ignored Joseph's irritation and Paola's confusion. Calmly, without giving either of them a chance to turn around, I led them back across the courtyard.

"Did you surprise —" Paola started to ask.

I turned and hugged her outside the gate. I held my breath while my eyes burned. After a moment Joseph's long arms wrapped around both of us. Then we made our way to Malakoff and the métro.

Paola and Joseph thought that you'd been up there, Margot. They imagined I'd stumbled upon you and Bou making love, and that this was yet another chapter in the confused melodrama of the Americans' relationships with the semidetached Bou. I let them believe that.

In the station entrance on Grande Armée, Paola held me once more. French people coming off the top of the wooden-stepped escalator walked carefully around us, especially when Joseph picked us both up against his chest.

"Eh, Dan," he told me when we were back on the ground. "You'll see. It's better this way."

His eyes sparkled under the tunnel lights. He gripped my hand.

"Better to know now," he repeated, "before you have given her everything."

Whatever Joseph was alluding to, Paola knew nothing about

it. That was clear from her expression. I knew he was talking about the woman in Le Havre who had been his fiancée back when he'd been engaged to be a truck driver.

"We must accompany Dan home," Paola said. "He should not be alone until he is tranquilized."

I looked at Joseph. He steered Paola downstairs toward their train.

"No. He must make a decision."

"But he is in disequilibrium," Paola told him, looking helplessly back at me.

"Go on," I said.

Halfway down the long flight of stairs, Paola began posing Joseph not one but a series of pointed questions.

Wolf Boy

I waited across Berlioz under the roofed doorway of number fourteen. The light in your bedroom window was tinged cherry by the curtains. Tears came and went, and afterwards the night cooled my cheeks. Beck didn't appear until after midnight. I'd planned to let him walk through the gate, then step out of the shadow and charge him.

He shuffled across the cobblestones, his trombone case in one hand, his saddlebag against his hip. He was talking steadily to himself. He wore his smoking jacket and had his safari hat tipped far back on his head, which gave him an Australian look. I didn't want to knock him down. I had to stop myself from calling out his name and asking him to come and wait with me. But wait for what? His own arrival?

He closed the gate and plodded away. The numbness that had carried me from the métro back to your apartment had given way to an ache that one moment was in the middle of my chest, the next in my throat. I wished more than anything else, as I climbed your stairwell, that I had a lemon Italian ice from Fast Break Pizza on Westcott Street. I'd scrape the first wooden spoonful out and lay it far back on my tongue. Then I'd be all right.

I climbed to the third floor. The apartment door, scuffed at boot level, asked me what I was doing in front of it again. I knocked and Bou answered, looking frightened. She wore your blue terry robe. It reached her thighs.

"Dan," she said, embracing me carefully, as if I were bandaged.

I followed her to the chaise.

"You know what Mam said to me once? *I don't know how men find the time.* She was talking about Tom Lautner, who had just left his wife, Rusty. Their son Dylan was in fourth grade with Jason. Rusty found out Tom had been seeing Mrs. Prine, who groomed their Airedales, for six years."

I settled into the curved end of the chaise. Bou leaned against the back. She rubbed my feet. She looked calm now.

"Mam meant only a man could consider it fun to undertake something as exhausting as being with two women at once," she said, "let alone at a pet salon. She told me that having Jason and Nathan in the house was already like carrying on two affairs under the roof she shared with Poppa. The last thing she could imagine herself sneaking around after was another lover. She said she might find a secret hideaway where she could go to be alone, even if she had to lie that she had a dentist's appointment or whatever, but not a place where some other man would be waiting for her."

"When was this?" I asked.

"I was five. I was her confidante."

There was a smear of chocolate on Bou's thumb from a florentine. When I looked at it, I felt an invisible hand tightening around my larynx. I looked into her eyes.

"Mam was my best girlfriend," Bou said. "But Poppa, I'm afraid, was another story. I wanted to steal him away from Mam so bad I kept making maps of where we could go together. Mam still has them. I thought Poppa and I would be in the clear if we could make it to Guyana. Jason and Nathan were as clever as I was, trying to swipe Mam from Poppa and each other."

"Did they make maps?" I asked.

"Nathan built a house for him and Mam in the attic. He modeled it after the bomb shelter but added a few amenities, such as extra pillows. He kept insisting there was only room in it for him and Mam. Jason told him the attic was the worst place during a bombing. Then Nathan would get a shifty look in his eyes, because he knew he was planning to take Mam up there when there wasn't any war."

"That would leave you with Poppa and Jason."

"Exactly. That's why I helped Nathan find pillows. I was desperately in love with Poppa. I could tell he was struggling, too."

I took her hand and pulled her toward me. I licked the chocolate from her thumb. I loved her more than ever. I felt as if she and I had been through a tough time and now we were sure of each other again.

"I can't even see straight," Bou confessed. Beck had left half an hour before, I showed no signs of moving, and Zubir would be giving you a ride home in an hour or two. I was sympathetic, but I still took Bou's other hand and pulled her closer.

"How are you?" she asked with quiet emphasis, her hand on my chest.

I couldn't think what to say. I closed my eyes for a minute. Then I told her about the lemon Italian ices, how after DanceWorks rehearsals for our big February performance, even on the coldest nights, I'd pick up a cup on my way up Westcott and finish it at home in front of Letterman. She didn't see the connection.

"No, I mean . . ."

I looked at her. She was so glad, still, in her body, the way she always was after lovemaking. And she and I hadn't made love.

"I feel," I said, and then noises came from me. I was crying but also making sounds that weren't my own, yelping calls such as a wolf boy, raised in the wild, might have made. Bou kissed me. My yelps became whimpers and then, blissfully, human sobs.

"Do you want to go for a walk?" she asked gently. I nodded. She led me to the bedroom. I sat on the floor. Bou collected clothes from around the room. I was still making noises, and I listened to myself with tentative pride. I'd always imagined my emotions were locked deep inside me where even I couldn't find them. I was wrong. There they were.

I concentrated on breathing. Just when I thought I'd made it, a new set of sounds surprised me. My chest rose and fell in waves. Bou knelt next to me and held me tight. I let my sobs overtake me so she could feel them. She stroked my hair with both her hands. When I was quieter, she finished dressing. We didn't talk until we were outside.

We walked in the direction Beck had taken. Through my tears, the night was too beautiful. The clouds, tinged with lavender by the city light, hung in an eggshell sky. At the turn of Berlioz and Marchand, the street lamp shone through the palmate stars of the horse chestnut leaves, turning each a dusky salamander green. Locust trees waved before us like undersea plants.

I was happy. Bou was completely mine for the first time in weeks. Every few feet I stopped and let her kiss the tears from my cheeks.

"I'm so sorry," she said. Her voice freed new tears. I prayed they would never stop. My happiness was in proportion to my pain. I understood that, and chose it all.

"You know I love you?" Bou was asking. I did. We were starting over. I was so sure of this I stopped weeping, and all of a sudden Bou started.

"Why did you —"

"I don't know," she quavered. We sat on the yellow bench of the bus shelter on Malakoff. Spasms shook Bou's long body. "When I thought I was pregnant. In St.-Raphaël. We —"

"Shh."

"I want to tell you. We were in St.-Raphaël and I thought I was pregnant. Beck and I took a long hike down this beach made of smooth stones."

I watched her lips but didn't listen. She was saying something about Beck.

"We watched the little waves and smoked a joint. We talked about you. Beck said you take care of him. He told me you two are like brothers."

She was speaking plainly, but I couldn't concentrate. Beck had praised me beside the Mediterranean. I held her head in my hands and she closed her eyes for a moment. She opened them and they were the color of campfire smoke.

"We hiked up until we were off the stones under some trees. We were fooling around the way the four of us do, but there was just him and me. One minute it was a wrestle. The next it wasn't."

I reached with my thumbs and wiped two tears from her cheeks.

"You and Beck?"

I thought she must be talking about you and her, Margot. You two had become lovers again. Beck had explained all that to me.

"I never thought I could take Beck seriously," Bou said. "But he was a different person."

"Hmm?"

"He changed. The way someone you know as a friend changes when you . . ." She looked down.

Slowly, working backwards, I thought about what she'd been telling me. She and Beck had been together already in St.-Raphaël. When I'd surprised them that night, it wasn't the first or the only time they'd been together. I took my hands from Bou's head, first the right, then the left.

"He's such a baby," she said, "and so strong at the same time."

I studied her as packets of information began to fall into place. The day Beck had slept so late and been so miserable, he'd been trying to tell me that he and Bou had fooled around. He'd decided, or been told by Bou, that he should tell me about that. But he couldn't do it.

"I'm not in love with him, but I could be."

I saw now why Bou had been proud of me the morning

she'd come over and surprised Germaine and me. That day she'd thought I was such an open, unpossessive guy. I'd told her, or she'd thought I'd told her, that Beck and I had talked and that everything was all right.

"He feels awful. He thinks he's taken me from you. I keep telling him I can't be traded like an old car. He doesn't get it."

My eyes were completely dry.

"I told him you and I were fine. I said he'd just have to believe that. But he keeps acting like a criminal."

That son of a bitch, I thought. Not only hadn't he told me what had happened, he hadn't admitted to Bou that he'd been too scared to do it.

"We decided to be friends again, but you know how that is. It's hard to forget —"

"How good it feels?"

Bou's face closed all at once. Her lips pressed to lines. I thought she was going to stand up and leave me there at the bus stop. For one brief moment, I didn't care. But she drew a deep breath and took my hand.

"You're angry again. Margot said you wouldn't just stop being angry."

"What does Margot have to do with this?"

"She said I had a responsibility to tell you what had happened. That you'd have to make your own choices."

She nodded, as if that covered it.

"That's why I was glad," she went on, "that Beck told you about it. He didn't want to at first, but I thought it was better that you two talk."

"Beck didn't tell me shit."

She looked puzzled.

"He didn't tell me you two had slept together. He said you and Margot were lovers again."

"Damn it," Bou said. "Why are you two always talking about me and Margot? Margot and I don't need —"

"What?"

"Don't need you two always talking about us."

She looked past me toward Grande Armée. Her hand in mine was as cold as a trout. She drew it away. We glared past each other.

"Since you've been back, have you and Beck —"

"Not till tonight. We were just going to talk. Beck wanted to —"

"I don't give a damn what Beck wanted."

I didn't ever want to see him again. I'd trusted him. Bou had never told me she wouldn't sleep with anyone else. She'd told me just the opposite. But I gave Beck none of the leeway I granted Bou. Brother, my ass. Beck was my enemy.

We stood and walked toward the tower of the Concorde building, its radio antennas bristling into the sky.

"Do you still want to sleep with him?" I asked casually. I was better at this than I would ever have believed. Bou drew back to see me in the streetlight. I looked her right in the eye.

"I don't think it's a good idea."

"No?"

"Margot says there's a fragile bond between you two. She says you and Beck aren't sure of the nature of your friendship."

I nodded as if this weren't complete bullshit. We walked away from the sea smells of the brasserie.

"She says that you two treat my body," Bou told me, glancing down at it walking along in its billowing blue pants and T-shirt, "as a battlefield."

We both smiled.

"She does?"

"Yup."

"What else?"

"She said if you two weren't dickheads, this experience might bring you closer."

"Closer?"

How could Beck and I become closer through loving Bou? Beck had lied to me and stolen my girlfriend. That was the way I saw it. I forgot for the moment that Bou was your girlfriend, or no one's.

"Men use women as shields. Also as weapons. She thinks that I could be a kind of bridge between you two."

Bridges, weapons, shields. I didn't know why you and Bou were confusing a simple question of right and wrong with all of military history. But I knew what I was expected to say.

"She's right," I said. "Beck and I are acting like idiots."

I tried to look thoughtful. I had to prove that I was open-minded. Bou and I walked slowly up to your gate. She said she was tired. I pretended that I didn't mind, that I didn't expect to come upstairs even for a few minutes, and that I wasn't waiting for her to tell me that she loved me, too, and would never again be unfaithful to me.

"I'm glad we talked," I said instead, as if we'd cleared up a minor misunderstanding. "I feel better."

Bou said she felt better, too, but she looked a little impatient.

"What's going to happen now?"

"I don't know," she said.

We kissed, but our mouths and our hands were still estranged. I was about to explain that there were three simple rules that she could follow if she didn't want to hurt me again. All she had to do was not think about anyone but me, not touch anyone but me, and come live with me as soon as she left Paris.

"We'll be all right now," I said instead. "You'll see."

Bou crossed beneath the budding linden tree, her shirt glowing, her harem pants flapping like a flag.

Last night I was trying to find Jennifer's house on Millaudon
Street when I heard Joel's soft voice.

"Dan," he said, walking up behind me. "I'd like you to meet
Tamara."

In her cream-colored suit and highlight perm, Tamara looked
like a grownup. She and Joel had started going out at the
end of high school, before he discovered meditation and she
started making money. I was so busy trying to reconstruct their
high school selves, I forgot for a moment we were all outside
Jennifer Sandler's house on a Wednesday evening.

"Are we late yet?" Joel asked. He, too, looked his age. His
hair was in a neat ponytail and his pants were pressed.

"What?" I said. I was pretending I just happened to be in
the neighborhood. I didn't even know if Jennifer had turned in
my evaluation yet.

"No, we're about right," I said when they kept looking at me.

That was when I realized that my dinner with Jennifer was
hardly a date. Joel had been invited, too, and probably the
other fourth-year, Steve. We walked across an organically neglected lawn and found the house number behind a camouflage of wisteria.

"Come on in," Jennifer greeted us. "Marx, get your butt out
of the way."

Marx, an Irish setter, stood right in the middle of the hall like
an old-guard Communist halting reform. Jennifer walked back
to the kitchen and we followed. Damn it, I thought. I'd blown

this little dinner invite all out of proportion. It was just a work party.

"Steve can't make it," Jennifer said, climbing a stepladder. "He's finishing a project." She searched through a cupboard and tossed me a bag of tiny alphabet pasta.

"It wouldn't have anything to do with ritodrine, would it?"

"I think it might," she said, climbing partway down. "Did he tell you?"

"We threw around a few ideas," I said to the back of her knees.

She handed me about fifteen linguine, which had been leaning all by themselves in a huge jar. She jumped to the floor, took the linguine back, and added them to a steaming pot. Then she emptied in the miniature alphabets and tossed the empty bag back on the counter with three other bags of pasta that had already been scrounged.

"Steve's a worker," she said with almost inaudible mockery.

I sat down with a smile on top of my frown of disappointment. Steve had gone for my research bait with Pavlovian gusto, just as Marx did now when Jennifer offered him the ricotta stuck to the plastic carton. That Steve was downtown almost made up for the sad truth that Jennifer considered me just another of her little students.

She layered the motley pastas with tofu, creamed spinach, ricotta, shaved parmesan, sauteed green peppers, onions, and mushrooms. She described what she was making as lasagna, which she didn't season so much as sow, creating an aromatic green cloud of dried herbs. Tamara pointed out a trifle smugly that Joel wouldn't be able to eat the dish because of the milk. Jennifer shrugged and opened another of the kitchen's enormous cabinets. It contained an arsenal of powders, grains, rice crackers, pills, and juices.

"Everybody," she said. "Doug."

For a minute I was sure she meant the cabinet itself. But it turned out that a muscular man had just entered the room barefoot. He was one of Jennifer's housemates, and he offered to fix Joel up with whatever macrobiotic brew was going to be his own dinner. They talked germs and grams for a while, until they agreed on an appropriate sludge. Then Doug led us out the back of the kitchen to an enclosed patio, where he lived in a hammock and carved sculptures out of huge bald cypress and black willow stumps, using power tools. He hauled the wood out of the bayou, by hand probably. Then he imposed just a hint of form on them and gave them modest titles, such as *Study in Line and Circle III,* a ten-foot octopus of shining red root.

Jennifer settled against Doug's side while he explained his vision. *Fine,* I thought, *rain on my parade.* Jennifer didn't need me. She had a dog, a Doug, and could cook. Her life was complete. I decided I'd tell Kate that she just wasn't my type.

We had time while the lasagna baked. Jennifer led us out the side door through a maze of overgrown catalpas. We walked the deserted streets to Audubon Park, where Marx had more friends in one square acre of squashed lawn than I'll have in my entire life. He moved from acquaintance to acquaintance, sniffing rears, then noses, wagging his brush of a tail, and smiling an Irish setter's smile, full of Marxist charm. Jennifer wandered after him, brandishing a well-chewed Frisbee. She threw it at him, but he didn't catch it once, not even when no leap was involved.

She talked to half a dozen other doggy mothers and fathers while their grossly mismatched animals copulated and defecated. Watching her, I liked her too much again. It was the way she corrected Marx's social behaviors, with the curt efficiency of a single mother. She spoke one-word commands to him, softly knuckling his head when he ran to her moaning for affection. She looked faintly Asian in the dusk. Her eyes narrowed when she smiled, and her lips rounded into a geisha bow. I had no choice but to imagine kissing her, the nape of her neck held in my palm. Meanwhile, I was talking to Tamara about the pilgrimage she and Joel were planning.

"We'll visit Gandhi's birthplace at Porbandar, then the Circuit House in Ahmadabad," she told me.

Jennifer was wearing her hair down, another new and unfair advantage. I'd never seen her hair, except tied back under hospital light. It was the color of caramel over ice cream.

"Can't you get him to go anywhere fun?"

"Singapore," Tamara said, "on the way home."

"What's in Singapore?"

"Electronics and silk. Tailors."

"Good," I told her. "Don't let him turn your vacation into a quest for boredom."

Jennifer threw the Frisbee to an adolescent cocker spaniel who could catch. She tried to get Marx to study this, but Marx had no ambitions as an outfielder.

"We're going to Benares, and then out to Sarnath to see the Deer Park," Joel chimed in. "Then we'll head up to Hardwar for eight days of meditation and ritual baths."

"Is it cheaper if you just meditate?"

"He's kidding, honey," Tamara said, pulling Joel's arm. Joel gave me his patient, Colonel Sanders smile. I looked past him.

Jennifer was lying on the ground, with dried grass and magnolia leaves all over her sweater. She scoured Marx's chest with her nails. He played doggy air guitar with his hind legs, and sang a groaning song of love.

The other housemates, Mitch and Karen, arrived home during our dinner. Their son, Ted, was ten months old and looked just like Yul Brynner — pointy ears, Mr. Clean head, penetrating blue eyes. Except for *Excuse me*'s and *Oh, that looks good*'s, his parents politely ignored Jennifer and the rest of us. They did both have extended chats with Marx, I noticed.

I was still determined not to let my feelings about Jennifer get out of hand. On the way back from the park, I'd almost been able to stop wanting to touch her. In the middle of dinner she grabbed Ted, set him on me, and fed him a jar of vegetable chicken followed by a dessert of crushed banana and milk. He pointed his spoon at me while I was making my largemouth bass face. Then he pointed straight at Jennifer. *Great,* I thought. *He knows.*

After his meal Jennifer burped him by putting him on the floor and crawling all the way around the house with him. They made a big circle from the kitchen down the front hall, then left through the parlor out of sight. I could hear their progress through the TV room, but nothing more. I was wondering if I'd ever see either of them again when Yul butted through the swinging door across the kitchen from me. He put on an impressive four-legged sprint straight under the table, Jennifer half a length behind, both of them giggling madly.

"Watch, Ted," Mitch told him sternly. He pulled his son from his sanctuary by his left leg, heaved him into the air, then set him on my lap. Everyone set Ted on my lap. "It's time for walking," Mitch said. "Walking, as opposed to crawling."

He demonstrated a few robotic toddler steps around the kitchen. Ted shrieked and pointed at Jennifer with an invisible spoon. *Why walk when I can crawl with her?* was obviously his point. I could only agree.

Jennifer deep-sixed the dishes into a crowded sink of gray water. She said Doug would wash them on Friday — it was his week. Joel and Tamara said they ought to be going. In a last-ditch effort to remain peacefully isolated in my self-contained reality, I attached myself to the broker-fakir couple as they headed for the door. My strategy was that of a bike racer drafting the leaders until he makes his final breakaway. I followed Joel and Tamara halfway across the lawn, then went for broke. "Goodnight," I said, and just walked. I made it across the weeds and all the way to the Corolla. I had my crush subdued, if not crushed. That was when Jennifer caught up with me.

She took my arm and led me back across the lawn and up two flights to her bedroom. *Oh well,* I thought.

Her bed had the sprung buoyancy of a '57 Chevy Bel Air back seat. We sat on it while we went through a thick album of mostly loose photographs. Jennifer's ex, the Seattle chemical engineer, looks a lot like Superman. I nodded noncommittally over the dozens of shots of him and Jennifer conquering mountaintops in the Northwest. I tried to make it clear that while I wasn't fond of chemistry, I was sure I could have mastered the field if I'd put my mind to it. I also wanted it understood that though I'd never climbed a mountain that required the use of crampons and such, I could probably do that, too.

At last we cleared the ex away. We started on the two hundred or so photos of Jennifer's family in Milwaukee. On top were an older sister and brother and their spouses, all in their thirties, and three nieces and nephews, just out of diapers. Further in, at about twelve years back, a Marxlike dog appeared between single, twenty-something versions of Jennifer's sister and brother. The dog, not Lenin, but Max, had died while Jennifer was away at college.

By this time we were lying down under a blanket of photos. We dozed for a while. I woke up just after midnight and maneuvered myself off the wobbly bed. Jennifer made a snuffling noise, squinted at me, and either smiled or wet her lips. I'm hoping both.

Marx, in his capacity as butler, escorted me downstairs to the door.

I don't know what to think. Did Jennifer and I have a date, or was I just the last one to leave the work party? All I'm sure of is that I'm going to call her when I get home tonight. I checked the schedule, and we don't work together anymore. That makes it easy for us if she wants to go out. If she doesn't, that makes it easy for her to say no.

She said yes. My excuse for calling her just now on company time was that I wanted to report good news. I heard the nurses talking this morning about a kid they delivered three weeks ago, who screened positive for PKU. Today we got the assays back from the metabolic lab. Phenylalanine and tyrosine, both consistent with hyperphenylalalinemia secondary to transient tyrosinemia. I asked them if Jennifer knew about the kid and they said she did. I called Jennifer, and she thanked me for thinking of her and said she had been worrying.

Before I could ask her if she wanted to get together, she said she wants to take Marx to the swamps on Sunday. She wondered if I might like to come along.

I told her I believed I would, Margot.

Exit With Bone

"Where you going to live?" I asked Beck.

"Zubir's," he said.

"You can stay here."

He didn't answer. He hadn't been home in a week. When I called Berlioz, he was always there. Sometimes I heard the honk of his horn, other times the bray of his voice. The two sounds were curiously similar, as if Beck's instrument had learned to talk and his voice to play. *Life is fine over here,* one or the other was always saying in the background. *I'm eating well, drinking lots of wine, and sleeping quite comfortably, thank you.*

"Let me have Zubir's number in case Brian calls. I told your mom to call you at Berlioz yesterday. Did she reach you?"

He didn't answer. Was Beck living at your place? He was there when I called after ballet at twelve-thirty. He was there at dinnertime, when loneliness overcame me and I made my second call to beg Bou to let me come over. Every evening for a week she'd said she needed more time. She didn't want to see me with you and Beck around. He was still there at eleven or even midnight, when I made my third call. You understood how hard it was for me to limit myself to three, but Bou was impatient, probably because I wouldn't let her get off the line and kept making her tell me she loved me.

"Beck, there's no reason you can't stay here."

"You'd like that, wouldn't you?"

Bou wouldn't admit that Beck was living there. Did he sleep on the couch? On the low bed with you two? I didn't mind that, but I couldn't think of him alone with Bou. Now he was packing to move in with you for your last week in Paris. I was sure of it, but I had to hear it from him.

"I know you didn't mean to hurt —"

"You don't know anything, Dan. You never did, and I doubt you ever will."

"I don't blame you for what happened."

"Listen. You have a perfect right to try, and I emphasize *try,* to beat the living crap out of me. But don't preach to me."

"Why did you come here if you don't want to talk?"

"I'm packing. Zubir's picking me up."

Only one fact confused me. If Beck had come from Berlioz and was going straight back with his stuff, why had he brought his bone with him? Maybe he really was moving to Zubir's.

"I don't hate you."

"You do."

Truthfully, I didn't know anymore. For two days after I'd found him with Bou, I'd been sick with rage. But then I started brainwashing myself. My premise was that I was still with Bou. This meant that Beck wasn't a serious threat to us. From that ridiculous conclusion, it was a small leap to the idea that I should forgive him.

"We can live here together until June," I told him. "Then we'll both leave."

He didn't look up. He was trying to cram all his cassette tapes into his three biscuit tins. I pointed to the suitcase, where his trombone mutes and army boots were nestled into a collection of bowling shirts. There was a perfect spot for the extra cassettes.

"Please shut up."

I did, though I was just pointing. The man was unapproachable, which was ironic since I was the wronged party. I retreated to the loft and observed him from above. It was nearly seven and the sun caught him in a broad orange stripe. I decided to try the humorous approach. I had to get some information.

"This is the only way you can get to Zohra, isn't it?"

He hauled clothes out from under the cot.

"You're going to sneak into the women's quarters, or wherever she is out there in Maisons-Laffittes, like Ali Baba."

Beck tied up a pile of *Coda*s with twine. I tried to picture him with Bou. He wasn't ugly, simply Beckian, with that curious, sea-mammal strength of his. I could see how they'd fit together.

"Bou says you weren't going to meet her anymore. She says Monday was the last time."

"Shut. Up."

"Why?"

"You still haven't caught on, have you?"

"No."

"We're not buddies, Dan. Everything's over."

"That's not true."

Nothing had changed. I had to prove that to him and to Bou. If I could accept Beck, my banishment from Rue Berlioz would end. The second exile was much harder than the first one, in February, had been. Then, you had decided I should stay away, and had carefully explained your reasons to me. Now Bou postponed my return day by day, and there weren't many days left. When this banishment ended, I wouldn't be able to go back to Berlioz. Berlioz would be gone.

"I'm not saying I'm not angry," I said.

"You don't know what anger is."

"If you hadn't been trying to break it off, it would be different."

I couldn't talk for a while. My throat was constricted, my chest pounded. Beck was right. How could I still be with Bou, since I never saw her? Well, she did visit me every other day, but never for long enough. Beck kept packing. I slowly recovered the faraway land in which I dwelt.

"In three weeks," I said calmly, "we'll all be home. Bou and I will go up to New Hampshire —"

"Don't talk about Logs, Dan. I'm tired of hearing about that horse farm. The only real estate of Bou's you'll ever see is the patch between her legs."

"Get out," I said. "Now."

"I'm trying."

He stuffed all his laundry into a duffle bag. I climbed down from the loft.

"You're no different than I am," I told him. "You fell in love with her."

He wheeled to face me. "Like hell."

"Don't pretend you don't love her."

Beck turned back to his task.

"You'll never learn," he said quietly. "Luckily, she'll walk out on you. Otherwise you'd spend your whole life believing this nonsense."

"We'll work things out."

"Give it up, Dan. You're trying to follow Margot's credo in the secondhand form you've gotten it from Bou, but you've misunderstood. Margot's not talking about sixties-style, 'Here, take my chick for a ride in your love van,' orgiastic nonsense. Margot doesn't have the slightest interest in free love. Nothing about her love is free. Haven't you noticed how hard she works to be with Bou?"

He sat down on his duffle bag and pulled me down next to him.

"Listen," he said through his fingers, into the sun. "That woman is the only romantic I've ever met. She's not a sentimentalist. She's not a voluptuary. She's simply convinced that two people can become so intimate that they no longer distinguish between each other's pleasure."

I was sitting on one of Beck's boots. I shifted closer to him. His bare legs poked, massive and orange-haired, from his cutoffs.

"Margot's been reading these linguists," he told me. "These gals make up words, put slashes and hyphens all over the place. They de-center. They don't play fair."

"Who?"

"The French, the Dutch, the Yanks. I've been reading these mommas all week. The ringleaders," he whispered, "have decided that feminine love is without the subject-object axis.

Feminine sexuality knows no borders. Feminine thought is within and without the body."

He hugged his knees. He looked frightened.

"What are you talking about?"

"I'm talking about you and me, brother. There's a growing consensus among enlightened women that we're not *comme il faut*. Those ladies want us out, big time."

"Margot doesn't —"

"No, not Margot. But who's to say she'll be in charge on revolution day? I'm afraid her role models are a little more hard-core. They've sent out invitations to the barricades, and danglers were not on the preferred list. *Tu piges?*"

I shook my head.

"It's payback," he said. "Siggy started it when he spread those hopelessly phallo-ontogenetic rumors. You know, that the joy button is a miniature trouser puppet, and that infuriating one about the hierarchy of orgasms. Ever since, women have been biding their collective time while they built their own theoretical apparatus. They've got it now, and they know just where to point it."

He held his hand to his forehead and smiled grimly through the sun at me, as if this were a moment we shared.

"New Woman will reach full psychosexual consciousness just about the time New Europe comes out of Maastricht," he told me. "Then it's bye-bye to Old Boy, with his network of enslaving impulses. Don't kid yourself. It's not as if you can take a refresher course and come out a spanking New Boy. Alas, your problem is right smack in the middle of your primitive brain. You just can't think right. You see lines, not circles. You work in binary, yes-no blinders. If you were a woman, you'd have a chance of discovering that meaning lies in the round, mobile play of *différence* and *désir*."

"Beck, I don't know —"

"You want Bou to love only you, don't you?"

I nodded.

"She's supposed to dote on you by day, light a candle in the window for you by night. She's to be your girl or nobody's, marriage or give me back my frat pin. All that's very, very binary."

He shook my arm, as if to soften the bad news.

"I'm afraid you're no more capable of change than you are of sharing Bou with me."

I straightened up and looked at him.

"You're not —"

"There you go again. You want to know whether I've been slipping it to her. How quaint. You're full of Superbowl fury just because I made a passing reference to the gal you love best. But can't you see, you pathetic, deluded, public-school putz, that you and I started going after each other a while back?"

He straddled the duffle bag to face me. He stroked his beard fuzz.

"I'll translate the situation into ethology, so you have a ghost of a chance of seeing it. You and I, we're two bighorn sheep on a panoramic mountaintop. We're rearing way up on our hind legs to slam our curling horns together until our peach-size, testosterone-swollen brains rattle around in our bony male brainpans like a couple of stale biscuits in a tin can."

Gently, he dropped his head against mine. It made a soft thunk. We settled deeper into the duffle.

"We've forgotten all about the woolly little mothers waiting back in the pasture," he murmured against my chin. "We're caught up in a frenzy of mutual self-destruction. We're ramming machines! Let's at least do it right."

He lifted his forehead off mine and studied my eyes from five inches' distance. When his head hit mine the second time, it made a distinct thwack. I frowned.

"Our job," he said happily, "is to crack skulls over Bou. You might ask why we should bother at this point, when the estrous cycle has pretty well played itself out and all good North American bighorns are migrating to the low country to hoover as much data as possible before the MCAT winter comes and freezes us into bald-assed oblivion."

"What about your TV? Do you want me to return it?"

"Exactly," he said. "We do it because there's absolutely no reason. We go for it, I exit, and we both preserve a shred of dignity. I know it's too late, both in the century and in the year. I know there's no place for a threadbare concept like honor in this ambiguity-riddled decade. But we'll do the best we can."

"Stay," I said. "I've got ravioli and —"

"It's too late," he told me. "I've wronged you. You'll realize that soon."

He stood impatiently and hauled me to my feet. I tripped over the duffle bag. He steadied me.

"You just want to fight," I said quietly, "so you can sleep over there."

"That's the spirit. You're close. You smell blood and semen. Your brain is steamy with territoriality. Give me your best shot." He closed his eyes and turned one fuzzy cheek to me, as if for a kiss.

"Have you been sleeping with her?"

He opened his eyes and frowned.

"What if I say yes? That would do it. All I have to do is give you a single seamy Polaroid of my robust form dominating Bou's sylphlike figure, and you'll clobber me."

He knelt and began arranging his chemistry books in one of the milk crates.

"I don't suppose it would suffice if I suggested that the three of us were all tangled together, nights, in a de Sade confusion? Why, only yesterday Princess Bou manipulated my gallant lingam with her jasmine-scented *mouchoir,* while with an outsized and conveniently handled espresso cup, I titillated Countess Margot's glorious yoni."

I ignored him.

"No, you won't go for one of those Twister-style, 'Gidget Goes to Babylon,' boudoir finales."

I found his Lehninger under a tangle of sheets and added it to the box.

"The only way for me to find the man in you is to tell you

I've been at Bou while Margot was in the tub, conditioning her hair. Something mundane."

He stood and pulled me up with him.

"Fine," he said. "I'm banging Bou regular as payday. I wait till Margot's out of the apartment. Sometimes I can't hold off that long. I bother her during dinner. Now hit me."

He stood in front of me, his eyes closed. The sun sparkled on his orange lashes. I knew, for the first time in eight days, that he wasn't sleeping with Bou.

I caught him under the eye so hard I couldn't straighten my thumb for a month. He didn't fall or even stumble. He just turned his head back to its original position from where my punch had rotated it.

"Crazy Jew," he murmured, opening one eye. "I had in mind a gentlemanly slap, not a bouncer's roundhouse."

Gingerly, he touched himself. I led him to the kitchen. We crowded together over the sink to look in the shaving mirror. As we watched, the left side of his face contused. After twenty seconds, his whole head was lopsided. Not a drop of blood flowed.

I held my fingers under the cold water.

Lasts

Rue Roubo had come undone in the spring sunshine. The windows of the plumber's shop were wide open. From the furniture refinisher's came the high whine of the jigsaw. At the corner, Madame Baranger's little potato sniffed suspiciously along the feet of the men drinking wine outside Les Trois Canards. Bou and I turned up Faubourg St.-Antoine. I hugged her tightly to my hip. This was to be our last walk in Paris before we met again in Massachusetts.

"George," I murmured. "Tell me about the Boutique."

"Once upon a time there were two branches," Bou said, her eyes in the middle distance. "The original Boutique, under the dining room table, was jointly managed by Monsieur Jim and Mademoiselle Cream."

"Cream?" I asked, peering into Pizza Carolina to see what sort of nonsense people had on their pizzas today. One woman had a six-inch stalk of broccoli. Her companion had a runny broiled egg.

"Jim created window displays and minded the register. Cream, who had the creamiest skin even though she was invisible, was in charge of Junior Fashion."

Bou looked tousled and lovely. I kept zooming in close until she blurred. Then I'd either kiss her or not kiss her, stand up straight, and wait for her to come back into focus.

"All the ladies lied about their sizes and Jim corrected them, but it didn't matter," Bou said.

"Because the only real clothes were Aunt Emily's hats," I finished for her.

We passed Jean-Pierre Mauduit's *boulangerie,* closed for Monday. I lay my head on Bou's shoulder and timed my steps carefully so I wouldn't get my ear banged.

"There wasn't much business downstairs after the first rubber, so we opened the second branch under Mam's desk at the top of the stairs."

"Under different management."

"Under the management of Monsieur Henry and Mademoiselle Emily."

"Emily?"

"Emily, Aunt Emily's make-believe daughter," Bou explained. "Because Aunt Emily doesn't really have any girls or boys. She isn't married."

"Why?"

"Oh, Lennie, you remember, because she's shy. Because she doesn't like to see people she hasn't known for a long time. The same reason she likes her cloches and *capelines.*"

We walked past the Hôtel des Pyrénées, thinking about Aunt Emily's low brims. Suddenly a flock of sparrows bounced down all around us like Rice Krispies hitting a kitchen counter.

"Mademoiselle Upstairs opened for the Christmas rush."

I didn't mind that Bou left out the description of the seventeen real hats, six of which Aunt Emily had designed herself, eleven of which she'd ordered from New York. Our bedtime story was already carrying us back to America.

"Once the game started, business was slow. Only Mrs. Saltonstall always bought the scarlet glass-cloth tambourine with the peacock eye, as soon as she started winning."

"Not with real money."

"No, but she made her point. The others forgot all about me once lunch was over. That was why I climbed to the second branch and grabbed their ankles when they were on their way back from the guest bathroom."

"At the very top of the stairs."

"It was a prime location," Bou admitted. "I wouldn't let go till they bought two items."

We waited for the light at Rue Paul Bert. Bou told me how, when bridge club disbanded, she locked up both stores and helped the kitchen maid, Barbara, set the table. At dinner, Poppa checked her accounting out loud.

"And after dinner he walkety-walked you on top of his shoes to the stable."

"And he brushed my big horse teeth and he put me in my stall, which was really my bed. You see?" Bou said proudly. "You do remember."

"And then Mam came up and kissed you goodnight, and left the door open just enough so that the light coming through it looked like a tree, except dark on the outside and light on the inside."

"An inside-out tree," Bou confirmed, as we stepped into the coolness of Faidherbe-Chaligny station.

The story ended. I could almost have fallen asleep, my head against Bou's shoulder, my feet already crossing the ocean.

Porte St.-Denis stood solid and noble in the sun, like a modest Arc de Triomphe. We walked Rue St.-Denis, pausing beside a mannequin store full of nude mannequins with elegant wrists. At the *boulangerie* on Rue des Petits Carreaux, Bou studied the coconut *tartes de l'île,* the dense *mirlitons* topped with toasted almonds, the raspberry *bavaroises,* and the lemon *tartes princesses* topped with browned meringue and powdered sugar. At last she turned her shoulder to all those and chose a two-level, chocolate-cream-filled *religieuse.* While the girl wrapped it we stood aside. Customers crowded past us to grab the last of the bread.

"Still nervous about Lincoln?" Bou asked. I kissed her gratefully.

"I don't think they'll like me," I said.

"They won't know what to make of you."

"Why?"

"Too earnest."

"I'm not earnest," I said earnestly. The bells on the door jangled beside my head.

"Oh, they'll like you once they get to know you. They'll pretend at first. They're very good. You'll never know."

We took the pastry and shared it as we walked Rue Réaumur.

"Does Mam know all about us?" I asked.

"She wanted to know if I have protection in case I want to 'go all the way.' She's trying to be very mod. I told her I was on the pill."

"You did? What about Poppa?"

"I don't think Poppa ever knew Mam was on the pill. Last Christmas he found Margot and me in bed and told everyone at the dinner table he'd caught us girls cuddling. Bess and my cousins were over. They giggled."

"Interesting. And Jason?"

"He kept eating."

Sunlight drenched us. High-revving French cars hurtled past as if engaged in an urban road rally. We built the idea of home.

"I'll caddy for Daddy and the boys," I told her. "That will pay for my nightly calls."

"I'll pay for calls," she said. "And planes."

"Deal."

We were almost to the corner of d'Aboukir when Bou stopped, cupped her hands to her eyes, and peered through the reflections into a shop window. I stretched my arms around her and propped my chin on her elbow. Together we chose her wedding gown.

We climbed halfway up the steps of the Bourse and sat. The crowd below swarmed between two French flags, one perched on the green, minaret-topped column plastered with posters, the other above the mouth of the métro 4 Septembre. I explained to Bou that we were currently having a last, or nearly last, conversation in Paris. There were an infinite number of lasts. The trick was to define things closely enough. A last conversation while walking in one place was different from one while walking somewhere else.

"So this makes you sad?" Bou asked. She was distracted.

"In a way."

There were the skies to take into account, I told her. I pointed out that this sky was slowly turning cotton-candy pink on the horizon, while the expanse above us was the blue of the enamel dishes Brenda used for our picnics in College Hill Park. There was wind out of the north at what I guessed to be about eight thousand feet, and though there was only the lightest breeze at ground level, cumulus humilis formations rushed past as if in an accelerated nature film. Bou nodded, but her eyelids were fluttering. All of this taken together, I quickly concluded, made the talk we were having into one particular kind of last, a conversation about lasts under traveling chromatically graded clouds. What I didn't know, and therefore didn't try to explain, was that this was our last last.

"You mean," Bou said, rousing herself, "this conversation is like a film where the character realizes she's in a film that she's watching?"

"Not exactly," I told her. She really hadn't been following at all.

"So what's about to happen in the film she's watching is about to happen to her?"

"I'm afraid not."

I wondered if I should start over. I decided that instead I'd explain the whole idea again in America. We could have the same conversation at Logs in the middle of June, except that we could talk about firsts, and of course the sky would be very different. I felt contented and empty of explanations. Then Bou wrecked everything.

"You really popped Beck a good one."

Below us on the sidewalk the French hurried past, shoes clattering, jackets open, as if they were fleeing the scene of a disaster.

"He said you two aren't going to see each other anymore."

I stared straight ahead while my face changed temperature.

The skin of my cheeks stiffened.

"What else did he say?"

"Nothing," Bou said, but then added cautiously, "He told Margot that you two duked it out when he came to get his stuff."

"I don't want" — I looked at Bou — "to talk about it."

Beck had been dead right, as always. Almost as soon as he'd left two days before, I'd begun to hate him. It was a sweet, new hatred, and I fell into it as if I were falling in love. After a single night, my passion was full-grown. It had been born the moment my fist connected with the side of his head. You see, Beck offered me himself as an enemy right when I needed one.

"He sits around chewing toothpicks and saying he could have been a contender. His bruise turned green yesterday."

"You saw him?"

"Sure. He was pretty funny. Well, Margot didn't think so. She's afraid you're going to hurt yourself."

"Let's not have a last conversation about Beck. Let's have a last conversation about another subject."

"You really did clobber him. He looks the way Nathan did when Jason hit him with an oar."

She picked up my hand, and I winced as she poked at the knuckles. I hadn't known I was going to slug Beck until I did. But in that one moment, blood began to sing in my ears. That music never left me all afternoon while I helped Beck pack. He didn't talk much, but I could tell he was proud of me.

"What set you off?" Bou asked in an artificial, breathy voice. "Was it about me?"

"This isn't funny."

I knew that Bou was more worried than ever that she'd screwed up my friendship with Beck. This was her way of trying to hide it. Still, she had no idea what her words did to me. She was a madwoman waving a loaded gun.

"Come on, Dan. Talk to me. Beck and I haven't slept together, if that's what you're thinking."

"Could we drop it?"

"Sure. You know what bothers me? I know you both blame all of this on me. I'm the loose woman who came between you two. That's what you think, isn't it?"

A broad-shouldered Cary Grant look-alike in a light blue suit made his way down the steps past us. He stepped through the spear-topped fence and fought his way through the crowd toward the newsstand.

"This is fundamentally about you two, you know that. Margot says that your fight had nothing at all to do with me. Dan, would you talk to me? Maybe you and Beck will be better friends now. When Jason hit Nathan, they didn't make up for four days, but then they went on a hiking trip to Pequawket Mountain and wouldn't let me go along."

I took Bou's hand in my stiff fingers and kissed it.

"Why did Jason hit him?" I asked.

I felt very powerful. Bou was right. In a way, I did want to talk about Beck and how I'd punched him. I just wanted Bou to say very specific things.

"Nathan called him a commie. Jason hated that. His politics were way to the right when he was in junior high."

"So Jason hit Nathan with an oar."

"Just a dinghy paddle. Jason thought the communists wanted to put Poppa in prison and make us all wear baggy uniforms. Nathan knew he was playing with fire when he called Jason a Red."

Her hand was long and cool. I held it to my cheek and kissed the white inside of her wrist.

"Beck just walked in," she said. "You came at him from behind the door. He never saw you coming."

"Exactly." I was trying reverse psychology.

"No, I've got it," Bou said. "Beck told you he was leaving you for another man."

Every time she said *Beck,* my cheeks tightened a notch. It was as if I were a kettledrum and Bou was tuning me, Beck by Beck.

"I don't want to talk about this."

I tried to kiss her wrist again, but she snatched it away.

"You do think I've done you wrong. You and Beck have it all figured out, don't you? You're the sensitive, faithful lover. I'm the promiscuous bimbo with no moral sense. Is that it? Are you two happy now?"

Her voice was all quavers. There were tears in her eyes.

"You're still trying to punish me," she said. "You won't stop, will you? I never wanted to hurt you."

I thought about this. She stood and walked, one foot at a time, down the steps of the Bourse. First she stepped with her left foot, then caught up with her right.

"I can't talk about Beck," I said.

She turned. "Are you going to hit me now?"

"No."

"Am I supposed to apologize again?"

"Bou, he told me to hit him."

"What?"

"He said," I mumbled, "that we'd both feel better."

"Feel better? Damn him. Do you know that he won't talk to me? He won't even look at me. He acts like I've got the plague. But he comes over to your place and invites you to belt him. You two are unbelievable."

She paced up and down a stone step.

"Margot was right. I'm just the girl you fight over. What I want, what I think, has no meaning at all. I thought Margot was reading things into this, but she's right. You two are bonding over me, becoming best friends."

Was Beck that bad? He must have been pretty cold to have made Bou so angry.

"Bou. We'll be back in the States in a week. We won't have to —"

"Worry about Bou's little moods? I'll be back where I belong then, with a boyfriend and my parents to look after me?"

"I didn't say that."

"That's what you think. Did Beck tell you that? Just get her home. Then she'll settle down."

"Forget Beck. I don't want to think about Beck. This is our last day." I held out my good hand.

"If you say one more thing about last days, I'm going to kick your butt."

"Sorry."

"You try to orchestrate every moment of life. Can't you just relax? You don't have to choreograph every minute we spend together."

"You're right."

"You're just saying that so you can have another perfect moment. You want me to come rest my head on your lap while you tell me what the sky is doing."

"Yes. Come lay your head in my lap. But first kiss me."

I closed my eyes. Bou's salty lips surrounded mine. I thought the argument might be ending, but when I reached out for her, she wasn't there. I opened my eyes and saw her headed for the street again, still taking the steps one foot at a time, like a toddler.

I meant to follow her. I was about to stand up when she stopped and looked around, as if at this late date she was considering establishing a third branch of the once prosperous Boutique Mademoiselle, right there on the steps of the treasury building.

"Hey," I called. "Come back here."

She looked up at me.

"I'm sorry, sweetie. Beck really has been treating me like dirt all week. I know it's not your fault, but I'm tired of it. I have to get to Pascal's."

"Now?"

"It's quarter of," she said.

"I'll come over tomorrow while you're packing. Margot said —"

"No. You're meeting Margot for coffee."

"That wasn't sure."

"Meet her. Don't come over. Let us close up the house."

She trotted quickly back up to where I stood, and kissed me again.

"So this is it?"

"Yes, you maniac. The last kiss on the last day in the last Paris, and all that."

I must have had a stricken expression on my face.

"Don't look so sad," she said. "It's only a few days."

"Seventeen."

She walked back down the steps, like an adult this time. I decided again to follow her. But I also decided to stay right where I was. I was determined, in a new, uncertain way, not to bother her the way I had been. I thought this was important if we were going to start out on the right footing back in the States. That's why, when I saw she didn't want me to escort her the few blocks to her goodbye dinner with Pascal and the other actors, I made up my mind not to impose myself. It didn't occur to me that I'd never see her again.

She reached the sidewalk and turned, one hand in the pocket of her black jeans. She waved and I waved. I remember thinking that she expected me to come with her after all. I waited for her side-to-side wave to turn into a forward-back, come-over-here motion. But it didn't. She turned and crossed the sidewalk. Everybody was going the other way, toward the métro. Bou's shoulders filled up Jason's yellow shirt. She made her way steadily upstream into the crowd. I stared after her like a bedridden child at a window. She waved once more, stalled at the corner of Rue Feydeau. I was about to follow her despite myself. I thought I'd made my point, and suddenly I couldn't stand to let her go without another goodbye. But Bou turned the corner, and I stood beneath swift clouds.

Jennifer picked me up at eleven on Sunday.

"Sorry about the delay. Marx was chasing tail."

Squirrels, she meant. His five-minute walk had turned into a half-hour hunt. Now he lay in the back of her Buick wagon on a pile of towels, rocking with the car's lazy turns. The car was a family castoff with Wisconsin plates and a loose interior roof that wobbled on bumps. Jennifer asked me why I lived way out in Terrytown. I told her that I'd taken my apartment first year, when I was too stupid to know better. I'd been intending to move to Dana's place for my last year. Then, when I graduated, I'd go north with her furniture, and we'd make a home together in Philadelphia. But in the end we'd broken up and I'd stayed in Terrytown alone. Jennifer nodded, and I knew she was thinking about her own changed plans. I remembered from the barrage of photographs I'd seen on her bed that she and the chemical engineer had shared a house in Madison, and they had probably planned to live together in Seattle.

We reached Lafitte just before noon. Jennifer put on a tennis hat, purple-lensed glacier glasses, and a pair of particolored hiking shoes. She led Marx and me down one of the trails, which were really boardwalks built across the marsh. Palmettos with scarred green arms stood guard at regular intervals over soggy ground, but the boardwalks gave the place a jaunty, holiday feeling, as if a little piece of beachfront had fallen into a tar pit. Jennifer and I talked about whether I should do OB.

"Why not?" she said. "You're good at it. You like it."

I just nodded, but I was listening hard. I'd never considered choosing a residency on the basis of criteria so sensible as what I liked and could do. I worried that once I was pigeon-holed into one branch of medicine, all the other specialties would look better than mine. If I did OB/GYN, I'd wish I was in medicine. If I went for medicine, I'd wonder whether I could have made the grade in surgery, and so on. I explained this to Jennifer.

"That's true," she told me.

She threw an invisible ball as far as she could. Marx clattered off. A stand of red maples broke the marsh on our right. Closer to the river stood an ancient pair of oaks. I wanted to grab Jennifer's hand and fiddle with her fingers, but I didn't.

"OB's different," she said. "We're the only part of the hospital where new people get born."

She stuck the hand I wanted to play with in her mouth and blew, and Marx charged back around a curve in the walkway and straight at us. Twenty feet from Jennifer he started braking like a cartoon critter, his nails skittering on the boards as he back-pedaled, his head rearing upward just before he crashed into her knees.

"Good boy," she told him, and thumped his ribs.

We rounded Marx's curve. The land sloped to the river. A single bald cypress broke the water to the north, its conical trunk squatting in pale duckweed. If I wanted to learn more after I finished OB, Jennifer said, I could always do a fellowship in perinatal. That was what she was planning to do. I could be a student forever.

I asked her something that had been bothering me ever since I started seriously considering obstetrics. Didn't she think that men in the specialty were obnoxious? After all, OB/GYN was entirely for women, so why shouldn't women run it? Jennifer hiked along, her hands in her pockets, her hat flopping over her ears. Yes, she said, most of the guys who go into OB/GYN think they're making a big sacrifice. They think they're God's gift because they aren't scared of women. Yes, she said, nodding to herself, most of them are obnoxious, there's no denying it. Only a few men have a place in OB, but she'd decided a few weeks back that I was probably one of them. I had to learn to take charge in the delivery room and not to get distracted. I had to quit the crybaby stuff.

I looked at the boards as they ran between my feet. She knew about the tears that flooded my eyes during deliveries. She'd seen them.

"You always start out that way," Jennifer said, looking up at me. "If you're good, I mean. You get wrapped up in it."

Yes, I thought.

"But after the first couple hundred births," she said, "you learn to keep your working mind separate from the part that wants to laugh and cry and holler hallelujah. You don't lose it. You just time it better."

Marx led us down to the river. We crossed a bridge and took a set of steps down to the far bank. I looked along the banks for alligators, but all I found were beer cans and sunken bald cypress logs.

"You've got eight weeks to make your match list, don't you?" Jennifer asked.

I nodded. She tugged her glacier glasses down, like reading glasses, to look at me. Her eyes were green and brown.

"That's why you're not sure," she said.

"You've got it," I told her. "I knew when I interviewed in October it was either peds or OB. Last month I knew it was OB. Now I'm thinking tropical medicine."

"Get out of here."

We did get out of there, Margot. And I was sure.

Cabala

"You must give her time," Germaine said.

It was June tenth, the dance company had the month off, and I was lonelier than I'd ever been in my life.

"She will find her way," Germaine said. "If the two of you are —"

I raised my hand. Germaine paused tolerantly. She'd been in unshakably good spirits ever since you three had left nine days before. I stood beside the dusty, sky-blue bowl and studied Dad's instructions once again.

"She called you this morning," Germaine guessed. I nodded. Bou had called at six, midnight in Lincoln, just as she had on her second night home. That first call was bliss. She was lonely for me, lonely for France. She wanted me to hurry back. We'd spend the whole summer together, not just July. Maybe I should come to New Haven in the fall, get an apartment, find a part-time job there instead of in Poughkeepsie. As soon as we hung up, I called Joseph and told him to borrow his cousin's *Deux Chevaux* two days earlier than we'd planned.

"She has reconsidered," Germaine said. "She thinks perhaps she should be alone."

I nodded again. I simply couldn't talk. A Y-fitting connected the toilet bowl to the vent and soil lines. I brushed flux on the ends of the joint, unrolled a few inches of solder, then tinkered with my torch.

My bags were packed. I'd planned to put in the toilet, say goodbye to the dancers, and leave in two days. But that morning everything had changed. Bou was in a quiet, distant mood. I knew as soon as I picked up the phone that I'd lost her. She talked about Paris as if it had been years instead of days since she'd left. She told me not to come see her yet. She wanted to spend more time in Lincoln. Maybe we'd go up to Logs in August, before she went back to school. She wasn't sure. The newlywed cousins might want to stay there then. We'd better just wait and see. Suddenly she was saying goodbye.

Wait, I said. What had happened? Had she seen Beck? No, that wasn't it. Had she seen you? She said you were in Lincoln.

"This is your home now," Germaine said.

I asked her to turn away, lit the torch, and worked the flame in circles until the copper fitting heated blue. I fed solder around the toilet side of the pipe joint. The rim sucked up the metal the way Dad said it would. Germaine's voice came to me from the tiled floor.

"The swiftest flight," she said, "is stillness."

I didn't hear from Beck until a month after I put that toilet in. The day before Bastille Day I received a yellowed postcard from New Canaan. On the front was President Nixon giving the peace sign, and on the back were five scrawled words — MCATS AMERICAN COLL SEPT APR.

I stayed in Paris. In the fall I took the test, and then again in the spring. Without that second set of scores, I would never have made it into a top-twenty school like Tulane. Beck knew I needed two tries, and was telling me to delay med school a year. That's why he wrote APR and not just SEPT.

In August you sent me the first of your careful letters. You and Bou were spending the month in New Hampshire. In the fall, you were going to live together in Saybrook. You two were back where you were always meant to be. As much as I was hurting, I was glad.

Through my goggles Germaine was a squat violet gargoyle. I shut off the flame. All summer Germaine tended to me as if I were one of her walking wounded. In June, her prescription for me was Jewish ghost stories, one a day after lunch.

"Before the destruction of the First Temple," she began, "the prophet Jeremiah discovered numbers within Verses, words within the Word. The Hidden Book foretold a history of defeat and diaspora. Jeremiah prayed to God to grant him his former ignorance, but the secret of Cabala was his."

I stepped into the main room. The place was pristine. No cot, no foreign beer bottles, no piles of dirty and cleaner clothes.

"Two thousand two hundred years later, in the time of Isaac the Blind, a band of murderers threatened the Jewish quarter of Prague. For six years the bandits came at Pesach and accused the elders of wetting the unleavened bread with the blood of Christian children. These men murdered families and stole even the holy objects from their houses. On the eighth night of the month of Nisan, Rabbi Judah Loew ben Bezalel created the Golem."

I sat beneath the window and rested my back against the wall.

"The Golem slept at the edge of the cemetery, visible to all but Rabbi Judah as a ridge of earth. On Pesach night, the murderers made their way along the Street of the Krasnohorske. Rabbi Judah took up his stylus and etched the Sign of Life in Death upon the Creature's forehead."

In December, Dad and Brenda were married. By the time they arrived on their honeymoon trip in January, the loft had a ladder, the kitchen had cabinets, the bathroom had a shower, and the long front window had electric-glide curtains.

"The Creature awoke. At once its eyes flowed with tears, dark as honey, as it beheld the beauty of Earth. The tears held no salt, for the Creature was neither man nor beast. *Tell me, Master,* it said. *What is this place? This,* said Rabbi Judah, *is the world.* He showed the Golem the mountains, the plains, and the distant sea."

Catherine choreographed a new piece in the fall. She gave

me a solo. In the spring we toured France again, making almost the same stops as the year before.

"*Tell me, Master,* said the Golem. *What manner of being are you?* Rabbi Judah said, *Like you, I am composed of clay. Unlike you, I carry in my bosom a spark of the divine. Tell me, Master,* said the Golem. *What must I do here?* The Rabbi said to the Creature, *You must kill a Man.*"

I closed my eyes. Germaine's words were punctuated by the sonar peeps of the swallows flitting over the roof gutters.

"*Tell me, Master,* said the Golem. *Is not this Man divine, as you are? He is,* said Rabbi Judah. *But he is blind to his divinity.*"

In February, Paola and Joseph were engaged. Joseph decided to speak only Italian in preparation for marriage, and drove everyone mad all spring. In the beginning of June, he and Paola left for Verona. A week later I followed on the night train. Paola's entire family met me at the station. I was best man.

"The Golem stood as high as the House of Prayer," Germaine told me. "The drunken bandits approached. Rabbi Judah clasped his right hand and raised it overhead. At this signal, the Golem seized the first of the killers. Rabbi Judah brought his raised fist to his left palm. The Golem reached into the murderer's chest. Weeping, the Creature tore the murderer's heart from his body and forced the organ into the man's mouth. This was to ensure that none would ever again speak the blood accusation."

I rubbed goose bumps from my arms.

"*You are divine,* said the Golem as the last mortal gleam left the murderer's eyes," Germaine placidly continued. "The murderers fled. The wagon they had brought to carry stolen goods instead bore away their companion. Rabbi Judah extended his hand, palm downward. The Golem lay flat upon the earth."

I stayed in Paris another year, but I never stopped missing you three or feeling left behind. Not one day.

"Beside the Creature," Germaine told me, leaning down

320

from her chair, "six centuries of the dead lay one upon the other. *Master,* said the Golem, *let me walk about.* Rabbi Judah said, *You will walk again. Now you must sleep.* He erased the Sign of Life in Death from the Golem's head. The last of the Creature's tears wet the earth. Its final breath, red with dust, settled among the headstones."

I savored the peace that Germaine's stories brought to me. Then I stood and walked to the bathroom. The pipes had cooled.

"Tomorrow," Germaine promised, following me, "I shall tell you the story of Joseph della Reina, who could see through the eyes of dogs and whose enemy, the king of Greece, wasted with the drinking sickness in his twenty-seventh year."

I turned on the water main. Water trickled through the pipes, then into the tank, with the sound of distant bells.

Less than an hour until midnight now. The contest for the First Charity Baby of 1993 is in hot contention. The last birth was forty minutes ago. Three women are trying to have their babies fast, but not too fast. A midnight-minus-one-minute baby won't make the papers tomorrow, but neither will a midnight-plus-ten baby. We're supposed to act like this is any other night and not 'hurry or slow the labors, but we can't help watching the clock.

Livia Brown is only six centimeters dilated, but pushing hard. Kate thinks Livia and her husband have cash on this blessed event. I asked her why she thinks so. She says Mr. Brown is right beside Livia, looking more anxious than any father of four has a right to.

Then there's Rebecca Larson, an obese twenty-four-year-old who had twins three years ago, who's already at nine centimeters. If I had anyone to wager with, I'd put my money on her. She told me, with a straight face, that she thinks having only one baby will be no problem. Her closest rival, Patricia Lee, is a thirty-one-year-old primigravida who doesn't give a damn about the New Year's competition, but who does want to deliver as soon as possible. Clinton ordered a second shot of Demerol half an hour ago, but she's not comfortable. I tried to cheer her up and she almost bit my head off. She keeps cursing out someone named either Slim or Sam, I can't figure out which. He's not here, but from Lee's mutterings, I gather he's responsible for all this trouble. Kate calls him Slam and says he's probably at Jackson Brewery, kissing a complete stranger beneath a storm of firecrackers.

I am not quite as far along as I'd hoped myself. I just ran up to the nineteenth-floor balcony, which has a nice view all the way to the Levee, where the fireworks display has started. But I didn't stay for even five minutes, because I've got to finish writing to you before I leave at seven tomorrow morning. Livia will deliver between one and two. I'll be lucky if I'm done by four. Then I'll still have to print out two copies of the *BOU, BECK,* and *MARGOT DOC*s, on the wide, striped paper, which is all we've got up here. I send one direct to you and the other to Bou via Mam in Lincoln. Beck will get his on INTERNET tomorrow at about eight o'clock.

But Livia and I aren't worrying about the details right now. We both ignore the possibility that our big moment has passed, that there might not be any fireworks when we finish. Instead we turn our eyes to the window, where the sparkle and bang float through the midnight sky, and push steadily on.

Jennifer and I went dancing the night before last. We were supposed to have dinner first, but when I picked her up she wasn't hungry, and I hadn't thought about food since I'd called her in the afternoon. We went straight to Wild Tchoupitoulas and stayed on the dance floor for two hours. Jennifer dances like she's running across an endless plain to an even drumbeat no one else can hear. She strides in place, her arms rising and falling, while around her people are double- and triple-timing her. Her shoulders and hips make delicate angles, sending signals in semaphore.

That was her regular, slowish dancing. But just before we left, Jennifer taught me how to very slow dance. From the outside, very slow dancing must have looked like two people standing still on a dance floor. From the inside it felt like time itself had taken a breather while the ceiling fans drew Jennifer and me softly away from the floor. From there we steered ourselves unhurriedly moonward, using the alternative energy source generated by the brush of her lips across mine. We even did it during a fast song.

We ate after midnight at the Hummingbird Grill, two blocks off Lee Circle. In the overflow room, a cop played one of the poker machines, while at the counter in the main room, his partner talked to a solemn, drunk woman about cameras. Jennifer and I sat on the same side of a window booth. She ordered a steak po-boy, I had a cheeseburger and fries to share, and we drank a pitcher of Bud in fifteen minutes. We lifted our mugs with our free arms while our other arms held each other. Outside on the brick sidewalk, in the red strobe of the hotel sign, a plastic male mallard nested in a straw basket. We talked shop as usual. I said I wasn't sorry to be saying goodbye to Dr. Grant, and Jennifer said that Gus is the finest OB at Charity, that what he lacks in bedside manner he more than makes up for in the OR. I said I believed her, but the way he treated me and Joel gave us the willies. *Grant scares all the fourth-years and interns intentionally,* she said. *It's his way of teaching.* I told her I didn't like it. *But you learned, didn't you?* she asked. I said I'd learned more from her.

There we were, talking about Charity, but I didn't wonder if we were on a date. We reached her house after one and found Ted wide awake. He was riding Mitch around the living room. He looked happy enough, especially when Jennifer gave him a beery kiss on the lips — Ted, I mean. But Mitch claimed that every time he put him down, Ted would wait just long enough for him and Karen to fall asleep before bursting into heartfelt sobs that quickly became terrified shrieks. Mitch's theory was that Ted was confusing being alone at night with being dead, an error with which I'm not unfamiliar.

Jennifer and I put Mitch down instead of Ted. Then we carried Ted back down to the living room and made him stagger back and forth between us across a distance of one meter, his current maximum range. Seeing Ted walk and squeal made me wonder what Jennifer's baby would look like, especially if he or she was also my baby. Jennifer didn't talk to me while

Ted was walking his four fast steps. Then all at once she looked up. *What?* I asked. She just looked, as if we were slow dancing with a baby and a few feet of air between us. I sent Ted to her. She caught him, spun him around, and sent him right back.

The New Year's babies are out. At 23:46 Rebecca Larson, two hundred and forty-three pounds, and Patricia Lee, one hundred and thirty-six pounds, were in the last stages of labor. Joel was delivering Patricia, whose husband still hadn't shown up and whose mood hadn't improved at all. I cringed by the brown-tiled wall when she screamed at Joel, just because he'd asked her to relax and push at the same time, which is what we tell everybody. Midnight crept closer. It looked like Patricia might land right on the money, but no one dared tell her how lucky she was. Her husband, Slam, arrived promptly at 00:02, but her baby didn't. Slam hadn't been at the Brewery or down on Bourbon Street, as Kate had suspected. He said he'd come straight from the bus station, and he had his suitcase in hand.

Meanwhile, in Delivery Two, Dr. Clinton had decided that his best chance at making the morning news was Rebecca Larson, the big woman who'd had twins three years before. Clinton shamelessly coached her about how to pace herself, and Rebecca wanted to be famous as badly as he did. At 11:56, Clinton had Kate hold up his stop watch, while Rebecca pushed and grunted like a weightlifter. Kevin No-Middle-Name Larson popped into Clinton's greedy mitts at 00:03. We all cheered. Clinton handed Kate his Polaroid and she took a shot of him, Rebecca, Kevin, and the hospital clock, which he set back to the historic moment. *Photo opportunities are made,* Clinton informed us, *not met.* Then he dialed the *Picayune* and Channel Four.

Joel Stayton Nash, master of the Third Plane of Enlightenment and exalted seeker after the True Path, delivered Patricia and Slam's baby at 00:11. The Lees didn't name their daughter Resolution, as I quietly suggested while I cleaned her up.

They decided instead on Brittany, which they don't realize is last year's fashionable name, along with Stephen for boys. Patricia's going to be angry again when she finds out.

Clinton was in the hall with Andre Trevigne from Channel Four by the time Livia Brown's water broke, in a clean rush, at quarter to one. Kate and I shut the door on the Mardi Gras racket in the hall, and Kate propped Livia up with an extra pillow while her husband massaged her freezing feet. Livia waited calmly. She knew that everything was going well, but Mr. Brown looked awful.

Livia's baby presented neatly occiput left anterior just before one. *Is it time?* Livia asked. I told her it was. Her next contraction came sharp and long. Kate chanted encouragement. The baby's head cleared. Livia rode her next wave hard, rising right up off the table. *That's it, honey,* Kate said, talking her back down. The baby's front took shape in midair, with me surrounding her. Then all her parts came flying out and I inventoried them as they arrived. *Beautiful girl, beautiful girl,* I heard Mr. Brown and Kate saying to each other. Livia was laughing. Her husband sat right down on the floor. Kate clamped the umbilical cord high and low and cut it. The girl and I started breathing. I cleaned up her long legs, her back, her belly. The hallelujahs I'd been holding back brimmed in my eyes. *Damn,* I thought, blinking steadily. Mr. Brown tried to get up a few times. Livia held out one hand toward her girl. With the other she reached down to Mr. Brown. Mr. Brown reached my height. I handed Livia her baby in the cleanest of flannel blankets. *Beautiful girl,* Mr. Brown and I said to each other, wiping our eyes on our sleeves and peering down at her. He kissed his wife.